WHERE DEAD THINGS STAND

PARANORMAL ARCHAEOLOGY DIVISION
BOOK 2

ERNEST DEMPSEY

PREFACE

WHERE DEAD THINGS STAND

Portions of this story contain factual events and people. To protect them and their families, names and specific locations have been changed. But the core of these incidents and those affected are real.

PROLOGUE
PATAGONIA, 1766

A ravenous wind whipped up across the snow-covered mountain slope, flinging icy barbs across Father José Garcia Alsue's face. *Just another of God's tests*, he reasoned, or tried to.

Each new merciless gale that screamed down across the hard-packed snowfield stirred the air with tiny shards of ice that cut across the few patches of exposed skin like minuscule bits of broken glass. Combined with the cold, the wind stung his face where the scarf and hood failed to cover him, and the only consolation he could find in those moments of strife were the prayers he'd been uttering since they left the relative heat of the valley below.

It was one of the warmer months of the year in this part of the world. Had Father José been a man given to complaining or had he possessed an ungrateful nature, he might have cursed nature for its unnecessarily bitter response to his visit.

He stopped and waited, turning his face away from the brunt of the wind. His eyes had been slits since they'd left the camp four hours before to begin their ascent up the mountain. Down there, the temperatures had been accommodating, if not borderline pleasant.

He'd never found the climate in this part of the world to be particularly appealing. It was rarely hot, and the warmth summer brought was typically a tepid, humid soup. But it was nothing of the kind up here on this mountain. For a moment, Father José nearly longed for that humid soup below.

Father José waited patiently, leaning on the staff he'd brought along for the expedition. He gripped the cloth wrapping around the top part of the dense oak and lowered his face close to it as if it could provide shelter against these merciless elements.

At least facing down the mountain the blowing ice shards didn't seem to sting as much. Still, he pulled the black scarf up over his nose and tightened it a little more under the hood protecting his neck and head.

He'd forsaken the cassock he usually wore during the mundane duties he performed throughout his life—the studying, praying, and listening to those who would visit him for confession. Now, he wore rugged clothes—thick brown trousers, fur-lined boots, and a similarly lined dark blue coat, cinched in the front with buttons and a strap.

Despite wearing the appropriate attire for such an expedition, the clothes seemed to do almost nothing to stave off the intrepid chill.

The cold cut through the layers and touched his skin with a thousand icy fingers, sending constant shivers through his body.

"Are you all right, Father?" A man's voice knifed through the howling wind, barely reaching his ears.

The speaker might have been a hundred yards away or more in normal circumstances, but Father José knew his guide was mere feet behind him.

"Yes," José grumbled. "Just catching my breath, Ignacio. How are you faring?" The frigid air gripped his throat with frosty fingers, making shouting over the noise of the wind a strenuous task.

The younger man stared at him from under his hood, bowing his head low to keep the ice and snow out of his eyes.

"You need not worry about me, Father," he replied.

"Are you saying I'm too old for this sort of thing?" He met Ignacio's gaze through the freezing wind, with his eyes barely cracked enough to let in the dim, gray light from the eastern sky.

The younger raised his head slightly, startled by the notion he might have just insulted a man he so revered.

"I didn't mean—"

"I am only joking, my young friend," José said with a nod. Despite the effort required to speak, the Jesuit priest thought it worthwhile to settle the young man's nerves.

José thought it odd, though, that the guide was the more nervous of the two.

Making such an arduous trek up the mountain in these conditions would have been safer with more men in support. It wasn't the tallest peak in the world, but up here the temperamental weather and thin air could pose immense danger to those brave or foolhardy enough to take on the challenge.

But the priest's mission had to remain a secret, and he'd repeatedly made Ignacio swear to God that he wouldn't share a word of this venture with anyone.

People had called José a fool for years. He understood why. Had he been one of them observing a priest obsessing over legends, stories, and forgotten histories, he likely would have done the same.

He wasn't a vengeful man. By his nature, as a priest, his foundation was one built on forgiveness, mercy, and grace. On top of that, his motives were pure, unlike so many other treasure hunters who'd searched for the fabled city since the dawn of civilization.

Their hearts were set on the deadly sin of greed. They came to this land, and others all around the continent, in search of gold, gems, and anything else the sacred city could offer to satisfy their hearts' avarice.

That's what it was always about, after all—what a man can get if only he had enough money. It was a human flaw as old as time itself. And it ran in direct contrast to Christ's teachings in the sixth chapter of the Gospel of Matthew.

José had pondered over that verse more times than he could count. He'd prayed on it, read and reread it, to the point where the words of the text were the first thing he saw in his mind every morning when he woke.

"Seek ye first the kingdom of God, and His righteousness; and all these things shall be added unto you."

The verse echoed in his mind even now, whispering to him over the roaring winds and splinters of snow and ice.

It warmed him against the cold in a way no cloak ever could, and it renewed his purpose, the drive within that pushed him up the mountain.

Thoughts of those who'd scoffed at him fueled pity from the pious man. He felt sorry for them in a way few others could.

José wondered more than once if anyone else would dare to seek such a treasure for the reason he sought it. He prayed for forgiveness dozens of times for even contemplating the irony of it all.

While all the treasure hunters who'd come to this continent searched for fame and fortune, a life filled with lavish spending, women, drink, and anything else their hedonistic minds could conjure, the Jesuit priest's motivations were pure.

He sought the sacred city to open its gates and pour its riches into the world for all to share. He viewed it as the way to ease the suffering of the poor, the starving, the naked, the hopeless. Where so many failed in their quest to slake their thirst for material wealth, he would succeed and bring heaven to a fallen world.

José looked up into the charcoal-black sky. It churned and broiled with the fury of a tempest, as if kneaded by the invisible hands of God himself. Everything related to weather moved faster up here, and José prayed it would change for the better soon.

Time was running out.

Daylight encroached on the dark horizon to the east. It was faint, but every passing second brought the sunrise closer.

They could not delay further.

José looked up the white slope toward the rocky peak a few hundred yards away. It might as well have been twenty miles in these conditions.

He braced himself against the cold, shoring his coat tighter around his skin. Father José nodded toward the mountaintop. "Come, my young friend. We're nearly there."

The two pushed forward, the tips of their boots dragging across the crusty snow's surface.

Every step José took felt like he bore the weight of two men on his shoulders. His leg muscles burned from his thighs all the way down to his calves. "Thank you, Lord, for that warmth, at least," he muttered through his scarf.

He checked back over his shoulder now and then to make sure Ignacio hadn't fallen behind. The guide was half his age but seemed to be struggling against the elements and the rugged terrain.

The priest quietly wondered how many times the young man had actually been up the mountain, but he relegated that question to the back of his mind.

José needed a companion. Nothing more. He knew precisely where he was going. After dedicating his life to the research for this quest, the only thing left to do was reach the peak.

He stared ahead at the craggy peak. The jagged outline of the rock formation shot into the sky, towering a few hundred feet above the slopes where the snowfield met barren rock. It looked as if an ancient, cracked hand reached up out of the mountain, forever pointing its bony finger toward the heavens.

Or maybe he was just hallucinating.

José had heard of that happening to people in some of the higher elevations, but this wasn't that high. Or maybe he'd miscalculated.

No.

He shook off the notion. He'd prepared for this. He knew more about this spot than anyone else, even the indigenous people who occupied the surrounding areas. He wasn't hallucinating. It was fatigue. That was all. Just his mind playing tricks on him as a result of the exertion.

Isn't that the definition of hallucinating?

Again, he forced out the distracting thoughts by twisting his head rapidly back and forth.

Fifty yards from the base of the formation, he felt his feet grow heavier. Each time he tried to raise the boots and move another step forward, it seemed as though they were wrapped in heavy chains, binding him to the mountain by some unseen force.

He looked back again at Ignacio. In the weak light radiating through the sky, he saw pain in the younger man's eyes.

José wondered if he should send the guide back down the mountain, tell him to go get warm.

The weather had been decent when they broke camp and started up the mountain. Overcast, sure, but warm. Nothing like this. Even though the priest knew the climate on the mountain could change rapidly, he'd never heard of it swinging to this extreme. Not at this time of the year. Winter? Maybe. But not in the middle of summer.

He knew the truth—a secret he could not share with the young guide.

This was no ordinary change in the weather. Nature wasn't lashing out at him on its own accord.

This was a test. A crucible to measure whether or not the priest was worthy to gain entrance, to behold what had not been seen by human eyes for generations.

How many others had reached this spot only to fall short? José figured there were few who'd even figured out the location.

Uncertain of the outcome of this perilous mission, he'd taken precautions so—should he fail—someone else could follow his path and emerge victorious.

"No." He perished the thought and took another heavy step forward.

He kept his eyes fixed on the rock formation. The pronounced, gnarled peak curled its tip toward the east.

Another step.

He labored for breath. The wind blasted across his face and body, striking him on the left side as it swirled like a vortex, spiraling into the furious clouds above.

"I am worthy," he said. "I am worthy."

He repeated the phrase. Again, and again, with each agonizing step.

The wind pushed him, as if God himself forbade him draw near the peak.

"I am worthy," he repeated, as if the words would somehow dispel the storm and clear a path to his goal.

If anything, the weather worsened. Snow and ice whipped past his face, and the rock formation all but vanished as his visibility shrank to almost nothing. He looked down, barely able to see his boots.

A new fear speared his heart as he leaned over at a severe angle against the wind. There was no cliff here, but if the velocity got any stronger, he might well be blown off the mountain. Even with no perilous drops up here, the outcome of such an accident couldn't be good.

"Protect us, Father," he prayed. "For the sake of your children."

The sky grew brighter to the east. He was so close, but the minutes were few before the sun would break the horizon. Even though he wouldn't be able to see it through the angry storm overhead, that didn't matter.

The rule was absolute.

"Under the finger of Inti at sunrise," he muttered. It was a phrase he loathed to speak. To even consider uttering the name of the pagan god of the Incas felt blasphemous to him. He forgave himself and allowed the name to pass through his lips for the simple fact that it was a name and nothing more—a name as empty and powerless as their supposed sun god himself. It could have been the name of a city, a country, a food. There were plenty of things and places named after pagan deities all around the world. It meant nothing to him. After all, those false gods never did anything but crumble as their impotent powers proved empty time and again.

"José," a woman's voice called out to him. The sound halted him instantly.

That could not be. There was no woman up here.

He turned around, expecting to see Ignacio just behind him, figuring that his guide had been the one to say his name.

Fear rippled through his body, tingling his extremities. It felt like a hammer dropped into his gut.

"Ignacio?" He shouted into the wind, but there was no sign of the younger man. He'd been right behind him just a moment ago. *Hadn't he?*

José questioned himself. He'd been looking back repeatedly for this exact reason—to make sure Ignacio hadn't fallen behind.

The priest couldn't even see beyond the reach of his own arm. There was no telling what happened to the young guide.

Perhaps he'd given up and retreated back down the mountain to calmer weather. José could hardly blame him. Every instinct in his mind told him to turn back, too.

"Priiiiiest," the woman's voice hissed again.

He twisted his head round in every direction but didn't dare adjust his feet. He couldn't see anyone, and the rock formation was but a mere shadow looming before him.

"The Lord is my shepherd," he spoke the familiar verse from the book of Psalms.

Daylight encroached through the clouds overhead, turning the black, roiling madness into a lighter shade of gray.

His conscience told him to cease this madness. To turn back and find Ignacio and make sure he got back to camp safely. They could always return here when the weather cleared.

Except he knew that wasn't the case.

This could only be done on one of two days per year. Here in the Southern Hemisphere, the summer solstice was the best option—the only option in José's mind. He shuddered to think how bad the weather would be up here six months from now.

Ignacio was fine. He'd simply gone back down the mountain. That had to be it. José had to press on. The sun was about to breach the horizon any minute. If he missed this chance, he would have to wait another year before returning. And anything could happen in that amount of time.

Heaven forbid some greedy treasure hunter figured out the clues and got here before him.

He shook off the thought, faced the peak's silhouette ahead, and marched forward.

Guilt riddled him as he clomped up the slope toward the rocks.

"Priiiiest," the voice taunted him again.

He refused to acknowledge it this time. Whatever demon was trying to turn him away, he would not allow it to dissuade him.

His feet felt even heavier now. The muscles in his legs were on fire. But he pressed forward.

"One more. One more." He repeated the words with every step.

Then, after what seemed like hours, the steep rock wall of the peak appeared before him.

He reached out with his left hand and touched the jagged surface, bracing himself against it.

The howling wind roared with even greater fury—a final protest against this mortal's intrusion.

José twisted his head to avoid the direct onslaught, then shuffled to the right, feeling his way around to the front of the formation.

The instant he stepped under the shadow of the arched stone finger, the weights on his ankles vanished, and he found refuge from the infernal wind that had ceaselessly tormented him.

He breathed hard, sucking in gasps of the cold, thin air. He wanted to wipe the ice from around his eyes, but that would prove futile since his gloved hands were covered in the same frozen particles.

José leaned his back against the hard rock and stared out into the swirling, icy wind. His heart pounded, both from the effort it took to get here and from the anticipation. He'd made it. The sun had not yet risen, and now he stood exactly where he needed to be to witness the greatest miracle in the last two thousand years.

A thread of guilt snaked through his chest for losing sight of Ignacio. But the guide was young and healthy. He'd be fine. Most likely, he was already clear of the storm and getting warmer by the second.

"Priiiiiest!"

José closed his eyes to the haunting sound. It was louder now than before. "Protect me, oh Lord. For I am thy servant."

The voice called to him again.

He summoned a dose of anger from his belly and pried open his eyes to face the apparition. But there was none to be found.

He looked left and right, but nothing lingered beyond the relative stillness in the shelter from the storm.

"You're imagining things, José," he said to himself, trying to dispel the paranoia.

Suddenly, the wind beyond his refuge stopped. The snow and ice that had been blowing relentlessly now hovered in midair all around him. The wind's howls ceased. And straight ahead, to the east, the clouds began to part as the dim light of dawn broke through, parting the storm like Moses at the Red Sea.

"Yes," José said. "Yes. This is it. Oh, thank you, Lord. Thank you for this blessing."

Sunlight sprayed onto his face. The levitating snowflakes and motes of ice glistened like millions of diamonds dangling around him.

"Father?" A voice spoke to José's right. He recognized the sound of Ignacio's voice, but it was distant, hollow.

The priest turned and saw his guide standing a few feet away, almost within arm's reach.

"My son," José said. "Behold! We bear witness to a miracle." He pointed toward the sun, but Ignacio merely stood there, staring at the priest with vapid eyes.

Something wasn't right, and a new chill swept across the priest's skin.

"Ignacio?"

The guide didn't move. He didn't respond. His body seemed to involuntarily waver slightly, as if blown by some undetectable breeze and out of his control.

José glanced back toward the horizon, fearful of missing the moment he'd been waiting his entire adult life to witness.

The snowflakes and ice motes still hung in the air, suspended in animation, glittering in the sunlight.

The priest turned back to the younger man, and nearly jumped out of his skin. Somehow, Ignacio was only inches away now. His previously brown eyes were covered in a hazy opaque glaze.

José leaned close, concern brimming within. He reached out his right hand and touched the guide on the shoulder. "Ignacio?"

Ignacio's right hand shot up in a blur and latched on to José's wrist, clamping down on it with the power of an alligator's jaws. He tried to shake free, but he couldn't budge.

"Priiiiiest! Why have you come?" Ignacio's lips moved, but the voice that hissed through them was not his own. It was the woman he'd heard before.

Father José quivered. His head shook in fear. He'd been trained to perform exorcisms in the past, but it was far from his area of expertise. One thing he felt certain of—Ignacio was possessed. But how?

"Why have you come?" the spirit demanded, its voice thundering across the mountain.

"I... I...." José struggled to find the words. "I have come seeking the sacred city."

"Why do you seek the city?"

The priest continued to struggle to free himself of the icy grip on his wrist, but his desperate attempts were in vain.

"I wish to share its splendor with the world, and ease the suffering of those in need."

For a moment, whatever had control of Ignacio remained silent.

"And yet you do not bear the key to unlock the gates of the Wandering City."

José frowned at the statement. "What? What key? I found nothing about a—"

"None shall behold the sacred city without the Key of Inti." The supernatural voice boomed, causing the priest to cower.

He winced and covered his left ear with his free hand.

"I... was unaware. Please. You must let me open the gates. The people—"

"Be gone, Priest. You have proved yourself unworthy."

Ignacio's grip loosened. The glaze over his eyes evaporated in an instant. Behind him, and all around the peak, the suspended snow and ice abruptly dropped to the ground. The clouds overhead dispersed, and the bright morning sun beamed upon their faces.

Ignacio blinked a few times, then looked out toward the sunrise. "What... what happened, Father?"

Tears welled in José's eyes. The relief he felt for Ignacio did little to salve the pain of his failure.

What had he done wrong? How had he missed this key the spirit spoke of? He looked out to the horizon as the blazing sun climbed into the clear blue sky. Under any other circumstance, he might have appreciated the spectacular view.

But not today.

Today, he had let down the entire world.

1

CHILE, PRESENT DAY

Michael Buford had never seen anything so spectacular, and terrifying, in his life. He'd been all over the world, hunting treasures, artifacts, and relics from numerous civilizations. He'd seen mountains, beaches, valleys, and fjords that boasted some of the most beautiful scenery he'd ever beheld.

But this place, this valley, had just moved up to the top of his short list of favorites.

He stood on a patch of grass, just above the edge of the forest, staring out at the mountains, the shimmering lake below, and the sleepy town nearby. Streaks of white clouds smeared the blue sky, which the water mirrored with a blurry reflection that van Gogh would have appreciated.

Up here, away from the rush of the "civilized" world, he felt different. The phrase *new man* was as cliché as any, but it was the prevailing sense that overwhelmed him in this place.

It was little wonder to Buford how so many of the ancients regarded this region as sacred, and as a gateway to the gods.

He inhaled a deep breath of fresh, cool air. It tingled his nose, cleansing him of the impurities he'd grown up with, and still indulged, in the city. There were no pollutants here, nothing but the cleanest air on the planet.

In some ways, Buford wished he could just forget all about his crazy obsession and simply enjoy this place for what it was. Here, he didn't have debts or other pressing matters that life seemed to throw in his way without respite.

Here, he had no problems.

He could find a place to live down in the village, work as a carpenter or a bartender or pretty much anything else. Heaven knew he'd done most of those jobs at one point or another.

But he was a man of integrity. He'd pay off the creditors back in the States. And if he had to return there and go back to a normal 9-to-5 job, so be it.

But that was the fear, his greatest torment.

He'd lived his life as a free man for the last two years since quitting his corporate gig as head of a marketing team. That job had given him more stress than benefits for over a decade.

Buford's friends asked him on multiple occasions when he'd burned out in that career, and he always told them the same thing: "Day three."

Marketing was a difficult job. Lucrative, sure, but he was always firing at moving targets. Social media had changed the game from the old days of Google AdWords and SEO, which had changed the game from its old days of billboard, television, radio, and magazine advertising.

Those things still existed, sure, but not to the powerful extent they once had as sole providers of much-needed traffic to businesses.

Buford had expertly and deftly navigated the minefield as the digital age brought in new marketing techniques. He'd mastered the "content is king" model, and created teams of writers, videographers, and artists that dominated the space for his company.

But that was always one of the biggest problems. It wasn't *his* company. He was an employee, just like everyone else.

Sure, he got bonuses every quarter, and at Christmas, but at the end of the day, he was just as expendable as anyone else, and he always had to answer to someone above him, all the way up to the president and CEO.

The pressure is what got to him. Pressure to perform, to exceed expectations, to keep building up market value for the company. It was a perpetually shifting bull's-eye, and eventually he reached a point where he realized he couldn't play the game anymore.

Numbers had slipped, which was natural during times of transition—particularly in the marketing field—but it was the perfect excuse for him to walk away and try something he'd always been passionate about.

History was one of those things he'd loved since childhood, which also caused him to question why he went into marketing in the first place.

Money, as it so often was for so many people, was the answer. But now, he was doing something that stirred his soul, that caused his heart to beat just a little faster.

His wife had left him a year before he quit, leaving him alone and a shadow of his former self. It was one of those moments where you either fall prey to the darkness, or you follow the light leading you out of it.

So, he took the leap and became a full-time treasure hunter.

He figured he had enough money in the bank and a few assets to live comfortably for two years, including some cash for emergencies.

The expenses had accelerated, though, as they often did. He had spent more on food and travel than he'd originally expected, but he had a lead on something that no one else—as far as he could find—had ever uncovered.

He had found it three months before turning in his notice at work. Had the clue never made its way into his possession, he probably would have stayed at his job.

Standing there on the slopes of the Patagonia, the view also reminded him that his playtime was up.

He'd ventured all over the world in his search for the Wandering City, and now he was in the place he believed he'd find it. But the mountains gave him nothing but pristine vistas. While a treasure in their own right, pretty views wouldn't pay the bills.

Part of him wished he'd never found that blasted tablet with its curious glyphs and ornate depictions of a city of the gods.

He'd been on vacation in Cuzco, the former seat of the Incan Empire. While avoiding the street vendors offering smoked guinea pig and other foods he found unusual and disgusting, he discovered a stall where a man was selling trinkets he claimed were authentic Incan artifacts.

Over the years, Buford had spent much of his free time studying the Incas, and while not an expert, he wasn't stupid either.

The replica jewelry and pottery was good, a little too good. And Buford respectfully declined the opportunity to buy any of it.

But then the owner of the stall had persuaded him to look at one more item, a tablet he claimed came from the heart of the Andes, one that would lead him to the greatest treasure ever known.

Of course, Buford was beyond skeptical at the man's outlandish claims, but the guy was speaking his language as a treasure hunter, so the American decided to indulge the old man.

The seller produced an old, leather-bound book. At first blush, Buford guessed it was some kind of journal.

One thing Buford knew was that this was unlike the rest of the seller's baubles and doodads. But what was it? And why did this guy know he'd be interested in such a thing?

As the American gazed upon the cover, he found himself entranced by the design burned into the leather. It was the symbol of the Jesuit order.

"Do you know what that is?" the old man asked, pointing to the center of the book with a bony finger. He was a hunched-over guy, with thin gray hair and traditional Peruvian clothes, though his featured the weathered, bland colors of gray and black.

Buford said that he did. The sun with the letters *I-H-S* contained within it—along with a cross above the letters and three nails below it—were something the American had seen several times before in his studies of secret societies and religious orders. The Society of

Jesus, or Jesuits, fell into the latter category. Along with forming universities and high schools, they did an enormous amount of mission work around the world, sending their priests to every corner of the globe to found parishes.

There were some, too, who performed research in various subjects, one of which was archaeology.

The price the old man asked for the journal was small enough—within Buford's shrinking budget—though he would not allow the American to have a peek inside at the pages.

Buford considered haggling with the guy but decided to just pay up since the seller had given him something no one else did—a renewed sense of curiosity.

Within hours, that leather-bound book had led Buford into a rabbit hole from which there was no escape. There were strange images contained on its pages, notes from a man hundreds of years before who searched for something called the City of the Caesars.

The book's author seemed obsessed by the subject, and by something he'd written down dozens of times in its contents—the Key of Inti. He'd even noted that this key was the secret to unlocking the gates to the lost city.

Buford decided the fabled place was probably nothing more than a myth, but the key, on the other hand, might be worth a hefty sum. Based on the notes from Father José, the priest believed this key was actually a jewel, and while it was impossible to guess the size of the thing, such an artifact would likely be considered priceless.

Buford felt certain he could come up with a number.

Countless hours of studying the journal of Father José Garcia Alsue had led him to this spot, in the Patagonia.

But the site offered no reward for the treasure hunter's quest.

That realization sent a thud through Buford's body, as well as a sense of absolute dread.

He was broke, and in significant debt. Going back to his old job wasn't an option, not that he wanted to. But what else could he do? Marketing was all that he knew other than history.

There were other companies he could work for, or perhaps he

could go into business for himself, though the risks involved with that were just as big as the one he'd taken to end up here, standing on this spot in the Patagonia.

Buford exhaled slowly.

He knew he was close. So close he could almost grasp it. But he was missing something, a piece of the puzzle he'd overlooked.

Impossible. He'd virtually memorized the entire diary.

He took out his phone and flipped through the images he'd taken—snapshots of the notes from Father José Garcia Alsue's journal.

Buford had also created a copy of it, adding the contents to his own notebook. This process further imprinted the original's notes in his mind.

He stared at the screen in his hand, swiping until he found the image he was searching for. "Devil's Point," he said out loud, noting the Spanish script written by the hand of Father José.

Buford spun around, his eyes sweeping the surrounding landscape. Behind him, a rock formation jutted out of the loose earth. The outcropping matched a drawing from Alsue's diary, complete with the mountain ridge behind it and the patch of forest below.

"What am I missing?" Buford wondered. He narrowed his eyelids to slits and peered at an object drawn amid the trees—a small black obelisk.

He'd hunted for the object, without success. Alsue mentioned it several times in his diary, and how he believed it was crucial to discovering the first of four symbols that would lead to the key.

Buford took his eyes off the screen and looked down the slope toward the forest. *Perhaps it's in there somewhere. I just have to find it.*

Seconds later, he found his feet carrying him almost on their own accord, downhill toward the trees.

Something inside him—a hunch, or perhaps simply desperation —told him that this obelisk was what he'd been missing. If it had been drawn in these trees, perhaps that's where it was hidden, possibly even by Alsue.

Doubt snaked through his mind. He'd come through the forest to reach the rock formation on the slope—the three prongs of the devil's pitchfork, as it was described in Alsue's journal.

A note in the corner of the page had befuddled him since the first time he noticed it. Now, it stood out to him. "Only two may come," Buford read it out loud, then peered down at the forest again. "What does that mean?"

He recalled reading Alsue's account of an expedition up to the top of one of the nearby mountains. Its memory was tucked away in a part of the journal with entries of a more personal nature—a place where the priest vented his frustrations and recalled parts of his journey.

He and a local man named Ignacio had climbed to the top of a mountain in the summer, though there was still a permanent snowfield near the summit. Buford had thought the climb must have been arduous for a priest beyond his prime and a reluctant local guide.

Buford knew next to nothing about mountain climbing and the gear required to reach one of the regional peaks. He knew to make it to the top of the world's tallest pinnacles, expensive equipment, clothing, outerwear, and even oxygen were needed.

While these peaks weren't as high as K2 or Everest, they were still extraordinary challenges for a couple of amateurs from the eighteenth century.

"Only two may come," he repeated under his breath.

Did that mean only two people would be permitted to discover the lost city? If so, had that already happened? Such a discovery would either be kept in utter secrecy by the finder, or it would have become the biggest story in history.

Buford had considered this dilemma multiple times during his search and decided he would do his best to keep things quiet if he uncovered the location of the city itself. Even finding the supposed key would need to be handled with discretion, particularly if it were something valuable that he could sell to a collector.

"What am I doing?" he said, shaking his head. He'd felt an overwhelming sense of doubt clouding his mind. *I'm just going to go back into the woods and see if I can find this...whatever it is.*

He checked the image one more time, studying the obelisk as if looking away from it might make it disappear.

If there were a monument of this kind in the woods, he hadn't seen it before. But with all the trees, it would have been easy to miss. He'd have to search more diligently.

Buford trudged down the slope, his hiking boots kicking the loose stone and scree ahead of him. He stopped at the edge of the forest and hesitated, staring into the shadowy, lush green undergrowth beneath the dense canopy.

He noticed the odd absence of birds chirping. No squirrels chittered in the branches or scampered around the trunks. The forest was eerily silent, save for a cool breeze that trickled through it, giving only the slightest brush of sound.

Buford swallowed, suddenly afraid—of what he didn't know.

He set his boot down on the forest dirt and stepped into the shadows. As he looked back over his shoulder and up the mountain, he thought he heard a woman's voice whisper in his ear.

"Only two may come."

2

ATLANTA

This was a first.

Tommy Schultz stared at the email subject line in the list of messages stacked in his inbox. He had heard or seen the request before—in person, on the phone, and even through emails like this. But he'd never received that request from a Chilean dignitary. Much less a high-ranking member of Chilean government.

He stared at the name: *Sofia Carrera.*

Tommy didn't recognize it, but that could be said of 99 percent of foreign politicians.

As founder and head of the International Archaeological Agency based in Atlanta, he frequently met leaders from around the world. Through his efforts, and that of his agents, the IAA had recovered and secured hundreds of important artifacts and relics over the years for dozens of nations.

Thanks to the IAA, many pieces of forgotten history had been returned to the light, and were now available for the public to study and witness in various museums and exhibits in their native lands.

The subject line of this email, however, carried a sense of urgency that most did not. Usually, there was some kind of greeting or salutation. Not a blunt plea.

Tommy opened a new window in his web browser and typed in the name attached to the official email address from the Chilean government. The instant he saw the first result, Tommy's jaw slacked a little.

Sofia Carrera was the interior minister of Chile.

Given that he was personal friends with a former American president, and familiar with the current one, he didn't get starry eyed at the idea of a nation's second-in-command sending him an email, but it also wasn't the sort of thing an ordinary person like him would ever get accustomed to, either.

Satisfied the email was legitimate, and armed with a surface knowledge of who had sent it, Tommy opened the message and read over it.

"Mr. Schultz. I hope this message finds you well. If you are unaware of who I am, my name is Sofia Carrera. I am the Interior Minister of the Republic of Chile.

"In recent years, we have been experiencing a number of strange disappearances in the Patagonia. I realize that at first glance you might wonder why I would reach out to you regarding such a thing."

He bobbed his head. "Yeah, pretty much."

They would have resources, agencies dedicated to such issues. But that knowledge only hammered home his curiosity.

"We have done our best to uncover the reason for these disappearances, but as yet have failed to discover the cause. It is my hope that you are able to help with this plight. Please call me at your earliest convenience. I know you must be wondering how someone in your position could help with this sort of situation. If and when you call, I will explain further."

Tommy rubbed the bridge of his nose with his thumb and forefinger. Then he transitioned to his eyes. It was too early in the morning for this. Actually, it was too early for anything.

He reached over and grabbed his hunter-green coffee mug from Kiawah Island's Ocean Course and took a sip.

The hot, creamy white coffee that had been part of his morning ritual for over a decade still brought calm to his nerves and a jolt to his senses.

Perfection, he thought.

After another swallow, he reread the message and noted the phone number at the bottom, where her name and title stood out in bold letters.

She was right in her assumption that he wondered what possible help he could be with a missing-persons issue—several missing persons from the sound of it.

The woman's cryptic message struck a chord with Tommy's curiosity, though, and he figured she would clarify everything were he to simply call.

He checked the time, then looked up what time it was in Chile. For all his world travels, Tommy still had trouble remembering what country was in which time zone.

Fortunately, he learned that Chile just happened to be in the eastern time zone, same as Atlanta.

He noted when the email had been sent. "Six yesterday evening," he muttered.

Tommy imagined the interior minister must have been at the end of a long Monday when she reached out.

He wondered what might have triggered the correspondence but figured he'd get those answers when he called her back.

His phone sat on the desk next to the keyboard, waiting for him to pick it up. He resisted for a minute, still not ready to take on something of this magnitude—whatever *this* was.

He shook his head, raised the mug to his lips, and drew one more drink of coffee. Then he set the mug down, picked up his phone, and entered the number.

He listened to it ring three times before a man answered. "Office of the Interior Ministry," the guy said in Spanish.

Tommy knew enough of the language to get into trouble in a cantina in Tijuana, or to get him food, directions, and assistance if needed.

"My name is Tommy Schultz," he said in English, opting to go with what he knew best. "The interior minister asked me to call."

"Ah, yes," the man said cheerfully, as if he'd been waiting for this call since he arrived at the office. "She has been hoping to hear from you."

Tommy knew the duties of such dignitaries were vast, and he was half-surprised Interior Minister Carrera was in the building. Then again, it *was* early. Visiting schools or factories or sitting down with other lawmakers probably had to wait until after 9:14 in the morning.

"I'll put you right through, sir," the secretary said.

The line went silent. A few seconds passed before he heard a click followed by a "Good morning, Señor Schultz. Thank you so much for responding so quickly to my message."

"Good morning to you, Madam Interior Minister. It isn't every day I get to my office and first thing I see is an email from someone in your position."

"Yes, I can understand it must seem somewhat daunting, though given your reputation and your list of clients and friends, I'd say you must be more accustomed to such a thing than most."

She'd done her research. Beyond just a quick browser scroll through the IAA about page on their website. Or maybe she'd had people on her team do it. Had Chilean intelligence officers vetted him before giving her the go-ahead to send the email?

Tommy rubbed his forehead. His early morning mind was playing games with him, and he quickly refocused.

"I must admit, I am intrigued by the email you sent," Tommy said. He considered informing her that locating missing persons wasn't their deal but decided to let her speak first since she'd promised in the message to clarify everything once they were on a call.

"I apologize for being so cryptic, and I'm certain you are wondering why I would request your help with something like this. But I didn't want to put it in writing."

He could understand that, in so much that the internet and even the cell signals were far from secure. There were encryption tools that helped with such things, but if it could wait for a live conversation over the phone, that was the safer option.

"Not a problem," he replied. "So, tell me about this mysterious situation you have going on down there."

She drew a breath before beginning. "Over the years, there have been a series of strange disappearances in the Patagonia. Specifically, in the Avsén region, where the Queulat National Park is located. As you might expect, some of the missing persons were tourists on holiday."

Tommy *did* expect that to be the case. The American national parks experienced similar issues, with multiple people going missing seemingly every year. Sadly, many of the disappearances were children.

Conspiracies abounded, of course, about what may have happened to the victims. The usual suspects were always included—aliens almost always being at the top of the list. And the detractors, predictably, had their "common sense" explanations about people getting lost in the woods, dying from exposure or animal attacks.

Tommy wasn't ready to commit to any of those ideas. He'd seen too many things in his time with the IAA that modern science couldn't understand or explain. He maintained an open mind about nearly every possible explanation, yet the pragmatic side of him always assessed everything with a healthy dose of skepticism.

He doubted her theory about the disappearances in the Patagonia had anything to do with the more extreme side of possibilities such as alien abduction or other paranormal activities.

"Experts," she continued, "have attributed the disappearances to natural causes, as I'm sure you can imagine."

"Yes, ma'am. Same thing here." He listed the typical explanations he'd thought of a moment before.

"Correct. But there is a problem with this line of thinking. I don't know how it has played out in your country, but here we have found none of the bodies. If someone died from exposure or by animal attack, logic would suggest there would be human remains somewhere."

"I've thought the same thing as well," Tommy echoed. "I've often wondered how people can just disappear without a trace. There are certainly animals that would pick a body clean, but you'd think there would be some bones, a skull, something left. That said, we're talking about huge areas in these national parks. After a certain time, I imagine it becomes extremely difficult for investigators to locate anything. And on top of that, searches get called off, which leaves discovery of any remains to pure chance by a random passerby."

"Exactly," Carrera agreed. "Which has left us with no leads over the years."

The tone in her voice changed slightly, elevating at the end of the sentence, leading Tommy to believe that she was about to add something else—a detail that would fill in the gaps her email left open.

"Until now."

3

"You found something?" Tommy asked. Anticipation simmered within him, tingling his skin from head to foot.

"Yes. As we discussed, most of the people who vanished were visitors, though there were a few who were from that area. But the most recent was an American."

American? Tommy wasn't extremely surprised by that. He'd known several people who visited the Patagonia region to hike through the forests and climb the mountains. It wasn't really his cup of tea, but several of his outdoor-enthusiast friends treated a trip to the Patagonia as a bucket-list kind of deal. He, however, had seen enough adventure to last a lifetime and knew that more always lurked around the corner whether he wanted it or not.

His curiosity gave way to concern as he realized the point of this call might have less to do with archaeology and more to do with one of his friends being the missing person the Chilean interior minister mentioned.

"It's... not someone I know, is it?" Tommy ventured. He knew Sean wasn't down in South America at the moment. He was safely at his beach house in the town of Rosemary Beach on the Florida Panhandle's famous Emerald Coast.

"I don't know," she admitted. "His name was Michael Buford."

Tommy didn't recognize the name, or having ever even met the guy. "I don't believe I know him."

"Based on what we've learned, he was more of a treasure hunter than an archaeologist. I doubt you would have ever come into contact with him unless he'd visited one of your exhibits or perhaps asked for help at some point."

The latter definitely hadn't happened, though Tommy may have shaken the guy's hand at some point. Treasure hunters, anthropologists, and archaeologists often shared a host of commonalities, including the events they attended.

Still, Tommy couldn't recall ever hearing that name. He wished Sean were in the building. His nearly eidetic memory would come in handy for something like this. Sean almost never forgot a name and face.

Tommy also found himself feeling a touch jealous that Sean and Adriana were on his favorite coastline in the continental United States.

"Anything's possible. And I'm not the best with names. That's more my buddy's thing. So, this latest person to disappear was a treasure hunter." Tommy connected the dots quickly. He jumped to the next logical question. "Was he in Chile looking for some kind of treasure?"

"We believe so, yes."

"Lots of old stuff down there in South America. Beyond the known history such as the Inca and pre-Colombian civilizations. You start getting into the Caral civilizations, and you're talking 3,500 BC, and probably older. We know a good bit about their cultures, how they developed into larger civilizations, but there is still much to learn."

"Yes, Mr. Schultz. I know. I live here."

Tommy winced at what she could have mistaken for mansplaining. It hadn't been, however. This kind of thing just excited Tommy.

He'd seen new information suggesting the Aboriginal tribes knew of ancient peoples in South America, even traded with them. Some said this relationship flourished prior to the Ice Age, or what they called the "cold time."

Tommy figured she was going to ask him about some golden idol, a crystal skull, or perhaps giant formations of stones visible only from the air.

"Any idea what this Buford was looking for?"

"Yes. But I must warn you, based on my limited information on the subject, and abject ignorance in the field of archaeology, it sounds pretty far-fetched."

"I've forged a reputation on far-fetched. Hit me with it."

She took a breath and sighed. "Have you ever heard of the Wandering City of Patagonia?"

Tommy leaned back. He scratched his chin and thought. That was one he'd somehow missed. He suddenly felt inadequate.

"No. That's one I haven't heard of."

"I'm not surprised. Few I've spoken to have, either. But perhaps you know it by one of its other names: Trapananda, Elelín, or the City of the Caesars."

Tommy thought. He hadn't heard of any of those. "Sorry. I don't think I've come across those before. What is it?"

"I'm surprised. But they are mostly regional legends. Perhaps the stories haven't made it that far north. You've no doubt heard of Cibola, El Dorado?"

Tommy fought off the urge to laugh, thinking back on some of his earliest adventures with Sean. "Yes, ma'am. That one I've heard of."

"It is a similar story, except that the fabled city of gold was in a permanent location based on most of the myths."

That much was true, though Tommy knew of a few stories that suggested the city moved around.

"So, I guess that's why the name?"

"Correct. The Wandering City of Patagonia is an old legend. Some researchers believe it existed as far back as a few thousand years ago, before most records of the early civilizations here."

Tommy kept his lips tight. Based on his own research, built on the foundation of several others, he knew the history of South America dated further back than a mere few thousand years. But those were semantics. And he needed to get to the point of this conversation so he could return to his coffee, and a subsequent refill.

"So, this guy Buford," Tommy was surprised he'd remembered the name, though it had been a struggle. And he had just heard it. "You think he was looking for this Wandering City? What makes you believe that?"

He rotated his chair and looked out the window. Centennial Olympic Park sprawled across the street of the same name. The last of the autumn leaves had abandoned their skeletal branches, leaving the trees naked for the coming winter.

"As I mentioned before, prior to this disappearance, we had no leads on any of the victims. With this one, we do."

Tommy nodded and scratched his chin. He channeled his favorite fictional radio psychiatrist. "I'm listening."

She obviously didn't catch the phrase, or his tone.

"Buford's journal was found in a cabin he'd rented in the nearby city of La Junta. This book contains details of his research and theories about the Wandering City. There is a recurring theme in his notes. It borders on obsession."

"That tends to happen to some folks when they go down the wrong rabbit hole. What was this common thread?"

Tommy stood and stepped closer to the window. The lanes of the street below overflowed with traffic. The park, however, was relatively empty, as was to be expected this time of year. Workers were setting up a stage in the field below the famous Olympic fountains. A big Christmas celebration was scheduled for the weekend, only ten days from the holiday.

"He mentions something called the Key of Inti. Do you know anything about this artifact?"

"Artifact? Can't say that I do. But you said it's called the Key of Inti? As in the ancient pre-Colombian sun god? It's represented by a yellow sun. The same one that's on the flag of Argentina."

"And the second flag of Peru," Carrera added. "It's also featured in the coat of arms of Ecuador and Bolivia."

She was just full of new information he'd somehow missed through the years.

"Interesting."

"Yes. It seems Buford was focused intently on this key. He had notes about possible locations for it, but he never mentions finding it."

"And you believe he was looking for this artifact when he disappeared?" Tommy guessed.

"The last lines in his journal indicate he was going to head into the mountains in search of it. He specifically notes a location above the lake called *La Punta Diablo*."

"Devil's Point," Tommy muttered. *A bit overused if you asked me,* he thought. "But search and rescue didn't find anything in that area."

"No. I must get to a meeting in ten minutes. So, I will be blunt, Señor Schultz. I want your help in uncovering this mystery. If anyone can solve the riddles mentioned in this journal, it's your agency."

The statement flattered Tommy. But he, perhaps pridefully, believed she was correct. There were few other organizations out there who'd been able to do what his had done, and in so many theaters of operation.

"I'd love to take a look at this journal," he said. "But it's coming on the holidays here. It's a time of the year when we're sort of winding down. Most of my agents have already taken off on vacations. It's pretty much just me, the security guy, and our receptionist. And she leaves on Friday until the new year."

As he said it out loud, Tommy realized what a softy he was to give so much time off to those in his building. But they earned it. And he'd always believed in treating people like people, not just employees.

"That is unfortunate," she said. He wasn't surprised by the disappointment in her voice. But there was nothing he could do.

June was home, and they spent more time apart than together, or so it seemed. He wasn't going to screw this up. If the interior minister needed his help, she could wait until the new year.

"If it can wait until January," he offered, "I'll be happy to put together a jaunt down there and have a look. Or you can scan the pages of the journal and I can analyze them from here."

She sighed. "I don't know if I'm comfortable with that scanning thing. As for the timeline, I feel like we need to move this along quickly. If for no other reason than for Buford's family, and those who've lost loved ones. Solving this could bring closure to many, and that isn't something I want to put off."

Tommy could understand that. And her statement pulled on his heartstrings more than he wanted to allow.

There was one other possibility. He didn't think they'd say yes, but it was worth asking. "I do have a couple of agents who might be able to help," Tommy said. "They specialize in stuff like this when they're not doing research. The Paranormal Archaeology Division was designed with these kinds of cases in mind. The agents who work under them are with their families, but these two don't have kids, and might be persuaded if I run it by them. It's worth a shot."

"I would be more than grateful, Señor Schultz."

Tommy chuckled. "My dad is Señor Schultz. You can call me Tommy. As for the two agents, I'll have to check with them. Can't give you any guarantees."

"Life gives few guarantees, Señor... Tommy," she corrected herself.

Isn't that the truth.

"I'll reach out to them and see what they say. They're snowboarding in Utah at the moment, but they're usually pretty fast to answer my messages."

"Thank you for your help. I look forward to your answer, either way."

"No problem."

She said goodbye and ended the call.

Tommy lingered by the window for a minute, watching the cars crawl along Centennial Olympic Park Drive. He imagined some of the drivers were already late for work, while others were pushing their luck.

He turned around and picked up his coffee, took a sip, and set it down. Then he opened the text messaging app, looked up the message thread with Alex and Tara, and began typing.

4

UTAH

Alex Simms cracked open his eyes, waking from a dream about an auburn-haired angel surrounded by falling snow, sparkling in bright sunlight.

"Good morning," a sweet voice said to his right.

He rolled his head over and found the angel from his dream lying next to him, staring back—her eyes the color of deep jade, glistening in the cracks of sunlight slipping through the curtains near the bed.

"Good morning back," he managed.

He reached over and touched her ear with the tips of his fingers, brushing a loose strand of hair behind it.

"You were in my dreams," Alex added.

She scoffed with a grin. "You know, you already married me. You don't have to use cheesy lines like that. But it is sweet."

"Cheesy?" He looked hurt. "No, I mean I really did just have a dream about you. You were standing in a field of snow, bathed in sunlight. It looked like you were on top of a mountain or something."

Tara maintained the suspicious expression on her face. "You're not just trying to come up with a line you thought I'd like to wake up to in the morning?"

He shook his head vehemently. "Absolutely not. And given the inquisition I woke up to, I think I might want to go back to the dream."

"What was I wearing?"

"What?"

She leaned in close until her face hovered over his, their noses nearly touching. "What was I wearing?" Tara repeated.

"Uh. Just normal clothes. You know. Like a jacket and pants?"

"Hmm. That doesn't sound sexy." She wore a look of disappointment on her face.

"No," he defended quickly. "It's not that. I mean, it wasn't that kind of dream."

"Oh." She rolled back over and propped her head up on her palm. "So, we were like, out for a hike on a mountain?"

He shrugged, scooting up the bed a little to lean against the headboard. "Yeah. I guess so. I didn't really get the full context. You were standing there. Then you woke me up." He held her gaze. "But it feels good knowing I don't have to wake up from this—"

"And there's the line," she cut him off with an eye roll.

He giggled. "Okay, you have to give me credit on that one. Especially because I thought of it on the fly, and just having woken up. I'm still groggy."

She nodded and pulled him close, cupping the back of his neck with her fingers. "Yeah, I guess that one was pretty sweet."

Their phones buzzed on the nightstands on either side of the bed.

He blew it off and pressed his lips against hers. She still smelled of the fragrant soaps and shampoo from the hotel shower. He inhaled her deeply, and it filled him like the most potent drug in the world.

The phones buzzed again.

They parted by an inch.

"Who is texting us right now?" Alex asked.

"I have no idea," Tara answered.

"Just ignore them," he persisted.

The phones buzzed again.

"We really should keep those on do not disturb in the night. It's shocking we forgot to do that."

"Isn't it?" He sighed and rolled over to look at the device. Lines creased his forehead when he saw the name on the screen. "They're from Tommy."

"Why is he, of all people, texting us at this time of day?" she wondered. "He's like the only person who knows where we are, and what time zone we're in."

"Must be important," Alex reasoned. He opened the message app and read through the last six texts from their boss. "He's been texting us for the last three hours."

Tara rolled over to the nightstand on her side of the bed, picked up the phone, and unplugged the charging cord. "Jeez. Yeah, that's a bit above average for him."

She sat up against the headboard, too, exposing the loose-fitting pink Dolly Parton T-shirt she'd worn to bed.

They simultaneously read through the messages in silence. Alex finished first thanks to his head start but waited until she was done to say anything.

Hey, when you two wake up, give me a call.

It's about a gig down in South America.

PAD material.

I know y'all are probably still asleep, and it's your vacation, but it's a high-priority client.

Missing persons involved.

Are y'all still sleeping? Call me when you wake up.

"It's not like Tommy to be so insistent," Tara said when she was done. She noted that the first text and the subsequent five were separated by two hours.

"I guess we need to call him," Alex suggested.

"I thought he was shutting down HQ for the holidays."

"He was. Whatever this is must be important." Alex looked over at her. He still admired her just as he had from the first time he laid eyes on her. "You want me to call him?"

She nodded. "Might as well. Doesn't look like he's going to stop messaging us until we do."

"Yeah. I guess not."

Alex tapped on the contact info, then the number for Tommy's cell phone. It started ringing a second later.

Two rings in, Tommy answered. "Hey, Alex. I hope I didn't wake you two."

"Nah, we just got up. To a pile of texts from you."

"Sorry about that. I wouldn't have bothered you if it weren't important."

"Good morning, Tommy," Tara said. "You're on speaker, by the way."

"Oh, hey, Tara. You guys having fun out there? How's the powder?"

"Some of the best in the world," she said, wiping the early morning fatigue from her voice with a smile.

"Yeah, it's hard to beat Utah pow-pow." He paused for a second to make the transition to the purpose of the call. "Look, I know y'all are on vacation, and I wouldn't bother you with this if it didn't come with a sense of urgency."

"It's okay, Tommy," Alex said. "We know. So, what's going on?"

Tommy sighed. There was an air of relief in the sound. The couple imagined he must have felt guilty about making this request of them so close to the holidays, and while they were on vacation. But they all knew each other well enough from years of working together. Any reluctance Tommy might have felt would quickly melt away.

"I received a strange email this morning when I got to the office. From the interior minister of Chile."

Tara snorted. "Do you ever have a normal day when you go into work? Just open up your email, and you don't have a message from the second-most powerful person in a developed nation waiting in your inbox?"

"Yeah, I would say that isn't typical, but it does happen from time to time."

"So," Alex said, running fingers through his thick, brown hair, "what did she have to say? You mentioned in your texts something about missing persons."

"Right. I did. I hadn't heard about this, but there have been several people who have vanished in the Patagonia over the years. It's not totally unsurprising considering how many visitors travel to that area each year."

Tara and Alex knew he was right about that. The area played host to hikers, climbers, mountain bikers, and campers. With the advent of social media, it seemed even more like people flocked to regions like the Patagonia simply for the likes and follows of posting pictures from exotic locations.

The couple had often wondered how many of those influencers actually enjoyed the places they went, or if they were simply posers.

"That sort of thing happens in the wilderness," Tara commented, unknowingly echoing Tommy's thoughts from earlier. "Far too often, unfortunately. People think they can handle the elements or won't get lost. Things can change fast out in the wild."

"Yeah," Tommy agreed. "You're right about that."

"No offense, boss," Alex cut in, "but what does this sort of thing have to do with us? We're not really a missing-persons unit. And surely they have their own agencies down there for that sort of thing."

"They do. I spoke to the interior minister this morning. Nice woman. Her name is Sofia Carrera. Their agencies have done all they can to solve this mystery, but much like the disappearances in our own national parks, they haven't been able to solve many, if any of them. But that isn't why she asked for my help. I doubt she expects us to find any of those who vanished. Some of them have, unfortunately, been gone for quite some time. The most recent person, however, caused her to think we might be able to help."

Tara and Alex shared a glance, both of them curious as to how this sort of thing would have anything to do with them.

"A man named Michael Buford disappeared somewhere in the mountains this week. He's an explorer and a treasure hunter. Either of you ever heard of him?"

Both shook their heads after another look at each other for confirmation. "No," Alex answered first. "Doesn't ring a bell."

"It didn't for me either. I just figured maybe one of us has met the guy at some point."

"Did you ask Sean?" Tara suggested. "Maybe he knows him."

"No, I haven't asked him yet, but I will. What I do know is that he was looking for something, something that probably doesn't exist."

"Probably doesn't exist is kind of what we do, isn't it?" Alex said.

"Which is why we're talking right now. It seems Buford was hunting for something called the Wandering City of Patagonia. Ms. Carrera said it goes by a few other names, the most common being City of the Caesars. Either one of you ever heard of it?"

Again, the two shared a blank glance, then shrugged. "Nope," Tara said. "You're zero for two today, chief."

Tommy chuckled. "Yeah. I didn't know about them either. I find it a little remarkable none of us have heard of this place, but that doesn't matter for now. I've done some research on this Wandering City for the last few hours. There isn't much online about it. From what fragments I could gather, it's a mystical place that appears and disappears."

"I've heard of stories like that," Tara said.

"Same here," Alex added. "There are a few similar to that out there. So, this guy Buford believed it was real and was trying to find it?"

"Seems that way. Carrera told me they have a journal he left behind while investigating an area in the mountains. They found it in his cabin."

"Did she send over digitized images of the contents? Would be interesting to look at that."

"No, she wasn't willing to risk it. Apparently, this is sensitive infor-mation. I don't know if she doesn't want more treasure hunters flooding the area and putting more people at risk, or if she's genuinely concerned that there might be some kind of mystical, supernatural thing going on."

The last part hooked the couple.

"So," Tara said, "let me guess. You want the two of us to fly down to Chile and see what we can learn?"

"I hate to ask," Tommy said, his voice sincerely apologetic. "And if you can't, I'll tell Carrera she has to wait. In fact, I did tell her that, but she insisted it needed to be soon. Wants to get closure for the families of those who lost loved ones."

"Sounds like she believes whatever is in that journal might help with that."

"Correct. Again, say no if you want to, and I'll let her know. No pressure from me at all. If we wait a couple of weeks, that's fine by me."

Tara and Alex looked across the bed at each other. Neither seemed bothered by the request at all, but they also didn't want to upset the other by abandoning their vacation and heading to another continent.

Alex signaled first with a shrug and a nod. "I'm okay with it if you are," he whispered. She smiled back at him and bobbed her head, evidently excited at the thought of the new challenge.

"Okay, chief," Alex said. "We're in."

"Are you sure? Again, I don't want to—"

"Tommy, do you always try to turn away a yes when you get one?" Tara interrupted, giggling a little as she spoke.

"No. Sorry. You're right. Thank you both so much. You'll need plane tickets. I'm assuming Salt Lake will be the closest international airport. I'll make sure you are taken care of, including the accommodations you paid for there in Park City."

They knew they wouldn't have to even mention that to him, and probably wouldn't have brought it up if he hadn't.

Still, it was a nice gesture.

"There's something else you need to know about this journal." Tommy paused for a breath. "It seems Buford was looking for something specific. Again, I haven't seen the pages from his notes, but it appears he was searching for an artifact known as the Key of Inti."

5

The couple didn't respond, staring blankly at the phone as they waited for more information.

"I take your silence to mean you don't know what that is?"

"I've heard of Inti," Tara offered. "Inca sun god. Prevalent in several nations."

"Isn't that the sun that's on the flag of Argentina?" Alex guessed.

"It is," Tommy said. "And I said the same thing." He chuckled. "Inti was worshipped long before the Incas. The Caral-Supe civilization is the earliest known culture in that region, specifically Peru. They helped establish the Andean civilization, which is one of only six 'pristine' civilizations in the world."

"That means they were created independently without outside influence, yeah?"

"Correct, Alex. And impressive, for sure. There were three, and according to some experts, four major Andean cultures between the Caral and the Incas. The Chavin, Huari or Ware, the Tiwanaku, and the Cuzco kingdom. There were others, of course, to a lesser extent. But one thing they all had in common was the core of civilization laid down by their ancestral founders—a system to feed the people."

"So, you're talking about developing an agricultural system, right?"

"Yes, but theirs was complex. It depended on the widely varying extremes of both the weather, the seasons, and the land itself. From Peru to Chile and into Argentina and Bolivia, there are regions that are quite inhospitable. Yet these ancient people figured out a way to make it work using a hybrid system of hunting and gathering and growing crops such as maize and other vegetables. But the key to it all, no pun intended, was the sun god."

"Right," Alex said. "Without the ability to harness the sun and its power to grow food, they would have remained hunter gatherers."

"Exactly. So, just as with many ancient civilizations, the sun figured prominently in their religions and worship practices. That's probably how Inti was born."

Tara and Alex knew plenty about helio worship, or the deification of the sun. As Tommy suggested, it had been prevalent in belief systems from ancient Egyptian religions to the practices of ancient Sumer to many that followed. The sun was still revered, although in a different way, by the pagan practices in ancient Rome, an empire built on the back of agriculture.

"Do you know anything about such a key?" Tara asked. "I've never heard of it." Alex shook his head in agreement.

"Unfortunately, no. And I've been looking around online all morning. Malcom couldn't even find anything about it."

The AI known as Malcom was a powerful addition to the research capabilities the IAA possessed. They'd been ahead of the curve creating it and had produced an artificial intelligence capable of scouring the world's databases in seconds.

In recent months, AI had stormed the headlines of most news outlets and YouTube channels. Some people feared the worst—the singularity that would become self-aware and take over humanity. While many believed that the advent of AI would ring in a new age of scaled production, health, and capability for the world.

Tommy had been one of the latter, and one of the first to deploy the power of AI into the realms of history and research. Malcom had even learned ancient dead languages, scripts, hieroglyphs, and symbology to provide almost instantaneous results for queries on the subjects.

"If Malcom couldn't find it, then does it even exist?" Alex posited.

"Funnily, I'm thinking more and more that's a legitimate question," Tommy admitted. "Nonetheless, this guy Buford found something about it, which means there must have been records of it somewhere. Malcom not being able to find it only suggests it's not digitized yet."

It was one of the glaring weaknesses of AI in general. Sure, there were theories that the systems could figure out how to take control of cameras, phones, and other devices to glean real-world analog information. But as of yet, Malcom hadn't done that, and Tommy believed that wouldn't happen.

"So, we're going to do this one real old-school, huh," Tara realized.

"Yep. I mean, obviously use your tech when you can. Just because the Key of Inti isn't recorded somewhere online doesn't mean you won't be able to find out more once you get to that journal. Follow the breadcrumbs. Buford must have left something that could lead to it. Start from where he was, and work backward. Almost always works."

"Almost?"

Tommy laughed gruffly. "Nothing works every time. Except Novocain. Give it time. It always works."

"Nice. *Remember The Titans*," Tara noted.

"Great film. Anyway, you two don't need me to tell you how to do your jobs. I just figured this sounded like the kind of thing y'all were into, particularly the spooky disappearance part."

"It definitely sounds as if there could be a paranormal element to it," Alex conceded. "We'll check it out and let you know what we find."

"Cool. Just so you know, Carrera wants to take point on this. She'd prefer any information you're able to gather be sent straight to her. Between you and me, I'd prefer it if you keep things quiet for now."

"Understood."

"I just don't like answering to someone else. Especially someone from a government. No one wants a politician looking over their shoulder at every move. You send me what you find, and I'll drip out what I think is appropriate for her until, or if, we find anything conclusive."

"Thanks for having our back on that one," Tara said. "What will the interior minister say, though?"

"Frankly, we're doing her a favor. And during the holidays. If she doesn't like how things are progressing, or how we go about it, she's welcome to find someone else. I don't have any misgivings about you finding any of the people who vanished. Obviously, the ones that have been gone for years are lost to the mountains. It's doubtful even Buford is alive, though it's certainly possible. The weather down there is nice right now, so dying out in the wilderness would likely come from an animal attack, or possibly dehydration. He'd have to get pretty lost out there for the latter to happen. But it could happen."

"We'll do our best, chief," Alex said. "Just let us know when the flight is leaving, and we'll be on it."

"Will do. I don't know if Carrera will meet you at the airport, or if it will be some of her people. I would imagine the latter. Interior ministers tend to have busy schedules. She likely has to delegate pretty much everything."

"No worries, Tommy," Tara said. "We'll play it by ear. Anything else we need to know?"

"No." Tommy went silent for a second, thinking to make sure he wasn't forgetting anything. "I think that's about it. I'll send you the flight details ASAP. From there, I won't bother the two of you too much. Just let me know if you need anything along the way."

They said their goodbyes and ended the call.

Tara and Alex looked up at each other. Their eyes filled with uncertainty, tinged with a splash of excitement.

Sure, they were giving up their vacation on the slopes, but the mystery Tommy had dropped in their lap was every bit as good, if not more so, to the two history enthusiasts.

"The Key of Inti," Alex muttered, as if saying it so he wouldn't forget. "Sounds like this Buford character believed it was real."

"I guess we should start by learning as much as we can about him since Malcom wasn't able to get any info on the key," Tara suggested.

"Good idea. But first, what would you say to some coffee and a croissant?"

She smiled back at him. "I'd say I love you."

6

SANTIAGO, CHILE

Arturo Bravo strode down the wide corridor, passing white marble columns with swirls of black twisting across the curved surfaces.

His long black hair hung over his ears, bristling slightly in the breeze generated by his movement.

He kept his brown eyes locked on the two white doors straight ahead, paying no attention to the sandstone tile floors that offered muted taps against his shoes with every step. Arturo ignored the ostentatious walls, too, painted with black and white stripes.

He'd seen it before. More times than he remembered.

When Manuel Orasco brought him here for the first time, Arturo had marveled over the show of wealth. He'd even wondered what it would be like to live in such splendor, at least for the duration of his first visit.

Little did he know he'd quickly grow tired of the opulence, the waste that was spent on this.

His tastes, as he learned, were much simpler.

That wasn't to say he didn't enjoy the best of what life had to offer. His home was luxurious but tasteful, and much smaller than Orasco's sprawling estate.

Arturo had a view of the ocean and the beach below. His four-bedroom penthouse had more space than he needed, though he'd managed to figure out uses for all of it.

Growing up in the *campamento* slums, he'd never imagined having all that he did now. So many of his childhood friends were either dead or still languishing in those shanty villages.

He stopped at the doors, checked his white button-up shirt to make sure it was still tucked into his black slacks, and adjusted his Rolex Submariner.

The part of him that grew up in abject poverty still felt as though he didn't belong in a place like this, that he was an outsider, and no matter what he did or how he dressed, he'd never truly belong.

Maybe that was okay. He was a tool, a resource to get things done.

Arturo knew his role. He embraced it in many ways.

Manuel Orasco was a highly respected businessman, one of the wealthiest in this part of the world. Running security and intelligence for such a man came with its benefits.

Security was a loose term regarding Arturo's role. Sure, he played the part of bodyguard, occasionally driver, and overseer of details for events like large parties Orasco hosted.

But now and then, the tycoon needed to get his hands dirty—except the man either didn't have the stomach for killing, or simply required plausible deniability. Either way, there had been more than one occasion in which Arturo was ordered to eliminate a problem.

He had no qualms about it. To him, taking another life was a simple thing—a black-and-white cause and effect. He felt no guilt over it, no remorse of any kind. He was paid to do a job, and he did it as well as anyone.

Arturo raised a fist and rapped on the white door to the right of center.

"Come in." The muted familiar tone of his boss's voice reverberated through the thick wooden barrier.

Arturo turned the brushed bronze handle and pushed open the door. He stepped inside the familiar study where his employer spent so many of his days and nights, poring over numbers, data, and news.

The room was as opulent as the rest of the palatial mansion. High ceilings with dark timber beams forming square sections contrasted with the white paint between. A fireplace and sitting area with two cabernet-red leather chairs sat angled in toward a coffee table. The table sat atop an oriental rug.

Silver sconces lined the walls, fixed into molding that matched the colors of the beams above. Paintings hung between the light fixtures, featuring images inspired by the Inca Empire. Some displayed ancient temples set in jungles or high in the Andes. Others portrayed the Inca people, the most eye-catching of which was that of a priest in full regalia.

Arturo closed the door and looked to his right.

Orasco sat behind a giant wooden desk. A relief of a jaguar prowling through the jungle stood out on the façade.

Arturo's employer fit the image of a powerful businessman. Orasco wore a suit and tie whenever he was working, even though the man was in his own home. The expensive outfits might as well have been a part of him. They were certainly a part of his persona.

He exuded confidence and power, and Arturo knew that wasn't by accident. Orasco lived by the creed that you become what you express to the world.

It would have been easy for a man worth billions to come into his office wearing a track suit or pajamas, but as far as Arturo knew, that had never happened.

Orasco's black hair was cut tight above his ears and combed over to one side. His matching mustache was thick like a push broom, hearkening back to the way powerful men of ages gone by had looked.

"Good morning, my friend," Orasco said. "Please. Come. Sit." He extended his right hand toward a pair of chairs that matched the ones over by the fireplace.

Arturo obeyed and walked the ten steps over to the chairs and sat down in the one on the left.

"Cigar?" Orasco offered. He stood and flipped open a glossy, cherry humidor to the right of his computer monitor.

"I don't usually turn down that offer," Arturo said with a cool grin. "You have good taste, Arturo."

Orasco picked out two of the hand-rolled Nicaraguan cigars and then closed the lid. He passed one across the desk to Arturo, who leaned forward and accepted it with a grateful nod.

The two men pulled the caps off the ends in lieu of using a cutter or a punch. Orasco lifted a black torch lighter, pressed the button, then touched the blue jet flame to the tip as he spun the cigar around in his fingers until the entire end glowed bright orange.

Satisfied the cigar was lit to his liking, he took a few puffs and then passed the lighter over to Arturo, who copied the same process.

A gray cloud loomed around them, though that would be sucked up by the air filtration machine hanging from the ceiling over the deck. A matching one was fixed to the ceiling above the chairs by the fireplace, and was why the room didn't smell like a cigar shop despite countless stogies being burned every week.

"Thank you for getting here so quickly," Orasco said. "You're always so quick to respond."

"There was a little traffic, or I would have been here sooner."

Orasco creased his lips in a smile but didn't bare his teeth. "Always seeking perfection. It's a good quality to have, my friend. And one of the reasons I knew you were the right choice for this position."

Arturo blew out a puff of smoke. It plumed up into the air and swirled slowly above his head.

"Thank you, sir," he replied. His answer was curt and to the point, which was another characteristic Orasco appreciated about the man.

Just in his early thirties, Arturo had worked his way up from the gutter, and that didn't happen by having a weak drive, lack of focus, or caring about social conventions.

"I'll get straight to it," Orasco continued. He slid a piece of paper across the table and nodded at it, indicating that Arturo should pick it up.

He did and studied the printout for a second. The image of a sun with shimmering, wavy rays was printed on it, along with some text below it.

"The Key of Inti?" Arturo said after reading it.

Orasco pinched the cigar with his teeth, tightened his lips to take a drag, and then removed the smoldering cigar from his mouth to exhale the smoke. He turned and took a step toward one of the eight massive windows along the wall. The panes were framed with dark wooden molding and golden curtains that hung on each side.

He looked out through the glass at the ocean beyond as if appreciating the view, though Arturo knew the man was deep in thought.

"I have been searching for something for years now, since before you came into the organization. Have you ever heard of the Wandering City of Patagonia?"

"No. Should I?"

Orasco rolled his shoulders and took another puff. "No. It isn't a well-known legend."

"What is it?" Arturo asked. He blew rings of smoke out of his mouth that hung in the air above him before melting into the rest of the fog.

"A mystical city. A place with unimaginable wealth. It is a kind of heaven on earth."

Arturo shifted uneasily. The man already possessed unimaginable wealth. And his estate was very much a paradise in its own right.

During his time as an enforcer for the cartel, Arturo had witnessed the fall of many powerful men, and almost always for the same reason—greed.

Their dissatisfaction with life led to a constant seeking of more—more money, more women, more material possessions, and more power.

And the more they got, the more consumed by this pursuit they became.

"You must be thinking I already have enough wealth for ten lifetimes," Orasco guessed correctly. Before Arturo could defend himself, the boss continued. "I would probably think the same thing if I were in your chair right now. But this kind of wealth is different. It would be infinite compared to the supply of money in the world right now. This kind of wealth could change the map of the world."

There it was again. Greed. Arturo wondered if he should start putting out feelers for another job once Orasco's empire fell in the pursuit of some mythical city of gold.

"If I were to obtain the location of the city," Orasco went on, "I would be the most powerful person in the world. And you would be my right hand, Arturo."

The man was trying to play to Arturo's ego but in a subtle way. Arturo was satisfied with his life now. He didn't care to move up, or down, the ladder anymore.

The only thing he sought from life now was his weekly dose of cocaine, pleasurable company, good liquor and cigars, and a little excitement now and then.

"Do you know what you could do with that kind of power, that kind of wealth, Arturo?"

The guest didn't reply.

"Anything you want," Orasco answered for him.

"With all due respect, sir, I do not wish to seek more than what you have already given me. You pay me extremely well."

"As you deserve," Orasco injected quickly.

"And I appreciate that. But my life is simple. I do not seek power. But I am in your debt. For the rest of my life, I will serve you. I know you will always take care of me, as you have done. So, if you tell me to do something, I do it. And I don't question it."

Orasco nodded, thoughts drifting through his mind like the clouds far off in the distance over the ocean. "I know. You're the most loyal person I've ever had in the organization. Which is why I am putting you in charge of this, a most crucial operation."

Arturo was wondering when his boss was going to get to the point of this visit.

"Recently, an American treasure hunter named Michael Buford went missing in the mountains near La Junta. Do you know the town?"

"Only by name. I don't believe I've ever been there."

"Doesn't matter. What does matter is what this treasure hunter was looking for." Orasco left the statement hanging for a few seconds.

"You think he was searching for this Wandering City?"

"I know he was." Orasco nodded, took another puff, and then faced his guest as he leaned against the corner of the desk. "He left a journal in a cabin in La Junta. That book is the key to everything. It contains his notes, research, and theories."

"You said he disappeared," Arturo noted. "What happened to him?"

"No one knows. Many people go missing in the mountains every year."

Arturo accepted the answer. He knew that was the case, but his initial suspicion was foul play. He shifted to his next question. "How do you know about this book?"

"It seems our interior minister is interested in the city as well. When investigators searched Buford's cabin, they discovered the book and reported to her people."

The interior minister? The epiphany caught Arturo off guard. He was accustomed to dealing with high-profile individuals, sometimes as targets, but the second-most powerful politician in the country was a new one for him.

"Sounds as if you aren't the only one looking for this Wandering City."

It was an easy conclusion to reach. What other reason would Carrera have for meddling with an investigation into a missing American—unless Buford was someone important? But from the sound of it, he was just another guy searching for lost treasure.

"Indeed," Orasco allowed. "I don't know why the interior minister has an interest in the lost city, but the fact that she had the journal delivered straight to her tells me all I need to know. Furthermore, she has requested help from the International Archaeological Agency in the United States."

"More Americans?" Arturo said with distaste. "Why? And what is this agency?"

"They handle recovering artifacts around the world. They've been known to find some now and then as well. Their methods, however, come under scrutiny since some of their agents tend to leave a trail of bodies behind them."

That last part intrigued Arturo, but he kept it to himself. He also wondered how Orasco knew so much about all this. How had he been aware of the journal going to Carrera, and the call to this agency in the United States?

There was only one answer.

Orasco's reach was extensive. He had people everywhere. From cops to cabinet members, and all points in between, Orasco had his ears wide open across the country, and probably the continent. Arturo figured that helped the man stay ahead of the competition in a volatile energy market.

The threat of green energy hadn't done much to Orasco's oil margins. Nor would it. The man had diversified, creating new branches of energy research to capture the whole market from biofuels, hydrogen cells, and fields of solar panels to quench the panic of those swarming to the electric vehicle segment.

Having people in key positions of influence, or observation, was vital.

It seemed his interests ventured beyond business.

"My mole," Orasco said, "said that a team from the IAA is going to be landing here in Santiago tomorrow morning to investigate Buford's journal."

Arturo inclined his head, raising his chin slightly. "What do you want me to do?"

"I need the Americans dead. Get the journal. That book, and now those two from the IAA, are the only threats to my plans. But my person inside the government tells me that Carrera is making sure they keep all of this quiet. Even so, I don't trust politicians. They're sloppy. They let their power go to their heads in a way that makes them believe they are invincible. That's when mistakes happen."

"You're not asking me to eliminate her, are you?" Arturo asked. There was an apprehension in his voice that was out of place for a man with his skills and background. Taking out a high-ranking government official, especially one in Carrera's position, wasn't just a run-of-the-mill hit. That was a political assassination, and with it came serious logistic and strategic issues.

"No, no. Nothing like that. Carrera is up to something, and whatever it is, I don't believe the president knows. She's keeping a tight lid on it. What *it* is, I have only ideas and theories. Those will have to wait for now. There's no point in discussing them."

"Understood, sir."

That was all Orasco needed to hear from the younger man.

Arturo was clever, and always thinking one step ahead. And he was a killer through and through, willing to do whatever it took.

Orasco's preferred method of operation was, and always had been, to let people do what they did best and use their skills for his own advancement.

It was how leaders of industry had forged their legacies throughout history. Henry Ford had been such a thinker, using the strengths of a group of experts around him to grow his business—and answer questions and solve challenges when he could not.

"Remember, we cannot permit the journal to fall into someone else's hands. Get the book, take care of the Americans. I don't have to tell you how to do that. You're truly gifted in that regard. I have an archaeologist working on finding solutions from the original journal."

"Intersting," Arturo said. "Has your archaeologist had any luck deciphering the riddles?"

Orasco's face darkened. "No. And my patience is wearing thin with him."

"Would you like me to... handle him, too?"

"Not yet. I can give him a little more rope, but if he can't figure it out in the next forty-eight hours, it will be time to cut him loose and find someone else."

"Understood, sir."

"I'll send you a text message with the flight details for when the Americans are to arrive. My mole will also let me know where they are planning to meet since I doubt they'll discuss this matter at an official government site. That's all the business for now, Arturo."

Orasco planted the cigar between his lips again and took a pull. The smoldering tip glowed fiery orange again.

Arturo took that as his cue to leave and started to stand.

"Please," Orasco insisted, holding up his left hand. "Stay. Enjoy your cigar. You've earned it, my friend. We both have."

Arturo nodded. "Thank you, sir. I appreciate it."

"I know you do, Arturo. I know you do."

7

Alex and Tara walked off the sky bridge and into the terminal of the Arturo Merino Benítez International Airport. They hadn't been sure what to expect regarding their welcoming party. All Interior Minister Carrera had told them was that she would meet them beyond the security gates when their flight arrived.

They'd flown out of Salt Lake City a day after the call from Tommy regarding the mysterious disappearances in the Patagonia. Tara and Alex had a feeling he'd delayed the flight by a day because he was a nice guy and wanted them to have one more day of vacation before abruptly heading back to work—and in the field no less, outside the comfort of their lab in Atlanta.

Normally, he would have sent the IAA private jet to pick them up and deliver them to South America, but Tommy had already given their two pilots the rest of the year off, and told them he'd only call if it was an emergency.

The flight down had been in first class, which was the next best thing to a private jet. Hardly insufferable.

They veered to the left and trekked toward the baggage claim and ground transportation. When they neared the point of no return for security checks, both noticed the entourage of security agents surrounding the walkway on both sides. One face, in particular, stood out from the men in black suits.

Interior Minister Carrera stood between two of the guards. A look of concern hovered over her distinguished air. Her dress was as red as the blood she'd drawn in years of politics, her black-brown hair coiffed as perfectly as if she'd just stepped onto a stage. Neither a hair nor a single thread was out of place. And she knew it.

When she saw the two Americans, Carrera quickly changed her expression to one of a welcoming smile and waved at the two as if they were longtime friends who hadn't seen each other in years.

Tara and Alex waved back awkwardly before they passed through the checkpoint.

"Bienvenidos," Carrera said, still wearing that politician's smile as she extended her hand toward Tara. "Thank you so much for coming."

"Not a problem," Tara answered.

When Carrera finished shaking her hand, she offered the same to Alex.

"It's not every day we get a request like this from someone in an office like yours," Alex said.

"Yes, well, I realize my station is an important one, but I'm a person just like anyone else. Speaking of, I could go for a coffee right now. Would you two like one?"

The Americans both said they would. It was still early afternoon, and they were accustomed to taking coffee anytime between the hours of 7:00 a.m. and 5:00 p.m., sometimes later if they were working on a big project down at the lab—which wasn't all that infrequent.

The interior minister ordered two of the security agents to take the visitors' backpacks. "They can carry those for you."

"It's okay," Alex protested. "I don't mind. But some help with our check bags would be nice."

Carrera bobbed her head once. "Very well. We'll get your bags, and then get coffee. I know a place not far from here that I think you'll enjoy."

Just landed, and they were already getting the royal treatment from the nation's second-highest ranking official.

The security team led the way down a set of steps and then over to the baggage claim area, where multiple carousels spun their conveyor belts slowly around, carrying suitcases and bags through their orbit until plucked up by the owners.

Dozens of people hovered around the carousels of the most recent flights. Most of the travelers watched the black rubber flaps of the tunnel as each piece of luggage spit out onto the conveyor belt to begin its loop.

"They are usually pretty fast here," Carrera said. "Fifteen minutes, and we'll be in my car and on our way."

She was right. Within the prophesied amount of time, they had collected their bags and were sitting in the back of a limousine, facing the rear, where the interior minister of Chile sat with her legs crossed and hands folded over her lap.

"You know my favorite coffee place, Victor," she said to the driver.

"Sí," the man replied.

Carrera was surrounded on both sides by guards with sunglasses. Both men stared out through the heavily tinted windows, constantly on high alert.

Alex wondered what that kind of life must be like, always worried someone was going to try to kill your boss, and if things got bad enough, you'd instinctively take a bullet for them.

There were few people on earth to whom he'd give that distinction. His wife was one. His family. Friends, sure, and that included the crew from the IAA. But doing it for someone you barely knew, and only because it was your duty... He figured he could do something like that if he had to but was glad he didn't have to make that decision.

"I trust your flight was comfortable," Carrera said in an effort to make pleasant conversation.

"Yes," Tara answered. "Very comfortable."

Alex merely nodded his agreement.

"I must say, I do appreciate your willingness to help with this matter, particularly in light of the fact it is the Christmas season, and your boss told me you two were already on vacation."

"We don't get out much," Alex said. "But this sounded too interesting to pass up. Can you tell us anything about the circumstances surrounding the disappearances?"

She smiled shrewdly, the corners of her lips stretching—her signature expression when getting serious. "Right down to business, then, I see. To answer your question, we know little about what might have happened to the people who disappeared prior to Michael Buford. His journal is the only lead we have, and I doubt it would serve to help us locate the others."

"Tommy said he was searching for the Wandering City of Patagonia," Tara stated. "I would think there are few people anymore who would dedicate much time to that kind of pursuit."

"Yes, well, people are full of surprises, aren't they, Ms. Watson."

"You can call me Tara, and him Alex," she corrected, immediately hoping she hadn't offended a foreign dignitary.

She received a disarming smile. "Very well, Tara. First, we get coffee. I need to shake the fog from my brain. I've been in meetings all morning and into this afternoon. Fortunately, I was able to clear my schedule to meet you both. I'm grateful I didn't have to delegate that one, especially since I have asked so much of you to come here during your vacation time."

"Seriously," Alex insisted. "It's fine. We're more than happy to help, and very curious about this whole mystery."

"Yes, well, it certainly is that," Carrera said. She looked out the window to the right and at the passing buildings. Pedestrians walked on the sidewalks, oblivious to who was driving by within earshot.

"Do you go out in public like this often?" Tara asked, changing the subject. She'd read a little about the interior minister on the flight down but wanted to know more. The notion that this powerful woman would simply ride over to a local coffee shop for a cup would be unheard of back in the States.

"Whenever I get a chance. It takes a little more planning than it did before I was interior minister, but I think it's important that leaders don't separate themselves too much from those they lead. Could it be risky to do so? Yes. But if you're good at your job, and you help the people, what do you have to fear?"

Tara thought about the answer. It was, perhaps, oversimplified, and maybe even a little naïve, but she'd never heard a politician speak that way. She could understand how Carrera had such high approval ratings, and why so many considered her to be the next in line to lead the nation of Chile.

The car slowed down, and the driver turned right into a parking area situated under the shade of four huge trees—one at each corner. Decorative string lights stretched across the parking lot, joining in the center.

The driver found a spot in the back corner next to the white building and shifted the transmission into park.

He spoke into his radio and looked back in the mirror, speaking to the interior minister. "Team two is checking the perimeter now Madam Interior Minister."

She thanked him with an appreciative nod.

The two Americans wondered how many times a day she went through this exact protocol. It wasn't as if she could simply get in a car and drive down to the nearest grocery store and get a dozen eggs if she ran out.

Then again, did she ever run out of anything?

It was hard to imagine that to be the case, though the notion did make Tara giggle as she pictured Carrera about to make an omelet and discovering she didn't have enough eggs.

"Sometimes I miss the days before all this," Carrera confessed. She waved a hand around as if indicating the car, the guards, and the general waste of time.

"All clear," the driver said.

The two security men on either side immediately opened the doors, stepped out, and stood by the car for ten seconds, each surveying the surrounding area along with men who'd taken up positions in every corner.

Carrera motioned for her two guests to exit first, and then she followed.

They didn't know if that was part of the protocol or just her being courteous.

The hot sun beat down on them from high in the western sky. It cast long shadows across the street from the buildings on the other side, but that shade missed the driver's chosen parking spot by a good ten feet.

The two guards from the car surrounded Carrera as she walked toward the front corner of the two-story white building. The window frames were the color of dark chocolate, with matching shutters on either side.

The group rounded the corner to find four more agents standing near the entrance to the café twenty feet away.

A few pedestrians on the other side of the street recognized the interior minister and started waving excitedly. She waved back to them with a sincere smile on her face and then walked through the door to the coffee shop as one of her guards held it open.

A cool rush of air wafted out over the visitors as they entered a café unlike any they'd ever visited before.

Straight ahead, the atrium split off in three directions, providing a room to the left for indoor seating, one to the right near where the drinks were made, and what appeared to be the most popular—the inner courtyard.

The central space was accessible through two open doors opposite the café entrance. Inside it, trees grew up to the second floor, their leaves casting shade down below at all hours of the day.

Vines ran the length of the wall, all the way to the terracotta roof. Flowers grew from planters cut into the ground at the base of the building, and in several large black pots that filled the space on gray tiles near the outlying metal tables.

The coffee bar and pastry shop were to the right along the wall. Four baristas hurriedly made drinks and warmed food for the line of patrons.

Carrera didn't try to cut in front of anyone. She found her place at the back of the line and waited like everyone else.

Several of the customers sitting around in the immediate area at wooden tables started whispering and taking out their phones for pictures of the famous politician. For the most part, Carrera ignored the attention and remained focused on the barista taking people's orders at the end of the counter.

The moment she made eye contact with the young man, he smiled and nodded at her. "I got you," he said cheerfully.

The two people in line ahead of her turned around, curious, and maybe a little annoyed at who might be getting special treatment. When they realized who it was, their eyes grew wide, and they offered to allow her to go ahead of them.

"No, thank you. Please, enjoy your coffee. I'm in no hurry."

The patrons couldn't believe they were standing here in a coffee shop with the interior minister. To be fair, neither could Tara and Alex.

Nothing like this would ever happen back home.

After placing their order, the three took their coffee, waved goodbye to the starry-eyed customers, and left the building.

Alex felt a little disappointed. He'd wanted to stay and drink his cappuccino in the courtyard, but they had to talk business, and a public place like that was not the optimal spot for such a conversation.

Back in the car, the interior minister raised her cup of coffee as if to say, "Salúd," and then took a sip.

The two Americans raised their cups as well, and touched them to their lips.

So far, their trip to South America was off to a rather surprising and pleasant start.

8

Most of the government buildings in Chile had been designed with Old-World Spanish architecture and would have fit in across the Atlantic had they been flown over and dropped in the middle of the Iberian Peninsula.

One glaring exception was the congressional building, designed in the neoclassical fashion handed down from Rome via the Enlightenment.

The facility Tara and Alex were taken to was nothing like either of those examples.

They were taken to a nondescript gray building with narrow windows surrounding the perimeter, all the way up to the fourth floor. The place looked like a brutalist relic from communist Russia.

The interior felt just as impersonal and sterile. Inelegant, narrow halls, steel boxes for elevators, and walls the color of concrete.

The conference room Tara and Alex sat in was one of the few things they'd seen with at least a touch of design. The walls were a darker version of scarlet with white curtains draped around the windows. The wooden conference table looked like a relic from the 1980s, and the chairs around it were made from a darker wood with no cushions and nearly 90-degree backs.

It was a strange place to have a meeting. At least that's what Tara and Alex thought. And the precarious picture of the current president hanging on the wall without any other decorations in the room only made it weirder. Both wondered to themselves if the chairs were uncomfortable by design, a sort of subtle method of forcing politicians to get to work and not waste taxpayers' time.

If that were the case, it was pretty ingenious.

They'd been sitting there for the last thirty minutes, scouring the pages of Michael Buford's journal—studying the notes, the symbols, and the riddles.

When the Americans finally stopped at the last page and looked up, the interior minister tilted her head to the side, an inquisitive expression on her face.

Alex felt the immediate reality of the powerful woman staring expectantly at him and his wife. It was the first time they'd been alone with her since being picked up at the airport. Her security detail waited outside in the hallway after being convinced that she needed to be alone with the team from the IAA.

Tara wondered if that sort of request would be honored back in the States with the VP and the POTUS, but the agents couldn't be around all the time. People had to sleep, and have at least a little privacy.

The Chilean agents hadn't protested in the slightest and had obeyed the order without hesitation, each one filing out through the two doors on either end of the room.

Now, both Tara and Alex acutely sensed how the room seemed too big for a meeting of three. Several empty chairs wrapped around the long table. The only sound between flipping pages or an occasional clearing of the throat had been the quiet hum of air blowing through the two vents in the ceiling.

"What do you think?" Carrera asked after giving her guests a moment to collect their thoughts and catch their breath.

The couple exchanged a glance. Alex motioned to her with a nod that she should speak first, and then the two faced Carrera.

"We'll need to take more notes on this," Tara said. "It's difficult to put a guess on any of it on first pass."

Alex agreed. "It definitely seems as though this guy, Buford, was convinced he'd figured out the location of the Wandering City. Which, to me, is still unusual in this day and age. But it's worth looking into."

"His theory on gateways to other dimensions is what intrigues me the most," Tara added. "This isn't the first time we've come across this sort of thing."

"Yes," Carrera drawled. She lifted the bottle of water sitting on the table in front of her and untwisted the cap. "Intriguing." She continued staring at her guests as if she were sizing them up.

For what, neither Tara nor Alex was certain.

The interior minister took a drink from the bottle, replaced the cap, and set it down with a refreshed "ah." She folded her hands on the table as she spoke, lacing the fingers together. "I'm familiar with your work on the Hell's Gate project. That was a similar theoretical framework, yes?"

The two snapped a surprised look at one another.

The Hell's Gate mission had been classified after everything went down. The gunfight, the portal—all of it had been immediately swept under the proverbial rug.

At least, that's what Tara and Alex thought. Then again, people in the position Carrera held played by a different set of rules. They could get things others could not, and laws or restrictions were more like a blurry set of easy-to-ignore guidelines.

"Don't worry," she said in a reassuring tone. "Your secret is safe with me. As I'm sure you can imagine, I am privy to such information if I want it badly enough. No one else outside this room, other than those involved with the project, know about it."

Alex wasn't sure how much he believed that. First, because she was a politician. He trusted them about as much as he trusted his ability to breathe underwater. Second, if she were able to access that information, so could others with similar clearance.

He knew there was no point in arguing the matter, or protesting it either. She knew. It was probably why she'd called them in the first place. Experience in dealing with supernatural or paranormal phenomena was hardly common, and often looked upon as a fake science similar to the way people viewed the Ghostbusters in the movies.

Only quacks believed in some of this stuff. That was the prevailing view.

But Tara and Alex worked between the lines, where science and archaeology connected at an intersection of ancient, forgotten knowledge that was far ahead of where the history books gave credit.

The simple fact Carrera had used resources and time to get them here to South America meant she had bought in—and wanted to know more.

"Tell me," she said, "what you know about this sort of dimensional science."

Tara rolled her shoulders. "It's been long believed that there are eleven, and possibly more, dimensions. There are multiple theoretical constructs for this, along with many equations that suggest it to be true. Since time is stacked instead of linear, it's possible that beings could be crossing over the same planes without ever coming into contact with one another. The multiple-dimension solution allows for two entities to occupy the same space, simply at different times, though time must only be considered a human construct and not an absolute."

She took a deep breath after finishing and let it out slowly.

Carrera pulled her hands back and crossed her arms. "Impressive," she said. "So, the question remains: Do you believe that there could be an interdimensional gate somewhere in the Patagonia?"

"We already found one down here," Alex blurted. For a second, he regretted the admission, then soon remembered that she had already accessed that information. "Stands to reason there could be others. Many believe that these kinds of stargates are all over the world. It's what the movie and television show was loosely based on."

He waited to see her reaction, but the mention didn't appear to spark anything from her memory.

"The stargate idea is that there are these portals all over the world. Some think they connect us to other dimensions; others believe they could be doorways to other planets and civilizations."

"As in aliens," Carrera clarified.

"Correct. Again, all of this is theoretical."

"Except for what you discovered."

Alex shifted in his seat, suddenly feeling uncomfortable.

Tara remembered the events of that day—the visions, the energy, the fear, and the otherworldly visions.

She counted herself lucky not to be traumatized over it. She'd slept fine after the experience, perhaps even better than she had before. Why that was, Tara didn't know.

"We discovered what we believe was a portal to another dimension, yes. Unfortunately, it was destroyed before we could conduct any thorough research."

"But you did see something, yes?" The interior minister pressed the issue, almost demanding the answer of Tara.

"We don't know what we saw," Tara said. "There were lights, colors, but nothing definitive. It was not... normal. I know that much. But as to what was on the other side of the portal, that remains a mystery."

The response seemed to appease the interior minister, though it did not satisfy her. She'd obviously hoped for something more, visions of another highly advanced race perhaps.

"I believe the Key of Inti that Michael Buford was searching for will open a similar portal, one that leads to the lost city."

"So, you think that this Wandering City is real, then," Tara stated. For someone in such a high office to buy into such a mythical concept, and admit it openly, was unusual, to say the least. In some countries, such a position would be grounds for expulsion from office, or worse. Places like Mali, Iran, and Pakistan came to mind.

"I think we should be open to many things we do not fully understand. The ancients had access to powers we are only now beginning to unlock. All our technological advancements pale when compared to the abilities people so long ago possessed. If we can somehow find a way to harness those powers, we can advance the human race into the future.

"Imagine a world with clean, abundant energy for everyone. No restrictions due to poverty or pollution. What if the riches of another civilization spilled into our own and helped us create not only a better world, but assisted us in reaching new ones?"

Her soapbox erected, and standing atop it, Carrera seemed satisfied with her dreamy speech. Perhaps it wasn't a disguise. Maybe she really felt the way she spoke, but with these types it was difficult to tell.

"So, what do we do next?" she asked.

"Well," Alex began, "we would need more time with this journal."

"Done. Take as much as you need."

"We'll also need transportation," Tara added. "I'd like to get a look at this site where he said he was going in his last entry."

"La Junta? Of course, I'll have one of my people drive you around. They can also serve as additional security. Not that I expect you'll be needing protection."

"That's really not necessary," Alex protested. "It's very generous, and we appreciate it, but we can get a rental car and drive ourselves wherever we need to go."

"Yeah," Tara agreed. "We'd hate to keep one of your people on a leash like that."

Carrera's right eyebrow lifted as a silent way of telling them this was not negotiable. "I insist, in part because I don't want that book getting lost. And don't think it's because I do not trust the two of you. But that book holds the key to all of this, to finding closure for the families who lost loved ones, and possibly to a brighter future for everyone."

"We'll see what we can do," Tara said, standing. "I trust you've made copies of this?" She held the book up over the table.

"Yes. I have made copies. No one else has access to them."

Two cell phones sat on the table next to her water bottle. Tara had wondered what they were for, and assumed the numbers attached to the devices were given out only to a select few in government.

She pushed the two phones across the table to her guests. "Take these. There is only one number programmed into them. It goes directly to me. Do not use them for anything else other than to give me progress updates. Your driver, Antonio, will also be reporting directly to me."

"Antonio?" Alex said as he took one of the phones.

"He's been in the security service the longest. He is set to retire at the end of the year. This will be his final assignment."

Tara didn't know if she should feel grateful for the help or insulted that the woman only offered the guy who already had one foot out the door.

She opted for the thankful route. "We appreciate that. Thank you."

"Antonio has been all around the Patagonia, and the Andes range. He was a guide before he joined the security service. You'll find him to be invaluable."

Carrera stood, collected her water, and turned toward the door. "I trust you have everything you need. We have reserved a hotel room for you here in Santiago for the night. Any other arrangements can be made by Antonio. Simply tell him what you need, and he will do it."

This Antonio was starting to sound like a concierge with an automatic rifle.

Carrera walked to the door and pulled it open. Two agents waited just outside, and stiffened at her abrupt appearance in the doorway.

"Antonio will be waiting for you outside. I have one more meeting this afternoon before I am done for the day. Raul here can show you out."

She motioned to a man about Alex's height, with ten more pounds of muscle, and a buzz cut so close to the scalp it was nearly clean shaven.

Raul simply nodded and motioned to the left. "Follow me," he said in a thick accent.

Tara and Alex obeyed, walking away from the Chilean interior minister. Tara looked back over her shoulder as the woman disappeared around a corner in the other direction.

She wasn't quite sure what to make of the woman, but Tara had to admit: she was a real leader.

9

Antonio leaned against the front passenger door of the black Mercedes sedan; hands folded across his belt in the way that chauffeurs do when waiting for their employers.

He wore the same suit and tie as the rest of the security detail, but in a way that said, "I don't really care anymore." The tie was a little looser, the white shirt tucked in but ruffled, and the black jacket hung over his right shoulder, gripped by a loose fist.

His hair was longer than any government security guy Tara and Alex had ever seen. As they neared the man, they noticed tattoos on both wrists where the sleeves had shored up his forearm.

He had dark-tanned skin, a hint to his mixture of indigenous and Spanish ancestry, and the lines across his face told of both his age and experience in what must have been a perpetually high-stress job.

Now, though, he didn't appear to have any worries, only that the day would pass too slowly.

He took a deep breath as the two Americans approached and pulled the toothpick out of his mouth. His narrow eyes allowed only a peek at the nearly black orbs within, making it impossible to get a read on whether he was annoyed to have been assigned babysitting duty, or if he simply didn't care.

The suit jacket dropped down over his arm and almost brushed against the ground as it swung up and over his forearm. He stepped to the side and opened the back door to the car.

Antonio wasn't a tall man, but neither was he short, standing around five feet, six inches. His broad chest and thick shoulders made him appear larger, and the unwelcoming scowl on his face perpetuated that threatening mirage.

"Hey," Alex said. "You must be Antonio. I'm Alex, and this is Tara."

He inclined his head, grunted some unintelligible greeting, and continued waiting.

Alex offered his hand to the man, but Antonio turned and walked around the front of the car as if he hadn't seen it. The Americans watched as the enigmatic man slipped a pair of aviator sunglasses onto his face, opened the driver's door, and slid inside.

For a second, neither Alex nor Tara knew quite what to make of the meeting.

They didn't have time to ponder it.

"Are you two getting in, or are you just going to stand there?" Antonio grumbled.

Tara pressed her lips together and nodded at her husband. "This is going to be loads of fun."

"Yeah," Alex agreed.

She climbed into the back seat first and he followed, closing the door behind.

The first five minutes of the drive felt like Chinese water torture but without the pleasant dripping sound. Antonio didn't strike them as the talkative or friendly type. Even though he'd only said one sentence to them, those sparse words had conveyed a lifetime of hardship, irritation, and apathy. Maybe his career had driven him to this point, or perhaps it was his upbringing.

No one said a thing as Antonio sped through traffic, driving the car in and out of lanes as he passed slower vehicles.

Tall apartment buildings passed by outside the windows, towering over low-slung businesses around and beneath them.

People-watching was difficult with how fast Antonio was driving, and more than once Alex and Tara had to grab the handles over the doors to keep from smacking into the sides. Then again, pedestrians looked like pedestrians no matter the country. The only factor that changed was their clothes, depending on the national fashion trends.

Here, Chileans dressed similarly to people in most American towns, with few subtle—almost unremarkable—differences here and there. Jeans and T-shirts seemed to be in style along with cargo shorts and tank tops for both men and women.

It reminded the two Americans in the Mercedes of so many European cities they'd visited, both while working for the IAA and on personal trips.

Neither Tara nor Alex dared risk starting a conversation with their driver. Based on the greeting he'd given them outside the government building, the man was in no mood to converse with a couple of tourists from the United States.

That was the look he'd given them when they met him. It was an expression of disdain and irritation, one that said, "Let's just get this over with." While the interior of the late-model sedan was luxurious —with black leather seats, brushed steel appointments, and carbon fiber details on the rails and doors—there were few other frills that might have been included on the ride.

We could have just called a rideshare, Alex thought. He didn't dare make the comment out loud for fear of the repercussions that could be brought on by the driver, who had, quite possibly, killed someone, or multiple someones, in his past.

With minutes to waste on the ride, and no chitchat coming from the driver, Tara decided to open the journal and have another look inside.

Alex watched her pry open the pages, flipping to the first where Buford had discussed his thoughts on the theoretical purpose of the Wandering City of Patagonia.

"Couldn't wait until we got back to the room, huh?" Alex said.

He looked up in the rearview mirror and caught Antonio's disapproving glower and abruptly realized how that might have sounded to the grumpy driver.

"Oh sorry. We're looking at Buford's diary."

The man grunted, shook his head, and reverted his gaze back to the road as he stepped on the gas and accelerated past a white van with a plumbing logo of a little man in a hat and overalls holding a wrench. The plumber behind the wheel scowled at the sedan as it zoomed by, the man clearly not happy with Antonio's aggressive driving style.

Alex refocused his attention on the book in Tara's lap and scanned over the lines again. When she was finished, Tara flipped to the second page and tapped her finger on one of four symbols drawn on the paper.

"It seems Buford believed these emblems play some kind of role in discovering the lost city," she said. Her finger rested on a four-sided cross with a hole in the center. The rest of the images looked as though they were drawn within windows.

An Incan figure was scribbled next to it. The image could have been a man, or some kind of monster, but they guessed it was more likely one of the Inca deities, as were the other two below it.

"You recognize these?" Tara asked.

"Not off the top of my head. But they shouldn't be too difficult to look up. Probably Inca gods, or important figures."

The statement caused Antonio's head to twitch slightly to the right. They didn't notice him looking back at them for two seconds, the only show of curiosity the gruff man had allowed so far.

They might have enjoyed that as opposed to the cold, stony vibe he exuded. But the moment was gone, and they remained fixed on the book.

"These look like clues," Alex noted the lines written on the adjacent page.

"Yes. And it seems he mentions them repeatedly."

She flipped back to the front of the book and noted a line near the bottom corner. It had been written in a smaller font than the rest of Buford's script.

"*This journal is both a copy of Father José Garcia Alsue's notes as well as my own ideas.*"

Alex looked up in the mirror as if wary of prying eyes and ears. The two of them had kept something under their lids since the conference room—an unspoken question they'd decided not to ask the interior minister.

Tara turned the page.

"And this is where he begins his description of the four corners of the Inca Empire. Chinchaysuyu to the north, Collasuyu to the south, Antisuyu east, and Cuntisuyu going west. Each of these roads led to a different quarter of the empire."

The driver's head twitched again, and this time Alex caught the man's interest in the subject.

"Have you ever heard of those, Antonio?" he asked, risking the driver's ire.

The man only grumbled and stepped on the brakes before flipping his turn signal to indicate his intent to swing left into the hotel parking area.

"Guess not," Tara muttered. "I've never studied these places before. Or even heard the names."

"Same," Alex said.

The car bumped up over the sloped curb and into the hotel parking lot. The concrete gray walls of the ten-story building were smattered with a mosaic of colors across the face, both on the end, and the main façade. A wide awning stretched out from the main entrance. The covering was propped up by rounded concrete pillars at the end. The underside of the awning was covered in stained wooden planks. Decorative trees, shrubs, and flowers filled the landscaping, surrounded by pebbles instead of mulch. A palm tree stood in front of each pillar, the broad leaves waving in the coastal breeze.

They remained silent as Antonio swung the car around to the left and under the awning behind a white Lexus SUV.

He hit the brakes again, causing the two occupants to lurch forward, and then shifted the transmission into park.

"We're here," the driver announced unceremoniously.

He shoved open his door, stepped back, and opened the passenger door behind his, then walked around to the back to get the bags that had magically been deposited there while Tara and Alex were in their meeting with the interior minister.

He flipped open the trunk as the two Americans stepped out. Antonio lifted their luggage out of the cargo hold and set them on the ground with a clunk before slamming the lid closed again.

"Your reservations have been made," he said. "You only need to tell the front desk who you are, show them your passports, and they will give you your room keys. Will you be needing anything else?"

He folded his hands over his waist in a forced show of manners.

"No," Alex said. "Unless you'd like to come up for a drink and help us solve this riddle."

The response produced a flinch from the man, and Alex wasn't sure if it was because he'd never been offered such an invitation before, or if it was simply due to the annoyance of the job.

He stood there, awkwardly, without responding. He looked uncomfortable, like maybe he needed to go to the bathroom.

"It's okay if you don't," Alex added quickly. "No pressure. But if you'd like to join us, I'm sure you've been given our contact information."

"Yes. I have your phone numbers. If you won't be needing anything, I'll park the car."

"Oh, so you're staying here?" Tara asked. "At the hotel?"

Antonio took a long, beleaguered breath. "Yes. I am staying here as long as you are. Wherever you two go, I go."

She chuckled. "That's a quote from the book of Ruth in the Bible."

He stared vacantly at her from behind his sunglasses.

"You know, her mother-in-law was talking about moving?"

No response.

"Anyway, that's cool. If you do happen to be interested in lending a hand with this stuff, you're welcome to. We're going to brush up on our history of this region, something I'm sure you know about since you grew up here."

Antonio inhaled, then sighed sharply. "I have no desire to help the two of you with some foolish treasure hunt. My job is to take you where you want to go and make sure you don't get into danger. The only reason I'm here is because the minister ordered it. I have one month left on my contract, and then I retire. So, I would appreciate it if you two didn't find yourselves in trouble."

They listened to the hard response and bobbed their heads, mouths gaping. It was the most he'd said since he picked them up.

"Understood, chief," Alex said cheerfully. "We'll try not to get into trouble."

He walked past the driver, pulled the handle on his roller bag, and slung his rucksack over his right shoulder.

Alex leaned close to the man, and when he spoke, his voice was barely above a whisper, in a conspiratorial tone. "But just so you know, trouble does tend to find us."

10

Arturo followed the car from the moment the driver picked up the Americans. He'd sat along the street, pretending to be on his phone while keeping a watchful eye on the back door to the building.

When the two Americans appeared again, he waited patiently. A lion lurking in tall grass, camouflaged and hungry for the kill, he remained still, undetected, even up to the point where the driver of the other car pulled into the Hotel Maduro.

Tailing marks was usually an easy task for him. His tried-and-true methods of hanging back far enough to observe and not be noticed had worked every single time he'd been given this kind of job.

But the other driver in this instance was a total maniac.

The guy had driven faster than Arturo expected, which made following the car without being noticed all the more difficult, and he wondered if it were possible the other driver knew he was there.

The man weaved in and out of traffic and far exceeded the posted speed limits, to a dangerous level, especially in the busy streets of downtown Santiago. The only thing that seemed to slow the guy down was the stoplights he ran into at the intersections.

Arturo had been lucky the driver hadn't run through any red

lights; otherwise, he would have been left behind and lost sight of his target. He could have found them eventually, but that would have taken time, and he preferred to get things done as quickly, and as efficiently, as possible.

When the other car indicated it was turning into the hotel, Arturo slowed down, passed by, and then deftly swerved his sedan into a parking spot along the sidewalk in front of a boutique clothier.

He watched from an angle half a block away as the driver exited the car, opened a back door for the occupants, and then removed their luggage from the trunk.

The man didn't look happy to be there. He wore a constant scowl on his dark face, and Arturo could see the lines above, under, and stretching out from his eyes.

He was older than the Americans, probably in his late fifties or early sixties, just based on a guess. But he was fit and looked as if he'd been keeping up with physical training for much of his life.

He was shorter than both of them, which didn't mean anything to Arturo. He'd fought against men who were smaller than him on many occasions, and most of the time their stature didn't matter when it came to hand-to-hand combat—not when the loser won a one-way ticket to the grave.

Based on the driver's suit, Arturo guessed the guy was part of a government security detail hired by the interior minister. Either their standards had slackened, or the man simply ignored them knowing that he only had so long to continue working until he could call it quits. *This guy has impending retirement written all over him*, thought Arturo.

Maybe that was the reason for the grouchy expression that hung across the man's face like a weathered tapestry.

Arturo didn't care, other than he needed to make such assessments when dealing with a potential enemy. He'd learned long ago that the phrase *know thyself* was only second to *know thine enemy*.

He'd grown up on the streets, never afforded the luxury of learning conventional martial arts techniques put on display in movies or in MMA fights. But he'd learned his own style of defensive and offensive combat, methods hewn by years in the crucible of hard knocks and survival of the fittest.

There had been things he picked up along the way—samples of Brazilian jujitsu, a touch of Krav Maga here and there. He simply added those skills to his growing repertoire, and deployed them as needed.

His primary style of fighting, however, was based on constant movement, a sort of fluid dance he'd used for years. While some taught that stillness was a powerful foundation for combat, Arturo believed that remaining motionless—while potentially an unnerving thing to witness in an opponent—also made for an easy target.

He believed that keeping an enemy guessing, uncertain, was the more effective approach.

Arturo watched the Americans say goodbye to the driver and walk in through the entrance beneath the hotel awning. The driver returned to his seat behind the wheel after closing the trunk and drove the vehicle out the other side of the covered entryway, and toward the back of the parking area.

The lot was small, only allowing for a dozen or so cars to park there, but more spots were provided in an underground garage accessible through an entrance at the other end of the building.

The sedan's brake lights glowed bright red as the driver slowed down to get a ticket from the automated kiosk. Then the car disappeared down into the dark.

Arturo waited to make sure the guy wasn't simply going in and coming back out as part of a ruse to flush him from his position. After two minutes, though, Arturo decided the driver was parking, which meant he was going to stay here at the hotel with the Americans.

It was an unusual situation but nothing he couldn't handle. Killing two or killing three didn't make a difference to him. It merely changed the method he would choose to get it done.

Separating the three would be best, not counting the present moment. Arturo didn't know what room the Americans were in, nor the one their chauffeur would use. The hotel staff could be bribed for the information, of course, but he preferred to handle this alone. It was simpler that way.

Other hit men were sloppy in that way, always taking shortcuts to get the job done quickly, which often resulted in a much more complicated, lengthy process. If he bribed a concierge for the Americans' room number, he could eliminate the Americans easily by waiting outside the room until they left, then put a bullet in both of them before they could get a foot out into the hallway. But then he would have to take out the concierge later. Loose ends needed to be cut off.

He'd done that one time to a guy named Marco in Viña del Mar, a coastal town to the northeast of Santiago. The man had been a contractor whose housing business had cash flow problems—as did so many around the world—during the pandemic. He'd borrowed money from Orasco as a last resort, then foolishly lost it all on a couple of bad land investments he thought he could sell off to other developers.

When word got out that Marco had skipped town, Orasco sent Arturo to find him. It hadn't taken long for Arturo to learn where Marco went. He'd planned on taking a boat out of Viña del Mar with what cash he had left.

It wasn't a terrible plan from the point of view of the boss. Taking a flight would have put his name on manifests and other lists Orasco could access with his seemingly infinite string of connections. But a private charter boat was different. Those places were happy to take a little extra cash to write down a fake name on their rental sheets.

Arturo had made use of that sort of service numerous times, though his jaunts out into the ocean weren't pleasure cruises, or to escape.

They were to ditch bodies.

Which is exactly what happened to Marco.

The contractor had booked a hotel room for one night in the town before heading out on the yacht the following day, presumably to skirt up the coast to another city such as Antofagasta and then either change vessels there or rent a car to go the rest of the way up to Peru, where he could book a flight and leave the continent.

The mistake Marco made was the hotel room. Had he simply escaped to Viña del Mar and gotten straight on the first charter north, Arturo would have never found him.

But Marco *had* booked a hotel room. And the moment word got back to Arturo exactly which town, hotel, and room number, he drove to the coastal town and took care of the problem.

Arturo waited for nearly five hours outside Marco's hotel, watching people come and go through the front doors until he finally saw the target return—dropped off at the entrance by an Uber. Marco had even hired the most expensive ride the app offered—in this case, a black Mercedes S Class.

The lowlife had the audacity to beg Arturo not to kill him, even stooping so low as to remind the hit man that he had a wife and kid.

Arturo knew about the family. He'd considered using them as leverage, but he preferred not to do that. Women and children were one of his few boundaries when it came to taking out Orasco's trash.

He'd done it a few times, but only out of necessity. And he would have used that strategy on Marco, but he knew better. Marco was already skipping out on his wife and daughter. He probably hadn't even told them he was leaving. No goodbyes. Just dipped out.

Of course, the call girl that got out of the car with Marco and accompanied him into the hotel didn't help the man's plight.

When Arturo burst into the room, he caught the scumbag on his back with the hooker on top of him. She'd turned her head toward the door only in time to see the puff of smoke pop from the suppressor's muzzle.

The look of utter shock, then fear on Marco's face as the woman slumped off of him and onto the floor was as priceless as it was pathetic.

It had been almost satisfying to force Marco to take the boat he'd rented out into the ocean, where Arturo put a bullet through his forehead and watched the body topple into the inky blue water.

The ocean would take care of the body. They'd sailed ten miles out from the coast to make sure of it.

Arturo had considered making Marco suffer simply due to the fact he'd had to stand outside Marco's room for so long. The fact Marco was an insufferable worm only made the killer want to torture him even more.

But he hadn't. In the end, Arturo had made it quick, which was more than Marco deserved. Arturo took solace in the fact that he hadn't had to listen to any further sniveling.

He returned the boat, skipped by the rental office on his way out, and left Viña del Mar with no one knowing what happened.

The charter rental office would eventually find their boat parked at the docks, and find the keys left in the ignition. They would assume the anonymous man who rented it simply brought it back and left in a hurry. And since they'd already been paid, why would they care?

It was as clean a kill-and-ditch as Arturo could ever hope for.

This one, however, would be nowhere near as simple.

There were three targets, and no doubt the bodyguard would be sleeping in an adjacent room, or perhaps one across the hall. Either way, it left room for more errors than Arturo cared to consider acceptable.

He had an assortment of tools at his disposal tucked away in the trunk. Guns, knives, and enough zip ties to wrangle a horse. But he decided another option would probably be best.

It could be messy, and there would definitely be collateral damage, but that was the only plan that ensured success in the most efficient way possible. There would be no witnesses, and he'd be out of the area long before the Americans and their chauffeur died.

His mind made up, he waited for traffic to pass, then pulled out of his parking spot, performed a quick U-turn, and guided his vehicle into the parking lot of the Hotel Maduro.

11

D
r. Juan Avila stared at the journal, as if that act alone would reveal the truth behind the secrets contained in the ragged pages.

He'd worked out the meaning of the symbols, all four relating to deities or important icons from the Inca Empire. He even understood the correlation to the four quarters of the kingdom. But what he hadn't been able to sort out was where to find any of these places.

His initial instinct was to find the Key of Inti, but he had to locate three other artifacts first, the first having been discovered by the man who'd written the journal in his hands.

Juan knew where to go once he had the final artifact. Father José Alsue hadn't had the Key of Inti when he ventured to the summit he described in his journal. It was only after the venture that Alsue realized he needed to find four other artifacts before the location of the key would reveal itself.

The priest had spent the rest of his life trying to locate the artifacts, all in hopes of gaining entrance to the mystical Wandering City of Patagonia. He'd succeeded in locating one item, a rose quartz sculpture of a four-sided cross with a hole in the center. But he was old, and the rigors of scouring the Patagonia and the Andes for the other three artifacts was simply too much to bear.

Juan didn't necessarily believe the lost city was even real, but Orasco had been insistent he come to work for him. Resistance had been futile.

Orasco made Dr. Avila an offer he could not believe, and he had happily walked away from his position as a university professor.

The moment Juan set foot in his new research facility, though, he regretted ever having left the school. Or even entertaining Orasco's generous offer. It hit Juan just how much trouble he was in when he'd told Orasco he wouldn't let him down.

Orasco's response had been, "Oh, I know you won't. No one ever does."

It was the way he'd said it that unnerved Juan, and hung over him like an IV bag with a 1,000-cc drip of liquid anxiety.

He'd felt the pressure only grow since day one, and every hour that passed without a viable solution to the journal's riddles only pushed him deeper into a pit of fear.

Juan studied the diary intently, flipping the pages to see if there was something hidden that he'd missed, some clue that would give the coordinates to at least one of the three artifacts.

He glanced over at the crystal sitting on his workstation atop a black microfiber cloth.

It was beautiful, cut from ancient pink crystal that some believed contained vibrational frequencies as old as the earth itself.

It was about the size of his hand, and had been expertly carved and smoothed to a glossy shine on each side. The front and back of it featured detailed grooves carved in straight lines extending out from the immaculate hole in the center. It was a perfect circle by every measurement Juan had taken, and he marveled at how someone so long ago had been able to do it with rudimentary, primitive tools.

The crystal mocked him from the corner of the table. It meant nothing without knowing the location where it needed to be taken.

Juan had searched the areas that had once been thriving Inca civilizations, but there was only so much he could do. He was just one man, and Orasco demanded the impossible.

The region occupied by the Inca had been vast, covering parts of four countries, and extremely difficult terrain in many places. Not only that; there were still undiscovered communities, towns, and perhaps even cities. The rainforest hid its secrets well.

Orasco didn't understand any of that. Or if he did, the man simply didn't, or refused to, see reason.

He demanded results, and if those weren't produced....

Juan shuddered at the thought. He'd lost focus on the work again by worrying. He reminded himself that worrying never helped anything. He'd heard a plethora of quotes about that as a younger man, and as an adult. Now forty-five years old, he found his concerns to be far worse than he ever could have imagined. Simply telling himself not to worry over the problems was like trying to catch a gnat with a butterfly net.

He knew the stories, what the price of failing Orasco would be. He'd heard them before he took this job, but the money was too good to pass up, on top of that, he got the overwhelming impression that Orasco wouldn't take no for an answer.

"How's it going, Doctor?"

The smooth, deep voice nearly caused Juan's soul to jump out of his body. He turned around and looked up.

"Señor Orasco. I... wasn't expecting you."

Juan's employer towered over him. He peered down with eyes like a bird of prey, circling a rodent on a wide-open prairie.

"Who were you expecting?" Orasco's voice filled the lab, echoing ominously off the walls and glass cases containing various artifacts. The lifeless glow of the fluorescent bulbs overhead reflected off the man's tanned skin in a way that made him look like death incarnate. The only thing he was missing was the reaper's dark robes. Instead, he wore a white suit with a black tie. The outfit contrasted the man's soul like oil on paper.

Juan's lips trembled. He knew Orasco could see it, could smell the fear oozing out of every pore across his body. Something about the man's expression gave Juan the sense that he actually enjoyed it—toying with the people beneath him. And everyone was beneath him in this country.

The only ones who weren't were in the government, but Juan knew even many of them had bent the knee to Orasco's financial support, and thus found themselves in his pocket.

"No... no one," Juan stuttered. "I wasn't expecting anyone. That's why you startled me."

Orasco looked around the lab, momentarily taking his eyes off the archaeologist to survey their surroundings. He'd given Dr. Avila everything he needed—the latest equipment to date artifacts, the most powerful computers money could buy, tools, money for travel, even a penthouse in one of his buildings.

He'd provided everything someone in Juan's position could possibly dream of in their line of work.

Orasco saw the gleam in Juan's eyes when he first saw the laboratory. The excitement leaped out of him despite every effort to contain it.

"I have a question, Doctor," Orasco said, folding his hands behind his back as he paced over to a machine that dated materials based on patina.

He paused and then looked over at Juan, who sat with his back bent over in a crooked arch. His face was drawn, and pained, completing the look of a defeated man—a man who who'd run out of time.

"Why do you disappoint me?" Orasco asked.

The pointed question sent a spear through Juan's chest. He swallowed, trying to come up with a response, but had no idea what he could say to something like that.

"I... I just need a little more time, sir. This is very old, and the riddles—"

"Are what I am paying you handsomely to solve!" His voice boomed through the lab like thunder. Juan thought he saw the computer monitor on his desk shake from the vibration.

The archaeologist cringed at the sound and then cowered like a frightened child.

"I have given you everything, Juan," Orasco continued. "And what have you given me in return? Nothing!"

"I'm doing everything I can, sir. I really am. But these notes, I just need—"

"You just need to produce results, Juan. Where are the other stones? Where is the key? That's all I want to know. I don't want to hear that you need more time. You've had two months to work on this. It's just a little book!"

He jabbed a thick finger at the book.

"The priest... He spoke in circles. None of it makes any sense. He talks of a place to the north, one to the south, one to the—"

"I've read the journal, Juan," Orasco boomed. "I know what it says. What I don't know is why you, an expert in the field, can't seem to interpret the meanings."

"We don't study these kinds of things in school, or in our line of work. I learned how to interpret ancient scripts, hieroglyphs, not these kinds of things." Juan stopped talking, suddenly acutely aware that he'd just told a dangerous man that he no longer had any use for him.

Orasco raised his chin and stared down at the man over the bridge of his nose. "So, you're telling me you can't figure it out, then?" He cracked his neck to the right, then left.

"No. I believe I can. I just—"

"Need more time?" Orasco finished.

Juan knew that answer wasn't going to satisfy the man. He'd been given two months and hadn't made much progress.

They were lucky to even have the crystal on the table. As he considered the object, an idea formulated in Juan's head. "The crystal," he said, looking at the artifact with renewed hope in his eyes. "That's it."

"What's it?"

Juan stood up. His mind ran ahead of his feet as he stepped over to the crystal and stood over it, gazing down at the sculpture.

"Don't you see?" he asked, never taking his eyes off the artifact.

"All I see is wasted time and money, Professor. You'd better not be jerking me around."

"Of course not," Juan protested, firing an insulted shot of flame from his eyes. That was a risky move. He wasn't exactly in the best position to beg, or be offended. Sincerity was the only thing that could save him in that moment. "It makes perfect sense. The crystal represents the center of the empire."

"So?" Orasco crossed his arms in a show of patient insistence.

"Cusco," Juan said as if the answer should have been obvious. "It was the capital of their empire."

All he received was a blank stare.

Juan sighed, exasperated with his boss. "This crystal represents the capital, the center of everything. And the four branches of the cross are for the four quarters of the empire."

Orasco clenched his jaw. "I've heard this part, Juan. You'd better tell me something new." He took a threatening step toward the archaeologist.

Juan twisted his head to the right, noting the guard standing just outside the open door. Even if he wanted to run, he'd never get past the door. And where would he go, anyway? Orasco's tentacles reached everywhere.

"Yes. I assumed you knew about the four corners. But as it relates to Alsue's journal—that's the part I was missing."

Juan hurried back over to where the aged leather-bound journal sat on the edge of his desk.

He picked it up carefully. Even though he wore white cotton gloves, Juan respected the history of every piece and knew that any careless mistake could ruin the fragile pages contained within the book.

The first three pages contained notes from Alsue. Some of the lines felt like the ravings of a madman, obsessed with wild fantasy. But there was a poetry to the priest's words, too. The way he described the city sounded as though he was conveying a vision of heaven beyond the pearly gates.

Juan had read the description more times than he cared to recount. He'd unintentionally committed most of it to memory simply by repetition, hoping as he pored over it time and time again that some unnoticed clue would leap out at him and point him in the right direction.

Those pages had failed to reveal a secret—at least none that he could find. The fourth page, however, contained the first of Alsue's clues.

The priest documented his journey throughout the book. His quest had led him across the Andes and the Patagonia in a search for four artifacts, crystals similar to the one now resting on Juan's desk.

That one had been easy to find, though the means of acquiring it had been unethical at best. The archaeologist still felt ill about it, unable to squash the uneasy feeling that tortured him over the matter.

Juan had surmised the location of the first crystal, the Cusco Cross, by sorting out a single line on the first page of the journal. It read, "The beginning lies at the end with me."

It was a cryptic line to open the book. Juan had pondered it for two days, pining over the riddle. The conclusion he reached was one that both excited and unnerved him—they needed to exhume the body of Father José Garcia Alsue.

But before Juan and any assistants Orasco would provide could dig up the grave, they first had to locate it. That was no easy task considering the oldest cemetery in the area was the General Santiago Cemetery established in 1821, well after the death of the Jesuit priest.

Juan spent sixteen-hour-days poring over local records—count-less pages of centuries-old books kept in nearly forgotten archives. While the task had been long and somewhat tedious, the archaeologist had loved every second of it.

Spending time in the old archives, researching the names of so many people who lived in the area centuries before, was like looking through a window into the past. He imagined the lives they lived, their challenges, triumphs, tragedies, jobs, families—everything that happened in a person's life between the date of their birth and the day of their death.

There were stories in the dashes between dates, tales that most would never hear, and that he could only conjure from a pondering mind.

Had Juan not been so pressured by Orasco to produce results, the archaeologist could have spent months in those vaults. But that wasn't possible. He had a job to do, and on the third day of his search, he found the information he desired.

Father José Alsue had been interred in a small local cemetery less than a mile from the General Santiago Cemetery.

The city was littered with such neglected resting places, grave-yards fallen into ill-repair with faded names on crumbling head-stones, sunken earth where mounds once stood, and overgrowth of trees, shrubs, weeds, and grass.

Alsue's resting place had been named the Cemetery of Our Holy Lady, though that title had slipped into distant memory as the decades passed. It seemed no one in the present knew it was called that, and the only way Juan was able to find it was thanks to an old map of the city he discovered in the archives.

The name had nearly faded into oblivion on the aged parchment, but it was enough for Juan to glean and pinpoint on a current GPS map on his phone.

Orasco had assigned two of his bodyguards to help with the exhumation of the body, which Juan felt grateful for since grave robbing was something people in his line of work did not approve of.

But he justified it by telling himself he wasn't the one doing the digging, and with the reminder that pulling up Alsue's body could lead to the greatest, most stunning find in all of history.

They went after dark, on a night where the half-moon cast a haunting glow across the derelict cemetery.

The three men waded through weeds and undergrowth, searching for the priest's name that Juan felt certain would be unreadable. They spent just under an hour on the hunt. The entire time, Juan felt certain someone in one of the apartment buildings

across the street, or one of the one-story businesses behind the cemetery, would see the trespassers and call the police.

But no sirens ever blared.

It took another two hours for the men to dig down through the
packed dirt before they reached the stone vault. Their efforts were
rewarded when they pried open the lid of the casket.

Juan knew he'd never forget the sight of the four-sided, crystal
cross resting on the tattered robes of the priest's rib cage.

The archaeologist felt a wave of paranoia crash over him as he
lifted the crystal, clutched in the bony fingers of the dead Jesuit
priest, from the body.

Covering up the crime took less than half the time it had required
to dig up, and the three men disappeared into the night with the artifact safely in their possession.

Since that victory, Juan had only encountered walls blocking his
progress to solving the mystery. Until now.

He pointed to an image on the page in his hands and held the
journal out so Orasco could see it.

"Do you know what this is?" Juan asked, excitement rippling
through his voice like an electrical current.

Orasco shook his head. "No. That's what I pay you to know." The
man was out of patience, and his irritated tone conveyed that
sentiment.

"This is a drawing of a stone that is in the oldest structure in
Cusco, the Coricancha Temple."

The blank expression on Orasco's face told Juan the name didn't
register.

Suppressing his own annoyance, Juan went on. "It's one of the
oldest buildings in all of Peru. This stone was an altar, and is part of
the remaining original stonework built by the Incas."

"And how does this stone help us?"

Juan carefully turned the page and pointed at another image of
the crystal above the altar.

"I believe this drawing is meant to tell us what to do."

"Which is?"

The archaeologist almost rolled his eyes but managed to keep a somber face. "We place the crystal on top of the altar."

"And then?"

"According to this, three keys will be revealed." Juan touched another image below the altar. It portrayed three windows, each with an Inca symbol contained within. "With those three, we will unlock the location of the final key, the one that opens the gates to the Wandering City."

12

Tara lifted her black-rimmed glasses and rubbed her weary eyes.

Two cups of coffee each and three hours of studying the journal had produced no clear answers to the mystery contained within the pages.

Alex paced over to the balcony door for the umpteenth time. The steady lights of the sprawling city glowed against the starry night.

It was almost eleven local time, and both of them were feeling the effects of the hour, as well as the fatigue brought on by travel.

"We've been through this book half a dozen times," Alex said. "Why is this so hard?"

Tara curled her lips to the right in a half smirk. "Probably because the person who created the original clues didn't want anyone to find it."

"Unless they walked the path he walked."

Alex's response was a reference to Buford's journal, a note the treasure hunter had taken from someone else—Father José Garcia Alsue.

Information on the priest had been difficult to come by. Scant references to the man online yielded little assistance. Tara and Alex had even put their AI lab assistant, Malcom, on the task but only to a disappointing end. Malcom's greatest asset was speed, able to deep dive through databases around the world in seconds. Its biggest weakness was anything that had only been recorded in an analog format.

"The beginning starts at the end," Tara repeated the phrase she'd spoken multiple times throughout the evening, as if saying it once more would magically manifest the answer.

It didn't.

Alex paced back to the workstation next to the entertainment system opposite the bed and looked down at the journal splayed out on the desk in front of his wife.

He flipped the pages back to the beginning and then stopped where the first drawings appeared.

"We know this cross is important," he said. "And we know it relates to Cusco."

"Correct. And the four quarters of the empire."

"Right." He turned to the next page. "And this makes it look like we're meant to combine it with whatever this thing is." He tapped on a drawing of what appeared to be a pedestal with four corners. The sides of it were curved in on the above view, almost giving it the shape of a rudimentary star.

"Again, that one was easy enough. Buford says the keys will be revealed." She sat back in her chair, slouching a little as she crossed her arms. A yawn escaped her lips. "But what *is* that thing? And where do we find the cross?"

"That has to be the part on the first page of this journal, the part about the beginning. But where is that?"

It was beyond frustrating. Both of them felt like the answer was right in front of them, but their tired minds couldn't work out the solution to the problem.

Alex took a step away from the desk and started back toward the balcony again. He'd always found pacing to be a useful way to shake the cobwebs loose in his brain, get the blood and ideas flowing.

"So," he said, "Buford's last entry says he's going to Devil's Point.

Clearly, he believed whatever that thing is at the beginning of the journal was located there. Then he disappears without a trace."

"I mean... it's possible he was correct, located the entrance to the Wandering City, and that's where he is now—in some other dimension or realm beyond ours."

Alex stopped in midstride and looked back at her. "Well, if that's the case, what are we doing here?"

She chuckled. "I don't think that's what happened. Devil's Point is near La Junta. This cross suggests that Cusco is where we should be looking."

"That narrows it down," Alex drawled. "That city is not small."

"No. It isn't," Tara agreed. She sighed. "I guess we could start with a search for the oldest buildings or structures in Cusco. That might get us somewhere. If this lost city has something to do with Inca legends, and based on all these drawings we have to assume it does, it would make sense to start with some of their cultural centers or temples."

"Good idea." He took out his phone, opened the app to access Malcom, and tapped the call button.

The AI answered immediately. "Hello, Alex. How goes the search for the Wandering City?"

"Not great, but we were wondering if you could help us with a quick search."

"Of course. What do you want me to find?" The AI's British accent sounded so real, with barely a hint of robotic pentameter that would suggest it was a computer and not a person. Most people wouldn't even notice.

"Can you give us a list of the oldest structures in Cusco?"

"Certainly. One moment."

"Actually," Tara interrupted, "give us the three oldest ones."

"Did you catch that?" Alex asked.

"I did. The oldest temple in Cusco is Coricancha, built in the fifteenth century by the Inca Emperor Pachacuti. Though there is debate about the age of the original stones within the structural compound. Some believe it is much older than that."

"That's interesting. Can people still visit that place?"

"Yes. The original stonework is frequented by tourists. It is located in the lower levels of what is now the Church of Santo Domingo. Much of the temple was destroyed by the Spanish in the sixteenth century."

"They certainly did a number on this continent," Alex groused.

"Indeed. Would you like me to continue?"

Alex and Tara didn't answer immediately. They stared at each other, both thinking the same thing.

"Not yet," Alex answered. "Could you send both of us images from this temple? We'd like to have a look at what's there."

"Certainly. Copying images now." Three seconds passed. "Sent."

Alex's phone vibrated in his hand, and Tara's dinged on the desk next to the journal.

"Will you need anything else?" Malcom asked.

"Maybe. I'll get back to you. Thanks, Malcom."

"We appreciate it," Tara added.

"Happy to be of assistance. I'll be here if you need me."

Alex closed the app, ending the connection.

"Sooo," she said, elongating the word. "I guess that means we need to go to Cusco?"

He nodded. "It's the only starting point we have. Maybe that's what the journal meant. Start at the beginning of the end. Perhaps that temple is symbolic of where the Inca Empire began and ended when the Spanish destroyed it."

"Could be. But that doesn't answer the question about that four-sided cross. We still don't know what that is, or where to find it."

"No. It doesn't. I hate to waste time and the minister's money flying over to Peru on a weak lead, but it's all we have to go on."

"Better than sitting here in this hotel for days on end," she countered.

"True." He glanced at his watch. "You want to go out and get a drink? I'm tired, but I don't want to go to sleep yet."

She stretched her arms over her head and yawned again. "Yeah. Sure. I could go for something. All this definitely calls for a nightcap."

"We passed a bunch of bars on the main strip earlier. Probably wouldn't take more than ten minutes to walk there."

"Sounds good." She stood up, ran her fingers through her auburn hair, and grabbed the black clutch sitting on the desk. The little bag contained some cash, a few company credit cards, her driver's license, and her passport. "Let's do it. I guess we'll let the minister know our plan in the morning. I'm sure she's asleep by now."

Alex grabbed his wallet off the desk, stuffed it in his back pocket, and walked over to the door. He turned the latch and pulled it open, then froze at the sight of the man standing just beyond the threshold.

When the man spoke, his voice filled with jagged rocks. "Going somewhere?"

13

"Antonio?" Alex stared into the bodyguard's disapproving eyes. Even the light radiating from the hotel room and the hallway all around him seemed to turn to shadow around those two black holes. "What are you doing here?" The question followed a deep, uneasy swallow.

"Unfortunately, my job right now is to keep an eye on you two. So, I'm doing that job. You didn't answer my question."

Tara joined Alex in the doorway and forced a welcoming smile. "Hey, Antonio. We're just going out for a drink."

"I know."

Alex's face turned into a sour frown. "What do you mean, you know? How could you know? Wait. Were you standing here all night, listening to our conversation?"

He expected the answer to be yes, and immediately began to wonder if this guy ever even slept.

"No. I was in my room. As I said, my job is to keep an eye... and ear on you two."

Tara sounded almost excitedly curious at the insinuation. "Wait. Did you bug our room?"

Alex turned his befuddlement her way. "Why do you sound like you think that's okay?"

She shrugged. "I dunno. Sounds like spy stuff."

"I don't have your room wired," Antonio said, his voice losing its grim reaper tone to be replaced with more of a matter-of-fact one. "That's the old way. We use remote microphones now."

"Cool," she said.

"No," Alex protested. "That is not cool. What if we were... you know?"

Antonio arched his right eyebrow and cocked his head to the side, as if begging Alex to finish the question.

"Well, you know," Alex finally said, unwilling to lay out the explanation.

Tara giggled. "Yeah, that would be creepy. But I'll be honest, you know we're both too tired for that."

"Still."

"Unless you want me hearing your most intimate moments," Antonio said, "I would refrain from those activities until our job is done. Believe me, I don't want to hear it any more than you want me to hear it."

"Fine. But I don't like this."

"Nor do I. Where are you going?"

"I thought you said you could hear everything," Alex countered, a little irritation layered in the question.

"I heard you say you're going to a bar up the street. Which one?"

"I don't know the name. I just saw several. Thought we could figure out which one when we got there."

Antonio's head swirled toward Tara. "Is he always like this?"

She grinned. "Most of the time."

"Hey," Alex said, "whose side are you on?"

Tara giggled. "Does this mean you're driving us to the bar?"

Antonio sighed. "I don't have a choice."

"Good. Can you recommend one of the bars around here?"

He peered back at her, silent for a long five breaths. She couldn't tell if he was going to advise her to figure it out—or make a suggestion.

"There's one called Maca Brava. I hear they make good drinks."

"Great. Let's go."

She slipped by Alex and the security guard and out into the hallway. Antonio watched her as she ambled away as if she didn't have a care in the world.

Alex rolled his shoulders.

"Is she always like this?" Antonio asked.

"Pretty much." Alex looked after her and waved a hand. "I guess we should follow."

"You will follow me."

"I thought you were supposed to have our backs or something."

The Chilean cast a smoldering look at him. "You don't know where I parked."

"Oh. Right," Alex said, feeling foolish.

The silent elevator ride down was always awkward, no matter who was in the lift. But this one was probably the most awkward Alex had ever taken in his life.

This stranger who'd been assigned to "keep an eye on them" as he'd put it, had been listening to every word of their conversation in the hotel room. It was unsettling to say the least. Not only that; Tara was acting like it was no big deal.

Alex wanted to have a conversation with her about it later, ask why she seemed so okay with it, but he knew that discussion, as with the previous, would be heard by the grumpy security man.

He decided that for the rest of their trip in South America, nothing would be private.

The elevator doors opened with a ding when they reached the lobby level, and the two men waited for Tara to exit first. Then Antonio allowed Alex to step off the lift after her, pulling up the rear.

"Where'd you park?" Alex asked, deciding to be as amicable as possible.

"In the garage at the end of the lot. Second level."

"Strange they don't have an elevator that goes directly to the parking deck."

The old guard didn't echo the sentiment, nor did he disagree. He simply kept close behind his two charges as they led the way through the lobby and past the concierge desk. The young woman behind the counter had black/brown hair down to the shoulders of her dark blue and black uniform. She smiled at them as if to offer a "good evening."

Alex gave a nod and a smile to her as they walked by and out into the warm Santiago night.

"This way," Antonio said, pivoting to the left and continuing his march toward the garage.

The wind from the west blew across their faces. It washed away the warm air with cool tendrils blowing on unseen waves. For some reason, it sent a chill across Alex's skin, and he inadvertently shivered.

"You okay?" Tara asked, grinning at his soft reaction.

"Yeah. I'm fine. Just a little chill in that breeze I wasn't expecting."

She didn't think anything else of it as they passed a row of cars to their right. Antonio turned right at the end of the sidewalk, then left along a white line painted next to the exit lane of the garage. He followed the path down the ramp and then turned left into the stairwell.

"It will be faster if we take the stairs," their babysitter said.

Alex looked into the dimly lit garage with the sloped ramps leading down below ground level. There was something foreboding about it, or perhaps he simply thought that because the hour was late and no one was around—no one he could see, anyway.

Antonio jerked open the blue metal door to the stairwell and stepped inside.

The sense of danger Alex felt heightened as he and Tara followed him. The concrete steps were smudged from years of foot traffic. The light blue cinder block walls had a dingy look to them, and the place smelled of stale cigarettes.

"I guess this is the hotel smoke hole," Tara said.

"Yeah, for like the last decade," Alex agreed.

Antonio didn't add to the complaint. Instead, he quickly descended the stairs, his feet moving in a quick staccato. He didn't look back at them when he arrived at the next landing. Instead, he pushed open the door and stepped back out into the parking garage.

The dank air in the subterranean parking area seemed fresh compared to that in the confines of the stairwell, and the Americans found themselves taking a few deep breaths to purge the remnants of the old tobacco-laced shaft.

Antonio turned to the left and continued along the row of parking spots, some empty and some occupied with cars.

With so many empty, Alex wondered why the man hadn't taken one of those, but assumed the spots had been full when he'd arrived.

At the corner where the ramp went up into the above level, Antonio continued around to the right, passing several more empty parking places.

Tara looked over at Alex with the same questioning frown on her face. Alex merely offered an *I don't know* shrug.

Once around the corner, they saw the black Mercedes sedan sitting at the very end of the garage, parked in the farthest corner from the stairwell.

"You afraid someone might scratch it?" Alex asked, keeping his tone light.

Antonio answered without looking back. "That, and I like to walk. It keeps you young."

The response shut down the inquisition, and they walked the hundred feet to the end of the garage in silence.

Antonio opened the back door for Tara then climbed into the front seat as Alex closed the door after her, then walked around and opened the other side. *At least he's a gentleman to Tara,* Alex thought.

He got in the car, strapped on his seatbelt, and waited as the driver did the same and then pressed the ignition button.

Nothing happened except a muted click. If the sedan's cabin hadn't been so quiet, it might have gone unnoticed.

Antonio froze for a second, then pulled his finger back from the button.

Tara noticed him seize up. "Everything okay? Will it not start?"

"Get out of the car."

"What?" She almost laughed.

"Get out now!" he barked and flung open the door.

Antonio moved faster than they'd seen him in their brief encounters with the man. He stepped out of the car, grabbed the handle on Tara's door, and flung it open. "Quickly!" he demanded.

After two heartbeats of hesitation and confusion, she unfastened her seatbelt and slid out of the car. Alex did the same on his side and hurried around the rear bumper.

"Get away from it!" Antonio ordered. "Now!"

"What's going on?" Tara asked, fear suddenly gripping her voice with dry, icy hands.

Alex took her arm and pulled her backward toward the wall and the empty parking spots opposite where the sedan sat.

Antonio ushered them faster, keeping his body between them and the vehicle.

When they reached the other wall, he then guided them back down toward the corner, putting as much distance between them and the car as he could.

Alex looked back over his shoulder at the man, and then the car beyond him. "What's happening? Where are we going?"

Antonio didn't answer until they were around the concrete pillar at the corner and the car was out of sight.

He searched the other vehicles parked in the garage, scanning the interior of each one from his vantage point. A look of frustration swept over him. He stole one more look back around the corner at the Mercedes, then exhaled.

"Do not move," he said as he took the phone out of his pocket and looked up a number in his list of contacts.

"Are you going to tell us what is going on?" Alex demanded.

As the security man pressed the phone to his ear, he simply said, "There's a bomb in the car."

14

"What?" Alex asked, cautiously taking a step back while pulling Tara by the shoulder.

Antonio ignored them as he continued to look around the garage. What he was trying to find, the two Americans didn't know.

"Pedro. I need you to come to the Hotel Maduro. Yes, now." He paused. "Yes, I know how late it is."

Tara and Alex listened to the conversation in Spanish.

"How soon can you be here?" Antonio paced one step to the right, then pivoted and took a step the other way. "That fast? Good. Thank you, Pedro. I owe you one. Oh, and if you have one, bring a tool kit."

Antonio ended the call and slid the phone back into his pocket.

"Okay," Tara said. "First, how do you know there's a bomb in the car? And second, who would be trying to kill us?"

The bodyguard narrowed his eyelids. "I was wondering the same thing. Have you told anyone else you're here and what you're doing, other than your boss and the minister?"

Both shook their heads.

"No," Alex answered. "None of the other IAA agents know we're here, either. Our boss said to keep it quiet."

"You're certain you've told no one?"

"Yeah. We're sure," Tara said.

Antonio seemed to accept the answer, albeit reluctantly, like swallowing a warm beer just for the buzz.

The bodyguard leaned to his left and looked back around the pillar. The car still sat where they'd left it, no explosion. Just the eerie silence of the garage and the sound of machinery whirring in the background.

Pedro told Antonio he would be there in fifteen minutes. He made it in eleven.

They heard Pedro's racing pipe before they saw him round the corner in a red souped-up Honda Civic. The car was dropped low to the ground for aerodynamics and had a raised spoiler on the back. The black-rimmed wheels housed wide tires that jutted out beyond the fenders, and the windows were so dark they made it appear as if the interior was an empty void.

EDM music pulsed from within the confines of the car as it approached.

"Your friend sure likes to make an entrance," Alex said over the growl of the engine.

Antonio didn't offer a response as the tricked-out Civic curled into a nearby parking space.

The driver killed the engine, and the others watched the subtle, almost undetectable movements inside the car as Pedro unfastened his seatbelt.

The door opened, and a man who looked like he was in his mid-fifties stepped out.

Tara and Alex hung their mouths open wide.

When Antonio initially made the phone call, they didn't know what or who to expect. But they certainly didn't expect a middle-aged guy driving a street racer.

Pedro's peppered black hair was thick and done up in a way that made it look like a dark flame. It matched the long, thick beard hanging from his jaw. He was strong, with thick biceps, dense forearms, and broad shoulders that stretched the black Henry Rollins T-shirt he wore.

The guy looked like he belonged in a biker gang, not in a car like this, and he certainly didn't look like the friend of a guy who worked security for the interior minister of Chile.

Antonio smiled for the first time since the two Americans had met him. He walked toward Pedro, raised a hand, clasped his, and they wrapped their free arms in a bro hug.

Pedro slapped Antonio on the back and then took a step away. "How have you been, my friend?"

"You know. Just counting down the days until I retire." Antonio looked around the man to the car. "Looks like you're enjoying your early retirement. Not doing any illegal street racing, I hope?"

Pedro laughed. It was a deep, booming sound that echoed through the concrete tomb of the garage.

"This?" He jerked his thumb toward the car. "This is just a show car. I wouldn't think of using it for illegal street races."

"I hear those races can be lucrative," Antonio hinted.

"They are. From what I hear." Pedro added the correction quickly. A little too quickly.

"Like you need the money. You do it because you miss the old days."

That comment produced a derisive snort. "I don't miss them. But life can get pretty boring in retirement. I like to keep things interesting."

"I heard you had a girlfriend who is fifteen years younger than you for that job."

Pedro allowed a mischievous grin to creep across his face. "Well, she certainly keeps me guessing. But I figured it was either a car like this or a motorcycle. You were always the motorcycle guy."

That last part took Alex and Tara by surprise, but neither said a word. They simply watched and listened, saving their questions for later.

"So," Pedro said, "what's going on? Not like you to call me at this hour and make a demanding request to come meet you in a parking deck like this. If you wanted to get something to drink, I could have met you at a bar."

Antonio acknowledged the question with a nod. "The minister has me watching these two while they do some kind of historical mission for her."

"Really?" Pedro leaned around his friend and sized up the two Americans. He waved and then returned to his original, straight posture. "Must be important if the minister is behind it."

"I guess so. It feels like babysitting."

"I'm sure. But what does any of that have to do with me meeting you here?"

"Did you bring the tools?"

"They're in the trunk." Pedro tilted his head back toward the rear of the car.

"Thank you." Antonio leaned close and spoke in a hushed tone, though his two charges already knew what he thought. "I think there's a bomb in my ride."

"A bomb?" Pedro blurted the words. "Sorry."

"It's fine. They already know."

"What makes you think there's a bomb?"

Antonio glanced back toward the Mercedes before he answered. "I went to start it. Pressed the ignition button, and nothing happened. But I heard a click."

Pedro's eyes widened. "They rerouted the ignition to a detonator."

"That's what I'm afraid of. If I had tried the button one more time, we might be at a barbecue as the main course."

Pedro muttered something profane.

"Exactly."

"So, what's your plan? You're not thinking about removing the explosive, are you?"

Antonio stared at him blankly for a second, then said, "Yeah. I am."

"Just call the bomb squad. Have them take care of it. You're too old for this sort of thing."

"You might be," Antonio said with a laugh. "I, on the other hand, am in my prime."

Alex leaned close to Tara and whispered, "Doc Holliday. *Tombstone.*"

She swatted his shoulder. "Not the time, Alex."

He cringed. "Sorry."

Antonio looked over his shoulder at them. They both smiled like two kids who'd been passing notes in class when the teacher's back was turned.

"Guys like you and me are way past our prime, old friend. But if you have some sort of a death wish, be my guest." Pedro hit the button for the trunk on his key fob, and the back of the car popped open.

"Thank you," Antonio said.

The two walked back over to the rear of the car, and Pedro picked up a black bag with a long shoulder strap. "I'm guessing you'll need a screwdriver, wire cutters, maybe some needle-nose pliers."

"Hopefully, that's all we'll need."

"We? You're not thinking I'm going to get under the car with you, are you?"

Antonio smiled and shook his head. "No, I guess you have enough excitement with your race car and the girlfriend." He winked, turned with the bag slung over his shoulder, and walked toward the two onlooking Americans.

He passed them and then turned back toward the group. Hang out in front of the hotel, I'll meet you there when I'm done. This place is no longer secure."

"Understood." Pedro said.

The two men shared a curt nod before Antonio marched off toward the sedan, leaving Tara and Alex with a new babysitter.

"Okay, you two," Pedro said, his voice gruff and stern, "let's go."

The driver opened the back door to the Civic, while Alex walked around to the other side. Before he climbed in, Alex cast one last look back at Antonio just before he reached the Mercedes and felt immediately overwhelmed by the notion that it was the last time he'd ever see the bodyguard.

15

Antonio set the bag down on the asphalt next to the driver's-side door, made sure the band holding up his ponytail was in place, and then lowered himself to his hands and knees.

He craned his neck low and looked at the undercarriage and chassis. It was dark, and the weak, pale lights hanging on the supports and concrete overhead did little to lend a good view under the car.

Antonio took out his phone, switched on the light, and stuck it under the vehicle. It only took him a few seconds to spot the anomalous steel box attached to the frame.

The bomb was only eight inches long and four inches wide. A red-and-black wire ran from one end of it up into the electrical system that started the car.

The only time he'd ever seen this sort of thing was in the movies, and in training. He'd gone through several rounds of ordnance education with bomb disposal units and paramilitary groups, both from Chile and from the United States. Antonio saw how bombers used various means of rigging a unit similar to this one.

In one case, the bombs were fixed with buttons on the upper side that, in turn, fixed to the base of, in this instance, a car undercarriage.

The buttons kick-started a current that passed between lines. Once the buttons were removed from the base, the signal would cut and trigger the explosion. Cutting the wires would also sever the current, so this setup had three ways to kill you.

The third was the most obvious, and the one that would have killed Antonio and his two charges. The ignition interrupted the signal passing through the bomb, and boom. Adios.

To remove the explosive device from the base, a technician needed to supply the unit with a steady power supply to prevent the failsafe from detonation.

Antonio questioned whether or not he'd paid close enough attention, but there was no room for doubt when it came to dealing with explosives.

He steadied his breathing, taking and expelling the air evenly, which also had the calming effect of slowing his heart rate. The jitters weren't something a person needed to deal with in a scenario like this.

He laid his phone down on the ground, keeping the light pointed up at the bomb, and then retrieved the aircraft aluminum flashlight from the bag. He turned it on and set it on its end to add more light to the car's undercarriage.

Then he flipped over onto his back and got his head as close to the box as possible. He spotted the four screws holding the casing together, slid out, and removed the screwdriver from the bag.

While it wasn't impossible that the bomber had rigged the explosive case to detonate if manipulated, it was unlikely, and a risk Antonio was willing to take.

He inserted the screwdriver into the first screw and turned hard to the left. It took effort, but the screw loosened, and he went on to the next, planning on making sure he could get all of them loose before removing them.

It took less than a minute to complete that task and another two minutes to take all the screws out.

He set them in a cluster on the pavement behind his back and slowly lowered the covering of the box away from the car.

The light sprayed across the internals of the bomb, and Antonio immediately recognized the setup.

He wouldn't be able to simply cut the red or black wire as so many movies suggested. This was going to require a more advanced set of skills. And a battery.

He rolled out from under the car, opened the door, and flipped up the center console. He rummaged through the spare sunglasses, a packet of tissues, a Glock subcompact 9mm, spare magazine, and a bottle of hand sanitizer before he found what he was looking for—a two-pack of 9-volt batteries.

Antonio sat back down on the ground, opened the battery pack, and removed the two batteries. He stared at them for a doubt-filled moment, uncertain that nine volts would be enough to do the job.

He'd used it before with a training rig like this, but the bomber could have crafted a different setup.

Antonio shook off the concern. If he was going to die, in a ball of fire with no pain was probably better than coughing himself to death on a hospital bed or in a retirement home.

He reached into the tool bag and found a wire roll, used the wire cutters to cut two strips and sheer back the sheath, then wrapped a wire around the positive and negative nodes, then slid his right shoulder under the edge the car and held the wires up to the two primary connection points.

The box was fixed to the car's frame with a magnet and would come off with enough force, but in doing so Antonio might jar the battery or wires loose, and once that happened, with the power supply severed, the bomb would detonate.

"First things first, Tony," he grumbled.

He looped the positive wire around the corresponding node, then repeated the task on the negative side.

He slowly let go of the battery, allowing it to dangle by the wires as he retrieved a roll of duct tape from the bag. He tore off a strip, then secured the battery against a metal plate containing the ordnance.

Antonio stuck the battery to the rest of the unit with the tape, and then checked it to make sure it wouldn't come loose. With the new power supply hooked up, there was only one thing left to do.

He placed the tools back in the bag and scooted it away, then lay down on his back and reached under the car with both hands.

Moment of truth.

Antonio breathed steadily as he gripped the sides of the bomb. He wasn't an extremely religious man, but his observations of situations such as this, and others where life was on the line, always brought a person closer to God. Or at the very least, questioning their life choices.

He recalled a prayer from his youth, something he'd heard from a priest on a cold, rainy afternoon. "Though I walk through the valley of the shadow of death..." he said. Then he pried the device from the car.

16

Tara and Alex sat in the back of the Civic with their backpacks in the middle. They'd made a quick trip up to their room to collect their things, and with their escort, hurried back downstairs and stowed the larger items in the trunk.

Alex bobbed his knee up and down with the rhythm of a machine gun. Tara rubbed her thumbs with her forefingers in a constant, circular motion.

Their nervous ticks could have been seen by the worst poker player in the world. While they'd both been in life-or-death situations, and handled utter fear with remarkable stoicism, when someone else's life was in danger and the outcome beyond their control, that's when the nerves really kicked in.

Pedro, on the other hand, seemed almost immune to the fact that his friend was down in the parking garage trying to remove a bomb from their ride.

He'd noted their tension and tried to take their minds off it. "Do you have any idea who would try to kill you?" he asked.

"No," they both answered.

"I'm not going to bother asking what it is you two are doing for the minister. Whatever it is, though, it seems someone doesn't want you here."

He looked back at them in the rearview mirror, trying to pry more answers from them. Instead, all he got was a question.

"Why didn't he call the police?" Tara asked. "Don't they have experts for this sort of thing?"

"Yeah," Alex piled on. "Maybe Antonio has training for this, but—"

"Antonio," Pedro interrupted, "was not willing to leave something so dangerous in a public place. If that bomb were to detonate, it could impact the structural integrity of the hotel. People could die. That isn't something he leaves to chance. The cops probably would have taken longer to get here than me. Even if they had arrived sooner, it would have taken them time to block off the area and assess the danger. I imagine he also wants to analyze the device, perhaps see if he can figure out who might have built it."

The answer quieted the couple in the back. They hadn't expected the part about Antonio being so protective, but it made sense. He'd dedicated his life to watching over the lives of others. He covered it with a gruff exterior, hiding his sense of duty behind a grouchy, bitter façade.

"The good news," Pedro went on, "is that we haven't heard or felt an explosion yet."

Headlights raked the sky overhead, and then dipped, spraying across the hotel and the awning in front of the entrance.

Pedro saw the Mercedes appear over the lip of the garage ramp and then accelerate toward them. The car stopped in front of the Civic at an angle, and the front passenger window rolled down.

Antonio leaned over the center console from behind the wheel. "Follow me."

"Right behind you," Pedro answered. He'd kept the motor running, both to keep cool air funneling through the vents and in case they needed to make a quick getaway, which Pedro assumed would be the case.

Antonio drove off toward the street, then turned left. Pedro shifted the stick into first gear and followed him.

The apartments, hotels, and shops turned into industrial buildings the farther they drove from downtown, until all that surrounded them were warehouses and factories.

"Where are we going?" Tara asked. She had the feeling Alex wasn't willing to risk being the kid in the back asking, "Are we there yet?"

Pedro answered with a flick of his eyes in the rearview mirror and a glint that told her she would find out soon enough.

The bright lights of the city faded to the darker glow of the intermittent streetlights and the occasional lamps that hung outside the buildings.

The taillights of the Mercedes ahead of them brightened as Antonio applied the brakes. Pedro slowed to a stop as Antonio turned into an abandoned gas station and mechanic shop.

The place was protected with weather-beaten, corrugated metal walls and a matching roof. An old rusting sign hung over the entrance and front windows where iron bars covered the glass. Three garage bay doors were closed to the right of the cashier's room, set back about ten feet from the front wall.

The bay door on the left, and the one in the center, slowly began rolling upward.

Antonio drove the Mercedes forward, passing the old gas pumps in front of the main building. When the garage doors were high enough for him to pass under, he pulled the sedan into the bay on the left and waited for the Civic to follow into the center spot.

Pedro took the silent signal and parked the vehicle next to Antonio's.

The second Pedro's car was inside, the doors started closing again.

Fluorescent lights flickered along the walls and from the ceiling above, as if switched on automatically.

The sterile glow illuminated the garage interior, shedding light onto shelves of neatly arranged tools. Wrenches hung over one of the workbenches in the left corner, each one arranged in order from smallest to largest. Bottles of motor oil, fuel treatments, jugs of coolant, and even windshield wiper fluid occupied shelves between the tools and two stacks of tires in the far-right corner.

There was a door to the left, which the Americans assumed led into the cashier station, and a door set in the back wall, presumably to an office, and maybe a dirty old gas station bathroom.

Antonio exited his car and walked around the back. He opened the door to the empty register station, peered out the windows for a second as if expecting to see someone else, then stepped back into the garage.

Pedro and the two Americans climbed out of the Civic and waited.

"Were we followed?" Pedro asked. He sounded as if he were asking an inconsequential question.

"No. I don't think so. The streets are pretty empty out here at this hour of the night. Unless you saw someone."

"I didn't, and I was watching. We're clear."

"I'm going to sweep the cars just to make sure. Take them to the back."

Alex took a step forward. "What is going on here, Antonio? What is this place? And what in the world did you do with the bomb?"

Antonio's dark eyes smoldered. "This is my safe house," he answered. "I bought it cheap several years back when the gas station went out of business. It's under the radar, so to speak. No one knows about it. Except you three. Before tonight, only Pedro and I had been in here."

"Safe house?" Tara asked. "Why—"

"Because you can never be too careful. Especially when you work for the government."

There was more to his response, but she could tell from the tired expression on his face that he didn't want to say any more. Not about that, anyway.

"There is a bedroom in the back," he went on. "The bed has enough space for two. I can sleep on the couch."

"You don't have to—"

"That's how it is. Pedro, you can have the other bedroom if you want to stay. But I think we're good now."

"I don't mind sleeping on the couch. I trust your bar is still stocked?" Thirsty eyes accompanied the question.

"You know it is, my friend." He offered a subtle smirk. "But my guests don't sleep on sofas."

"Then, I'll stay for a night. You always have the best tequila."

"Show them the place while I sweep the cars for bugs. I'll be in shortly—that is, if I don't find anything."

The bodyguard flipped open the trunk of the Mercedes and ducked down, disappearing into the cargo area.

"Come on," Pedro said to Tara and Alex. "In here."

He walked over to the back door and flipped up a worn plastic panel near the doorframe. It was smudged with grease and paint and looked as if it hadn't been touched in ages.

But underneath, the covering hid a sparkling clean key panel. Pedro entered in a sequence of numbers, and the red light above the buttons turned green to the sound of a click inside the wall.

"This way," he said, opening the door wide for the couple to enter.

Tara led the group through the door and into a hallway. She and Alex had expected the place to be dingy, dusty, and possibly even infested with rodents or bugs. But what they found was a clean corridor. The beige tiles on the floor were old, the kind you'd expect to find in a nursing home or hospital in the 1980s. The walls were faux wood panels from the 1970s. While the place wasn't stylish, it had been kept in great condition, or perhaps refurbished to look brand new.

They passed a bedroom on the left that had previously been a manager's office, a renovated bathroom on the right, complete with a small corner shower, and another bedroom just past it.

The hall ended in a large space that had previously been a waiting room for customers who'd brought their cars in for repairs.

Instead of the old vinyl upholstered chairs, there was a long brown leather couch, two matching chairs, and a coffee table facing a flat-screen television hanging in the corner.

The bar Pedro had mentioned earlier was to the immediate right. Three stools sat underneath the stained wooden counter. Beer glasses lined the other side of the counter, along with a row of tumblers for stronger drinks. A steel refrigerator stood in the corner next to a sink and dishwasher.

But the star of the show was on the counter next to the sink and behind a glass-faced cabinet where dozens of bottles of every variety of liquor you could think of stood at the ready.

"Wow," Alex said, impressed. "I wanted to go to a bar, but I didn't mean a high-end one. That's a nice stash."

Pedro chuckled. "Antonio doesn't have a lot of fancy things. The Mercedes is government issue. But he puts his money where it counts."

"I'll say." Alex took a step toward the collection and pored over it, mesmerized. He ran his fingers down the neck of a bottle of Colonel Taylor single barrel, tilting it slightly to admire the label.

Tara directed her attention to the other side of the room where a huge L-shaped workstation fit into the near corner. A black leather chair sat behind the desk. Three curved computer monitors occupied the surface, connected to a tower on the floor to the right.

"This is quite the setup," she said, admiring the space.

"Yes, he did a good job with it. I think he uses it as his... How do you Americans call it? A man cave?"

She giggled at the term. "Yes. That's the one."

"He has an apartment in the city, closer to the government buildings. But he comes here on the weekends, or whenever he has some free time."

"Doesn't sound like he gets out of town very much," Alex noted.

"That's true," Pedro said. "But he says he's going to travel more once he retires. We'll see."

It was hard for either of them to picture the grizzled man sitting on a beach soaking up the sun or wandering through museums, art galleries, or ancient castles. But there were layers to Antonio that he didn't allow to be seen—unless they were peeled away one at a time.

Pedro walked around to the bar, flipped over an upside-down

tumbler, and pulled the lid off a bottle of Clase Azul tequila. He poured the golden liquid into the glass and looked to Alex as if to offer one.

"Sure. Pour one for Tara, too."

"Of course."

Pedro finished making the drinks, asked if the others wanted ice, which they declined, and then set the two glasses on the counter.

Tara joined the two men, picked up her glass, and waited for Pedro to offer a toast.

"Salúd," he said with a nod, then tipped the drink to his lips. He sipped it slowly, taking in only a fraction of the warm liquid, then let out a satisfied "Ah, that's good stuff" before making his way around the bar and over to one of the chairs near the television.

The door at the end of the hall clicked, then opened. Tara and Alex watched as Antonio stalked toward them, allowing the door to close automatically behind him.

"We're clean," he said. "No tracking devices on the cars." He pointed his next question at the Americans. "Did anyone speak to you at the airport, or between the minister giving you her information and meeting me?"

"No," they said at the same time.

"We haven't talked to anyone," Alex insisted.

"You didn't notice someone touching your things, did you?"

"No," Tara said. "We've had them in our sights other than when the luggage was on the plane."

"The luggage is clean, too," Antonio stated.

Tara choked on her tequila.

"Don't worry. I didn't ransack your bags. I just ran a scanner over them. If there was anything suspicious in them, I'd know. But it's possible there was something in one of your bags and you simply dropped it by accident once you checked into your room."

"I... didn't notice anything lying around," Alex said, though doubts filtered through his statement.

Antonio accepted the statement with a nod. "Well, we are fine for now. Did you get the journal the minister gave you?"

"Yeah," Tara said, slipping her backpack off her shoulders. She unzipped the bag and produced the leather book.

"Good. I have a suspicion whoever was trying to kill you also wanted to destroy that book."

"Why would someone do that?" Alex asked. "I thought she was keeping our presence here a secret."

Antonio thought for a second before dismissing the theory that bubbled to the top of his mind. "We will figure that out later. For now, you're safe. Finish your drinks, and then get some rest. You can return to whatever it was you were doing for the minister in the morning."

"Actually," Tara said, holding the book out with the pages open, "we need a flight to Cusco."

"Cusco?"

"Yes. May I turn on your computer?"

He shrugged. "Sure. Go ahead. Everything is in Spanish, though."

"That's fine."

Antonio looked a little surprised at the statement as he watched her move over to the desk, set down the book, and fire up the desktop.

The screens bloomed to life, each one featuring a different screen saver, all of picturesque settings from around the world. One was of a beach somewhere in the Mediterranean. The green-blue crystal water lapped against golden sand in white, foamy ripples. The image on the middle screen displayed a cliffside coastal town in Italy. The third was of the rolling dunes of the Sahara Desert.

Tara clicked the mouse, and the pictures disappeared, replaced by the background wallpaper. The center monitor displayed most of the icons.

She found the web browser, clicked it, and then entered the search for the temple in Cusco. The screen blinked, then produced a list of results. She selected the first one, and a website with images of the Coricancha Temple appeared.

Antonio floated over to the workstation, moving like a ghost. Pedro looked back at them over his shoulder, curiosity getting the better of him.

"This is the oldest temple in Cusco. Well, it's in the lower level of this place. We need to get here and investigate. I think we're looking for this." She pressed her finger to a drawing in the journal.

Antonio peered at the object—something that looked like a pillar with a wide square top and curved sides.

"Do you know this place?" she asked.

He bobbed his head and said that he did. "I have been there, but it was a long time ago. And I did not see whatever this is."

She redirected his attention to the screen as Alex walked over to the desk. Pedro had been sitting long enough, unable to resist a closer look, and joined the others by the computer.

"I think it's this thing," Tara said, hovering the mouse arrow over an eerily similar object in the middle of the screen. "This altar has something to do with what the minister wants us to investigate. Only problem is, we don't have the other piece to the puzzle."

"Puzzle?" Pedro asked. "I suck at puzzles."

The Americans chuckled. Even Antonio let a snort slip.

"We think that this object needs to be set on top of the altar," Alex said. "Notice the arrow pointing down from the four-sided cross?"

The two older men nodded.

"So, where is the cross?" Antonio asked.

"We don't know," Tara sighed. "But maybe if we can get to this place and do a little digging, we can figure that out."

"I don't think they'll let you do any digging."

"I didn't mean that literally," she said with a laugh. "Either way, we need to get to Cusco to check it out. After that, we may not have anything else to go on."

Antonio deliberated silently for ten seconds before responding. "I'll arrange the flight. We'll leave for Cusco in the morning."

Alex had been sitting on a question for several minutes now. About to burst with curiosity, he finally let it out. "I'm sorry. But what did you do with the bomb?"

Antonio put on a coy expression. He flicked his right eyebrow up before he spoke. "I put it in the dumpster behind the hotel and moved it far enough away that there would be no structural damage if it were to detonate. Then I called the police. Their bomb squad will have dealt with it by now."

"A dumpster?" Tara blurted.

"It was the safest, fastest option. I rerouted the power to the detonator, so it's unlikely it would have exploded anyway."

"Unlikely?"

He merely shrugged. "Yes. Now, if you don't mind, I need to make travel arrangements. You two should get some sleep. Tomorrow could be a long day."

17

"I never thought I'd be waking up in a bed in an old mechanic shop," Tara said as she rolled over and picked up her watch from the nightstand. She checked the time and noted it was nearly seven o'clock in the morning—not unusually late for them to sleep in considering they often spent late hours at the lab in IAA headquarters.

"That makes two of us," Alex agreed.

He stretched his arms and legs, lengthening the muscles to send blood pumping to his extremities. Then he rolled onto his side and checked the time on his phone, scratched his head, and set the device back down.

"You think they're up yet?" he wondered.

"I'm sure they've been up for a few hours. Guys like that come from strictly disciplined lives. I doubt either one of them has ever slept in. Well, maybe Pedro has since he's retired."

Tara slung her legs over the bed and reached down to the floor, where her jeans lay in a heap next to the nightstand. She stood up and slid into them with a graceful ease that Alex never got tired of watching.

Sometimes he had to pinch himself when he looked at her. "You really are beautiful."

She looked down at him with that smile she only shared when they were alone, like she saved it just for him.

"I'm glad you think so. You're not so bad yourself, Mr. Watson."

He blushed at the comment, grinned back at her, then planted his feet on the floor and picked up his jeans.

"You know," he said, "we're going to need some luck on our side for this."

"I know. I was thinking about that. Hopefully, seeing this altar first-hand will give us a clue about where to find the cross. Or maybe there's something in the Santo Domingo Church that can give us a clue."

"At the very least, we're going to Cusco. So much history in that city."

"Yeah." Her agreement felt half-hearted, as if the memory of their last adventure in South America still haunted her, tormenting her with hallucinations from the past.

"You okay?"

She snapped out of it, choked down the demons, and nodded. "Yeah. I'm fine. Just ready for some coffee. It smells like the guys already have some out there."

They finished getting dressed and emerged from the bedroom timidly, poking their heads out the door to see if there was any activity in the main room.

Unsurprisingly, the two older men were up just as Tara and Alex expected. The old friends sat at a small rectangular table painted a light teal color. The aluminum chairs around it were functional but lacked in design.

"Good morning," Tara said as she and Alex made their way into the larger room.

The two men hushed their conversation immediately in the way people do if they don't want whatever they were saying to be heard by intrusive ears.

"Buenos días," Pedro said.

Antonio merely bobbed his head once at her, then raised a white coffee mug to his lips as he watched the couple enter the room and stop by the bar counter.

"There's fresh coffee in the pot back there," Pedro said, raising his mug to point the way. "Just beware. We drink it strong."

"Good," Tara said. "That's how we like it."

They shuffled around the corner of the bar, found two mugs set out beside the machine, and filled the cups.

Alex raised the mug to his nose and inhaled deeply. "I love the smell of coffee in the morning."

"Beats the smell of napalm," Pedro quipped.

"Wow. Good reference."

Pedro shrugged. "Classic film about a horrific war."

"Indeed."

Tara noticed Buford's journal sitting on the table. It was open to the pages near the beginning that showed the images of the altar and the four-sided cross, along with the windows with the strange symbols.

"I see you've been doing a little reading," she said.

Antonio remained silent, but Pedro acknowledged the statement.

"I was curious. I hope you don't mind the intrusion."

She shook her head and ambled over to the table, set down her mug, and took a seat next to Pedro. "It's not our book. Find anything interesting?"

Alex joined her in the seat nearest Antonio, who'd been oddly silent. Even for him.

"All of it is interesting," Pedro confessed. "I'm not sure what it all means, but interesting, definitely. You believe this object here," he tapped on the altar, "is in Cusco?"

While Antonio hadn't shared his friend's backstory, they could glue enough of it together to figure that a guy like him was mostly appreciated for his physical attributes, and probably a particular set of lethal skills.

Finally, Antonio spoke up. "Pedro has keen interest in history. He studied it at university before going into the service."

"I'm no expert like these two," Pedro said, blowing it off. "Antonio told me no one is supposed to know about this, but he thought maybe I could lend some assistance."

"Sure," Tara said, leaning forward with her elbows on the table. "We found images from the old Coricancha Temple of an object similar to this. We think that the journal is suggesting that if this cross is placed on top of the altar, the locations of three of the other artifacts, or keys, will be revealed."

"Yes," Pedro agreed. "It seems the man who owned this book thought the same thing. Only, he said he was unable to find any of those keys."

"Did you read the riddles on the next page?" Alex asked.

"I did." Pedro turned the page and pressed it down so it would stay open. "Three quarters make the whole. Bring to the altar the earth, thunder and lightning, sea, and moon. Only then will the sun light your way to the blessed city." He looked at the others. "Three quarters? That doesn't make any sense. Bothered me the first few times I read it."

"Nonsense if you ask me," Antonio grumbled. "I can't believe the minister buys any of it."

"Don't pay any attention to him," Pedro dismissed, waving a hand at his old friend. "Do you have any ideas what the riddle means?"

"No. Not yet," Alex admitted. "And we don't have the cross to put on the altar. We were hoping that once we got to Cusco, we could maybe find it. Or at least get a lead."

"Sounds like a pretty big stretch."

"We weren't going to find anything here in Santiago," Tara said. "Everything about this mystery centers around Cusco. So, it makes sense to start there, even if we don't have much to go on."

"So, your plan is to fly to Cusco and begin the hunt for clues?" Pedro's interest continued to climb.

"Yes. And on the way I guess we figured we'd try to sort out the riddle you just read."

Alex and Tara both felt acutely aware of how ridiculous that idea sounded when he said it out loud.

Pedro blew it off with a non-judgmental shrug. "I've heard about a legend like this before. Of course, most people have heard stories of El Dorado and other mystical cities overflowing with treasures. Unfortunately, I don't know if I have any information that can help you. Though I find the riddle to be quite intriguing. It seems that you are to bring some kind of representation of three Inca deities to the altar before the fourth and final key is revealed."

"Wait," Tara blurted, nearly spitting out the gulp of coffee she'd just taken. "What do you mean, three Inca deities?"

Pedro searched her eyes, then Alex's, but saw that neither knew what he was talking about.

"Oh. Well, perhaps I can lend some assistance then." He spun the journal around and pointed to the three windows. "See these images here?" They leaned closer.

One window contained a portrait of a stormy sea crashing into the rocks along the shore. The second displayed a cloudy sky over a valley with lightning piercing through the center all the way to the ground. The third window showed an image of the moon, set amid stars over mountains. And the final picture portrayed a sketch of a deep, rocky canyon.

"These represent three key deities in the Inca religious system. Pachamama, the goddess of earth, symbolized by the canyon. Mama Killa, the goddess of the moon. And Mama Quiche, or Qucha, goddess of the sea. These"—he peered at them as he spoke, his finger resting on the page; then he turned and looked down at the paper and tapped his finger on one word—"all lead to the sun. Inti."

"The sun god," Alex realized. "He's mentioned dozens of times in the journal."

"Yes," Pedro said. "It seems that this priest Father José Alsue must have believed Inti was the final key, the last piece to the puzzle that would unlock the lost city."

Pedro leaned back, picked up his mug, and took a long drink of coffee, waiting for the two guests to reel in everything they'd just heard.

Both of them would have come to that conclusion eventually,

possibly on the flight into Peru. But Pedro had just potentially saved them hours with this revelation.

"How do you know all that?" Tara asked, happy to show him how impressed she was.

"I told you," Antonio answered for his friend. "He loves this stuff."

Alex started to say something, hesitated, and then mustered the courage. "You... wouldn't want to come along with us to Cusco, would you? I mean, if it's okay with the minister." He quickly added the last bit as he looked to Antonio for approval.

Antonio didn't move, but his eyes shifted to his friend, wondering what he would say.

"That's very kind of you, but I can't," Pedro said. "I have other things going on here. I help with a charity in town for poor kids. As much as I would enjoy investigating this, I have to decline."

The statement about helping underprivileged kids struck Tara's heartstrings. "Well, that's awesome. We really appreciate your input on this."

"Yeah," Alex agreed. "Saved us a bunch of time for sure."

"Happy to lend assistance," Pedro replied. "I'll follow you three to the airport to make sure you don't have any other issues."

"Gracias, mí amigo," Antonio offered.

"De nada." Pedro took another drink of the coffee. "The question you three should be asking is, who tried to kill you last night?"

That question had shaken Tara and Alex, but it hadn't broken them. They'd pondered it before going to sleep, even discussed it a little. Eventually, slumber called and would not be denied, though the answer never revealed itself.

Not that they believed it would.

They'd faced brutal enemies before, lethal villains who would just as soon kill an innocent person as pick up a coin from the street. Whoever planted the explosive in their car was just the next one in line.

To Tara and Alex, the question of why was just as important as who.

The surface answer to that was simple enough. Who wouldn't want to find a mystical lost city with unimaginable, infinite treasures?

Michael Buford had tried and presumably failed.

Beyond treasure hunters, though, the mystery remained as to who could be behind their attempted murder.

"I'll see about getting access to the security footage from the garage, but I doubt we'll see anything helpful," Antonio said. "Whoever did this wouldn't be stupid enough to show their face."

"So, I guess that leaves us with more questions than answers," Alex thought out loud. "For now, we have to move forward. Get to Cusco, see what we can learn, and go from there."

"You seem unfazed by the fact someone tried to kill you," Pedro noticed. There was a hint of admiration in his voice.

"It wasn't the first time."

Alex didn't feel like elaborating on their on-the-job training with Sean Wyatt and his wife, Adriana Villa.

The young couple had been put through rigorous physical tests through the years, along with self-defense and martial arts, and firearms training—not to mention the real-world danger they'd faced since working at IAA. They could hold their own in a fight, and had been in the field more than once, where those skills were put to use.

This wasn't the time to brag, though, and that wasn't in either of their natures to do. They also realized that there were far more dangerous people out there than themselves. The second someone got cocky was the second they got killed.

For this reason, Tara and Alex remained silently humble about their abilities.

"Well, you're lucky you have Antonio watching your back," Pedro said. "What time is your flight?"

"Two hours," Antonio said. "Speaking of, we should get going. Traffic can be problematic this time of day. So, finish your coffee. Then we'll go to the airport."

"We'll have some other things to figure out on the plane," Tara said.

"Yes," Pedro agreed. "Three riddles on the next three pages, one for each window. I wonder...."

He let his thought fall away.

"Wonder what?" Alex pressed.

"Nothing," he shook it off. "Finish your coffee. You three need to get going. I look forward to hearing about your discoveries."

"We gotta find something first. Could be we're just taking a jaunt to Peru for a tour of a museum and a church, and we'll find nothing."

18

Arturo arrived at the hotel before sunrise the next morning and found a parking spot directly across from the entrance to the hotel parking lot where he could see all the way across and into the garage.

There'd been no news of an explosion yet, but that was to be expected. The Americans and their caretaker had probably gone to bed early last night after a long day of travel and meeting with the interior minister.

It was only a matter of time.

Arturo lifted the paper cup of steaming-hot coffee and raised it to his lips. He inhaled the aroma, then touched the lid to his mouth and took a cautious sip. He winced at the scalding heat, and set it back into the car's cup holder.

"Too hot," he complained and removed the lid to let it cool naturally for a few minutes.

He kept an eye on the lot while he picked up the brown paper bag he'd grabbed from the café in the hotel he'd spent the night in. The place was only two blocks away, close enough that had there been an explosion and subsequent sirens of first responders, he would have heard every second of it.

Arturo removed the flaky pastry from the brown bag and took a bite.

He knew it could be a long morning. That was fine. He could sit here for hours. The targets would have to leave to get breakfast, or perhaps begin their search for the interior minister.

Either way, they'd be getting in the Mercedes. And when they did....

As the sun climbed over the horizon, people walked by on the sidewalk to his right, most not paying him any attention, and only a few daring to glance in through the windshield before quickly shifting their eyes away.

Arturo was no one to them. Just another guy in a car on the street, probably waiting for his wife or girlfriend, or sipping his coffee before going to work.

Cars passed on the street, and the longer the hours drew on, the more stuffed it became with lines of commuters.

He checked his watch for the hundredth time.

It was nearly nine o'clock, and there'd been no sign of the Mercedes, and equally disturbing—no blast.

He'd finished his coffee more than two hours before. Normally, he'd have already consumed three cups by now. Due to certain personal constraints, that wasn't an option in the current circumstances.

But the amount of time that had passed began to press on both his curiosity, and his bladder.

"Where are you?" he muttered.

He'd been patient, never taking his eyes off the hotel exit. Cars had come and gone, in and out, all morning—a slow trickle at first. And more people had left than arrived, but none of the vehicles contained the two Americans.

Arturo waited another ten minutes before he made up his mind to find out what was going on.

Was there another way out of the hotel?

He hadn't seen other exits, and he knew the garage only had one way in and out. If a cab or rideshare had picked them up, he'd have seen it.

But why would the Americans still be in their room? Sleeping in? Doubtful.

Arturo waited for a break in the traffic and then opened his door, stepped out, and trotted across the street.

He slowed to a steady walk when he reached the hotel lot and continued past the awning where two valets stood behind a pedestal. One was assisting a customer while the other guy sipped on a bottle of water.

They paid no mind to Arturo as he passed.

He reached the opening to the parking garage and followed the painted white line marking the path down into the below level lot.

A blue hatchback pulled up to the gate as he walked by. The driver inserted their parking ticket into the kiosk, the bar raised, and the car drove off.

Arturo examined the back seat and cargo area just to make sure his prey weren't hiding somewhere inside, but other than the driver, the car was empty.

He walked down the slight grade and into the main level, turned left, and made his way between the rows of cars on his left and right. Most of the spots were empty now, the hotel visitors having left that morning to continue their travels elsewhere, or perhaps go grab breakfast and coffee.

Arturo looked back the other way to make sure no one was watching, or had set up an ambush. He reached into the right side of his pants next to the pocket and pulled out a subcompact 9mm. He kept it in a conceal-carry holster at all times. The only exception being when he slept.

It wasn't the most powerful firearm in his arsenal. He had several other weapons in his stash with more stopping power, but they were larger, bulkier by comparison.

This one was thin, with a single stack magazine that—while offering less capacity—provided exceptional discretion.

He held the weapon low and to his left side in case another car appeared around the corner or down the ramp to the right. Then he quickly cut across to the other side and skirted along the row of cars and empty spots until he arrived at the cylindrical concrete pillar at the corner.

He stopped, switching the position of his pistol to the right to keep it out of view, and then slowly leaned around the pillar, peering down the length of the parking area to where the bodyguard had parked the night before.

Arturo blinked once. Twice. A third time.

Muscles in his jaw tensed and gripped his skull all the way around like invisible fingers squeezing his brain.

He shook his head in disbelief. "That's impossible."

Arturo felt a wave of panic hit him in the chest. His heart dropped into his gut.

Orasco would not be pleased with this latest development. He was a dangerous man; someone few would mess with. Powerful, wealthy, and intolerant of excuses, failure such as this would only mean one thing for Arturo.

The pleasant evening of smoking cigars in Orasco's study would be replaced with torture and, eventually, Arturo's execution.

He had to think.

Turning around in circles, as if the car might suddenly appear, he searched for answers, but the walls and the cars offered none.

"Where did you go?" he asked, knowing the garage would not give the secret away.

He had to think. Freaking out wasn't going to solve the problem.

First, how had the car not blown up? He'd been meticulous with the device. The instant the driver had started the car, it should have detonated and ignited the explosive agent.

"The driver," he realized.

It was the only answer that made any sense. The guard must have checked the car and somehow disabled the bomb. Arturo didn't even know if men in his position had learned how to do such a thing, but it was possible.

The only other solution was that Arturo had screwed up the bomb when he attached it to the wires.

Had he connected it correctly?

Of course he had. He'd done it a few times before to eliminate targets. It was a time-tested method, and his execution was flawless.

That left the driver theory.

Just knowing the how of his quarry's getaway was only part of the equation. How had they gotten away? And when?

He'd been there since dawn and hadn't seen the Mercedes.

The only logical answer was that they'd left in the middle of the night. There was no sense in fussing over what time. They were gone, and standing around wondering when they dipped wasn't going to make a difference.

He took out his phone and called Orasco.

The man wouldn't be happy that the Americans had slipped through Arturo's fingers. But if Arturo remained silent and didn't give an honest update, those bad optics could come back and bite him.

For all he knew, someone was watching him right now, a tail that Orasco had put on his hitter to make sure the job got done.

It had happened before, and to make an example, Arturo had killed the man and brought back his hand in a Ziploc bag to the employer.

It was a risky thing to do, and could have been perceived as a threat. But Arturo wanted his boss, and everyone else who might hire him, to know that he would not tolerate being second-guessed or micromanaged.

The macabre act yielded the desired results, and no employer since had ever put a pair of eyes on Arturo while he was working.

He surveyed the parking garage, searching every car for a snitch behind a wheel, but all the vehicles were empty.

The phone rang against his ear three times before Orasco answered. He sounded out of breath as if he'd been working out. Arturo doubted that.

"Hello, my friend. Do you have an update for me?"

"Yes. The marks have skipped town."

A deathly silence filled the call.

"That is... unfortunate. I assume since you're calling me, you must have some idea where they went."

"No, sir. I don't. But we can find out. You have someone on the inside with the minister."

"Yes." The answer sounded almost like a question.

"If the Americans flew somewhere, it's unlikely they would fly a commercial airline. Their flight would be a private charter, probably arranged by the office of the interior minister."

"You're asking me to get the passenger manifests and flight details."

"I am," Arturo confessed, knowing that it wasn't a good look. He leaned hard on the fact that he'd had the guts to actually call instead of dodging the problem, or scrambling to cover it up.

"That is a smart idea," Orasco said. "And I admire the fact you weren't afraid to call me."

Arturo felt relief spill into his torso, washing away the paralyzing sense of panic. "I just want to do my job. I could get that information on my own, but your mole can get it faster."

"I'll make the call and send you the information the second they get it to me. Don't let them get away again, Arturo."

"I won't."

19

Tara and Alex fought off the urge to melt into the beige leather seats aboard the Gulfstream G5.

The jet Interior Minister Carrera had provided wasn't all that dissimilar to Tommy's IAA plane. They were the same make and model, though Tommy's was the newer, more updated version.

Tara and Alex sat next to each other, while Antonio was seated across from them, facing backward.

Despite the luxurious comfort of the jet, Tara and Alex found it difficult to relax with the important task—and the man tasked with ensuring its success—staring them in the face.

They'd continued to study Buford's journal, particularly the pages that centered around where they were headed.

Placing the symbols on the altar was simple enough—if they *had* the three symbols. According to the book, the seeker of the city had to pass through a series of tests. Until Pedro explained the part about the three goddesses, Tara and Alex had only briefly examined those pages.

The couple shared the journal between them, each with a laptop open across their legs. The book was open to the page after the one with the altar on it. The one to the left featured a drawing of the window with Pachamama, the Inca goddess of the earth. A deity's face was superimposed over a canyon as if she were in the background watching over it.

The image on the next page of Mama Qucha was similarly designed, except she presided over the raging waters of the sea.

Each page contained notes Buford had scribbled down, copied from the diary of Father Alsue.

Tara read the first entry out loud. "Collasuyu, the southwestern quarter of the empire. The seeker of the city must complete the trials of Pachamama."

Then she read a side note: "Unable to locate Collasuyu. It could be somewhere in Chile, but I can't work out where. I'm also not sure what the trials might entail."

She looked at Alex. "Father Alsue's notes were pretty thin. All he said was only through Chakana the way is found."

"Chakana?" Alex wondered out loud.

"We knew we were going to have to look that up at some point."

Antonio watched them with amusement, as if he held the answer to the question.

"What?" Alex asked, noticing the mischief on the man's face.

It wasn't an expression he'd shown to them before, and it looked out of place on a tough exterior, like painting a Rembrandt on the side of a derelict steel foundry.

"The Chakana is *Arbol de Vida*," Antonio explained as if it were common knowledge. Maybe to him it was. But the two Americans had never heard the term before.

Arbol de Vida, however, they were familiar with.

Nearly a decade before, Sean and Tommy had found themselves in the depths of a dangerous mission in search of the fabled Tree of Life, a search that led them across multiple continents.

"The Chakana is the Tree of Life?" Tara asked.

"Sí. It's also called the Southern Cross."

"Why do I feel like you know more about this stuff than you're letting on?" Alex said.

Antonio put his arms out wide across the top of the chair back. "I don't. Pedro is the guy for that. I only pick up on a few things here and there. But the Chakana is something I've known about since childhood. And it's one of those symbols that's in the front of the book. The four-sided cross that represents the four corners of the empire, with Cusco in the middle."

Tara typed furiously on her laptop. She entered a search query, clicked the first result, and read through the information. "The Chakana was an important symbol to the Inca people. It was also a symbol of the collective unconscious of the people and served as a spiritual guide map."

She looked up from the screen, expecting Antonio to say something else. But his lips remained tightly sealed.

"The collective unconscious?" Alex said. "You mean collective consciousness?"

"No." She turned the laptop toward him so he could read the text. "See?"

He peered at the screen for a second. "Oh. Yeah, you're right. That's odd they worded it that way."

"The subconscious, or unconscious, is far more powerful than the conscious mind." Antonio said. "It runs many processes at once, all the time. Our conscious minds can only handle a few things. Thus, the unconscious holds the power to access greater spiritual understanding, and power."

The couple stared back at him with their mouths dropped open.

"What?" he said, raising his hands so the palms pointed up. "I read personal development stuff."

"Okay," Tara said, bobbing her head to show she both approved and was impressed. "So, the Chakana is a symbol that connected the people to this greater unconsciousness. Do you think it could be that this alternate state is actually where the lost city exists?"

"I have no idea. That's your department of expertise," Antonio said. "But that would make sense since no one has been able to locate it in the physical plane."

Alex chuckled under his breath, musing at the way he phrased it.

The man who was a hardened warrior, trained to protect Chilean leaders at all costs, was as deep as the many jungles of South America. Every time they thought they had him figured out, his bio complete, they cut through a swath of underbrush only to find more jungle beyond.

"Do you know more about the Wandering City than you're letting on?" Tara asked, risking a quick rebuke.

"No," Antonio replied. "Only the stories my grandmother used to tell me before I went to bed at night. Fairy tales, you call them in America. Nothing more than that."

The response he received from Tara and Alex wasn't what he expected. They both immediately perked up, ready to hear more about the man's past.

His face darkened, and they knew not to press him further.

"Back to the journal," Alex said quickly, "The next page refers to the goddess of the sea and Chinchaysuyu, the northwestern quarter of the empire. It seems Buford wasn't able to find it, either."

"Trials of Mama Qucha. A lot of these goddesses have mama in the names. I wonder if that's where we got the idea to call mothers that."

"Maybe."

Antonio merely arched a suspicious right eyebrow.

"It doesn't seem like Buford was able to add much to Alsue's document," Alex noted.

Tara turned the page to the last of the three clues referring to the windows or portals around the altar.

"Well, he was able to figure out the location of this one," she corrected, pointing at the name *Machu Picchu* above a drawing of the moon. "But it also says he didn't find anything there."

"Temple of the Moon," Alex said. He recalled reading about it at some point in the past. The ancient temple sat amid the stacked stone buildings at the incredible city high up in the Andes. "That's the one obvious part about all this. But here it says he realized after the fact he didn't have the key and thinks that's why he couldn't find anything out of the ordinary."

"Yeah. The guy went all the way to Machu Picchu. I mean, I would say that sucks, but he did get to go to Machu Picchu. Which is kind of a bucket-list thing for me."

She'd brought up a trip to the wondrous place multiple times to Alex, but they'd always found an excuse not to do it. Their trip to Utah had actually been a potential week for a journey to the city in the Andes, but they'd decided to go snowboarding instead.

Not that snowboarding sucked. They both loved it, and wished they could go more often. But Georgia rarely had snow, and never enough for any kind of winter sports.

Alex passed her a knowing glance. "Maybe this is your moment to finally do it," he offered.

"Maybe." She sounded unconvinced. "We have to see if we can find a way to open these portals. But without the cross, it seems like we're wasting our time just like Buford did."

They combed through the pages following the three about the windows and the trials that went along with them, then returned to the one with the moon goddess.

"Mama Killa," Alex said, leaning over to better see the writing. "Sounds like a rapper's name."

Tara giggled.

Antonio didn't get it and unleashed a confused scowl.

Alex took a deep breath and resisted rolling his eyes. "So, she was the goddess of the moon in their religion. Interesting that the other two trials are based on the earth, but that one is celestial."

Tara looked over at the surly security man. "You wouldn't happen to have anything to add about this one, would you?"

He shook his head, looking almost bored. "Only the stories my abuela told me. I doubt they would be helpful. I don't know much about the history of Mama Killa. You can probably learn more from the internet."

"Yeah, but I like having your input. You're a part of the team, after all. Whether you like it or not."

The statement unsettled him. He shifted at first, and then got up and walked away, heading to the bar at the end of the aisle.

"I guess he didn't want to talk about it," Alex said.

"Guess not."

They returned to the journal and focused on the page with the last of the three clues.

The trials of Mama Killa await beneath the moon.

"Seems kind of vague," Alex noted. "The others were pretty thin on details, too. What kinds of trials is this thing talking about?"

"I don't know," Tara said. "But you can bet they won't be easy. If we can get to the locations of them, we'll have to be ready for anything."

"Aside from the next part about returning to the altar with the three keys to receive the Key of Inti, the only other detail in this book refers to Devil's Point."

A rudimentary drawing of a rock formation on the side of a mountain stood out on the following page.

"But that's where it seems Buford gave up. His notes say that Alsue went to the top of the mountain near there but wasn't able to find the gates to the city."

"Because he didn't have the Inti Key," Tara added.

"Which we may not have either."

"If that's the case, we're going to end up with the same results as the priest. And probably Buford. Although hopefully, we don't mysteriously disappear."

20

CUSCO, PERU

Juan Avila stepped out of the white Land Rover and onto the cobblestone pavement in front of the Palacio del Inka hotel.

Orasco had spared no expense on Juan's behalf, providing the luxurious SUV, two guards—one of whom drove—and a suite at the five-star hotel.

While Juan appreciated the refinements, he also felt a mounting sense of pressure because of them. Like a footballer newly signed to a massive contract, expectations were higher than ever. And the archaeologist needed to produce results.

He closed the door and looked down the street right to left, watching the people emerge from their homes, businesses, and lodgings.

Juan knew they were all returning from their siestas; well, most of them. The tourists never seemed to disappear from the streets, perpetually wandering through the old city, night or day, to take in the many sights, sounds, smells, and traditions.

Siestas had never really been Juan's thing when he was a kid, but that had changed as he grew older. Now, he looked forward to the break in the day and wondered how he ever got along without one.

"I'll park the car and rejoin you," the driver said as the guard in the front passenger seat stepped down onto the walkway next to Juan.

That other guard, a stout man a few inches shorter than Juan, nodded and closed the door.

"Wait here," the guard ordered.

Juan didn't need the command. He'd heard what the driver said. But these guys operated as if they were reading through a manual. Everything was by the book, systematic. It didn't surprise the archaeologist, but it did feel awfully robotic.

The guard's name was Javier, and his body was as thick as his head. He looked like a walking fist. The driver, Mathias, was tall and thin, with a head that sat peering to and fro, like a vulture, on an elongated neck.

Orasco had insisted Juan take the two men with him, despite his protests. Juan claimed that he didn't need a couple of bodyguards shadowing him across the continent and that it would be a waste of resources.

The truth was, Juan didn't trust the two men. They'd been tasked with protecting him in case of an incident, or an unlikely attack, but Juan got the distinct feeling that both of them would happily turn on him and kill him themselves if Orasco so much as snapped his fingers.

Juan couldn't verbalize it to anyone, but he suspected that the two guards had been sent to make sure he didn't try to escape, or perhaps claim the lost city for himself.

The second part seemed obsessive. The first was terrifying.

Juan did all he could to maintain a sense of calm during the flight to Peru and the drive from the airport. Neither guard said much to him, even when he tried to spark up a conversation.

Not that the archaeologist had anything in common with the two men. He figured they were probably former military of some variety and had turned to private security as a way to continue the only line of service they knew.

The two men unnerved him in a way only rivaled by Orasco himself, and every second he was stuck with them only made Juan wish all the more that he'd passed on the offer from the wealthy magnate.

He mused silently at the thought. *As if telling Orasco no was an option.*

Juan looked out over the busy streets that met at a nearby intersection. He'd decided to visit the temple later in the afternoon with the logic that most tourists would visit the Santo Domingo Church earlier in the day and then filter out to the many bars and restaurants in the city after everyone reopened following siesta.

A puffy cumulus cloud drifted across the face of the sun and cast its shadow down on the city. The temperature dropped a few degrees as a result, and Juan appreciated the relief from the sun's direct rays.

He wiped his brow and looked back toward the lot, wondering how much longer Mathias was going to take. He saw the long, athletic man strutting toward them. He was at least six-foot-two and probably 220 pounds of lean muscle.

The two guards standing next to each other struck a harsh contrast, but Juan imagined that they worked well together, possibly able to communicate nonverbally if the situation called for it, though they both wore radios in their right ears, with lapel mics attached on the inside of their collars.

Mathias joined the other two and raised his chin. "So, to the church then?"

Juan nodded. "Yes. Unless you two want to stop and get a bite to eat before."

The two guards stared at him with stone expressions on their faces. They were lifeless, like statues, save for the steady rise and fall of their chests as they breathed.

"I suppose eating can wait until dinner," Juan said nervously. "Yes. Let's get to the church. Hopefully, there won't be any bothersome tourists around so we can work in peace."

"How far away is it?" Javier asked.

"Only a few blocks from here. We should be there in less than five minutes."

21

Antonio didn't like the idea of taking a cab into the city from the Cusco airport simply because he didn't want to depend on uncontrollable, external factors, and had insisted on getting a rental.

As he sat in the stop-and-go traffic leading into the city, Alex and Tara knew the man was questioning that decision—at least from a driver's perspective.

It didn't help that he'd wanted a sedan, and all the rental place had was compacts.

Not that Antonio could complain. He was driving, so he had the most leg room in the little four-door hatchback.

He followed the flow of traffic into the city and found a parking spot near the center of town, where the lanes filled with more people than cars as they poured into the Plaza de Armas, a huge public park in the center of the historic district.

The square had existed long before the Spanish settled in the city —at least five hundred years before—and had once been twice the size it was today.

Originally home to long, public meditation ceremonies among Inca nobility, today this part of town was anything but. Antonio turned right at a busy intersection after waiting for a dozen straggling people to clear the crosswalk. He drove away from the historic center on a less busy street and continued along the Avenue El Sol.

They passed street vendors selling everything from colorful scarves, round caps, and traditional Andean clothing to street food from steaming, greasy carts. Between the micro-businesses on the sidewalk, cafés and shops occupied the ground floor of two- and three-story buildings.

He slowed down—from a creep to a near crawl—and turned into a lot next to the Hotel San Agustín El Dorado. The white building featured stone archways at the base leading into the lobby.

"This is the hotel," he announced. "We can either leave our things in the trunk, or we can check in and then head to the church."

"It's getting late in the afternoon," Tara said. "We should probably go to the church now and then check in when we get back."

"Your call. But that's probably best. They will probably close the church in the evening. Siestas just ended for most of the city, which is another reason why it's so crowded. If we had been here an hour ago, you'd have found the streets mostly empty."

"Ah, siestas," Alex sighed. "I would love to have that as a tradition back in the States. Shut down all the businesses for a few hours. Everyone just takes a nap."

"I wonder if that would make people happier," Tara said. "Everyone is always in such a rush. Gotta do this or go there. Maybe if we had siestas, and the country just shut down for an hour or two each day so people could rest and recuperate, mental and physical health could improve."

"I nominate you for president," Alex joked.

Tara giggled.

Antonio rolled his eyes without them noticing. He found an empty spot in the back of the lot up against the building and parked between two vehicles that looked like they'd been driven to the breaking point. Having a new car in a city like Cusco wasn't the most logical of ideas. Minor accidents and scuffs were frequent, whether from the local cab drivers, tourists from all over the world, or from the many scooters and motorcycles that skirted in and out of lanes.

When he was satisfied with how close the front bumper was to the brick façade in front of him, Antonio turned off the engine and looked back at his passengers.

"You're sure about this, right?" he asked.

"About leaving the stuff in the trunk? Or going to Coricancha?" Alex said.

"Coricancha."

Tara and Alex nodded. It was a feeble gesture, masked with faux confidence.

"Yes, we're as sure as we can be," Tara answered.

He didn't buy it, but he also didn't have a choice. They were the experts, and he was just the babysitter.

They'd gone over the plan on the plane, but there were too many unknowns, factors he couldn't control without some recon of the area.

The plan was to get to Cusco, investigate the Santo Domingo Church, and then figure out the location of the first key.

He thought the whole thing was a waste of time. There was no key. At least that's what his gut kept telling him. And there certainly wasn't a real lost city that disappeared and reappeared across the Patagonia.

The more he thought about it, the more irritated he became. All his years of service to the office of the minister and the Chilean government, and this was how they repaid him? It was an insult. Like a thoroughbred put out to pasture for the remainder of his days, Antonio still felt the urge to run.

Then again, he hadn't done much running while he'd served the minister, or her predecessors. His job, for the most part, had been unexciting. Which was a good thing in his line of work.

But the threat of potential danger always lurking in the shadows, behind every face on the street, kept him on his toes—made him feel alive with a higher sense of purpose.

This. This was beneath him. A man with his skills and training shouldn't be used as a tour guide to a couple of crackpot Americans hunting for a mythical city.

And that was the part that drove him nuts more than anything else. The fact that the interior minister bought into this was sheer madness, and he couldn't wrap his head around it.

Antonio had seen a lot of things in his life. Some crazy, though most had been pretty normal and easily explained. The more outrageous occurrences had been the violence, both delivered by the hands of others and his own. But nothing like this. Nothing like mass disappearances and some magical city. The entire story smelled like what he thought it was.

Thanks to a long period of peace in Chile, his primary missions for the military were off the books, and often in conjunction with teams from the United States. The Chileans were meant to act as support but often were thrust into the forefront of dangerous missions—usually operations to take down cartels in bordering nations, though there was one in Colombia that took Antonio beyond the buffer of their neighbors.

Now, here he was. Chasing shadows of forgotten myths of a superstitious people. Why on earth the interior minister believed any of this was beyond him.

The only thing that caused a shred of doubt to Antonio's skepticism was that Carrera was in the government.

There'd been things Antonio and his team had done that were wiped from the records, never to be seen again. He knew it was like this in most countries, the United States being no exception.

But if things could be erased, others could be hidden.

Was there secret information in some classified archive he'd never heard of? It was possible. Unlikely, but it wasn't out of the realm of what a national government was capable of.

Perhaps the minister had stumbled onto something during an investigation. Antonio had served her since she attained the position, but he'd never heard mention of this outside of the last few weeks.

There was no point in contemplating it. He'd do as ordered and then ride off into retirement.

He climbed out of the car and opened the back door for Tara while Alex got out on the other side.

The sun brightened the colorful murals on the upper half of a four-story building to their right. It was late afternoon already, and long shadows reached across the parking lot.

"How far is this church from here?" Antonio asked.

Alex already had his phone out, looking up the walking directions to the Santo Domingo Church.

"Seven minutes," Alex answered. He stuffed the phone back into his pocket and tapped his jeans to make sure it was still there. It was an odd habit, but one that he'd picked up when one of his phones slipped through a hole in a pocket.

Antonio opened the trunk, removed two spare magazines from his rucksack, and then closed the lid again.

"Nothing for us, then?" Tara asked.

Antonio shoved one magazine into a holster in the back of his belt while he glowered at her. "No."

And just like that, the discussion ended.

He finished concealing the second magazine, checked the pistol in his shoulder holster, and nodded to the others. "Let's get moving."

Alex slung his backpack over his right shoulder then removed his phone again and checked the directions. "This way," he said, pointing toward the street.

The three walked to the sidewalk then turned left. Throngs of tourists of multiple nationalities surrounded them.

It was easy for Alex and Tara to pick out the Americans. There were telltale signs such as the patches on their bags, their clothes, or the way they walked with an adventurous yet naïve gait.

Most of them were younger, probably here on a gap year from college, doing the cliché backpacking through South America they'd read about in some blog post run by an out-of-work marketing consultant trying to earn enough money to repeat his own gap-year trip, but in middle age.

Alex led the group off the main drag and down a side street. The cobbled lane was narrow and designed for foot traffic, not vehicles.

Fewer people walked here than on the main artery. The pace here was slower, more casual. Visitors looked into shop windows, gazed at the colorful balconies, window frames, and doors set against beige walls and the gray-brown stones of the street.

"That was a little chaotic back there," Tara noticed, glancing back over her shoulder at the rows of people herded along as if guided by an invisible hand.

Antonio looked back for a second. "More tourists here than usual because of the festivities."

"Festivities?"

"They will have a celebration of the solstice here in a few days. It was a big deal for the Incas. Their descendants maintain the tradition. There will be a parade, food. It's quite the show."

"Sounds like you've seen it before," Alex said.

"No. But I've heard about it. Seen the pictures. It never interested me to come see it for myself."

The smell of roasted meat and vegetables wafted through the corridor, carried by a warm, dry wind.

"What's that smell?" Alex wondered, noticing the meat in particular.

Antonio chuckled. "You don't want to know."

Tara leaned close to Alex. "Guinea pig is a staple here. Remember?"

Alex cringed at the revelation. He remembered reading about that, but seeing it—or in this case smelling it in real life—made it a little too real.

"That is both sad and disgusting," he said.

They continued down Avenue El Sol then turned left at a cell phone store on the corner. The walk from the hotel took about what they'd expected before the Santo Domingo Church appeared at the end of the street.

A domed tower stood at the main entrance. Four pillars stood at each corner of its roof. The walls were made mostly of a drab brown stone but with gray blocks of varying darkness interspersed throughout the construction.

From the pictures they'd seen, Tara and Alex knew that many of the original temple ruins were on the other side, below the ground level of the church. Beyond the far end, the white two-story buildings of the monastery expanded the religious campus around the ancient structures.

A square plaza stood in the center of the property with covered walkways around the open middle.

Tara hoped she'd have time to see all of it but knew their first priority was getting to the ruins in the basement of the church and investigating the altar.

She and Alex both doubted they'd find anything interesting beyond general historical significance. This place had been visited by untold numbers of people over the centuries. If there had been a secret to find, it was long gone by now.

They crossed the street and kept walking, passing blue streetlight poles, and then the near corner of the church, where the curved blocks of the reconstructed temple wall met the more recent Spanish architecture.

They stopped at a thick wooden door at the entrance and paused. Antonio frowned at their hesitation and quickly reached out and pulled on the iron handle, jerking the door open wide.

"Sorry," Alex offered. "Just taking it all in."

Antonio didn't understand, and he didn't care. He just wanted to get this over with as fast as possible. Maybe once they figured out this place didn't have any answers regarding the lost city, they could all go back to Chile, and the Americans could return to whatever they had been doing in the States.

A cool gust of air billowed out of the church and washed over them as they stepped inside the dark, musty building. It smelled like most cathedrals they'd ever been in—a mix of ancient stone, dust, mortar, incense, and candle wax.

A priest in a cassock stood against the wall opposite the entrance. He looked about fifty years old, with a shaved head and dark, tanned features. He smiled at them, welcomed them to the church, and asked if they had any questions.

"We were hoping to see the Inca ruins in the lower area of the church," Antonio said, taking the lead.

"Of course." The priest raised his right arm and pointed down the wide corridor. "It's that way. You'll see signs pointing you down the stairs."

He returned his hand to the folds of his robes and resumed his statuesque position.

"Gracias," Alex said and tossed a coin into an offering bowl on a little table next to the priest.

"De nada, mí *hijo*."

The three left the man to his station and followed his directions down the hallway, passing several doors on their right, along with reliefs of Jesus, the apostles, and paintings of scenes from Christ's ministry. They rounded a corner at the stairs and followed a sign with an arrow pointing down at an angle.

"That was easy," Tara said.

"Yeah, but now comes the hard part," Alex countered.

They descended the dark stairwell illuminated only by dim lights in black sconces fixed to the walls, and by candles set in alcoves.

At the bottom, more light radiated into the space from the open archways connecting the downstairs to the courtyard. The walls in this area had been painted white, possibly to highlight the contrasting dark stones of the Inca ruins.

"Wow," Alex gasped.

"Yeah," Tara echoed reverently.

They stared down a narrow corridor between two rows of ancient buildings around eight feet high, and ten in a few other spots.

The structures were constructed of heavy stacked blocks with no mortar holding them together. The stone had been cut with laser precision and fitted together by superior craftsmen centuries before.

It was a remarkable feat to behold in the context of its age and workmanship.

Alex sidestepped to his right and looked through a window shaped like a narrow trapezoid. The stones forming the shape had been cut perfectly to allow for the opening.

As he stared through it, he realized that every subsequent room down the line had the same windows built into the walls, all the way to the other end where....

He froze at the sight of someone in one of the rooms. He didn't recognize the man—skinny, dark tan, perhaps a local.

Alex couldn't see much, but the one thing he noticed immediately was a glowing pink light radiating onto the man's face through the window.

"Hey," Alex whispered, tugging his wife over to the side so she could see. "Look at that."

She peered through the hole at the sight.

Curious about what had caught their attention, Antonio joined them and stared through the opening.

"What is—"

"Shh," Alex hissed. He nearly raised his palm to cover Antonio's mouth but thought better of it. He might not have gotten the appendage back had he done such a thing.

"Who is that?" Antonio asked in a quieter tone.

"More importantly, what is that?" Tara asked.

They watched as the man raised a pink crystal. From the side, it was difficult to tell the shape of the object, but they didn't need to see it. They already guessed what it was.

"Is that the four-sided cross?" Tara asked, feeling like she knew, and dreading the answer.

"We need to find out," Alex said. "Come on."

"Wait," Antonio halted him, stepping into Alex's path. "They're probably just conducting some old ceremony. There's a lot of that here in Cusco. They go through the same rituals the Incas conducted centuries ago as a way to honor tradition. What if that's what he's doing?"

"I'd like to see a ceremonial ritual," Tara said. "Wouldn't you, Alex?"

"Absolutely."

"We shouldn't bother them," Antonio protested. "Maybe we're not supposed to—"

"Be here?" Tara finished. "The area is not closed to the public yet. So, whatever is going on down there is fair game."

"Oh? And what about those two guys?" Antonio asked, staring down the corridor at two men who'd just stepped out of the stone room.

They both wore black suits and ties and matching sunglasses. One was tall, paler, and sinewy. The other, shorter and had a thick neck and broad shoulders. Both men appeared to be some kind of private security. Antonio figured they worked for the museum.

"Who are they?" Alex asked.

Before the other two could offer an explanation, the shorter of the two men saw them and inclined his head in a threatening, *buzz off* sort of way.

"Look," Tara said, ignoring the warning glare. She met the eyes of the two men with her firm gaze. "That guy has the crystal cross. If he places it on the altar and that thing actually works, the three portals are going to open."

"What do you suggest?" Alex asked.

She fumbled for an answer, searching the depths of her mind for an idea.

None of them had planned on this. They couldn't have anticipated a scenario where they showed up and someone else had the crystal cross, ready to initiate the ritual that would open portals to who knew where.

Questions pulsed through Tara and Alex's minds. The fact that, for centuries, no one had been able to figure this out, and now all of a sudden two groups were here at the same time was beyond all odds.

They had to think fast.

22

Alex stepped back out into the corridor before Tara or Antonio could say a word or even attempt to stop him.

He casually strolled along the walkway between the block structures, turning his head back and forth as if simply appreciating the history around him. He even slowed down and leaned in through one of the windows for a half second to make it appear he was checking out the interior of a room.

The ruse only lasted so long before one of the suits, the stocky man on the near side of the opening into the last chamber, stepped away from his post and toward Alex.

"This area is closed," the man said in Spanish.

Alex took this as a chance to play the stupid American. He smiled back at the man as if he didn't understand a word the guy said and kept walking right up to the point the man stuck out his right arm and blocked the way.

"No. It's closed," he said again in Spanish.

Alex lost the confused expression and replaced it with an irritated one. "No hablo Español," he lied.

The taller man behind the one blocking Alex's path turned and scowled.

"You are not permitted back here," the stocky one said in English.

"And why is that?" Tara asked, catching up and stopping next to Alex's right.

"Because it is closed for tourists."

"What's that guy doing back there?" she pressed.

The man pulled back his jacket to reveal a pistol tucked in a shoulder holster. "None of your—"

Alex lashed out in an instant, smashing his fist into the man's throat before he could finish his sentence.

As the goon stumbled back, desperately clutching at his neck, Alex reached into the guy's jacket and drew the pistol.

Tara flashed forward and kicked the staggering henchman in the chest. The blow sent the man reeling onto the floor, where he rolled onto his side, still grasping his throat.

The second goon reached for his pistol, but Alex stopped that idea cold, brandishing his new firearm toward the tall guy. "I wouldn't do that if I were you."

The man froze, thought better of it, and raised both hands over his head, his gun dangling from a thumb.

For the first time in his memory, Antonio was completely shocked.

One second, he thought Alex was foolishly walking into trouble. The next, the young American had taken a pistol from a threat, incapacitated him in the process, and kept the second gunman in check while his wife side kicked the first man to the floor.

It only took a second for Antonio to collect himself and quickly step ahead to the second gunman, drawing his own gun and relieving the other guy of his.

"Down on the ground," Antonio demanded. "Hands on your head."

The gunman complied, lowered himself to his knees and then onto his belly.

The pink light in the last chamber swelled, encompassing the entire basement with a radiant glow that seemed to pulse like a heartbeat.

Tara grimaced as if the light somehow pained her. She touched the side of her head. Her vision blurred, and for a few nauseating seconds she heard voices calling to her, sounds she hadn't heard since....

"You okay?" Alex asked. He moved over to her, touching the back of her head gently while keeping the pistol in his hand pointed in the stocky gunman's general direction.

"Yeah," she said, her focus clearing once more. The voices evaporated into nothing, though now a new sound filled her ears.

"What is that sound?" Antonio asked without looking away from his captive.

A dull hum echoed through the area. The sound vibrated the floor beneath them. Their heads tingled from the frequency.

Alex spun around the corner of the doorway to the last chamber and saw the man he'd noticed before.

The guy held the crystal cross over the altar. The room, the man, and the altar were all bathed in the pink hue. As he lowered the cross slowly toward the top of the plinth, the frequency changed. The pitch climbed to a higher din.

Alex winced as the center of his brain tingled from the sound.

"Stop!" he barked over the noise. He turned the gun away from the goon on the floor and trained it on the man at the altar.

The man turned his head around. It was a creepy, deliberate movement, as if he felt no fear, and possessed a total sense of control. He stared back over his shoulder at Alex with calculating eyes, as if he knew there was no chance the American would fire the weapon.

"You're too late," the man said in a thick accent. "It's already begun."

Alex couldn't conjure a compelling argument for the guy to not place the crystal onto the altar. Knowing what the journal said, he would have done the same thing.

"Get the stone away from the altar. I don't know who you are. So, don't make me shoot you."

The man's lips creased into a wicked grin.

The tone increased in volume and pitch as he lowered the crystal another inch toward the top of the pillar.

Now the noise was nearly unbearable. Alex squinted hard against the sound. He lowered the pistol slightly, covering one ear with his free hand—tempted to do the same with the other.

The man turned his head away from Alex and laid the crystal down on top of the altar. The noise heightened a final time, and Alex wondered how the guy could stand it.

Then, when the crystal cross touched the stone surface, the deafening noise instantly ceased.

The building rumbled to its foundation.

Alex took a step back toward Tara, who grabbed him by the shoulder as they watched pink light spray out from the crystal into three beams.

The lights hit the stone blocks of the wall eight feet away. Instead of small, focused spots, they began to expand, though the beams remained the same diameter.

Alex and Tara watched, enraptured at the incredible sight as the lights on the stacked blocks swelled into the shape of four arched doorways, each nearly as high as the wall.

Within each portal, a pink fog swirled and churned.

Tara clenched her jaw against a sudden sense of fear. This was way too similar to her experience at Hell's Gate, something she never cared to relive.

And yet here she was, standing before three portals that—for all she knew—led to another dimension, or some other plane in the cosmos.

The man at the altar stepped around to the side of it and then took another step toward the portal on the right.

"Don't move!" Alex shouted. "I don't want to shoot you."

He had no intention of shooting the man. The guy appeared to be unarmed. Alex couldn't shoot an unarmed man no matter how much his inner Clint Eastwood begged him to.

The man didn't turn around this time. Instead, he ignored Alex's warning and took another step toward the portal, then another. He stopped inches away from the swirling mist framed by the bright fuchsia light.

Alex tightened the trigger against his finger. He felt his pulse against the cold, narrow metal.

"Last warning, man. Step away from the—"

The guy glanced back over his shoulder at Alex. He wore an amused expression on his face, and a sinister mischief filled his eyes.

Without saying a word, he suddenly jumped forward and into the churning mist.

23

Alex and Tara stood by the altar, staring at the space in front of the portal where the man had been only a moment ago.

For a second, they couldn't react. They froze like pillars of salt, paralyzed by what they'd just seen.

They heard Antonio swear in Spanish. "Where did he go?" He peered at them, his eyes burning with furious bewilderment. He kept the pistol trained on the two goons on the floor, alternating from one to the other and back to make sure they didn't have any ideas about escaping.

Alex and Tara didn't answer. Instead, Alex broke free from his trance and rushed over to the portal the man had entered. He looked up and down along the sides, the top, and the bottom as if the man's disappearance had been some kind of illusion.

Tara took his side, also inspecting the empty space and the frame around the ethereal door.

This was no trick. The man was gone. He'd vanished into the portal, and they had no idea where it might lead, other than the theories they'd concocted based on Buford's notes. The two Americans stood on the portal's threshold, staring into the churning mist.

Inside, a crescent moon seemed to form, dissolve, and reform over and over.

"Do you see that?" Tara asked with a nod toward the anomaly. "That must be the one that leads to the Temple of the Moon."

Alex turned toward the middle portal. A different shape appeared and disappeared, this one of a desert canyon. Within the portal to the left of center, the image of a stormy sea congealed and then evaporated in the same, steady rhythm.

"We have to follow him," Alex said. "We can't let him get to the key."

Tara shook her head. She didn't want to enter the portal. If it were anything like the one at Hell's Gate, that was something she'd rather not experience again.

Alex noticed the fear draped across her eyes. "We have to stop him. It'll be okay. But if you want to stay here, I understand. Those clues were designed for someone to do this. We have to believe we can pass through safely."

"I can't let you go alone," Tara said. "You don't know what's on the other side. This thing could spit you out into the middle of space."

"What are you doing?" Antonio demanded. "You're not actually thinking about following him."

Alex and Tara looked back at him but ignored him.

"If you're going, I'm coming with you," she said, staring into Alex's eyes.

"You sure? I don't want you to have to go through that again."

"I go where you go. Remember?"

He smiled, leaned in, and kissed her on the lips. Then he grabbed her hand and faced the portal.

"Hey!" Antonio shouted. "What are you doing? Stop!"

Alex glanced back at the bodyguard. "We have to go through. We can't let that guy get the key. You can come with us or stay here with those two."

"Hold on a second."

Alex reached out his hand as if to stick it through the portal, a cautious test of the ethereal surface. But when his fingers reached the edge of the mist, it suddenly changed color to a bright blue. What seemed to be an intangible cloud solidified into a crystal barrier.

They saw the man who'd gone through. He stood somewhere on the other side, just out of reach.

He'd survived. On one hand, that was a good thing. It meant they could pass without fear of instant disintegration. But the bad news was they couldn't go through this one.

"What the—?" Alex blurted.

Tara brushed the tips of her fingers against the barrier. "I don't understand—" She stopped herself, remembering what the journal said. "Only one can go through each," she said.

Alex faced her. "What?"

"It must have some sort of way of closing once someone enters."

"Ah," Alex said, the realization hitting him. "So, that's the answer."

"Get away from there," Antonio warned. He kept switching his focus between the two Americans and the two men on the floor. He looked nervous, which was as foreign an expression to him as speaking Russian. Nothing unnerved him. Nothing except, apparently, supernatural phenomena.

Again, they ignored his commands.

"We have to split up, then," Tara realized. Her eyes locked on the portal in the center.

"What?" Alex asked. "We can't split up. We have to stay together. I'm not letting you go through that thing alone."

"We have to. It's the only way." Resolve had replaced the fear on her face. A moment before, she wasn't sure she could do this. But that uncertainty melted away with the sense of purpose that burned within her. "We can't stop that guy from getting the first key. The only thing we can do is get to the other two before he can."

"No. There has to be another way." He banged his fist on the crystal surface of the portal, but nothing happened. It was as hard as a diamond.

She tightened her grip on his hand to get his attention. "Alex. There is no other way."

"I don't want to leave you," he protested. "I know what that did to you the last time."

He could only imagine what she had experienced. But he heard her talking in her sleep, fighting through nightmares that had tormented her ever since Hell's Gate.

He couldn't let her go alone. He had to keep her safe.

"I know you're thinking you need to protect me," Tara said, reading his thoughts. "But I can take care of myself."

"I know," he surrendered unconvincingly. "But I don't want to lose you."

"I don't want to lose you, either. But this is the only way, and you know it."

A lump fell from his throat to his gut. She was right. It was the best plan. But he'd always felt like he needed to be close to her, even before they'd confessed their affections for each other.

"We're the only ones who can stop him," Tara added. "Just remember the clues."

"The clues were pretty vague. And we don't even know who that guy is."

"It's all we've got. You're right. We don't know who he is. So we need to be careful." She stood up on her tiptoes, tilted her chin, and kissed him again. Then she let go of his hand. "First one to their key wins."

Tara stepped past him to the portal on the far left with the scene of a raging sea painted in the mist. Alex followed, stopping in the center. He never took his eyes off her.

"You sure about this?" he asked.

"Not really," she admitted. "But the other guy made it through okay. We should be fine." She almost sounded like she believed the words.

Almost.

"Together on three?" Alex said.

She nodded. "Sounds good."

"One," he counted.

"What are you doing?" Antonio shouted from behind. "Step away

from... whatever that is." The sound in his voice carried the temptation he felt to turn the pistol at them. But he wouldn't use it. They
knew that much. It would be a hollow threat, and he didn't dare take
it off the two prisoners.

"Two," Alex said.

"Don't do it!" Antonio warned.

"Three."

Tara and Alex stepped forward as one into the portals. Antonio
watched, helpless, as they disappeared into the churning pink fog.

24

Arturo watched the entire scene play out beneath him. A wall of glass separated him from the ruins twenty feet below.

At first, he'd been tempted to shoot his quarry through the glass partition. The clear barrier was too thick, though, and would have easily stopped his bullets. Not to mention the fact that everyone in the church would have heard the report.

He regretted not attaching the suppressor before arriving at the church, though that would have changed his carry options. Regret wasn't going to help anything. Nor would questioning his prior decisions.

His second instinct had been to run down the corridor, descend the stairs, and kill everyone. But he'd been uncertain he would reach them in time. And then there was the problem of their bodyguard. He would make things difficult. The man was also armed, which only exacerbated the issue.

The best Arturo could hope for was a lucky shot, the element of surprise, or a stalemate shootout before the police showed up.

It was one of the few times Arturo had been indecisive in his career; since he was a teenager for that matter. The only other time he remembered seizing up like this was when he'd seen his sister gunned down by thugs in their ghetto neighborhood.

The gangsters hadn't been targeting her, or Arturo, but the siblings had been in the line of fire and his sister paid the price.

Arturo had frozen that day, and all he could do was hold her as the life leaked out of her fourteen-year-old body.

He'd only been a year older than her but felt responsible for her death. It was a freak accident. That's what he told himself. A random occurrence. It could have happened to anyone. But it happened to her.

That day, Arturo made a decision. He would never stand idly by and not take action. He also made another decision, one that would alter the course of his life. He became obsessed with revenge, of meting out justice to those responsible for taking his sister's life.

He knew such a path wouldn't lie in the light but in the shadows.

That day he began a new journey, one dedicated to learning how to kill. And how to hurt.

Three years later, he found the men responsible for his sister's death. There had been four of them in the car that day. He learned one of them had died as a result of a rival gang shooting. But he made sure that the three who were alive took a long, painful time to die.

When he was done, the scene he left behind served as a warning to any who might cross him.

Youthful and sloppy, he'd left the scene without thinking about how to properly remove all clues to his presence there. One of the investigators on the case had been able to track him down.

Instead of an arrest, the detective had offered him a job. The investigator was on the take from one of the local cartel bosses, and he had an eye for talent, the kind of talent the cartel truly appreciated.

Now, as Arturo stood behind the glass partition, staring down at the Americans' bodyguard as he watched over two men in suits, he felt a deep sense of regret at having failed his first creed—the oath he'd sworn to never stand idle again.

The two Americans had disappeared into some kind of strange portal, as had another man before them.

Arturo had never seen anything like it. He admittedly wasn't a scientist, and had barely scratched the surface of the subject in school. In fact, he never finished high school—much less attended university—when he left as a teen to pursue this other career.

Killing didn't require a diploma.

But science, at least what little he knew of it, couldn't explain what he'd just witnessed. It looked like some kind of magic. But magic wasn't real. It belonged in fairy tales, books, and movies.

Arturo didn't use drugs regularly, save for the occasional line of coke, and he never touched psychedelics. Yet the entire scene that just played out in front of him might as well have been one huge hallucination.

He knew it wasn't.

There was only one explanation, as insane as it seemed.

He'd doubted the existence of the lost city Orasco seemed hell-bent on finding. Arturo thought the entire idea foolish, a fantastic obsession of a man with too much money and an overactive imagination.

That judgment was just rendered obsolete.

Arturo wondered who the third man was, along with his two guards. If he didn't know better, he'd say they worked for Orasco, but he'd never seen the three before.

The boss had told Arturo about an archaeologist he had working for him. The man was supposedly an expert who could help him find the Wandering City, but Orasco's patience had worn thin with the man, and from the way he spoke about it, Orasco sounded as if he were about to rid himself of the liability.

It was possible the man who went through the portal first, and the two guards, were all working for Orasco. If that were the case, the boss would be more than just a little disappointed at how things went down, at least from the perspective of the two bodyguards.

The Americans didn't look like anything special. At first glance, Arturo figured they wouldn't be much trouble. Until he watched as the two expertly took down the two men in suits and then disappeared, each through a different portal.

There was another problem on top of all this: Orasco's fury would trickle down to Arturo, and after the mistake he'd made with the car bomb in Santiago, his employer's patience would be wearing thin.

Thoughts of self-preservation bled into Arturo's mind.

If the two guards reported back to Orasco, it wouldn't be a good look for them, but as the overseer in all this, Arturo would come out looking worse. And he knew Orasco didn't believe in third chances.

At the moment, there was no chance of them reporting to Orasco. They were prisoners of the Americans' bodyguard.

But he was running short on time, and if anyone other than himself, any tourists, had seen the miraculous and troubling incident with the portals, there would be investigators swarming the property within minutes. Not to mention the locusts from the local news media.

Arturo remained in the shadows, just outside of view from the basement level below, as he tried to forge a new plan of action.

It appeared the Americans tried to follow the first guy through the portal on the right. From his angle, it had been impossible to see why they'd been unable to go through after him. Then the Americans split up and went through the other two portals, each alone.

Arturo peeked around the corner again and peered down at the bodyguard as he focused his attention on the two prisoners. He looked back toward the portals for a second, as if trying to decide what to do.

For the moment, Arturo's only play was escape. He needed to get out of the church and figure out his next move. A plan ballooned in his head.

It would work for now, until he could think of something else.

He turned away from the glass and walked through the archway, back out into the main church corridor.

The priest at the end of the great hallway still stood at his station near the entrance. He seemed unaffected by what had happened down in the basement, as if it hadn't happened or he'd simply not noticed.

Arturo smiled and nodded appreciatively toward him, then stepped out into the warm, dry air.

It was an hour before sunset, and people were making their way either home or to restaurants and bars.

Arturo removed his phone from his pocket, tapped on the last call he'd made, and raised the device to his ear.

"I hope you have good news for me," Orasco said.

"I have good and bad news, sir."

25

"Get up," Antonio barked. "Both of you."

He brandished the pistol, first at the stocky one, then at the tall guy. "In here. Now."

He directed them both into the chamber where the altar and the three portals were. Only now, the beams of pink light were gone.

They, along with the portals, vanished the second Tara and Alex disappeared through the pink mist.

The two guys hesitated, both looking to each other for direction but finding none.

"I said get up," Antonio ordered and kicked the stocky one in the ribs.

The man huffed from the blow and dropped back down to the floor while the other picked himself up to his knees, then stood. The stocky one rolled over, swearing at Antonio, making threats he was in no position to fulfill.

"Get in there," Antonio repeated, waving the gun toward the room with the altar.

The men begrudgingly obeyed and moved into the chamber.

"Against the wall. Both of you. In that corner over there." He motioned to the far-right corner.

The men did as told and shuffled to the prescribed spot.

With them far enough way to not pose an immediate threat even if they wanted to, Antonio lowered his guard only slightly.

He looked down at the altar first. The pink crystal cross that the first man had set on top of it was mysteriously gone. It had disappeared the instant the two Americans walked into the last two portals.

Antonio rubbed the surface of the altar with his left hand. The stone was smooth against his skin, and there was no trace of the crystal that had been there only moments before.

"Impossible," he said.

"You have made a grave error," the stocky one said from the corner.

Antonio looked over at him. He could tell the man was still in pain from the shot to the ribs.

Above the two men, a glass panel stretched the length of the basement, serving as a sort of observation area for visitors. He thought he saw something in the shadows to the left, but after a few seconds figured it was just his imagination.

Surely, someone would have heard all the noise from before. The strange high-pitched sound had grown to a deafening level. Antonio was surprised no one had come yet to see what was going on.

At the very least, the priest they'd met at the entrance should have appeared by now. With the observation deck just above them, Antonio suddenly became acutely aware of the fact he was pointing a pistol at two men in suits.

Not good optics.

He needed to get out of there, regroup, and figure out what had just happened to the two people he was responsible for protecting.

There was one more thing, and the answer to that might just give him some of the others he needed—finding out who these two jokers worked for.

Antonio took a menacing step closer to the men. "Here's what's going to happen. You're going to walk down that hallway there, and you're going to do it quietly."

The shorter guy spat at Antonio, who merely exhaled calmly. He could have crushed the guy's face, but right here wasn't the place for that. He needed to get out of view, and he had just the place in mind.

26

MACHALLILA NATIONAL PARK, ECUADOR

t first, Tara couldn't see anything but the pink fog blunting her vision. She didn't know how long it took for it to clear, but the time that passed tortured her.

As the mist whipped around her, voices called to her. Initially, she didn't understand what they were saying. The words were in a language she didn't speak. They sounded ancient, haunting.

Then a woman's voice reached her ears and spoke to her in English. "The trials await you, traveler. The Key of Mama Qucha is yours, should you pass."

"What must I do?" Tara asked, a quiver in her voice. "How do I pass the trials?"

"Walk where men cannot, and you shall conquer the seas."

That's... not helpful.

She kept the thought to herself, fearful of offending whatever or whoever this voice belonged to.

"In all things, balance." The voice drifted off. Then a blast of wind blew over Tara. It swept the fog away, leaving her with a clear and unsettling view.

She stood on the edge of a cliff at least a hundred feet above the ocean. The turquoise-blue water darkened beneath her before foaming white as it smashed into the jagged rocks far below.

Her ponytail whipped around in the gusts, strands tickling the back of her neck. Tara wasn't typically afraid of heights, but passing through a mystical portal and being dropped off on a narrow ledge over a bunch of rocks by the ocean could unhinge even the most courageous of hearts.

Dark clouds blanketed the sky overhead. They moved quickly, turning in on themselves as if kneaded by invisible hands. The waves of the ocean rose and fell in tall, dramatic swells. This was no day to be out on a pleasure cruise—or sightseeing from the cliff above.

The toes of her shoes were only a foot away from the edge, and she immediately took an involuntary step back, expecting to feel the hard rock of the cliff catch her.

She reached out both hands behind her waist, anticipating the touch of rough stone, but instead her momentum continued backward.

The unexpected absence of the rock wall caused her to lose balance, and she toppled over backward amid a surge of panic.

Her initial thought was *This is it.*

But instead of a long drop, she felt her butt hit a hard surface. Her hands and wrists jarred against stone, only cushioning her landing slightly. The bright sunshine dimmed to a shadowy darkness around her.

"What in the world?"

She picked herself up and looked around. She was in a cave. On the edge of an oceanside cliff.

The walls on both sides were smooth, as if cut with a laser and rubbed painstakingly to a fine polish. The arched ceiling stood ten feet over her head at its highest point. She turned around and stared into the tunnel. The light from outside only penetrated a few yards in front of her before fading to pitch black.

Tara swallowed as she stared into the abyss. Something told her she shouldn't go in there. That she should stay put, that eventually she could hail someone. Maybe a boat passing by.

She returned to the ledge, this time a full three feet away from it, and surveyed the sea from north to south. There was no sign of any other piece of land. She wondered if this was some kind of island out in the middle of nowhere in the Pacific. Based on the color of the water to her right, however, she figured it was more like a small peninsula jutting out from the mainland. Still, there wasn't a sign of anyone in sight. She didn't even notice any seagulls clumsily coasting on the air currents over the water.

"Where am I?" she muttered. "Think, Tara. Think." She turned back to the cave and stared into the blackness.

A grim reality took hold of her. Its grip was cold like that of the reaper's icy, skeletal fingers grasping her shoulders and spreading a chilly fear throughout her body.

She knew she didn't have a choice. She couldn't jump into the water from here. The rocks would smash her into oblivion. Even if the jagged crags weren't down below, she doubted her chances of surviving a fall from this height.

If she were going to attempt going into the cave, she'd need a light to be able to see. But where was she going to—

Then it hit her. She felt the bulge in her pants pocket and realized she still had her phone. She slid the device out of the pocket and tapped on the screen.

She didn't expect the thing to work, wherever she was. For all she knew, she'd landed in another dimension—beyond the reach of any 5G network, to say the least.

To her surprise, she had four of the five bars showing in the top right. The device hadn't been damaged. All the apps were there. The screen looked fine.

Did she really have service?

"Only one way to find out," she said to herself.

She opened the phone app, tapped on Alex's number, then pressed the phone to her ear.

27

CASPANA, CHILE

Alex felt dizzy for a few seconds as the pink haze around him swirled incessantly. He couldn't see anything else, no matter how much he waved his hands around in front of his face.

The mist didn't feel like anything. It didn't have an odor. It was almost like it was some kind of a 4-D illusion.

Suddenly, a woman's voice spoke to him, seemingly out of the fog itself.

"The trials of Pachamama await you, traveler. Clever must you be, for the serpent is wise." The voice hissed the last part as if it were the snake itself. The sound sent chills across his skin.

"What?"

The answer he received was a gust of hot air blasting over his body. It felt like he'd opened the door to a giant oven, allowing the heat to escape.

Except now, he was in the oven.

The fog dissipated within seconds, and he found himself standing on a ledge overlooking a canyon. The hot sun in the west beat down on him, baking his skin and the hair on his head.

He instinctively took a step back, realizing how high up he was. "What the—"

He put out both hands to brace himself against the wall. His left hand found nothing but air. The right touched something smooth behind him.

Alex looked back and found he was a third of the way down the sheer cliff wall, standing on a narrow ledge in front of an opening.

He spun around and took a step inside the cave, eager to get away from the drop-off. "What is this place?" he mumbled, expecting no answer from the apparition who'd spoken to him moments before.

He got what he anticipated. The only sound came from the hot breeze blowing across his ears.

Pushing aside his fears, he returned to the ledge and risked a look down.

He eased back immediately. "Note to self. Do not do that again."

The landing where he stood was easily three hundred feet from the hard desert floor below. Another cliff opposite him was thousands of feet away, separated by the deep ravine.

Patches of sage cropped up in a few places on the barren plains. Several huge boulders dotted the landscape, too.

But there was no sign of life anywhere. And definitely no serpent he was warned about.

He spun around and peered into the black void of the cave, then looked up at the cliff wall above the entrance. If he wanted to scale the cliff to get out of here, it would be a free climb up a sheer rock face with few if any visible handholds and ledges.

Alex didn't believe he'd make it more than five or six feet before losing his grip and falling to his death.

He lowered his gaze to the tunnel. It would be cooler in there; that much he knew. He couldn't stay out here in the sun, baking all day. He needed to get into the shade at the very least and figure out his next move.

Cautiously, Alex put one foot in front of the other and stepped into the passage. The smooth archway had an almost polished look to it, but there were no designs, emblems, symbols, hieroglyphs, or runes adorning the edges.

Once inside and out of the sun, he paused, staring into the pitch black before him.

The words of the apparition taunted his mind. If there was a snake in here, he at least wanted to be able to see it. The last thing he needed was to venture blindly into a lightless cave and stumble into a pit of vipers, or whatever kind of venomous serpents they had here. Wherever here was.

His phone abruptly started vibrating in his pocket.

For a second, he thought maybe he was hallucinating. But it kept going, gyrating until he stuck his hand in his pocket and removed the device. He checked the screen. It was Tara!

He hit the green button. "Tara? Are you okay?"

"I'm fine," she said. "Sort of. Are you?"

"Yes. I'm okay. Although, I don't know where I am. It's some sort of canyon in the desert. Where are you? And how are you able to call me?"

"I'm by an ocean. In a cave high up on a cliff. And I have no idea how we're able to talk right now. This is all so crazy, but I'm going with it."

So she was in a similar place, but by the ocean. "I'm in a cave, too. Can you tell which ocean, or where you are?"

"Not really. I can't see any other land from here. Haven't seen any boats pass, either. It's weird."

"All I see here is desert. It's a pretty canyon. But there's no way to climb up to the top."

"I have a similar problem. Looks like whatever we're meant to do with these trials start in these caves."

He nodded. "Yeah. I guess the portals connect directly to these places. Would it be too much to ask for it to drop us off in a field of posies or something?"

"No kidding. I don't see any other way, Alex. We're going to have to complete these trials. But I have a bad feeling about this."

"Hey. It's going to be okay. You got this. If anyone can figure this out, it's you."

She chuckled uneasily. "I don't even know what *this* is."

He hesitated to ask the next question for fear of sounding crazy, but they'd just crossed through an interdimensional portal to a couple of remote places somewhere on Earth. He assumed it was Earth. He hoped it was Earth.

"Did... you happen to hear a voice when you came through the other side of the portal?" He managed to ask the question, though he was aware how it must have sounded.

"Yes. You heard it, too? It was a woman's voice. She said something about being worthy to receive the Key of Mama Qucha. Then it said I needed to walk where no man could, and I would conquer the seas."

"That's... not much to go on."

"I thought the same thing. What about you? What did she say to you?"

The question raised another in his mind. The she. Who exactly was this woman speaking to the two of them? Was it the same entity? Or was there more than one woman?

"She said I have to be clever, for the serpent is wise."

"Serpent? That doesn't sound good."

Neither of them was a fan of snakes. They didn't understand people who enjoyed keeping the reptiles as pets.

Alex had had a friend in college with a pet python. He'd watched his friend feed the animal a few times. It was a ghastly thing to behold. The friend would take a white mouse in a shoe box, shake it up to stun the rodent, then drop it into the terrarium.

The snake then coiled around the mouse and squeezed until the rodent could no longer expand its chest. On one occasion, Alex witnessed the creature actually flip over on its side and shove the mouse's face in its water bowl to drown the prey.

Alex had always thought snakes to be evil, but that solidified his opinion.

"Well, hopefully, it's just like a statue of a serpent. Or maybe some kind of puzzle with the image of a snake."

"Yeah. That's probably it."

He didn't believe her. But he hoped they were correct.

"At least we have our phone lights," she added. "This cave looks like the light is afraid to pierce it."

"I thought the same thing. It's like an unnatural darkness." He paused for a second and looked out across the canyon again. He didn't want to let her off the line. "You think we'll still have a connection in the cave?"

She hummed. It was a musing, contemplative sound. But when she made it, the noise carried a cuteness to it that only he appreciated.

"I was wondering the same thing. Put yours on speaker, and we can see. If we get cut off... be careful."

"You too." He flipped the phone around in his hand, pulled down the corner screen, and switched over to speaker mode. "Okay. I have it on speaker now."

He then tapped the flashlight icon in the bottom left, and the bright white glow of the LED cast a wide beam onto the shaded cave floor.

"Same," she said.

"Okay. Here we go. Good luck."

Alex stepped deeper into the tunnel. The light continued to shine on the path ahead, pushing back the shadows.

"You okay?" he asked.

"Yeah. Just inside now. It's cooler in here than—"

Her voice cut out.

"What?" Alex said.

No response.

"Tara?"

He looked down at his phone's screen and realized the call had been dropped. He thought about trying to call her back, but he saw the bars at the top of the phone had disappeared.

To make things worse, the beam of light from his phone no longer cast a circle onto the dark floor ahead.

Alex moved it around, even flipped it over to make sure the thing was still on. The light flashed into his eyes for a moment, and he flinched at the bright glow before turning it away again.

Curious, he took another step deeper into the tunnel, pointing the light ahead. Still nothing, as if the darkness swallowed the light.

Alex froze, uncertain if he should continue on.

He considered turning back, returning to the side of the cliff where the sun touched his skin and lit his path. There was no escape in that direction, though, and going back would be pointless.

His thoughts shifted to Tara. He wondered if she was facing a similar dilemma. Was she afraid? What kinds of things would she face on her end?

Thinking about that stuff would only distract him, and make whatever trials awaited ahead even more difficult.

He needed to stay focused.

The light was pointless now.

Alex kept it in his hand anyway, took a deep breath, and stepped forward into the darkness.

28

MACHU PICCHU

Juan wavered; his balance thrown off by the sudden transition to... whatever this place was.

"Why have you come?" a woman's voice asked.

It filled his ears as if it came from all around him.

Juan twisted his head back and forth, but all he could see was the mist dancing around him. He didn't know why, but it felt like the strange fog was judging him, peering into his soul. It was an unnerving feeling, one that made him squeamish.

"I... seek the key," he stammered.

"Why?" the voice thundered. "Why do you seek the key?"

Juan trembled. His lips quivered. "I... seek the city."

"Why?" the voice shouted again. It boomed and echoed as if bouncing off mountains. "Do you think it will bring you great riches? Make you powerful beyond human comprehension?" The voice grew quieter, almost gentle. "Will it make you happy?"

"I don't know," Juan confessed. His eyes brimmed on the verge of bursting with tears.

"Lies!"

"No. I am not lying."

"No one seeks the city without knowing why." The voice died off in a hiss. "To pass the trials of Mama Killa, you must bear only the truth. If you do not, then you will die."

The fog evaporated around him, and suddenly Juan felt alone, as if the presence of the voice had disappeared with the mist.

He looked around, and a new fear stabbed him in the chest and brought him to his knees.

He was standing on a ledge, high up in the Andes. Had he lost his balance, or taken a single step forward in the fog, he would have fallen thousands of feet to his death.

Juan braced himself with his palms on the hard ground beneath him and looked out to the left and right. He thought he recognized the mountains, but he couldn't be sure.

He'd entered the portal with the moon symbol forming and dissipating within the pink mist. His guess was that it would lead to the Temple of the Moon, or the key underneath it as the riddle in Alsue's journal suggested.

But this wasn't the temple. Was it?

He'd been to the Temple of the Moon at Machu Picchu before. As he looked out over the divide between the towering mountain peaks, he began to think he really did recognize the vistas, simply from a different angle.

Juan twisted around and saw the entrance to a cave, hewn from the rock in a dramatic arch. The cliff over it climbed another hundred feet to the top, but he couldn't see beyond the edge.

Fear squeezed his lungs. *How had this happened?*

He couldn't come up with a scientific explanation. Juan barely knew anything about such things. His expertise had been focused on history, things from the past. Not experimental physics.

He inched his way closer to the cave entrance, scooting along the rocky surface—too afraid to stand up again. It was a miracle he hadn't fallen before, he reminded himself.

Once he reached the threshold of the cave, he spun around and crawled headfirst into the shadows.

The sun hung low in the distance and cast its rays just a few feet into the tunnel on the floor and the walls to the left.

Inside the relative safety of the cave, Juan slowly began to steady his breathing. At least in here he wouldn't fall.

"Traveler," a voice hissed. It tickled his ears like dry fingers.

His head snapped around on its own accord, and he stared into the darkness.

"Hello?"

"Come, traveler."

The ghostly voice was different from the previous one. As before, it sounded like a woman, but raspier, more distant.

"Who are you?"

"Come and see."

"Tell me who you are, and I will enter."

He glanced back toward the edge. Juan was acutely aware that he lacked any position to argue with... whatever this was.

"Then you will die."

A gust of wind suddenly blew through the tunnel. It was cool, as if it came from the highest mountains, and blasted over him with incredible force.

Juan hunkered low to the ground, but he felt himself slipping backward toward the edge. He tried to lie flat, but the powerful gust continued to push him back.

He pressed his fingernails into the rock, clawing at the ground to attempt to keep himself from flying off the landing and down to his death. But it was no use.

Juan felt the toes of his shoes slip over the ledge as he kicked and pushed, trying to find purchase.

"Okay!" he shouted. "Okay! I will go. I will go. Please, just don't kill me."

He whimpered the last few words like a desperate victim of a serial killer.

The wind died in an instant.

"Come, traveler," the voice insisted.

Juan scrambled forward, still unwilling to stand until he was safe within the confines of the tunnel. Once inside, he braced himself on the left wall and stood.

He took a wary step forward toward the darkness, beyond the light of the sun, and paused. The cave wasn't just dark. It was black just beyond the border cast by the sun.

He pulled his phone from his pocket and checked the screen. Surprised to find the device still worked, he turned on the light and pointed it forward.

Goose bumps ran across his skin as he watched the light swallowed by the darkness.

"What evil is this?" he muttered. Regret immediately stabbed at his chest, and he feared he'd offended the apparition within the cave.

But the voice from before said nothing.

The silence should have relieved him, but instead it only made his anxiety spike higher.

Juan muttered a silent prayer as he stepped forward, uncertain if he would ever see the light of day again.

29

SANTIAGO

"I am starting to wonder if I made a mistake hiring you," Orasco drawled. His casual, matter-of-fact tone concealed the true venom within the words.

Arturo had expected that response. If he'd been in Orasco's shoes, he'd have probably said the same thing, and been feeling the exact same frustration.

He was professional enough to separate emotions and pride from doing his job. Still, he didn't appreciate the doubt verbalized by his employer. Things happened when working on a gig like this. The fact there were two targets complicated matters, and the Americans having a bodyguard with them at all times made it even more difficult.

It was nothing Arturo couldn't handle. He'd dealt with worse. Much worse. His typical targets were often far more dangerous people than a couple of archaeology researchers from the United States.

The fact they'd gotten away once, evading his car bomb, could be attributed to dumb luck. It certainly wasn't due to any sort of slip-up by him. He'd been meticulous, though after the fact he questioned whether he'd connected the device correctly.

He decided he had and that the only way the Americans and their babysitter could have gotten away was if the bodyguard diffused the explosive, or there had been faulty components.

Arturo tested everything, so he ruled out the latter. Which meant the guard driving the Americans around was the one to blame for his bad luck. It was to this bodyguard Arturo would deflect the blame for his two failures.

But Orasco would not merely accept an attempt at placing fault on someone else for not getting things done in a timely manner. The tycoon would see it as a sign of weakness. Excuses, to a man like Orasco, were simply not acceptable.

There was, however, an opportunity with the bodyguard.

Along with adding him to the list of targets, Arturo had another way of leveraging the man's unexpected appearance to his advantage.

"I tracked the Americans to Cusco, sir."

"Cusco?" Orasco said it in a strange way, as if it surprised him but not simply because of distance or location. It was the kind of tone that a person made when they already knew something.

Arturo kept going instead of questioning the man. "Yes. I followed them to a church. The Santo Domingo Church, to be precise. Their bodyguard was with them."

"Yes. A nuisance, that one."

"They weren't the only ones there, sir. There were three others. I was unable to make a move on the group."

"Three others?" Orasco paused. His heavy breath rattled through the speaker against Arturo's ear, and the assassin knew the man was contemplating something. "What did these others look like?"

That question was only a piece of what Arturo had hoped the conversation would produce.

"There were two men in suits. Uniformed guards. One tall. One short. The short one stocky, strong. The tall one was strong, too, but more of a lean, muscular look."

Orasco exhaled through his nose. There was a hint of frustration in it he probably hadn't meant to allow. "And the third?" he asked.

"Medium build. Middle-aged, probably forties. He looked like a scholar compared to the other two."

"Tell me what happened. What were these three doing?"

So far, Arturo had slipped by the tycoon's suspicions by offering information, details that he knew would pique the man's interest. Classic diversion.

"The scholar appeared to be holding some kind of crystal over an altar." Arturo stopped at an intersection and turned right down a side street where there were fewer people and where the only cars were those parked along the curbs.

"What happened then?" Orasco asked, trying to coax the story out of his hit man.

"The Americans and their bodyguard showed up. They tried to interrupt whatever it was the man with the crystal was doing. He appeared to be performing some kind of ritual, though from my angle it was difficult to tell."

Arturo looked back over his shoulder to make certain he wasn't being followed, then stopped next to a bicycle stand and waited.

He wasn't going far. Just out of sight from the church so he could come up with a plan of attack while he spoke to Orasco.

"While the man held the crystal over the altar, the two Americans, along with their bodyguard, approached the two men in suits. They disarmed both of them within seconds, and then moved toward the guy at the altar."

"Wait," Orasco said. "Did you just say the two Americans took down both of the armed men?"

The question was beyond mere curiosity. It contained a truth Arturo had suspected. Orasco knew who the armed men were. He'd probably hired them to watch over the third, which meant he also knew who the man at the altar was.

It had to be the archaeologist he'd hired to solve the mystery of the lost city.

Orasco was a man who covered his bases. He'd made mention of the archaeologist's lack of progress, and even alluded to possibly eliminating the man if he didn't produce something soon. The two bodyguards were probably serving a dual purpose. If Orasco sensed the archaeologist was simply stalling, the men charged with protecting him would flip to become his killers.

Arturo carefully crafted his next words. "Yes. I believe the two men were guarding the one at the altar. Those guards offered little resistance to the two Americans. I have to admit, I was surprised by that. They both appeared to be professionals, and they were armed on top of that."

"Were the Americans or their bodyguard armed?"

"He had a pistol, but the two of them weren't. Not that it mattered. They took the weapons from the two guards. The man assisting the Americans held the two guards at gunpoint while they went into the portals."

Orasco exhaled loudly through his nose in exaggerated, furious breaths.

"This... is troubling," Orasco said. "Do you know who those men were, Arturo?"

"No, sir," he half lied. "Should I?"

"Those men work for me." The confession came out of necessity. "The man with the crystal is the archaeologist I mentioned to you before. The other two were protecting him, though if he'd tried anything stupid, they had orders to dispose of him. I can find others like him. Time is more difficult to come by than men."

Just as I figured, Arturo thought. Through his experience, he'd learned how to read people and scenarios. Orasco, while wealthy and powerful, was—at his core—no different from anyone else. He had human desires, needs, insecurities, and urges.

And like anyone else, Orasco also had tells, little ticks or cues in their body language, or even their voice, that gave away everything. Sure, Orasco might have honed some skills and talents over the years —the ability to manipulate unsuspecting people being one of them —but in Arturo's experience, everyone eventually gave themselves away.

Arturo used the man's discomfort to his advantage. He'd now flip to the position of power in this conversation. "There's no way to know where that thing took your archaeologist...."

"Juan. Just call him Juan. He was supposed to call me when he found more information about all this. He told me they needed to go to Cusco, but I expected an update from there."

Arturo figured there was a plan of that sort. It was the same kind of deal he had with Orasco. Do your job. Report in.

"Odd that he didn't call," Arturo said, fanning the flames of doubt. "It seems like that should have been the first thing he did. He seemed to know what he was doing with the crystal and the altar."

"Yes," Orasco grumbled. "I'm sure he did. He must have known all this time."

Arturo had achieved what he wanted with the conversation. Instead of taking blame and getting flack for letting the Americans get away, his employer was now firmly focused on the impudent archaeologist.

Now for one more little diversion.

"Do you trust the two guards?" Arturo asked.

"What?"

"The two men you had watching Juan. Do you trust them?"

"What do you mean, do I trust them?" Orasco said again. "Of course I trust them. They work for me."

"Well, now they're prisoners. They're probably going to be interrogated by the police. Are you certain they won't turn on you? Or perhaps the police here in Cusco won't be a problem for someone with your reach."

That last part was a potentially dangerous stretch, but Arturo was playing with house money now.

"They are loyal," the boss repeated. "But every man has a price. Did they do anything illegal?"

It was the one hiccup in Arturo's plan for the two guards. But he'd already thought that through.

"No. Not that I could tell, other than their firearms. The Americans' bodyguard, however, carries himself like he works for the government. I'm just as concerned about him interrogating your men as I am the police."

"What does that have to do with me? I've done nothing wrong here."

"No. But if they tell this man who they work for, there could be trouble. Then people start looking in places they shouldn't. Then maybe they find something incriminating. Better to pull the weed up by the roots."

"I see your point," Orasco said. "They made a mistake. One that is more costly than you probably realize."

"Then help me realize it. I can intercept and eliminate the two inept guards you sent with Juan. But I need to know exactly what I saw in the church earlier. What were those three portals? And where did those people go?"

Orasco didn't respond immediately. Arturo took that to mean his boss was measuring his words, which meant the man was still not being completely open about everything.

"If you don't help me understand what we're dealing with, sir, then I can't help you."

"No. You're right. The truth is I don't know where they went. We discovered a journal, one written by a Jesuit priest centuries ago. His words suggest that whoever seeks the city must pass three trials. My guess is that the portals you saw each lead to a different trial. Until this week, we didn't know what we were looking for. It seems Juan's guess was correct."

He stopped talking, but Arturo sensed that Orasco had more to say. He only had to wait two seconds before the man continued.

"Our theory is that each trial leads to a different key, a key that we need to find the final key. The Key of Inti, sun god of the Incas." He shifted gears. "Tell me. What did these portals look like?"

"I didn't have a great view of them. I could only see the sides, and I didn't really know what they were until I saw Juan go through the one on the right. They were made of a pink light, formed from beams that came from the crystal he placed on the altar."

"It's unfortunate you couldn't see more."

"There's no point in lamenting over what can't be changed," Arturo said. "Is there nothing in that book that suggests where the portals might lead, other than the trials?"

"I don't know." Orasco sounded tired, and his response wasn't helpful in the least. "But it's possible that if they complete the trials, they must return to the altar."

That was what Arturo needed to know.

"Good. I can work with that. I'll stay here, find a place where I can keep an eye on the church, and when they come back, I'll handle it."

"That's a good plan. I am going to cancel my meetings for the rest of the week. I need to come to Cusco. If Juan truly is close to uncovering the mystery of the lost city, I want to be there."

Arturo considered asking the man if he thought that was a good idea but decided against it. He'd accomplished what he set out to do with this conversation. All thoughts of blame had been dispersed to the others involved, and he'd given a solution to his employer that seemed to satisfy the man.

There was one other thing, however, he needed to address.

"What would you like me to do about the two men you sent to protect Juan?"

Orasco grunted. "Yes. They could prove problematic."

"I am still close to the church. If the Americans' bodyguard takes them anywhere, or if the police pick them up, I'll know it. As I said before, I can intercept them if you like."

The boss only hesitated for a couple of seconds before answering. "Eliminate them both. We can't risk having any loose ends on this."

"Understood. I'll handle it."

30

The interior minister had grown tired of waiting. Too many hours had passed without so much as a squeak from Antonio. He'd only called to let her know that he and the Americans had landed in Cusco.

He'd been good up until today. He had texted her progress updates every few hours, just to keep her aware of what they were doing. She trusted Antonio. He'd been a loyal protector in the service since before Carrera arrived.

It was her idea to put him on the case with the two Americans. Them, she didn't fully trust. Their agency had a good reputation, however. They'd recovered and secured artifacts from all over the world, helping many countries to regain lost history and culture. Their founder, Tommy Schultz, had an honest reputation, and she thought it unlikely they would try to screw her over.

That didn't mean she had to trust the two agents he'd sent here. They were young, and perhaps ambitious.

They hadn't seemed like the sort to try to rip her off, but she also knew to never let her guard down. That's when people took advantage of weakness.

Carrera had contemplated calling him to see what was going on and get to the bottom of why his consistent stream of contact had been broken. She'd resisted, telling herself that they were most likely in an area with poor cell service and thus unable to check in.

But he had access to Wi-Fi calling, and with satellite coverage, that shouldn't have been a problem, either.

She paced across her kitchen floor and stopped at the black granite countertop adjacent to the sink, coffee machine, and white cabinets. She reached over to the corner where a half-drunk bottle of red wine stood next to a replica of an Inca ceremonial vase.

Carrera's job was one burdened with immense responsibility. And with that responsibility came a mountain of stress from the moment she woke to the moment she closed her eyes at night. Sometimes, especially lately, the faceless monster called anxiety still taunted her, ravaging her mind with a million untamable thoughts per second.

She pulled the cork out of the bottle, snatched a nearby stemless wine glass from a row of four, and filled two-thirds of it. She thought about recorking the bottle, but this was feeling like a finish-the-bottle kind of evening.

She set the cork by the bottle, tipped the glass to her lips, and looked out over the rim as the Chianti flowed into her mouth. She paused to swallow, continuing to peer out of the big bay windows across from her.

The mansion offered panoramic views of the city below. She walked over to the window and stood next to a dining table. The glass hung loosely in her fingers that cupped it from the base.

Standing here always gave her a strange sort of heroic feeling. Guilt teased her now and then, often causing her to reflect on how long it had been since....

She shook her head and took another drink, hoping the wine would drown the ghosts that haunted her.

It wasn't all the time. Only occasionally. She was too busy to allow nostalgia or regrets to interrupt her focus.

No one knew what she'd done. She'd been a rising politician, but her husband's gambling addiction was rapidly becoming a serious problem. And his debts were beginning to draw attention from the public. Carrera had been left with no choice. She needed him eliminated, for the greater good, so she could truly help Chile.

To arrange the accident, she went through Orasco, who was too happy to make a deal with the promise that he could cash in on the favor later.

She'd hesitated at first, but when she found out her husband was cheating on her on top of all the other reckless behaviors, Carrera had given the green light to the killing.

This ridiculous quest for a mythical city had taken up enough of her time, pulling her away from more pressing matters of state. Still, she knew what finding a city like that, full of infinite treasures, could do for her career—and her country, of course.

SHE FOCUSED ON HER BREATHING, keeping it slow and methodical as she'd practiced so many times during frustrating moments—often in meetings with high-ranking officials. The question that had dominated her mind for most of the afternoon kept flashing in her mind. Something was wrong. She couldn't pinpoint how she knew. She just did.

Antonio should have checked in hours ago.

Carrera tossed back the remnants of the wine and spun on her heels to return to the counter for a refill.

Paranoia snaked its fingers into her mind. *What if Antonio was dead? What if something happened to the Americans? Was it possible they'd—*

"No." She shook her head and spoke the word out loud as if the act would push back the demons loitering around her.

She grabbed the bottle and filled the glass again. She didn't stop until it was nearly to the top. Then she placed the bottle down to the side, clutched the glass, and started to drink.

Her phone stopped her just before the glass reached her lips.

The device vibrated on the counter, rattling against the hard granite surface.

She nearly dropped the glass, fumbling it for a second and

spilling some wine onto the gray tile floor. Cleaning it up would have to wait.

She grabbed the phone, noticed the name, and answered.

"Is everything all right?" she asked, trying not to sound too concerned, or like a person who'd been checking their phone repeatedly for the last hour.

"Sort of," Antonio said.

That was a response she hadn't expected from the man.

"What's that supposed to mean?"

"We ran into a problem in Cusco." He spoke quickly so she wouldn't be able to cut him off with another similar question. "We went to the church. When we arrived, there were already people at the altar I described in my last text. A man, and two men in suits protecting him."

"Protecting him?"

"Yes. And that's not all. When we arrived, the man they were protecting was holding a pink crystal. It looked like rose quartz, though I must admit I'm no geologist. He placed the crystal on the altar, and something very strange happened."

She felt her heart flutter, and her breath caught in her lungs as she waited for him to keep going.

"The crystal fired three beams of light toward the wall and created three portals."

"Portals?" she breathed. She could barely contain the volcano of emotions erupting inside her. Excitement. Wonder. Fear. They all dueled for her attention.

"Yes. I've never seen anything like it. The man with the crystal went through the first one. He disappeared, as if he'd walked through the wall to some other place."

Her eyes widened as she listened. "And the Americans?"

"They tried to follow, but the portal closed off. I tried to stop them, Minister, but they went through the other two. I was busy holding down the bodyguards."

More questions fired through her head like bullets from a

machine gun. Carrera was adept at compartmentalizing things. It was a necessity that came with the job.

"What did you do with those two? Police have them?"

"No," Antonio grunted. "I have them. I need a secure location where we can interrogate them."

"Where are you now?"

"At the church. There is a room in the basement I passed on the way to the altar. I hid them in there."

"You're not in the room with them?" She thought that to be a potentially careless mistake.

"They won't be going anywhere. There are no doors or windows. And I secured them."

She had no choice but to trust his assessment of the situation. She knew Antonio wasn't one given to half-measures or carelessness.

"I'll make a call. Do you want backup for the interrogation?"

"No. Keep this off the record. I want to know who these guys work for, and what they're up to."

It felt strange for him to be giving her the orders, but she felt no disrespect. She liked that he was willing to take charge. And she knew that Antonio would get answers, one way or another.

31

MACHALLILA

The darkness wrapped around Tara like a blanket that had been in a freezer for a few hours. She shivered at the chill in the air dragging across her skin.

Tara twisted her head around and looked back over her shoulder. She expected to see the cave entrance and the bright light of the sun tempting her to return to the relative safety of the ledge.

To her horror, the entrance was gone, as if the cliff had closed up and swallowed her.

She blinked a few times, hoping that she was just imagining all of this, or that she might wake from a dream and find Alex next to her in their bed.

But the darkness never retreated. It was absolute, and she'd never been so terrified in her life.

She reached out her right hand to touch the wall, but just like the tunnel entrance, she found no surface to use as a guide.

"Hello?" she said. "What am I supposed to do?"

No response.

She considered turning around, going back the way she came in hopes of somehow finding the entrance. Maybe she could scale the cliff. It would be dangerous, but was it any worse than being in this place? Whatever this was? She shook her head at the thought. The entrance was gone. There was no turning back now.

Tara focused all her energy on remaining calm. She'd been using mediation practices for several years, though she never could have imagined that would come in handy in a situation like this.

Now, however, she embraced her practices. She turned her attention to her breath. *In slowly through the nose. Hold it. Then release slowly.*

She closed her eyes. What was the difference anyway at this point? As she shut them, she expected there to be no change. The blackness all around her couldn't get any darker.

To her surprise, when she shut her eyes, everything changed.

She saw torches on the walls, hanging from golden sconces shaped like skeleton hands. Blue flames flickered from the macabre bowls, fiery tongues lapping at the darkness as if drinking it.

"Come, traveler. If your courage allows."

The voice hissed through her ears as though it came from inside her skull, and circled around her only to go back in again.

She opened her eyes, in no small part from the fear ripping her apart from the inside. Tara wasn't sure what she expected, but what she got was the empty, black void all around her once more.

"What the—"

She quickly closed her eyes again, and the scene returned.

"Only by faith will you see the way, traveler." The voice urged caution with its warning.

The words had only just sunk in when Tara froze where she stood, her feet on the edge of a deep chasm.

She looked down for a second before stepping backward. Her surroundings tipped and swirled, and for several seconds she felt like she might be sick.

She dropped to her knees; her eyes still closed. She was too scared to open them, which felt just as strange to think as the reality staring her in the face.

It was a hallucination. It had to be. What other explanation was there for such a phenomena?

"Be wary, traveler. You will only pass through to the other side if your faith and your courage are strong."

"Faith and courage?" Tara said. As expected, she received no answer.

She looked around again to reset her bearings. The floor at her feet was made from the same rock on the outside where she'd first arrived at this place.

The path narrowed into the center, spanning a seemingly bottomless gorge. She crawled forward to the ledge and mustered the strength to look down again. There was nothing below, as if the cliff fell through the earth and into a starless outer space.

She caught her breath and inched back. Her eyes fixed on the slim path stretching across the chasm.

Tara hadn't been much on faith over the years. She believed in a higher power, but what that consciousness was had remained faceless and nameless.

Exploring various religious ideas had been an enjoyable activity. She learned about all the commonalities, and the differences, between religions, including the religions that didn't believe in anything else out there in the universe.

Everything had changed a few years before when she and Alex were sent on an investigation to South America, not entirely unlike this one.

She'd seen things, heard things from another plane, a place she didn't understand, and wasn't sure she wanted to.

The visions that assaulted her that day had refused to leave her mind, like squatters unwilling to leave her property. For the most part, she'd endured the memory in silence.

Alex knew something wasn't right. He could always tell when she was trying to suppress something. He had a keen sense for things like that.

Fortunately, their work with the IAA drew her back into the normal routine of life. Immediately following the events surrounding

Hell's Gate, they found themselves in the lab once more, assisting Sean and Tommy with their next mission.

But rushing back into things hadn't allowed her to fully process what happened, what it meant, and what she'd seen.

Now, fumbling her way through this ethereal place with her eyes closed, she wondered what else was out there beyond human perceptions. If there were two such mechanisms that could transport a person into another realm, were there more?

Tara looked up to the ceiling of the place. She'd noticed it only with her peripheral vision, but now she stared at it, unable to remove her gaze.

The blue light from the flames radiated up to a massive domed roof. The diameter of the ceiling was half the length of a football field, and it shimmered like glass reflecting the hues. The icy surface was beautiful and mesmerizing and almost appeared as if it were alive.

Tara pulled her focus from the roof and looked down at the path again. The voice had alluded to some level of faith required to pass this test, but Tara doubted that meant in the traditional sense of the word. She'd been surprised that the voice spoke to her in English, and she wondered if it would have spoken a different language had she been from somewhere else in the world.

The voice didn't answer her thoughts, and for a second, she questioned why she should expect it to.

"This is so messed up," she muttered, taking a step toward the bridge. There was nothing for her to go back to, no way out provided by the tunnel.

Still, there was something comforting about being in the sunlight —with her eyes open.

Tara shook her head to rid her mind of the doubts. The voice had said this required faith. Doubt was the oldest and fiercest rival of that.

Did the faith the voice mentioned have something to do with walking around through an underground labyrinth with her eyes closed?

She didn't know, but standing around here on the edge of this cliff wasn't going to give her the answer.

Her mind made up, Tara raised her right foot and stepped out onto the bridge.

32

CASPANA

"Hello?" Alex called out into the darkness. "Is anyone here?"

His voice didn't echo. Instead, it seemed as if the black around him swallowed all sound as well as light.

He blinked his eyes and for a second saw a strange array of lights.

Curious, he closed his eyes again, this time squeezing his eyes shut to make sure he wasn't hallucinating.

"Whoa," he blurted.

Rows of red torches lined the tunnel on both sides, the flames rising from silver bowls held in skeletal, silver fingers.

"What is this?"

He opened his eyes again to make sure he wasn't crazy. The unwelcome darkness greeted him again, and he quickly closed his eyes once more, happy to stay in the light no matter how it was provided.

"This is weird," he said. Alex felt silly speaking out loud in the cave with only him to hear it. Well, he and the other entity that had spoken to him before.

He walked ahead, following the rows of flames flickering on the walls.

Alex thought of his wife and wondered how she was faring with this bizarre set of challenges.

Did she have to close her eyes to see, as well, or was her situation different from his?

He wished he could know, wished he could help her. He knew what a trial it had been to deal with the stuff she'd seen in Hell's Gate. He'd heard her talking in her sleep, trying to push away the nightmares of unseen spirits haunting her dreams.

"Through faith and wit, you shall pass, traveler."

The voice startled Alex, and he froze in place, realizing he was at the cusp of a bridge made of stone. It arched slightly in the middle, spanning a deep crevasse. Above, the red light from the flames ran in serpentine streams up to a glassy domed ceiling where it swirled like a vortex and cast the red glow down upon the bridge and across it to the other side.

"So, what am I supposed to do here?" he said, almost expecting an answer. When none came, he kept talking—mostly to comfort himself. "So, I guess I just walk across this mysterious bridge here." He leaned over and looked down and immediately regretted it. "Okay... that's a perilous drop to certain doom. Note to self. Do not open your eyes."

It felt weird to say it, but he knew that if he opened his eyes as he attempted to cross the bridge, he'd lose sight of it and risk falling off on either side.

Where the pit ended, he didn't know, but it didn't appear to have a bottom. Only a black, empty void stretched deep into the space below, surrounded by the cliff walls on both sides of the bridge.

"Faith and wit, huh?" Alex muttered. He guessed the faith part was having his eyes closed, which he also figured meant that would have to be the case for the entire ordeal.

He stepped forward onto the bridge. The second his foot touched the stone blocks, the entire place shook from somewhere deep within the earth.

Alex crouched low to keep his balance, touching his fingers to the hard stone. It felt wet against his skin. That sent a whole new set of concerns raging through his head, the most prominent one being slipping over the edge.

He looked out toward the other side of the bridge, except now the bridge was... moving?

"What the—?"

Sections of the bridge split apart. Some hovered to the left, others to the right, as if they'd come to life.

Alex stood upright, keeping his knees bent slightly to maintain balance. He watched as the sections of the bridge twisted in a steady rhythm as they shifted back and forth in what had to be the weirdest dance Alex had ever seen.

He followed the nearest section, watching it closely to see if he could pick up the pattern of its movement.

He'd have to jump to them to be able to progress across the gorge, but there was no way he could make the leap. Even if he timed it perfectly, he didn't have the ability to jump that far. No human did. Alex thought even an Olympic long jumper would probably fall a couple of yards short.

Then how would he get across?

He checked the other side, but all the pieces were moving too far away and too fast.

A wave of despondency hit Alex as he stood there gazing out at the wondrous sight. No one would believe him if he told them about this. They'd say he was crazy, or having a hallucination, or perhaps he dreamed it.

Tara would believe him. The rest of the IAA crew would, too, but no one outside that building.

That was part of the life, though. They were supposed to be the ones facing these kinds of things. It was their job, one that came with a requirement of being able to suspend one's perceptions of reality.

Still, this was a lot to take in.

Alex took a deep breath in and exhaled. There had to be a solution to this. He studied the movements for another minute. It didn't matter. The patterns, the speed—there was no way to solve it.

He'd only just entered the cave, and he'd failed at the first step of the trial.

Alex turned around and took a step toward the tunnel leading back out to the cliff. He stopped and stared into the corridor, which was glowing crimson from the flames along the walls. There was no point in going back out there. Even if he wanted to, he couldn't climb the sheer cliffs surrounding this place. He doubted he'd make it a few feet off the ledge before losing his grip and falling to his death.

Meanwhile, in here....

He twisted his head around and looked back over his shoulder.

"Whoa," Alex blurted.

The parts of the bridge had come together once again while he was facing the other direction.

He hurriedly stepped back onto the bridge. But the second he did, the sections broke apart and began their rhythmic dance again.

"Okay...." He grumbled skeptically.

Then it clicked in his brain. He took a step back, and the bridge reformed itself just as if it had never moved an inch.

Alex scowled at the puzzle.

Just to make sure he got it, he touched his shoe to the bridge and watched the thing disassemble. As soon as he pulled the foot away, it reconstructed before his eyes in seconds.

"Gnarly," he gasped.

It was the most incredible thing he'd ever seen. These giant stones that made up the sections of the bridge had to be over a ton each, and yet they were hovering—no, dancing around in midair as if they were feathers fluttering on a summer breeze.

The wonder of it all washed away after the third time testing the hypothesis. So, the bridge broke apart when he stepped on it. That wasn't helpful.

He needed to cross the bridge to get to whatever horrible thing awaited him on the other side. The thought didn't exactly make him feel a sense of urgency. But the sooner he could get out of this place, the sooner he could get back to Tara.

"Ugh," he grunted.

He worried about her. He hoped she was okay. Right now, though, he had his own problems to deal with, and he had no clue how he was going to solve them.

33

MACHU PICCHU

The darkness surrounding Juan felt unceasing, cold, and eerily alive. He could sense it all around him, almost able to touch it yet at the same time out of reach.

His lips quivered as he walked ahead, carefully shuffling his feet forward inch by inch. The cave made no sound, and it seemed even the gentle scraping of his shoes against the stone tunnel floor was absorbed by the darkness.

He breathed hesitantly, afraid he might awaken some monster hidden in the void.

Juan blinked slowly, trying to force himself to be brave. As he closed his eyes, he suddenly saw clearly.

The tunnel ahead of him appeared. Sconces in the shape of skeleton hands lined the walls. White flames licked the black air and cast an eerie, pale glow throughout the tunnel.

He opened his eyes again, but the darkness returned, and he shut them half out of fear.

"How is this possible?" he breathed.

With his eyes closed, Juan stepped forward, passing between the ghostly torches. The flames didn't make a sound. Not a crackle, hiss, or even the sound of the fiery tongues lapping at the air.

He observed them as he passed, inspecting each detail with a mesmerized curiosity. He didn't dare touch them. There was no telling what might happen if he did that. It was enough for now that he could see—well, sort of.

Juan emerged from the tunnel at a point where a bridge stretched across a deep chasm. He looked up at the pale light churning within a glassy domed ceiling fifty feet overhead.

The light radiated down onto the bridge, all the way to the other side.

"Through faith and truth, you shall pass, traveler."

Juan started, nearly jumping out of his clothes at the sound of the woman's voice. "What? Faith and truth? What's that supposed to mean?"

She didn't answer.

"Whatever you are, you're not very helpful," he complained. "I could use a better hint."

Still nothing.

"Fine. I'll figured it out then."

He assumed he was meant to cross the bridge, though he risked a quick glance back toward the tunnel entrance before testing it. The torches still burned behind him, but all signs of the outside world had vanished. It was as if the mountain had closed its mouth and swallowed him.

Juan faced the bridge again, and hesitated. It was old, and the stones stretching from one side to the other weren't held up by any supports from beneath. The arched design of the crossing provided its stability, but Juan didn't fully trust it.

The distance to the other side was at least a hundred meters, and there were no rails, no walls to protect him from falling off what he guessed was only a three-foot-wide bridge.

He counted himself lucky not to have a fear of heights, though he certainly felt less comfortable with it than ever before.

Juan leaned out and looked over the edge to see the gorge's bottom, except he couldn't find it. A new sense of fear punched him in the gut.

"Where's the bottom?" he mumbled.

There was no choice. It was cross the bridge or stay here until he starved to death.

Juan lifted his right foot and stepped out onto the stone walkway.

34

CUSCO

C arrera had been true to her word. Not that Antonio ever doubted her.

Within twenty minutes of making the call, two plain-clothes agents arrived at the Santo Domingo Church, found him in the storage closet, along with the two prisoners, and escorted the men off site.

Antonio hadn't needed to know the men's backstory, why they were in Peru, or how they'd arrived so quickly. They were there, and at the order of Carrera. That was enough for him.

They administered a drug to both men to make them woozy, but not knock them out.

They "assisted" the men out of the church as if they were both too drunk to walk on their own. The drug worked perfectly for that, and the men were stuffed in the back of the agents' SUV and driven to a safe house in the city.

Antonio didn't know if Carrera kept the place at all times, just in case, or if it was something she procured since their talk. The woman, it seemed, had connections everywhere, and layers of secrecy that even he didn't know about.

The house was a two-story villa near the historic district. He'd have preferred something out of town, perhaps in the hills over-looking the city, far from wandering eyes and curious ears.

They'd entered on a quiet side street, though, and no one had seen them arrive. More importantly, no one saw them drag the two guards into the house.

It was a modest residence, though it didn't appear anyone had actually resided there in quite some time.

The floors and countertops were clean in a way that suggested they hadn't been used often, or at all, in recent months. The furniture was minimal, both in design and supply. A couch with cream-colored cushions and a black wooden frame, a single matching chair, a black rectangular coffee table, and a flat-screen television mounted to the wall occupied the living room.

In the kitchen, white cabinets hung from the walls, with black handles as accent pieces. There were four clear glass plates in one, four pint glasses, and four sets of silverware in the drawer to the right of the dishwasher.

There was four of everything, again telling Antonio that this place had been furnished and then rarely, possibly never, used.

His curiosity begged to know who owned this place and how many like it there were throughout the city, and indeed the continent, but there were more pressing issues for him to focus on.

Antonio and the two agents dragged the men into the living room and deposited them on the couch.

The men were still groggy from the drug, though the thicker one appeared to be coming around first.

That didn't surprise Antonio. He expected the denser man to have a higher tolerance than the slimmer guy.

"I'll take him first," Antonio said, pointing at the shorter guard. He stepped behind the kitchen counter and opened the door to the cupboard under the sink. He bent down and looked inside. Extra rolls of paper towels, a packet of steel wool scrubbers, dish soap, a roll of red duct tape, a bottle of dishwashing detergent, and some glass jars. He took out the tape, stood up, and closed the door.

"Where you want him?" the agent named Paolo asked. He was a

man in his late twenties, medium build, with a hawkish nose and a sharp chin. His hair was cropped short and spiked to one side.

"First-floor bathroom should be fine. Just give me a minute. Keep your eye on them, yeah?"

"They aren't going anywhere," the second agent, a man named Raul, sneered. He was an inch shorter than Paolo, and slightly slimmer, though he looked just as athletic.

Antonio walked down a short hallway past the kitchen toward the back of the house. He passed the stairway leading up to the second floor and turned left into the bathroom. It was small but larger than a powder room. The room contained a toilet, sink, and a corner shower with white and black square tiles and a divider that jutted out so that no water splashed out onto the floor.

He set down the roll of tape next to the sink, then turned his attention to the toilet. Antonio flipped up the lid to the toilet seat, then spun off a bunch of toilet paper. He wadded up the tissue into a giant ball, and dropped it into the bowl. The paper filled the bottom of the basin, effectively clogging the drain.

He waited a minute, then pressed the handle to flush the toilet. As expected, the water couldn't escape through the tissue blockage, and the bowl slowly filled toward the top, stopping a few inches short.

Antonio watched as the water gradually receded through the makeshift dam. *That'll do,* he thought.

Satisfied with his handiwork, Antonio returned to the living room and nodded at the man he'd mentioned before. "Bring him in."

Raul yanked the dazed guard up from the couch, leaving the skinnier guy still slumped there on the cushions. The stocky guard's resistance was mostly due to gravity and his lack of motor control, and Raul struggled a little to keep the man upright.

Antonio knew how to wake him up.

He grabbed the goon by the back of the neck and helped Raul stabilize him as they ushered him down the hall and into the bathroom.

The man slurred his words, swearing at the two in a drunken-sounding Spanish. Once in the bathroom, his resistance strengthened. His legs stiffened, and he pushed back, twisted around, and took a wild swing at Antonio.

The punch missed badly as Antonio easily ducked his head to the side, then shoved the unruly prisoner against the wall to the left inside the bathroom.

Raul joined in pinning him there. The two overwhelmed the man's strength, despite his grunting, hazy protests.

"Let me go," he managed. "You two are making a huge mistake."

"I'm sure we are," Antonio spat. "You're going to tell us who you work for. There are two ways this can go. You can tell us right now and make things easy on yourself, or you can make it hard. That's up to you."

The goon spit on Antonio's face and swore.

Antonio acted as if it hadn't affected him. He cocked his head to the side, stretching his neck, then punched the guy across the jaw.

The blow stunned the man, whipping his head to the side on impact.

Antonio ignored the dull pain in his knuckles, twisted the man around, and shoved him toward the toilet.

With Raul's assistance, they forced the man down to his knees and shoved his face into the toilet.

The prisoner resisted. He gripped the bowl's rim and tried to push back up. Antonio remedied this by slipping both his hands off, which resulted in the henchman's head slamming into the back of the bowl with a thud.

His muscles weakened from the blow, which gave Antonio enough time to do the job.

He unwrapped the duct tape and strapped it to the back of the prisoner's head, around the bottom of the bowl, and back up again. The man's face was inside the bowl while the back of his head remained just above the rim.

Antonio continued wrapping more and more strips of tape until the man's skull looked like some kind of red vinyl mummy.

The prisoner's strength returned, but when he tried to push himself up and away from the bowl, he couldn't budge his head.

"When I get out of here, you two are dead." He added in a few obscenities for good measure, which did him no favors in the eyes of his captors.

"I gave you the chance to do this the easy way," Antonio said. He grabbed a hand towel from a silver rack on the side of the sink and wiped the spittle off his face. "You chose the hard way."

The man's expletive response reverberated off the toilet bowl, giving it a muted sound.

"Here's how this works," Antonio said, ignoring his remarks. "You probably noticed by now that the toilet is clogged."

Raul chuckled.

"When I press the handle, the water will rise, and when it gets high enough, you're going to have trouble breathing."

The stocky man swore again, and this time said something about Antonio's mother.

"Very well. Let's see if you still feel so feisty after this."

Antonio depressed the handle. The toilet gurgled and hissed. Then the water began to rise. The goon shook his head, trying to free himself from the sticky bonds. He probably pulled out a few hairs in the process, but he couldn't push his head away from the rising water.

"No!" he shouted in protest. "No!"

"You should probably take a breath," Antonio suggested as the water reached the tip of the man's nose.

The man's back expanded as he sucked in a huge breath of air and then held it. The water submerged his nostrils, then his mouth. He offered a muted sound, though he kept his mouth closed to keep the toilet water from entering.

Within ten seconds, the water stopped rising. At the twenty-second mark, it began receding.

After the water cleared the prisoner's nose, he blew out hard and hurriedly took in several gasping breaths.

More profanity echoed through the bathroom.

"Next time will be longer," Antonio warned. "You feel like changing your story?"

He held his finger over the handle, ready to flush again.

The man breathed hard, spitting between gasps. "Orasco. We work for Manuel Orasco."

Antonio inclined his head, unsure if he could trust the answer or if the guy was just trying to loosen the duct tape.

He wasn't sure he believed the guy. After all, he was desperate now, and the fear of drowning had taken him down more than a few pegs.

Manuel Orasco was a well-known businessman with connections, including in the federal government. Orasco had never formally been accused of any wrongdoing, but there were whispers in certain circles that he used strong-arm tactics, and even violence, to get what he wanted.

Bribery and extortion were other accusations that bounced off his stellar reputation like bullets off a tank.

Antonio shouldn't have been so surprised at the confession. Men like Orasco had their fingers in all sorts of pies. But what was his angle in trying to find the Wandering City? Pursuit of something so... mythical in nature didn't seem like something a man such as Orasco would chase, unless he actually believed it existed.

Anything was possible. But what did Orasco want with the city if he were to find it? What would he do with something like that?

Unfortunately, there were more questions than answers. For now, he needed to know if the man getting the Sandinista Swirly was being honest or just giving a name to spare him from another round of toilet water to the face.

"Is this true?"

"Yes. Yes. Orasco hired us to watch the archaeologist."

"And what was this archaeologist doing at the church earlier?" Antonio let his finger drag across the handle's surface.

"He had a crystal. Something they found before. I swear, we were just told to protect him."

There was something more the man wasn't saying. Antonio flushed the toilet again.

"No! No! Please!"

He watched as the water rose again, this time from a higher point.

It climbed all the way up to the tips of the man's ears. Veins in his neck bulged as he strained to pull his head out. As predicted, the water stayed at that level longer this time, and Antonio knew the man would be pushed to the limits of his lung capacity.

Again, the water slowly sank back down. And when it cleared his nostrils, the man took in huge, desperate gulps of air.

"I told you everything," he blurted. "Please!" He coughed, and the splashing sound of water in the basin told Antonio and Raul he'd already choked on a little.

He'd gone from a hardened blowhard to a babbling baby within two minutes. Simulated drowning had that effect on people. Antonio knew it was why so many black ops and terror organizations around the world used waterboarding to extract information from prisoners.

He also knew if he held the handle down a little longer, the man would succumb to the instinct to breathe.

"Don't lie to me," Antonio cautioned. "I can do this all day. Or I can just hold this handle down a little longer next time and let you drown in a toilet. Hardly a legendary way to go out of this world, I'd say."

"I swear. I've told you everything."

"So, when I bring your partner in here and give him the same treatment, is there anything he could say different? Because if that happens, I'll bring you back in here and finish the job." Antonio bent down and spoke into the man's ear, making sure the guy heard the clear threat in his words. "What are you not telling me?"

"He told us to kill the archaeologist once he had the Key of Inti," the man blurted. "And to kill the Americans if they showed up."

The Key of Inti. Antonio had heard the Americans talking about this. He'd considered it fiction, or a fragile hope that it really existed. Now, however, the notion of this mythical key was corroborated by this guy, and by extension the archaeologist he was assigned to watch over.

If he was telling the truth, that meant Orasco was up to something.

Antonio looked over at Raul, who offered a subtle nod at the man's response. But the weathered agent wasn't done yet. He understood that if this man worked for Orasco, he'd have to be willing to get his hands dirty. The wealthy tycoon certainly couldn't do that. He had a clean reputation to uphold, and this sort of thing was always hired out by someone in a position like his.

"What happened to the three who went through the portals?" Antonio asked. It was a shot in the dark, and he didn't fully expect the man to know, but he had to try. The Americans were Antonio's business, as much as he didn't like it. And he wasn't about to fall down on the job and lose his two charges on one of the last gigs he took before retirement.

"What?" the man said.

"The three portals at the church. The archaeologist and the other two with me went through those things. Where do they lead?"

"I don't know that. We had no idea what was going to happen. I swear. I just follow orders. Okay? I'm a hired gun, just like you."

Antonio inclined his head, raising his chin a little. It was a defensive posture. He didn't appreciate the insinuation, that he was nothing more than some goon off the street paid to protect and eliminate people.

Temptation weighed heavily on the finger hovering over the toilet handle. He could do it. At least he told himself he could. He'd killed before, though never in cold blood. But would this really constitute that? Or would this be more in the interest of protecting others?

Either way, he wasn't going to do it no matter how much his imagination entertained the notion.

"Surely you must have heard this archaeologist talking about where the portals might lead. It certainly seems like he knew what he was doing at the church with that crystal and the altar."

"If he did, he didn't tell us anything. He walked over to the altar and told us to watch the door. There was nowhere for him to go, so we didn't think anything of it. It's not like he could have escaped."

"And yet that's exactly what happened."

Antonio depressed the handle again and let the water flood up to the rim of the bowl again. The man's screams turned to muted gurgles when the water reached his lips. After waiting a few seconds, Antonio reached down and ripped the duct tape away from the bottom of the basin.

The goon fell backward against the wall, tape ripping from his hair in the process.

He coughed and gasped, spitting up water. His face dripped water all over his shirt and jacket, soaking the fabric.

"You want me to get the other one?" Raul asked.

Antonio shook his head. "No. He won't know anything else. I'm not sure they've broken any laws, so taking them to the police is probably not an option. Any ideas?"

"We have a place we can hold them until all this shakes out."

"Good. They may be of use to us later on if we need to try to pin something on Orasco." Antonio turned his attention to the man on the floor still recovering from the swirly. "If what you say is true, you would do well to talk when more questions are asked. You're expendable to a man like Orasco. Just remember that."

He turned and walked out the door with more questions than he'd entered with, but he wasn't going to get any farther down that rabbit hole tonight. This case had just taken an unexpected turn, and Antonio wasn't sure where to go with it next.

He did know one thing. Carrera needed to hear about Orasco.

35

Arturo sat in his rental car, watching the Americans' bodyguard usher the archaeologist's protector out of the church with the help of two other men. Even in their ordinary, everyday clothes, the two new guys reeked of cop. He chose a spot along the sidewalk seventy yards away from the church's nearest corner. From there, he could see everything but would also go unnoticed were any suspicious eyes to turn his way.

He'd been around enough police, usually on the wrong side, to tell the difference. In this instance, it was too easy. They may have been some kind of federal agents, though which division Arturo couldn't guess.

The way they looked both directions on the street, the turn of their heads, the keen yet aloof look in their eyes that tried to portray confidence but really showed uncertainty—all dead giveaways.

Then there was the way the three men attempted to make it look like the two prisoners were drunk. Most likely, they'd drugged them. It was just a guess, but the two men guarding the archaeologist had been completely functional earlier, other than the fact they couldn't take out a couple of weak-looking Americans.

The guard and two agents stuffed the two suspects into the SUV the agents had arrived in, which worked out well for Antonio. He'd planted a tracking device on the car while waiting to see what would happen next, and his planning as well as his intuition, had paid off.

He was lucky in a way, he knew. If the Americans' guard had decided to use the vehicle he'd rented, that would have been a problem. But Arturo's keen eye had recognized the reinforcements, and combined with the size of the vehicle—more than enough room to stow a couple of captives—he decided to plant the device on the SUV. A quick slip under the chassis, and the magnet grabbed on to the steel near the back-right quarter of the car.

Once the men were gone, Arturo checked the GPS tracker on his phone and watched the blue dot move down the street, then turn left at the next corner.

When they were out of view, Arturo started his car and pulled out of his parking spot.

He placed the phone in the cup holder below the dashboard. Enough of the screen was visible so he could keep a watchful eye on the targets as they fled the scene.

Arturo expected the car to head toward a police station, or perhaps a government building somewhere in Cusco. Instead, his quarry seemed to be heading toward the historic district, which was only a few minutes away.

He drove carefully, making sure he didn't catch up to the other car too quickly, while at the same time doing his best to stay close enough that if the men exited the vehicle and parked somewhere, he'd be able to see what building they entered.

When the dot on the screen slowed to a stop a block away, Arturo turned onto the next street and eased his vehicle into a parking spot next to the curb, sliding it in between an old motorcycle and a rusty gray two-door compact.

He peered ahead through the windshield but couldn't see his marks, though according to the GPS they were less than a hundred meters away.

Arturo killed the engine and waited, watching the sidewalk and the street up the slight rise.

The area was quiet, with only a handful of cars parked along the curb and no foot traffic at all. But he wondered what the Americans' bodyguard was doing here with a couple of cops, or agents or whatever they were. Maybe he'd missed his read. It was possible the bodyguard had called in a couple of thugs to help out with what he felt certain was turning into an interrogation.

His initial suspicion had been that questioning would be carried out by authorities. Now, he wasn't so sure.

THE AMERICANS' guard had taken a risk coming to a place like this, but his timing had been perfect. The houses lining the street were all quiet and seemingly unoccupied.

He saw movement. The driver's-side door opened, along with both passenger doors on the right. They dragged the men out of the back and ushered them into a two-story house. They moved quickly, one opening the door for the other two, and then shutting it again before anyone could notice.

Anyone but Arturo.

He immediately climbed out of the car, pocketed the key and his phone, and patted the left side of his jacket to reassure himself the pistol was still there. He felt the weight of it, of course, but he always preferred to recheck just in case.

It was one of the OCD qualities he'd always permitted himself since obtaining his first firearm. It was a security blanket, a friend by his side that would always do his bidding in a life where such human connections had been fleeting at best.

Arturo carefully closed the door and walked around the front of the vehicle. He didn't duck or crouch or try to sneak. Doing so could have drawn the kind of attention he preferred to avoid. Sneaking around always looked suspicious.

Instead, he ambled slowly to the curb, stepped up onto the sidewalk, and continued up the slight rise toward the SUV and the house his targets had just entered.

He glanced around casually, surveying the narrow street. Colorful homes lined the cobbled road and slim sidewalks. Many of the balconies were draped with flowers in boxed planters. Chairs and little tables sat on most of the stoops but were unoccupied. Curtains of myriad colors hung over the windows of the two-story homes and apartments. For all intents, the place had turned into a temporary ghost town.

No one was watching Arturo.

He strolled up the sidewalk, swinging his arms gently back and forth as if simply out for some fresh air.

Just ahead on his left, the black SUV sat silently next to the curb. As he drew closer, he could hear the engine block crackling as it cooled. A dog barked somewhere in the distance, but it didn't startle Arturo. His ears were attuned to the sounds of danger and able to ignore the random noises of the city.

He'd learned a lot growing up on the streets. That survival instinct of knowing who was around you, and what they might be up to, had been one of his earliest lessons.

He slowed down slightly as he reached the SUV and the two-story villa. Arturo scanned the façade of the semi-detached house. A narrow alley ran along the right side of it, allowing for only foot traffic. The left side of the home abutted another dwelling, this one painted in a light blue color with purple flowers hanging from the balcony rails.

Arturo noticed no flowers or even flower boxes on the stoop just above him on the home his marks had entered.

A safe house, he realized. The sparse decor on the exterior was probably mirrored by minimal furnishings on the inside. He wondered who owned the home but guessed it was probably used by local police, or government—in this case, the two agents who'd joined the Americans' bodyguard.

He heard sounds coming from the inside, but they were muted and unintelligible. Not that he expected to hear what they were saying without a little help. He could have used a field microphone that would have enabled him to zero in on the villa and its occupants,

but even then, their muffled words would have been nearly impossible to decipher.

So, he would have to wait it out until someone left the house.
Then he would make his move.

He walked a little farther up the sidewalk, paused, looked around
as if searching for a specific address, and then crossed the street. He
found a dark green park bench on the sidewalk behind a navy-blue
Volkswagen Jetta and sat down.

From there, he had a clear view of the villa's front door and
balcony through the windows of the Volkswagen, but was also hidden
enough that no one leaving the house would see him before he saw
them. He could quickly duck out of view for a second and then
reassess the situation.

Now, it was down to a waiting game for Arturo, and he had no
problem with being patient.

36

Antonio stormed out of the villa and back onto the sidewalk. Dusk was near, and soon the streetlights would flicker to life to replace the light of day for those out walking the streets of Cusco at night.

He surveyed the empty street, checking some of the nearby cars for any curious onlookers, but saw nothing. Satisfied no one was following him, he called Carrera and held the phone to his ear.

"I'm surprised to hear from you so soon," she answered after two rings. "What's the update?"

He looked across the street as he walked down the hill away from the villa. He appreciated the help the two agents had given him, but he didn't want anyone else hearing his conversation.

"I interrogated the... suspects," he said, wary that the call could be recorded.

"And?"

"They work for Manuel Orasco." He let the statement sink in before he went on. "One of them gave me everything. He said they were assigned to protect the archaeologist. And if necessary, eliminate him. It seems we have another player in this game. I'm not sure what Orasco has planned, but it can't be good. He's a shady character."

"Mmm," she hummed her agreement. "Indeed he is. So, he hired an archaeologist to try to find the lost city?"

"It seems that way." Antonio stalked around a curve and out of sight from the villa. "I think we should keep them a little longer, find out what else they know. I'm sure they'll be willing to tell us everything if we apply the right amount of pressure."

"Yes. Find out what you can. Have you heard out of the two IAA agents?"

"No," he said, regret in his voice. "I haven't seen or heard out of them since they disappeared into those portals."

He'd planned on returning to the church to investigate while the two agents in the villa watched Orasco's men. Maybe there was something he'd missed. Or perhaps the Americans, and Orasco's archaeologist, would be returned to the same place. There was no way to know, but he couldn't sit around doing nothing.

It wasn't his style.

He stopped at the next corner. He needed the fresh air, and some distance between himself and the villa.

Only a few more weeks, and he would be done with this nonsense. A free man, able to do whatever he wanted for the rest of his life. It had seemed like this last gig was going to be a walk in the park, a sort of swan song on the setting sun of his career.

It had turned into a disaster of unbelievable proportions.

He needed to think. And sitting in the villa with the two agents and Orasco's men wasn't going to clear his head.

A door creaked open behind him. Laughter and rock music spilled out. He turned around and saw the entrance to a pub slowly closing after an older man in a green sweater stepped out and turned left before crossing the street.

That's exactly what I need.

"I'm going to figure out what's going on," Antonio said, still eyeing the pub. He didn't need to tell her he was going in to have a drink. That part he could leave out. It wasn't necessary for the interior minister to know everything he did. His methods were his own, and if she didn't like it, she could figure it out for herself.

"I'll call you when I have more information," he added.

"Be cautious, Antonio," she warned. "If Orasco has been working behind the scenes on this, and it sounds like he has, then it's possible there are others in play."

"Good advice, Minister," he said.

"I have to take care of my best. Especially so close to you hanging it up. Can't have anything happening to you on the last month of your career."

"I appreciate that. I'll update you when I know more. I just wanted you to know about that snake Orasco. I don't know what else he's up to, but I thought it was best to inform you of his involvement. How long can we keep them at the villa?" He knew better than to ask who owned the place.

"As long as you need, though if you would prefer, I'll have someone bring them in to one of the local jails, I can make that happen."

"Maybe. Let me see what else I can get from them, and I'll let you know."

"I'll leave you to it, then."

He ended the call and checked the screen to make sure it was off, then walked over to the red pub door. The paint peeled off in a few spots, revealing a grimy white base.

One tequila, and I'll get back to the villa. He shook his head. If only it were that simple. He knew he couldn't do that. He'd never drunk on the job, and now wasn't the time to start, no matter how much a shot of tequila would settle his nerves.

He distracted himself by looking around at the other offerings of the city—a corner bakery across the street, a restaurant next to it, an apothecary kitty-corner to those. None of that would help him right now.

He was hungry but in no mood to eat, and he doubted the two agents would be ready to eat, either.

Antonio checked his watch. He'd been gone seven minutes. He

knew he probably needed to get back to the villa and formulate a plan. But getting some privacy while he spoke to one of the top leaders in Chile was just as important. Now that the call was done, he could head back and figure out the next move.

Only a few more weeks to go.

37

Orasco's phone rang for the second time in the last thirty minutes. He'd been expecting to hear Arturo's update on the situation in Cusco. The news was disappointing to say the least, but it sounded like his man had a handle on things and was going to get to the bottom of what was going on there.

This call, however, was entirely unexpected.

He'd cleared his afternoon schedule to do the one thing that always relaxed him. Now, as his personal assistant unbuttoned her scarlet blouse, he realized that wasn't going to happen either.

He exhaled in frustration.

"Should I go?" the young woman asked. Her pouty lips were the color of red wine, and as she finished the sentence, she bit the bottom one to tease him.

Orasco wanted her to stay. He needed this, and he certainly wasn't going to get it at home. He and his wife were still together, but it was a marriage built on a toothpick foundation with nothing substantial or real holding it up. He needed an image for the public, a family man with family values, and that public persona had helped him get everything he wanted—so far.

He'd liked his wife at one point. In fact, he didn't truly loathe her.

But the fragile walls of their relationship crumbled quickly when he refused to give up any of his vices, this one in particular.

Orasco liked women the way aficionados liked fine cigars or wine. He knew they were people and not objects, but he also didn't care. They'd paid him no attention when he was younger, and now that he was rich and powerful, he'd take full advantage of lost time.

"Yes," he said with regret cracking his voice. "Leave. I'll call you later."

"As you wish," she said, letting the blouse fall just a little more to give him a taste of what he was missing before she rebuttoned the fabric and sauntered out the door. She closed it behind, leaving him alone in the penthouse suite.

He'd come to Cusco for two reasons: to get away from responsibility, and to make certain everything went according to plan.

Was that a case of micromanaging things? Definitely. And he didn't care. That's how he operated, and if people didn't like it....

The phone continued to vibrate, as he knew it would. The caller wouldn't leave a voicemail.

Even though the number on the screen was obscure, and probably unmemorable for most, he'd committed it to memory immediately.

Orasco lifted the device, tapped the green button, and raised the phone to his ear.

"Hello," he said calmly.

"What took you so long to answer?" a modulated voice asked.

He detested the sound of the robotic audio mask every time he heard it. He thought it contrived, and unnecessary. It wasn't like he'd be able to identify the person by the sound of their voice.

"I had to have privacy. I was in a meeting." He wasn't lying.

"With your personal assistant, I presume. A man of your standing should be more careful, Manuel."

Orasco cringed at the insinuation. His heart beat a few ticks faster, and his cheeks burned. Not only was it a huge source of irritation that the mole knew about his personal life; he also hated the fact the person on the line used his first name so casually. Whoever it was behind the masked voice was, as far as he knew, beneath him.

They were an informant, his mole within the office of Sofia Carrera.

Orasco understood the caution. He was, after all, a dangerous man. But he wasn't going to turn in someone who could do the same to him.

"Why did you call me?" he demanded, trying to both divert away from the question and take a more commanding role in the conversation. A rat shouldn't run the show.

"Oh, I have questions, Manuel. Like, why did you send your archaeologist out into the field without my knowing? My employer was not happy to hear about this."

He frowned. A bead of sweat formed on his forehead over his right eyebrow. He thought he'd been careful. For three seconds, he wondered how she knew. The conclusion was obvious, though, and he reached it quickly.

He'd known about Carrera asking the IAA for help in the search for the Wandering City and had taken measures to counter that problem. Orasco hadn't initially believed time was a problem in his quest to locate the lost city. And it hadn't been, until Carrera obtained the journal that belonged to that stupid American treasure hunter.

"I didn't think you were going to tell her. Why would you do that?" He'd taken the offensive now, which was where he always liked to be.

"You know I have to run everything by her. Those Americans are dangerous. We don't want any of our own people getting killed, do we?"

The mole made a good point. He cared little about what happened to his hired help. They were, like most people, expendable in his eyes. But if they were killed or captured, and any had been careless enough to leave a bread crumb that could lead to him—then there would be problems.

"No. Of course not."

"Then you need to tell me when you do something like that again. We wouldn't want any—accidents."

He didn't appreciate the pause to emphasize the last word. There was a plethora of things he didn't like about this conversation, and he was beginning to think maybe he shouldn't have trusted the mole in the first place.

Orasco was slowly losing his grip on the conversation.

He wanted to tell the informant that they maybe could have done something on their end to keep the Americans from joining the hunt, but he kept it to himself, as he had with sending Arturo to eliminate the Americans.

Instead, he decided to take the neutral route, knowing that bravado would only breed the same from the other side.

"There was a man protecting the Americans. Who is he?"

The caller hesitated. "He's old security for the minister. Near retirement. Why?"

Orasco had kept a few things close, and this was one more. "Because I would hate it if our people crossed paths in the field and didn't know they were playing for the same side."

"He's not on our side," the mole corrected. "As you said before, like with the others, he is expendable. I, however, am not. If you want to pull this off, you're going to need to be smarter about the people you bring into this."

Orasco blew air out his nostrils like an angry horse. No one talked to him that way. No matter their station. The mole had proved themselves useful so far. It was they who'd reached out in the first place. Without them, he would have never known about the location of the first crystal, or obtained the journal of Father José Alsue.

He'd wondered why this mysterious person would reach out to him for help. Only one reason made sense. Ambition. The informant must have been some kind of intern working in the office of the interior minister, privy to all the information that flowed through.

They'd seen an opportunity to change their stars, and could think of only one person with enough power to help.

The alliance was a tedious one for Orasco, and he knew how it had to end. He'd play along, letting this mole think they had control of the situation. But once his people found the city, he'd take out the informant, and anyone connected to them.

"I never said you were expendable," Orasco claimed, shoving away the insult for a moment. "We need each other to get this done. And when we complete it, we'll both be wealthier than anyone on the planet."

38

MACHALLILA

The instant Tara's foot touched the bridge, the entire scene around her changed. The glowing ceiling above, the bridge, the torches on the walls of the tunnel behind her—all of it vanished.

A new scene appeared, and she found herself in a shadowy, lush jungle. Splinters of sunlight pierced through the dense canopy of leaves and branches above her. The tree trunks stood all around her, towering to the sky and casting an eerie shade to the forest floor.

Undergrowth surrounded her, too. Shrubs, plants with huge leaves, and tropical flowers sprang up from the ground, each desperately vying for a taste of sunlight.

Tara realized she was on a narrow trail. The beaten dirt path was only a few feet wide and appeared to have been forged by animals. A chill crawled up her spine.

What kind of animals?

She had no idea where she was or why the strange cavern had brought her here. She even considered that this might simply be an illusion, all playing out in her mind. Her senses begged to differ.

Not only did the sights seem very real; so did the smells of the forest and the sounds of the birds and insects above and around her.

Tara bent down and brushed her fingers against a dewy orange flower petal. The water moistened her hand, and she believed that if she tasted the droplets, they would be as real as everything else.

She didn't know how it was possible, how she'd ended up in this place. She could either fight it and lose, or accept it and try to move forward.

The trail wound past a wide tree trunk in front of her, then bent back around the other side and disappeared from view. She twisted around and looked back in the other direction. The path ran into a thicket of shrubs, almost as if the leaves and branches swallowed it.

One of the bushes near the path shook abruptly. Tara steadied her breathing. She loved the outdoors—usually. Because she'd spent so much time outside her whole life—except while working in the lab—she had developed a certain confidence when it came to wildlife.

The problem was, she didn't know what kind of wildlife this jungle supported—or even what jungle she was in.

The bushes continued to shiver and shake. The intensity of the movement surged. Tara took an unconscious step back. Then another. She instinctively reached for the pistol that typically remained tucked within the back of her belt. But it wasn't there. She knew it wasn't. The old habit had won out over logic.

She stuck her hands out wide as she continued to backtrack away from the shuddering shrubs.

Leaves and twigs snapped and cracked under her, and she dared to look back where she was going.

For a second, Tara saw she was nearing the wide trunk that forced the path to detour around it. Something snapped. Then she felt the ground under her foot give way as her foot sank suddenly.

She felt herself falling. Her body hit something flimsy where the ground should have been. Debris, sticks, and leaves rained down around her as she fell.

Tara didn't have time to wonder how far she would drop, or what gruesome death awaited her at the bottom. The earth stopped her momentum within two seconds of her losing her balance.

She winced at the hard landing, but it was just dirt. There were no rocks, no sharp spikes sticking out of the ground. It was just a pit someone, or something, had dug and covered with forest scraps.

"I doubt it was an animal who laid this trap," she said.

She stood and dusted her pants with a few quick slaps, then assessed her surroundings. Opaque spiderwebs covered the pit's walls all the way to the top—which she figured to be around eight feet, maybe a few inches less.

It was too high for her to jump out, but she'd noticed big roots on the ground earlier. If there was one close to the lip of the circular hole, she might be able to grab it and climb out. It was that or try to dig her way out with her bare hands, or with a few rocks she might be able to find.

Tara stepped over to the wall and leaped. She slapped her hands on the ground above, and for a brief few seconds looked out across the forest floor. Nothing but the bottoms of plants, some dead branches, and leaves appeared. Then she fell back to the ground, landing on her feet.

She took two steps to the right and tried again. She saw virtually the same thing as before, landed, and moved to her right.

Tara repeated the process until she was on the opposite side from where she started. She paused for a second to catch her breath. The humid, warm air of the jungle purged sweat from her body. She felt beads of moisture forming on her forehead and wiped it with the back of her sleeve.

She took a breath and jumped again. Her hands smacked against something other than dirt and leaves. A thick root ran along the ground in front of her face, and she grabbed on to it as gravity started pulling her back down again.

Tara froze there, holding on to the root with her feet dangling over the ground below. In front of her, only a few feet beyond her hands, was the most terrifying thing she'd ever seen.

39

"What the—" she muttered, too afraid to move.

She stared into the giant, creepy eyes of the biggest spider she'd ever seen in her life. The monstrous black creature stood at least five feet high, with a three-foot-wide body.

It straightened its legs and towered over her, staring hungrily down at its new catch.

She'd thought a human had laid this trap in the ground. Now she realized that was a painfully wrong assumption.

The webs along the pit walls should have been the first clue. But there was no way she could have figured it was built by a beast such as this.

Her instincts kicked in, and she released the root with both hands. The spider hissed, then snapped forward as if to bite her head with its enormous fangs.

She felt the wind blow over her as it missed the strike.

Tara hit the ground and immediately rolled to her feet, looking up for the monster.

There was no sign of it.

Her heart pounded in her chest as she searched frantically for the giant arachnid. She spun around in a circle, sweeping the top of the pit for any sign of its return. Her lips quivered, and her fingers trembled.

Spiders were one of her greatest fears, though she rarely saw any dangerous ones. A tiny one in the house now and then that she politely asked Alex to remove was about as scary as it got. She'd have killed for one of those little guys now instead of this thing.

She tried to reinforce that this was just a test, a trial of Mama Qucha. But it all felt so real. And that spider definitely looked real.

Something shuffled in the undergrowth above to her right. She snapped her head in that direction but saw nothing. Only a few small trees that shook. Had this been the creature in the shrubs from before? And was this its plan all along? Scare her backward until she fell into its trap?

Her gut tightened, and she found it difficult to take air into her lungs.

Then she heard a subtle noise. It sounded like large feet trying to shuffle quietly in the leaves and dirt behind her.

Whatever this thing was, it was extremely clever for a spider.

She spun around and saw the creature standing on the edge of the pit, staring down at her with ravenous hunger.

It rose slightly, screamed some unholy sound from its mouth, and leaped into the pit.

With the wall close behind her, the only place Tara could go was forward. She dove ahead, and hit the ground with a roll. She watched the monster fly overhead as she rolled to the other side of the pit.

The spider hit the wall behind where she'd stood, smashing its hideous face into the web-covered dirt. Its legs scrambled, kicking up debris from the pit floor.

It backed away from the wall, thrashing its head and body around in an uncoordinated fury.

She stepped close to the wall, bracing herself against it with her right elbow. Tara watched the creature continue to toss violently. It spun around and reared back as if to strike again, but she noticed its eyes were covered with web and dirt.

It was blind. But for how long?

Faith and courage.

The thought came to her as if from somewhere else, somewhere outside of herself. The second part of that clue—courage—seemed to resound louder.

What is courage? The answer came to her quicker than she thought. *Courage is facing our fears, and overcoming them even though we think we are too afraid to.* It sounded like something Sean or Alex or Adriana might have said to her at some point, but she couldn't recall who, if any of them, had.

Tara swallowed. She searched the pit for something, anything she could use as a weapon.

Eight feet to her left, a tree limb sat on the ground near the wall. The limb was around five feet long and had a sharp point where it had broken from its tree.

If she moved now, she could grab it before the spider noticed. But fear gripped her. She wanted to make the move, wanted to grab the only weapon she could reach, but something deep within her froze her in place.

The spider continued to claw at its eyes to free its vision. It had pulled away some of the debris already, and within moments it would be able to see once again.

Tara clenched her jaw.

What are you afraid of? Dying? That's going to happen if you just stand here.

Logic took over her brain. She knew it was the correct sentiment. Doing nothing never resulted in anything good.

If she moved, though, the creature might sense it.

She shuffled her foot to the left and felt it bump up against a rock about the size of a softball.

An idea flashed in her mind.

Tara reached down and picked up the stone. She reached back like she'd done with her father so many times in their backyard when she was a child and flung the projectile as hard as she could.

The timing of the throw was perfect.

The rock sailed toward the monster's face, and just as it lowered down, struck the hideous left eye, crushing it to pulp.

The spider screamed again, louder than before. Its legs scratched at the wounded eye; the other still mostly blinded.

Suddenly, Tara felt free of the fear that had held her motionless before. She darted over to the makeshift spear and lifted it in her right hand, bracing it with the left.

She took up a defensive position, pointing the branch up at an angle toward the maniacal creature. The spider backed up against the far wall, desperately trying to clear its remaining good eye.

Tara went on the attack, rushing across the pit floor with the sharp limb aimed at the monster's face.

Before she reached it, the giant spider lunged forward in a wild, uncontrolled strike. The head snapped down with fangs bared, narrowly missing her, and instead slamming into the dirt.

Tara reacted by adjusting the angle of the spike, leaped into the air, and thrust it down into the beast's hairy skull. The sharp point penetrated through its mouth and down into the ground, pinning it to the dirt below.

The legs kicked and flailed, and its body rocked back and forth like a mechanical bull. She held the limb for a second, until the dying monster rose one last time. Then she took two steps across its back, and jumped toward the edge of the pit.

Tara's elbows hit the ground above with a thud. Her feet still dangled over the lip of the hole. She quickly scrambled, pulling herself clear of the opening in the jungle floor.

Her chest swelled and fell rapidly, her lungs taking in huge gasps of air. Her heart raced as she turned around, half expecting the giant spider to somehow mount one more attack.

Instead, the creature slumped to the ground, its legs barely twitching.

She'd done it. She'd killed it.

Tara wished she could feel some sense of victory, but the reality of not knowing where she was in some foreign jungle—and how many more such creatures might await her—crept back into her mind, filling her with a renewed sense of dread.

Then, unexpectedly, the scene around her vanished.

She found herself standing between two obelisks on the other side of the abyss. Tara looked back across and saw the bridge spanning the immense gap as if the entire jungle scene and the fight with spider had all happened in her mind.

She took a step ahead, and blue torches lit along walls in another tunnel not unlike the one at the entrance to the cavern. The sapphire flames danced in their sconces, causing her shadow to ripple and waver as she passed.

A bright blue light radiated in front of her, thirty feet away atop a stone altar. She continued forward, into a chamber surrounded by smooth, squared walls.

As she drew closer to the pedestal, she realized the object emitting the blue light was a crystal in the shape of Mama Qucha she'd seen before. It was only eight inches tall and appeared to be flat—only a couple of inches thick.

"Well done, traveler," the voice from before said. "The Key of Mama Qucha is yours."

Tara took a step closer and stopped at the base of the altar. The crystal bathed her in blue light so bright it made seeing anything else in the room impossible.

She reached out her right hand to touch the sculpture's smooth side. The instant her fingers touched it, the light enveloped her.

40

CASPANA

Alex didn't feel comfortable walking backward across this magical bridge, or whatever it was.

In theory, it seemed simple enough—just walk backward across a bridge. Except the bridge was narrow, barely wider than his shoulders. That, and it just happened to span what appeared to be a bottomless chasm.

Every second that passed felt like days as he shuffled toward the other side, barely moving his heels inches with every step.

He didn't dare move faster. One wrong move, and he didn't know when he'd stop falling. If ever.

On top of that, Alex had more pressing concerns. He had to get back to Tara, if only to make sure she was okay.

Part of him regretted that they'd split up. But there'd been no choice. The portals only allowed one person to go through each. Which seemed to contrast a line he recalled from the journal—something to the tune of "only two may come."

At the moment, he couldn't let thoughts such as that distract him. He had to focus. And on not falling.

Alex had learned from his mother not to focus on the negative. So, instead of saying don't forget to do this or that, she'd tell him to remember to do the thing instead. It wasn't always easy. Life was full of challenges.

In this case, a literal quest. One he had to complete going backward.

He hoped this was the only thing he had to do to reach the key supposedly located somewhere through this portal, but Alex had a bad feeling there was going to be something else waiting for him on the other side—if he reached the other side.

The voice in the tunnel had said with faith and wit he would pass. Moving backward across a narrow bridge spanning a perilous gorge seemed to fit the faith part. Not to mention the fact that huge sections of said bridge had been moving around on their own whenever he turned and faced it.

He'd been moving for a while and thought surely he was at the halfway point, but the slight rise to the stones under his feet suggested he still had farther to go before he reached the downslope toward the other side.

It didn't matter. He'd take as long as he needed to get safely to the end of the bridge. It would do Tara no good if he didn't make it out of here at all.

Alex's mind drifted, wondering how many others had come through here before him... and failed. Distracted for a second, he looked down to his left, staring momentarily into the abyss below. Had others fallen into the chasm, never to be seen again? Perhaps that happened to Buford, or others like him.

Alex shook away the thought. Buford hadn't made it this far. He'd never found the crystal that other man had placed on the altar. If there were others who had come before Buford, however, it was possible those poor souls had indeed failed this trial and met their end somewhere in the seething darkness below.

So far, the only tricky thing about this had been going backward, feeling his way across. What was the big deal?

He felt the surface underfoot begin to level out. Hope swelled in his chest. He'd made it halfway. Just a little farther, and he would be to the other side. Had it taken him half an hour or more to get here?

Alex didn't care. As long as he got there, that was what mattered. He could make up time in other ways.

That sentiment melted as he looked toward the tunnel where he'd begun the journey across the gorge.

For a second, he thought he was hallucinating. Was the bridge... collapsing?

His eyes widened inside the shut eyelids as he watched the sections of the stone bridge that had magically separated, now dropping away—one piece at a time—into the black abyss below.

"You have to be kidding me," he complained.

The bridge sections fell one every three seconds, by his rough count. That meant they'd be to him in....

"Ugh." He grunted in frustration. Right now wasn't the time to work out the math. It was time to move. And faster than he had before.

He didn't like the idea of hurrying backward across the span, but he didn't have a choice.

The temptation to look back over his shoulder at the rest of the path nearly overwhelmed him, causing him to temporarily forget the repercussions. He stopped himself just as he was about to steal a glance.

Instead, Alex shuffled faster, scooting his shoes along the smooth stone surface. He quickly realized that wasn't going to cut it. The crumbling bridge was catching up to him. He needed to move faster.

Then he had an idea. He grabbed the phone in his pocket, held it up, and tapped on the camera app. He pressed the symbol to reverse the image to selfie mode and then stuck the device out to his left.

It was a risky move. He didn't know if the bridge, or whatever force had caused it to move, would consider the use of the camera cheating.

To his relief, the stone crossing remained intact.

Alex picked up the pace, walking backward in full strides. He wished he'd thought of this before, though it may not have mattered. It seemed the bridge collapsing only began when he reached halfway.

It was a sinister concept, lulling adventurers into a false sense of security before dropping them into oblivion.

Not Alex. He was going to make it.

The other side was in sight of his camera, only another forty yards away.

He could make it. He had to make it.

The bridge shook with each section that fell away. Alex looked up toward the crest and saw the collapse had just reached the halfway point, and it was gaining on him despite his renewed speed.

He moved faster, desperate to stay a safe distance ahead of disaster.

For the slightest of moments, Alex's movement changed, and his left heel dug into the stone.

He tripped, and tumbled backward to his left. He flailed for a second, dropping the phone in the process. It clattered on the bridge as he landed on his rear. Alex landed hard and bounced toward the edge. He stuck out his hands to slow his momentum, but his legs fell over the side.

Alex grasped for a hold on the bridge, but his fingers slipped across the surface. He shouted, something between a battle cry and a panicked scream, and dug his nails into the stone.

His fingers found purchase in one of the grooves between the huge tiles. Alex gripped with every ounce of strength he could muster with most of his body hanging over the edge of a perilous drop.

In this moment, he truly understood the meaning of the phrase *holding on for dear life.*

He glanced to the left and saw the bridge behind him continue to fall away. The huge blocks dropped in a faster cadence now. And they were closing in on him.

Alex summoned every last bit of his strength and pulled himself back over the ledge and onto solid ground.

He scrambled to his feet, grabbed his phone, and kept his back turned to the finish line. The screen, fortunately, hadn't been damaged when he dropped the device. But as he raised the phone to show him the way, he knew he wasn't going to make it.

The sections of falling bridge were twenty feet away. He'd have to run backward, and faster than he probably could forward.

He wasn't going to give up. But a sinking feeling flooded him.

Alex had a thought. If he couldn't outrun the bridge, maybe he could outwit it.

He got down on all fours, keeping his center of gravity low, and before the section of bridge adjacent the one on which he stood could fall away, Alex looked back over his shoulder at the destination.

41

The section of bridge Alex crouched on suddenly shifted. But it wasn't the dropping motion he'd seen from the other half of the bridge on his frantic attempt to reach the other side.

This heavy block moved sideways, as did the other pieces separating him from the landing. He started to stand, but the segment shifted forward, then back to where it had been in the same rhythm he'd seen before from the other side. Only this time, the sections on the second half were moving closer to each other, separating, and repeating the process. Each subsequent block was slightly lower than the previous, which would make it possible for him to jump from one to another.

He'd have to be careful, but it was the only plan he had. Alex kept his knees bent as the block swayed back and forth. He gave himself a couple of passes to get the rhythm down, and then when the stone neared the next section, he leaped.

The jump was only four feet, but with the beige segments moving, and at different levels, it was terrifying.

He landed on his feet and immediately dropped to his belly so the next block's movement didn't throw him over.

This one moved left to right at a diagonal track. Again, he allowed two passes before making the jump to the next stone.

Each one presented a different angle and movement, but they also moved together in sequence with one another.

Alex didn't try to figure out how. He just needed to get to the other side.

He timed the next jump and pushed off, this time landing harder than the others. His momentum carried him toward the front edge, but he quickly let his muscles go limp and fell to the surface. He grunted as his torso hit the ground, but it was better than falling over the side.

He looked out to the landing, then to the two remaining blocks.

"You can do this," he said, trying to build himself up. In truth, he couldn't believe what was happening, or what he was doing. It was easily the strangest scenario he'd ever experienced. And one of the scariest.

He recalled the scene at Hell's Gate. That had scared him more than anything. Not for his own personal safety but for Tara's. Alex didn't know what he would do if he lost her. He tried not to feel so attached, so codependent on her with his emotions, but he loved her more than he'd ever loved anyone.

It was a pure kind of love. He genuinely liked her, enjoyed spending hours and days with her. She was fun, caring, and beautiful. He doubted a guy like him would ever find someone like Tara again, and the reality was he wasn't sure he would want to, should something happen to her.

He sized up the next jump and leaped.

His shoes hit the surface of the next section, and he immediately crumpled as he had on all the others.

Once his weight was stabilized, he crouched and looked at the final block. It shifted left to right, while the one he was on moved forward and backward—intersecting briefly with the left half of the last one.

"One more, Alex," he breathed and waited for two passes before committing.

He leaned forward, took a breath, and when the block slowed down near the next one, Alex shoved off.

He aimed for the right half of the last stone segment, thinking like an American football quarterback—don't aim for the receiver, aim for where they're going.

The strategy worked perfectly, and he landed squarely in the middle of the moving platform. His elbows hit the surface with a thud, and immediately they throbbed with pain, but he didn't care. There was only one jump left, and he could make that one easily.

He let out a sigh of relief as he crouched and waited for the next pass. An odd sense of nostalgia caught him, and he turned around to look back across the span.

Suddenly, the moving blocks started dropping out of the air. One, then another, and another.

"Oh, come on," he complained.

Alex turned around and stared at the landing where the bridge had been attached before.

"Hurry," he said, though he knew that wouldn't make the thing go any faster.

Two steps back, the next platform fell into the darkness below.

"Come on. Come on. Come on."

As Alex neared the landing, the block he'd just been on, dropped.

He was only going to get one shot at this.

The landing jutted out between two obelisks. It would have been easier if the block he was on ran along a broader landing area, but that—he figured—was the point.

Nothing in here so far had been easy.

Alex waited until the last second, and as the platform passed the landing, he dove forward.

He hit the surface and rolled to a stop, propping himself up to look back.

The block passed the second obelisk and then nose-dived out of view. Alex was tempted to stand up and watch it fall, but he decided the farther he could get from this death trap, the better.

He stood up and turned around, facing away from the terrifying chasm, and stared ahead.

Another tunnel entrance greeted him against the backdrop of the cavern wall. Unlike the rough-hewn rock walls of the other side, this wall was smooth and adorned with images of canyons, people, and the recurring symbol of Pachamama.

He took a step forward. The move was reluctant, dragged by uncertainty. A light blinked to life inside the tunnel. It was the torches again, lighting the path.

Alex kept walking, now with a little more confidence. This part of the cavern felt more welcoming than the first.

He'd almost forgotten that his eyes were closed, but he wasn't about to reopen them now. No telling what might happen if he did.

Alex didn't feel any warmth from the torches as he passed, but he didn't need them for that. He just needed to see where he was going.

Ahead, a new light radiated from another chamber at the end of the passage. He couldn't stop looking at it and found himself moving toward it as if a moth to a bug zapper.

It was beautiful. As he drew closer, maybe twenty feet away, he noticed the shape of the thing emitting the strange, red glow.

"The Key of Pachamama," he whispered reverently.

"Yes, traveler. Well done. The Key of Pachamama is yours."

Alex barely felt his feet moving, but he continued forward until he stopped next to a cube pedestal. The crystal was in the same shape as the deity he'd seen during his research. It was roughly the size of his head, but flat and only a few inches thick.

It somehow levitated over the plinth, as if held in place by translucent lines from overhead.

The eyes carved into the crystal seemed to stare back at him. It was an unnerving thing to behold, but he also didn't feel threatened. He was supposed to be here.

Alex reached out his hands and held them there, hesitating to take the gem. He didn't know what was going to happen next, or what he was supposed to do once he grabbed it, but he had to take that chance.

He moved his hands closer to the red crystal and then grasped both sides.

42

MACHU PICCHU

The cavern around Juan changed the second his foot touched the bridge.

He looked around at what appeared to be a 360-degree movie screen that reached all the way up to the top of the domed ceiling.

The bridge was still there, but the chasm beneath him had disappeared.

He stared at the setting around him, spinning in place to take in the entire image.

It was a playground for children. A few dozen kids played all around him, on the swing set, the slide, the merry-go-round. Others ran around laughing or screaming with delight as they played their games.

It all seemed so... familiar.

A face appeared to his right, almost as if Juan were part of the scene.

He recognized the child. It was the eight-year-old version of himself.

"How?" he mouthed.

Juan watched as the child looked away from him, peering at

another kid playing by themselves over by a giant tractor tire sticking up out of the ground.

"What am I doing here?" Juan demanded. "Why are you showing me this memory?"

He received no response.

He watched as his child self walked over to the other kid. The child was playing with a toy truck, one that Juan had wanted for his birthday but never received. His father had been gone often when Juan was a boy, always out in the field on another expedition. His mother had pursued other interests—specifically, a banker from the city.

Little Juan stopped near the child and told the boy he wanted to play with the truck. The kid looked up at him, curiously at first, but when he saw the stern expression on Juan's face, he got defensive.

He stood up, collecting his toy in the process, and retreated a few steps. "No," the boy said. "I'm not going to give it to you, but we can share it if you get some of the other toys from the bin."

Adult Juan watched, disgusted by what would come next.

He'd largely forgotten this day from his childhood, and now he was being forced to relive it against his will.

"I said give it to me," little Juan replied. He reached out and snatched the truck from the other kid, shoved him against the tire, and walked off as the boy crumpled to the ground amid sobs.

The children and the playground scene evaporated into a mist that enveloped Juan.

"Why did you take that child's truck?" It was the same haunting voice from before.

"What?"

"Why did you take that child's truck, Juan? He wasn't bothering you. And his toy didn't belong to you. So, why did you take it?"

He looked around, but all he saw was the gray vapor surrounding him.

Faith and truth, he remembered.

"I took it because I wanted it," he said, shame filling his words. "I wasn't a good kid. I bullied smaller children, took their things sometimes. Everyone thought I was a well-behaved child, but I was terrible. I'm not proud of how I behaved. If I could go back in time and change it, I would."

The smoke around him blew away in a huge breeze, and he found himself standing on the bridge once more, though farther along it than from where he started.

Odd. I haven't even taken a step.

A new scene appeared around him. It was twenty-two years after his childhood, and he saw himself standing behind a podium wearing a black-and-white tuxedo.

He recognized the scene immediately.

It was a gala to celebrate his achievement of discovering a temple in the Amazon that had been covered by the jungle for centuries.

"Thank you to everyone who helped make this possible," his younger self said to a short round of applause. "I am so proud to accept this award from the Brazilian government on behalf of all those who worked tirelessly behind the scenes."

The medallion he held in his hand was a trinket compared to the generous sum of money he received from the government for his efforts.

Except most of the effort had been by someone else. Juan had been tipped off about some research another archaeologist was doing. Desperate and broke, he had done the only thing he could think of. He stole the research and moved onto the site before the other guy could get the permits.

That would still leave a loose end, though, so Juan arranged a meeting with the man under the guise of sorting out compensation.

Juan plied him with a few bottles of Chianti, and then followed him to the train station. Even with all the wine, the other man wouldn't agree to Juan's terms. The only thing he would accept was full credit for the discoveries made. He wouldn't even give mention to Juan.

The man was drunk when he arrived at the train station later that evening. Unbeknownst to him, Juan had followed him from the restaurant. Just before the train arrived, Juan shoved the man out onto the tracks.

It had been a grisly scene, and Juan played the part of the despondent colleague with an Oscar-worthy performance. The man's death had been an untimely accident—the result of too much wine and a little lack of balance on the platform.

In the acceptance speech, Juan even had the gall to thank the guy for being supportive of his endeavors.

The gala disappeared, and the fog returned, swirling around Juan.

"Why did you kill that man?" the woman's voice demanded. She sounded angry and vengeful.

"I was jealous," Juan admitted. "Okay? And I was desperate. I didn't have any money. No one would fund any of my projects. I was going to lose everything. I tried to reason with him."

The ground under him shook, and he felt himself lose his balance and tip to the right. He could see the bridge below him but nothing else. He feared he might fall over the edge, and so got down on one knee to brace himself.

"Lies!" the voice thundered.

"Okay!" Juan shouted, fearful of the repercussions. "I knew he wouldn't work with me. He was going to be a problem. So, I got him drunk. And then I killed him. Is that what you wanted to hear?"

The mist dispersed once more, washed away by another wind.

He saw the end of the bridge just ahead. It was only fifty feet away, marked by two obelisks, one on either side of the landing that jutted out away from another tunnel.

Juan breathed steadily, fearful of what other scenes—if any—the cavern might make him endure.

He regretted having to kill the other man. He felt the same about the little boy on the playground. But he'd done what he needed to do. Or at least what he thought he needed.

Juan lifted his right foot and stepped ahead.

Again, the scene around him changed.

43

Juan couldn't believe his eyes. He spun around in circles, taking in the incredible sights surrounding him.

He stood next to a creek with the clearest water he'd ever seen. Gold sparkled in the creek bed, glistening from the bright light cast down from the sun in a cloudless blue sky.

Precious gems lay on the ground all around him like they were common, everyday rocks. Fields of yellow and white flowers stretched up over the hills toward white-capped mountains in the distance.

Juan inhaled the fresh, clean air. It smelled of grass and mint with hints of vanilla.

Ten seconds passed without him realizing it. Then it hit him. Everything seemed so real, despite the illogical pieces such as the gold in the creek bed or the precious stones lying around on the ground.

This wasn't real. It wasn't a memory like the others. This was something else.

The previous two visions were from his past. Did that mean whatever he was seeing now was a glimpse into his future?

It looked like every depiction of heaven, Elysium, and all the other good afterlife places he'd heard of. The only thing missing were the angels playing harps while sitting on pillowy cotton clouds.

"Why do you want the key to the city? Answer rightly or remain where dead things stand." The woman's question was unexpected. Startled, he glanced around, but he didn't find anyone. As he had been since entering the portal, Juan was alone.

"What?" he asked, making sure he heard correctly.

"Why do you seek the lost city? Why should you be worthy to receive the key?"

Juan looked around, still keeping his eyes closed.

"Because... I am the one who deserves to find it," he said. It sounded cocky, but he felt it in his heart.

He was an archaeologist, and not the glorified kind such as the two Americans from the IAA. He'd spent years in the field, and countless hours in research. Awards and recognition were great, but discovering the Wandering City of Patagonia would make him wealthy, and a legend for all of time.

Was that such a bad thing?

The presence that had been speaking to him sounded as though she blew out a long, disappointed breath at the answer.

"A proud spirit."

"Not proud," Juan corrected, hoping not to incur some kind of divine wrath. "But I've earned it. I have worked hard, done what it takes."

He truly believed it. Even with the murder, the bullying, and all the other errors the cavern left out, Juan did believe he deserved it.

"What will you do if you are granted the Key of Inti?"

Juan stumbled over the answer. One of the first things he'd considered was killing Orasco. Juan wasn't stupid enough to think he wasn't expendable. He was hired help to Orasco. Nothing more. But with the immense wealth of the city, he would become powerful. No one would threaten him then. With that kind of wealth, he'd be untouchable.

After that, everything seemed like it would fall into place—a life of luxury unlike anything he ever dreamed possible.

Something told Juan those weren't the answers the voice was looking for. He was self-aware enough to know that if he said those things he would come off like a total jerk.

Thinking it might be better to go with a more politically correct answer, he held back on his initial comments.

"I... was thinking I could do something for underprivileged young people, get them interested in history."

The voice groaned, and with it the ground beneath him trembled.

"Lies!" she shouted.

The entire scene around him vanished. The fields around him, the little river, the sky—all of it was swept away in an instant, replaced by utter desolation.

Barren, dead trees filled a rotting forest to his right. The hills of flowers were replaced by a charcoal-gray dirt. Black rocks lay around on the ground, and the creek oozed with a dark red liquid Juan hoped wasn't what he thought it was.

The smell of decay filled the air. It was hot and humid, the kind of oppressive atmosphere that made it difficult to breathe.

What had just happened?

He thought he'd said what the voice wanted to hear.

"Hello?"

No response.

Fear gripped him. He put out his right foot to take a step forward but froze. He stood there, paralyzed, with his foot hovering over the abyss below. The blackness twisted and churned under him, as if begging him to jump in.

He couldn't go forward.

Juan spun around and looked the other direction and found that only a section of the bridge he'd been on before remained. The rest of it had disappeared.

A new sense of terror set in as he realized he might be stuck in this hellish place forever.

His chest tightened as a wave of anxiety squeezed him.

He looked around the dead landscape, searching for a way out, an answer that could free him from this place.

It hit him, then, what he'd done wrong. He'd lied about what he would do if he found the lost city. He offered an answer he thought might appease... whatever was talking to him.

He considered apologizing, but that would be insincere. He was only sorry because of the situation he found himself in, and that there appeared to be no way out.

Instead, Juan opted to go with the truth like he should have initially.

"I seek the city for fame and fortune," he said.

Juan knew how it sounded. The statement was full of shallow, materialistic greed. But it was the truth. He thirsted for recognition, for wealth beyond imagining, and power unlike any he'd ever had in his life.

Until that moment, Juan had always been someone else's pawn, a piece in the game to be moved by other hands. It was time for him to be the king for a change.

"I want power, wealth, a life of luxury."

"Yessss," the voice hissed. "Truuuuuth."

The world around him dissolved.

The end of the bridge was a few feet ahead, bordered on each side by two obelisks. Relief spilled into him. He'd done it. He'd passed the first test.

When Juan walked between the obelisks, a new tunnel appeared in the cavern wall ahead. As before, pale torchlight lit the way forward. He noticed strange carvings on the smooth stone around the tunnel's archway. Even with his expertise in such things, Juan couldn't decipher their meaning.

He walked through the tunnel, doing his best to keep his eyes straight ahead. A pale light glowed from a chamber at the other end. It called to him, pulling on his chest as if by some magnetic power.

As Juan stepped into the circular room, he realized the light radiated from a crystal sculpture of Mama Killa.

"Well done, traveler. The Key of Mama Killa is yours."

Juan blinked rapidly as he approached the glowing pale crystal. Adrenaline rushed through him at the sense of achievement, of victory, of power.

"Only two more to go," he said, and touched the flat edge on the side of the statue.

44

CUSCO

Arturo had to watch the front entrance to the villa for only fifteen minutes before he saw something interesting.

He'd been on stakeouts before that lasted for hours, sometimes even an entire day. So, he was surprised when the Americans' bodyguard appeared through the front door holding his cell phone.

Arturo maintained a cool, disinterested look from the park bench behind the Jetta. One concern was that the owners of the car might show up and drive off, leaving his spot exposed. Another was that it was difficult to hide behind such a small car.

But the car owners hadn't shown up. And now Arturo watched the bodyguard walk down the street away from the villa.

It was impossible to hear what the man was saying on the phone, but from the way he moved, the speed, the determination in his stride, Arturo guessed he wasn't coming back for a few minutes.

That was all the time he'd need.

Arturo stood up, glanced left to make sure no cars were coming, and then back to the right to watch the babysitter disappear around a curve down the street.

Once the man was gone, Arturo trotted across to the other side and slowed down at the front door.

He drew the pistol from inside his jacket and quickly attached the suppressor to the end of the barrel.

The bodyguard had left in a hurry, and it was fifty-fifty whether or not the other two guys had locked the door behind him. If they had, he'd knock and pretend to be the guy. If not....

He pushed down on the latch and found it unlocked. It was a rookie mistake and one he'd take full advantage of.

That assumption proved correct when he saw the first guy in the living room. He was one of the guys who'd helped bring Orasco's men here, and he stood over a tall, skinny man in a suit. The prisoner's hands were bound together behind his back.

"Who are—"

Arturo's muzzle spit three rounds at the man—two into the center of his torso, one into the middle of his face. The window and wall behind him stained red after the third shot a second before he hit the floor.

"Hey? You okay in there?" a second voice asked from just down the hall.

Arturo moved toward the sound. He assumed he didn't have to tell the prisoner to keep his mouth shut. Three steps into the corridor, he saw the other cop lean out of a bathroom door to the left.

His eyes widened, the only reaction he could muster in the split second before Arturo put a bullet through his forehead. The man collapsed to the floor with an arched, splattered trail of dark red on the wall behind him.

Arturo ducked his head into the bathroom and saw the stockier of the two men hired by Orasco.

"You okay?" Arturo asked, leaning his head back out to check the hallway.

The man nodded. It was a slight movement, barely a tilt of the head.

"How many of them are there here?"

After a lazy blink, he answered, "Three."

"You're sure. Only three?"

"Yes. I am sure."

"Good." Arturo closed the door to the bathroom and peered down at the soaked man on the floor. "I work for Orasco."

Hope sprang in the man's eyes. "He sent you?"

Arturo nodded. "Yes. And we need to get you out of here. But I have to know, did they question the other one? Did he say anything to them about Señor Orasco?"

"No," the guy answered. He twisted his head a little to emphasize it. "Only me. And I didn't tell them anything."

Arturo didn't need a lie detector to know the man wasn't telling the truth. It was in the defensive motion of his eyes, the muscles around them, the slight tension across the skin. Even the tone of his voice betrayed the dishonesty.

"Okay," he said. "Good. Do you think anyone saw you?"

"No." The man scrunched his face, frowning as he retraced his steps. "No. Only the priest at the church."

Another lie. Several people had seen him and his sloppy partner. The priest was only one of them, but he wouldn't be a problem. None of them would be.

"Glad to hear it," Arturo said. He raised the pistol and shot the man through the top of the head before he realized what happened. The muted click of the report wouldn't have reached the man in the living room.

The guy slumped back against the wall in the corner. His head settled against his shoulder, lifeless eyes now staring at the toilet paper on a chrome rack.

Arturo opened the door and stepped out into the hallway again. He only checked to the left once before returning to the living room. He knew the only thing the first guy had been honest about was the number of enemies in the villa, and one of them was down the street on a call.

"Who are you?" Orasco's skinnier henchman asked as Arturo entered the room.

"Did you tell them who you work for?" Arturo pressed. He kept his pistol low, by his side, but at the ready.

"No. They took him back there first, and—"

That was all Arturo needed. He raised the gun in his right hand, let the man stare down the barrel, and then burrowed a round through the guy's nose.

The bitter scent of spent powder filled the room.

Arturo scanned his handiwork—the body in the hallway, the two out here. The one in the bathroom was definitely dead, too.

He unscrewed the suppressor, concealed the pistol in his jacket, and cracked the front door.

He peeked out through the opening, checking down the street to the left for any sign of the Americans' bodyguard.

There was no sign of him, but he could return any second.

Arturo stepped out of the villa, eased the door shut until the bolt caught in the housing, and casually walked down the sidewalk. He didn't look back until he was a half block away.

Then he turned and peered up the street. Still nothing.

At the next intersection, he turned right. It would be a long loop back to his car if that was his plan. But it wasn't.

He'd ditch the vehicle for now. Too dangerous to stick around here.

Orasco would be pleased with how efficiently that had gone, and how quickly Arturo had erased the problems. Now he needed to find the archaeologist and the two Americans.

That could prove difficult given that all three of them had just disappeared into the glowing portals at the church.

Arturo needed to investigate the site. Perhaps there was something he'd missed, a clue that could tell him what happened. Maybe it was all a trick, an optical illusion of a grand sort.

He made up his mind and opened the Uber app to call for a ride. He requested the Santo Domingo church, and when he reached the next corner, stopped to wait.

45

Antonio watched as another bar patron pushed the red door open and stepped out onto the sidewalk.

The woman was probably in her late forties and wore a black dress with a puffed skirt and matching shoes. Her dark brown hair was pulled back tight in a high bun, and her silhouette would have stopped traffic. She didn't even notice Antonio, or if she had, she ignored him and walked away down the hill.

He didn't care. There'd be time enough for women after he retired. He was still thinking about the method he'd resorted to in order to get information out of Orasco's henchman.

He detested using torture as a way to get people to talk. Waterboarding was an illegal tactic according to the Geneva Convention, but what he'd just done wasn't technically waterboarding. It had similar effects, with slightly more abject terror and filth thrown in.

It never sat well with him, no matter how bad the person was he questioned. And the only remedy that ever worked for him was a shot of liquor—usually tequila. But whiskey would work, too.

The other part of him, the part that had strapped the man's head to the toilet bowl, knew that there were probably few other ways he could have gotten the necessary information from Orasco's man. The guy was being stubborn, and would only give up the goods if pushed to the breaking point.

Orasco was dangerous. Maybe the interior minister didn't realize it, but Antonio did. He knew that guys like Orasco had slews of skeletons in his closet. But no one had ever opened the door.

Antonio started back up the hill toward the villa with a renewed sense of purpose, and a clear vision of what he needed to do next.

He doubted there was much else he could glean from the two prisoners, which meant they would need to be moved at some point. Antonio didn't expect the two agents to stick around all night long, or to provide a rotation of new guys.

He'd talk to the agents, find out what they could do, and maybe the three of them could work something out without having to involve the interior minister. If Antonio could handle it without bothering her, he'd prefer to do it that way.

People had started emerging from their homes, some wandering toward restaurants or bars or to dinner parties at friends' houses.

Antonio didn't make eye contact with any of them as they passed. A car puttered by on the street, and a scooter followed shortly after.

He stopped at the front door to the villa, looked both directions, and then stepped inside.

Antonio froze just inside the house. The tall, slender guard was lying on the couch, his head at an odd angle, eyes staring up, not seeing the ceiling.

The agent who'd been guarding him was dead, too, slumped over the coffee table where a pool of blood dripped off the surface and onto the hardwood floor.

Very few things stumped Antonio, or shocked him to the point of inaction. But he didn't know how long he stood there in the doorway, staring at the violent murder scene.

His mind snapped back to the moment, and his years of training and fieldwork kicked in.

He quickly, and quietly, closed the door, drew the sidearm from his shoulder holster, and took a step forward.

Before he did anything else, he had to make absolutely certain the killer wasn't still in the house.

Antonio crept down the hall, moving like a lion on the prowl. The floor under him didn't make a sound as he neared the body of the man lying across the bathroom threshold.

The first potential danger, logically, was in the room with the body.

He stepped over the dead agent and into the bathroom and once inside found the body of the man he'd interrogated less than twenty minutes before.

How is this possible?

He cursed himself for not getting back faster, and now he wanted that tequila even more. Antonio didn't drink on the job. He actually didn't drink much at all, but this scenario was pushing him to the breaking point.

He needed to think, to clear his head and try to come up with a plan.

Now, two agents and the two men they'd apprehended were dead. But who'd killed them?

Antonio moved back into the hallway and down to the next open door. He stabbed the pistol through the opening first, checking left then right. The bedroom, like the rest of the house, was minimally furnished with a black bedroom set that looked like it came straight off the boat from Sweden.

He tiptoed over to the closet, jerked open the door, and stepped back, ready to fire if the killer was hiding inside. But all he found was an empty storage space. No clothes hung from the rods; no shoes lined the floor.

He left the room and went across to the next one. It was decorated in a mirrored set from the first bedroom, and again, he found it to be vacant.

Just because the first two rooms were empty didn't give Antonio cause to relax. He left the bedroom and made his way back through the living room, and into the adjacent master bedroom.

He stopped just inside and looked around, but he found nothing.

No one was here. He checked the attached master bathroom just to be sure, as well as the closets, but the place was empty.

The killer had come in, eliminated everyone, and left without a trace. And he'd done it in a very tight window.

That could mean only one thing—whoever did this had been watching the building. But how? This was supposed to be a safe house, a secret location few knew about.

The conclusion was inevitable. Someone must have followed him here, which meant—more than likely—the killer had been at the church, and possibly had seen everything that happened.

Antonio knew he couldn't stay on the scene. If anyone had heard the gunshots, they would have called the cops, who would be arriving any minute if that were the case.

He tucked his pistol back inside his jacket and stepped back outside.

A quick survey of the immediate area produced no signs of the killer, unless it was a couple of girls in their early twenties walking along the opposite sidewalk, giggling about something.

Doubtful.

He started to retrace his steps back to the corner where he'd finished his conversation with Carrera but decided to go the opposite direction.

He didn't recall passing anyone on the hike back up the hill, at least no one with the look of a person who'd just killed four people in a matter of minutes.

Maybe if he hurried, he could catch them going the other way.

Antonio took off down the sidewalk, wary of everything and everyone around him as he searched for the murderer. He passed a few people but no one aroused his suspicion.

He stopped at the next intersection and looked down both streets, then straight ahead. He turned around and looked back toward the villa. Again, nothing.

The killer was gone. Antonio knew that with all the alleys and side streets, and all the businesses in the city, there were way too many places for someone to hide if they were trying not to be found.

The city was a veritable labyrinth.

Another thought occurred to him. If the Americans somehow ended up back in the church, he would need to be there to make sure they were safe. That was his primary mission. Not chasing a killer.

That could wait.

For now, Antonio needed to get back to the church.

46

Sofia Carrera had always been second fiddle, the perpetual bridesmaid, silver medalist extraordinaire.

That was about to end.

She'd waited patiently for hard work and perseverance to pay off over time, but she'd always ended up in the same spot—second place.

Her position as the interior minister of Chile had been a microcosm of her life's experience. It wasn't an insignificant role. But it wasn't the head job.

That belonged to the president, a man who had appointed her to her position as a way to check another box on the diversity, equity, and inclusion chart.

The truth was, Carrera was far better suited to lead the country than he was. He'd known the right people, greased the right palms, and back-slapped his way to the top like everyone else who attained that position.

He didn't deserve any of it.

Carrera had gone about things the right way her entire life, tried to work her way up the ladder, got good grades in school, and became a successful attorney at a powerful law firm in Santiago.

But she'd run into the glass ceiling in that career, and so had diverted course into politics, where it seemed the same problems plagued her.

The call with Antonio had been unsettling, and Orasco's actions could upset her plans to find the city, extract everything she could from it, and position herself as the next leader of Chile.

Beyond that, she would have worldwide influence, and infinite wealth. No one could touch her then.

Orasco threatened to end any chance of that happening.

The man was reckless, and power hungry. He had no designs on getting into politics or leadership roles outside his own company. But that didn't mean he didn't meddle in political affairs.

Antonio had done well to handle things the way he had, especially given the unusual circumstances surrounding the portals and the disappearance of the Americans. Not to mention the archaeologist Orasco hired.

How had he gotten there before them?

She'd probably never get that answer.

But if that was true, and the archaeologist Orasco hired knew where to go, he might be ahead of them on the next steps as well.

Carrera paced back and forth. She ran her fingers through her dense black hair as she thought, trying to decide her next move.

She hated being in the middle of a waiting game. She preferred to be a woman of action. It was one of the reasons she hated being on impotent committees, and preferred total control.

At the moment, she had no control other than over her thoughts and emotions. With everything spiraling into chaos, even those proved to be difficult to tame.

She walked over to her desk, pressed a button on the phone, and leaned toward it. "Marta. I'm going to need to fly to Cusco. Have the flight ready within the hour."

"Yes, ma'am."

47

At first, everything around Tara turned as black as the abyss she'd crossed on that bridge.

But the darkness only lasted for a second. In the next instant, she stood in the basement of the Santo Domingo church next to the altar.

A flash, then another, spewed light across the space around her.

She turned and saw Alex standing to her right. He held a red statue in his hands. To her left, the other guy gripped a statue made from an opaque white crystal.

"You," she sneered.

He hugged the crystal to his chest and took a step back. Then he put on a disparaging scowl. "How did you two get those?"

"How did you get yours?" Alex demanded. He took a step forward and put himself between the other guy and Tara. "And who are you?"

The man alternated his focus, shifting his eyes back and forth from Tara to Alex and back.

"I completed the trials of Mama Killa," the man said. He had the look of a cornered badger.

"It seems each of us completed trials," Tara said. "So, what now?"

The three exchanged suspicious glances. It would have been a Mexican standoff had they been carrying guns.

Tara and Alex weren't accustomed to being unarmed. They usually carried some kind of weapon with them. But this trip had not allowed for that convenience. So, now they stood in a stalemate.

"I got here first," the man said. "Give me your crystals."

Alex let out an exaggerated and disingenuous laugh. "Yeah, that's not going to happen, pal. Try again."

"Then what do you suggest? I am not giving you my crystal."

"Boys, let's figure this out," Tara interrupted. She stepped back into the center, cradling the blue sculpture in her left arm. She looked to the stranger. "What is your name?"

He narrowed his eyelids to slits. "Why should I tell you?"

"Because if you want to get to the Key of Inti, we're going to have to figure out some kind of compromise."

"You mean share," he clarified.

"Look. You're going to need all three of these crystals to get to the key. So, unless you're packing a gun we don't know about, I don't see you taking these from us. Which means we're going to have to work together."

The man chuffed at the suggestion. "Work together? Why would I work with you two?"

"We are—"

"I know who you are. You're dancing monkeys who claim to be archaeologists. You're nothing like me. People like you give my profession a bad name."

"Okay," Alex protested. "Let's settle down. So, you're an archaeologist?"

"Astute observation. My name is Juan Avila." He watched them, gauging their reaction. "I can tell you've never heard of me. Like most real archaeologists in the world. We're all just faceless grunts to people like you. You're nothing more than glorified treasure hunters."

Alex and Tara exchanged a disappointed glance.

"Well, I'd say we're off to a great start here," Tara said. "It sounds like maybe you got some wrong information about us."

"You work for the IAA. Your boss, and his friend, are famous around the world for their discoveries. But their work is glamorized, and they always leave a path of destruction in their wake. Not to mention a trail of bodies."

"We would prefer things not end up that way," Alex said. "But now and then, there is no choice. We're not threatening you, Juan. We're offering to work together to figure this out. People have gone missing trying to find the Wandering City. We're just trying to track them down, and if we happen to find something else, cool. We'll share the credit for the discovery."

Juan let out another scoffing laugh. "I'm sure you would love to share the credit. Someone else does all the work, and you swoop in and say you did something."

"It's not like that at all, Juan," Tara said. "You can take all the credit if you want. This can be your discovery. We're trying to get to the bottom of this mystery. We were hired by the Chilean interior minister for this, but it doesn't matter to us who get the accolades. Don't you want to see what happens if we can figure out how to get the Key of Inti and open the gates to the lost city?"

Her calm demeanor and reasonable words seemed to settle Juan a bit.

Alex stole a glance up at the window overhead. The second he'd gotten his bearings, he considered that they might be seen by someone in the viewing area on the main floor.

Fortunately, he didn't notice anyone there when he looked. But that could change, and he felt a strong need to leave lest they get trapped here.

"We can work together, Juan," Alex said, adding to his wife's statement. "But we should get out of here. Who knows how long it will be until one of the priests shows up either down here or in one of those windows up there?" He pointed above.

He could tell Juan was considering everything they'd said.

"You can stand here and deliberate if you want to," Tara hinted, "but we're getting out of here. I don't think it's a good idea to stick around here holding these things. We're going to go somewhere we can sit down and figure out the next play. You can come with us. Or you can stay here and start answering questions from the priests and maybe the local cops. Choice is yours."

She tucked the crystal under her arm like a football and started toward the stone doorframe leading out of the room.

"Hold on," Juan stopped her. "You won't be able to find anything without the journal of José Alsue, which I just happen to have."

Tara's and Alex's eyes flashed to the bag strapped to the man's back. He noticed the movement and smiled.

"So, it seems while you two hold the crystals I need, I have the diary you need."

"Yeah, so we could talk about this here," Tara said with a gravy boat of snark. "Or we can find a quiet coffee shop. And you should know, we have a journal, too. A copy of Alsue's, to be exact."

Juan's face gave away his surprise. The subtle drop of the jaw, the eyes widening, the darkening skin color. All were tells that they had him. His only chance now was to call their bluff.

But he couldn't do it here, and they knew that. They'd already been standing there in the open for too long.

"Fine," he surrendered. "There is a coffee house not far from here. Not usually many people there at this time of night. A few students from the university might be there studying, but it will be quiet and we can find a place in the back where we will not be disturbed."

Alex and Tara shared a sidelong glance. It was a look that shared an unspoken sentiment. They couldn't trust this guy, and not just because of his behavior so far—the opening of the portals, the sinister way he'd looked at them before entering, the obvious deceit in his eyes and in his words.

There was something else to him, but they couldn't put their finger on it.

"The coffee house sounds like a good plan," Alex volunteered. "From there we can figure out the next move."

"After you," Juan said, motioning to the door with his free hand.

The Americans weren't about to allow him to get the drop on them from behind.

"We go together," Tara said, tilting her head in an upward nod.

"Very well. Together."

They went through the door, Tara first, followed by the two men walking side by side. Once on the path between the stone rooms, Tara joined Alex to his right, leaving him in the middle. She stealthily reached into her pocket and took out her phone.

When the home screen appeared, she tapped on a black app icon with a white M in the center.

Tara made sure not to let on that she was doing anything with her phone. If Juan saw, it might spook him and throw this entire, imperfect plan into a tailspin.

She typed in a simple query with her right thumb and hit the Send arrow.

"Archaeologists named Juan in South America."

Tara deftly slid the phone back into her pocket as they reached the door leading into the foyer with the staircase a second before Juan leaned forward to look at her.

She smiled back at him as innocently as she could.

He looked annoyed, but also aloof.

Before they would hit the sidewalk outside the church, their AI helper back in Atlanta would have the results of her query.

48

Arturo nearly walked right into the Americans—and the archaeologist Orasco had hired.

The three stepped out of the church when he was only twenty meters from the entrance. Of course, Arturo recognized them immediately, but none of them had ever seen him. To them, he was just another local out for an evening walk.

They turned in his direction after exiting the church and continued up the hill.

He'd been walking at a steady pace, but upon hearing the door to the church open had slowed down a little to appear more casual, just in case.

His adjustment had been impeccably timed, and neither the Americans nor Juan seemed to pay any attention to him.

He fished the phone out of his pocket and pretended to be checking his text messages as the three approached. Looking down at the device, he stepped closer to the curb to give the three more room to walk by.

The female asked something about the location of a coffee shop. From the sound of it, Arturo figured they must have discussed this previously.

He took five more steps toward the church entrance, then turned halfway around while staring at his phone. With his peripheral vision, he watched them continue along the sidewalk.

Arturo tapped on the last message to Orasco, and then typed a new one.

"I have eyes on all three targets. It looks like Juan is working with the Americans."

He sent the message and then started back up the hill behind them. They'd just reached the top of the bend and were now walking down the other side.

Arturo knew there were a few coffee shops in the area—not typically busy at this time of day, but still open for those looking to re-up their caffeine supply for a long night. He'd passed two on the way back to the church. Odds were, the three would pop into one of those if that was indeed their intention.

His phone vibrated as he neared the top of the hill. He looked down at Orasco's response.

He hummed at the answer.

"Understood," he replied.

It wasn't what he'd expected Orasco to say. He thought he knew what the man would want, but he'd only been half right.

It didn't matter to Arturo. Things were back on track as far as he was concerned, which would mean a healthy payday and more contracts from referrals in the future.

He slowed down as he began the downslope to maintain a safe distance from the Americans and the mutinous Juan.

They wouldn't suspect much even if they turned around to check behind them. But he'd rather play the odds on the side of caution.

The three ducked into a coffee shop with a black metal sign hanging out over the entrance. The logo featured a golden anvil and hammer, along with the words *Blacksmith Coffee Co.* in English, which he took to mean it was owned by either a British or an American expat who'd decided to try their small business luck in the Peruvian city.

Arturo had seen the place a few minutes before—the interior

occupied by a few younger people who looked like they might be students at the university.

He slowed his pace a little more and ducked into an alley between two buildings. Knowing where the targets were, he took the opportunity to replace the magazine in his pistol with a full one, attached the suppressor to the muzzle, and then concealed the weapon in his jacket before stepping back out onto the sidewalk.

There was no sign of the group, and it had taken him less than fifteen seconds to make the changes.

He kept walking until he reached the coffee shop, then turned, opened the door, and went inside.

49

A nauseating feeling spilled into Antonio's gut.

He'd nearly made it back to the church when he saw the two Americans emerge from the entrance, along with the man he'd seen go through the first portal.

For a second, he felt relieved. Somehow, they'd made it back through the portals and into the church.

How?

There was no way he could even begin to conjure an answer for that question. All he knew was they'd made it back—from wherever they went.

But the sense of relief faded into concern when he saw a man in a windbreaker pass them, then stop to check his phone near the front of the church.

The guy was from one of the South American nations as far as Antonio could tell, but which one he didn't know. What he did know was that this guy was trouble, and probably the hitter who'd tried to kill them with the car bomb in Santiago.

Antonio ducked out of sight as the man waited in front of the church. He gave the killer a few seconds, then peeked around the corner. The man had turned around in the other direction and was following the other three.

Antonio swore under his breath and stepped back out onto the sidewalk. If the guy had been following them, it was possible he would have seen what happened in the church. The man's appearance also explained the slaughter at the villa.

The timing was far too perfect to be a coincidence.

Antonio tailed the guy from a distance, staying close to the curb in case he needed to duck down out of sight should his mark turn around. With his original plan scuttled by the abrupt appearance, he had to improvise. His mind churned with ideas, though none of them were great.

He could try to catch up to the assassin, but that might prove difficult without giving away his position and intent. The man's abilities had been a full-on, bloody display at the villa. He'd entered the building, taken out two armed agents and the two prisoners, and left without being detected.

That was the mark of a pro.

Antonio would have to proceed with caution. One wrong move, and he, and the two Americans, could end up dead.

He skirted along the sparse row of cars to his left, moving on his tiptoes to keep as quiet as possible. He didn't dare run. Even if he remained as quiet as possible, the killer would sense him—either by sound or by some other perception it seemed those types always possessed.

Closing the gap between them was important, though, so Antonio kept a brisk pace. Fast enough to get closer to the assassin, but slow enough that he could dip out of sight in a fraction of a second.

The killer disappeared over the top of the hill twenty-five yards ahead of Antonio, who picked up his speed a little to keep the guy within view until he, too, reached the crest and began the descent.

Farther ahead, the Americans and the guy from the church basement ducked into a building with a black sign over the entrance. A second after, the killer dipped into an alley to his right.

Antonio wasn't sure what the guy was doing.

Was he going to try to go around to a back entrance?

Without knowing the killer's intentions, Antonio shifted over to the right under the awning of a pottery shop. The place was closed for the day, so no one would question his loitering. And the entrance was set back into the wall, providing a place for Antonio to hide while he waited to see what the other guy was going to do.

He didn't have to wait long.

He watched from behind the pink stucco corner as the assassin reappeared on the sidewalk. The guy was walking differently this time and had his right hand in front of him.

Another curse escaped Antonio's lips. The man was armed. He knew the look. That was how someone walked when they were carrying a gun in their jacket.

Without waiting another second, Antonio stepped back out from cover and walked after the gunman. He took shelter again when he reached the alley the killer had just used—probably to prep his weapon—and leaned around the brick corner in time to see the guy disappear into the same building as the Americans.

Looking at the sign, Antonio realized it was a coffee shop.

Tara and Alex had gone in there with the other guy, but why? And why were they together? As far as Antonio knew, that guy was the enemy. He'd been protected by two hired goons, goons that worked for Manuel Orasco. So, why were they cooperating?

Had they been duped into it? Or was there more to the story?

The fact the assassin had followed them inside complicated things significantly. Would the man be so bold as to brandish a gun in public? Or would he take a more subtle approach?

Antonio arrived at the coffee house and stopped near the edge of the window. He glanced inside and noticed the Americans sitting in the back-left corner. A server approached to take their order, but there was no sign of the gunman.

He considered staying outside and observing. That way, he could get the drop on the killer if he tried to follow the others back out of the building.

That idea sank like a boulder in a lake.

The killer had walked into the back of the shop via a short corridor that housed the bathrooms, and then nonchalantly eased into a chair at a table next to them.

To make things exponentially worse, none of them seemed to pay any attention to the venomous serpent that had just slithered into their midst.

50

Alex and Tara sat in a corner at the rear of the coffee shop, both in chairs that faced the doors and the windows by the sidewalk. It was an almost unconscious practice for them now—a habit picked up from their time with Sean Wyatt.

"I'll have a double espresso," Tara said to the server in near-perfect Spanish.

"Same for me," Alex added.

The young woman taking their order looked impressed at their aggressive taste in coffee at this hour of the day. She looked young, probably a student from the local university like the handful of patrons that sat in various nooks of the café.

"And you?" the server said, turning to Juan.

He looked surprised but quickly gathered his wits. "I'll just have a coffee."

She noted the order on a pad and walked away, heading for the counter, where two other people worked to prepare the drinks for customers.

The coffee shop was warm, both in temperature and in its welcoming, cozy atmosphere. Old brass sconces hung from the black walls in keeping with the proprietor's branding. Paintings of black-smiths hammering away at anvils and stoking the fires in their forges hung from the walls, along with pictures of blacksmith tools, swords, axes, knives, and armor.

The room was set up like some of the Irish pubs Tara and Alex had visited in Atlanta. Little alcoves with stained glass windows wrapped around booths to provide privacy or intimacy for patrons, while other tables sat out in the open, such as the one where Tara and Alex were.

And of course, the intoxicating aroma of freshly brewed coffee soaked the room.

A man in a gray windbreaker sat down to Alex's left and took out his phone.

Alex glanced over at him and recognized him from the sidewalk before. He figured the guy must have gotten turned around and was supposed to meet someone here for a date.

It was easy to get lost in the maze of alleys and side streets Cusco offered.

"So," Tara said, pulling out Buford's diary from her backpack. She set it on the table and peeled it open. "We have the three crystals. From what I remember, we're supposed to use these to get to the Key of Inti."

She and Alex had stowed their two crystals in Alex's bag before ascending the stairs from the church's basement while Juan had tucked his away in his jacket, unwilling to trust the two Americans with it.

Not that they blamed him. They wouldn't have given up theirs, either.

Tara noticed their counterpart didn't offer up his journal but said nothing.

She turned the page and stopped at a drawing of a wall with three windows. The sun shone above the window in the center. Familiar symbols hung in each opening—the three crystal statues the group obtained in the portal trials.

Under the first window the words *Uku-Pacha* were written. Beneath the second, Hana-Pacha. And the third, Kay-Pacha.

"We need to know what these words mean," Tara said. "Any ideas, Juan?"

He glanced at the page. "No."

"Those are the three representations of reality according to the Incas," Alex answered. The other two looked at him, surprised at the unexpected answer.

"What?" Tara asked for clarification.

"So, Uku-Pacha represents the underground, or what they believed to be hell, also where the dead are. Hana-Pacha represents heaven where the gods live. And Kay-Pacha is the human world, or the present moment. The three realities. They're at the Three Windows Temple at Machu Picchu."

The cappuccino machine gurgled and hissed from the bar as the barista steamed the milk. A low, rumbling metallic sound rumbled through the room in perpetuity as the machine extruded the espresso through its spout into white carafes.

Juan shifted uncomfortably. Tara caught the movement and wondered if he'd known the answer and kept it to himself, or if he was annoyed he didn't know it.

Their server returned carrying a round tray with three drinks on it. She handed out the beverages, setting them on the table in front of each customer, then politely asked if they needed anything else.

"No, thank you," Alex said in Spanish. She smiled at him, said she would check on them again, and walked away.

"How in the world did you know that?" Tara asked. She gazed at her husband in the dim light of the coffee shop.

He'd lifted the espresso to his lips and started to take a sip when her question stopped him. Confusion painted across his face. "How did I know how to say thank you?"

She giggled. "No. How did you know that about the three realities, and about the Temple of the Three Windows?"

"Oh. That." He took a sip of the hot drink and shrugged. "You know I always wanted to visit Machu Picchu, well I learned a bit about it. I don't know as much about the Inca Empire as I probably should, but their city in the mountains has been an interest for a while now."

Tara smiled at him. Appreciation radiated from her eyes. "You are a fascinating man, Alex."

"Thanks." He raised his glass toward her in toast. "So are you."

Juan rolled his eyes as he picked up his coffee and took a drink.

"There isn't much after this except for the last page," Tara said.

"Which we already know refers to Devil's Point," Alex added.

"Unless that was the incorrect assumption documented by the writer."

Juan listened to the two carefully, paying close attention to the conversation.

"You think Alsue was wrong?"

"Look at the last page," she said, flipping over to the image of a rock formation pointing out from a mountain. "It only says Devil's Point. Nothing else."

"After that, Buford made a notation that he was going to Devil's Point, but that was the last place he was going to look."

"And do you think he found what he was looking for there?" Juan asked. He'd remained silent, listening to the other two since they sat down.

"I was wondering if you were going to chime in at some point," Alex drawled. He was starting to feel like Juan was the kid in school who didn't chip in on a group project but then got the grade everyone else worked for.

"It's a fair question. Clearly, this Buford did not possess the crystals. So, there is no way he could have discovered the real location of the city. He obviously assumed he would find something at Devil's Point. But this man was looking for the wrong things in the wrong places."

His logic made sense, though it still didn't give them any answers.

"That might be true," Tara half agreed. She turned the page back to the two featuring the drawing of the three windows and the notes about it. "Based on this, it seems like our next move is going to Machu Picchu. How far away from there are we?"

"Around eighty kilometers," Juan answered with the oddly specific number.

"What is that in miles?" Alex asked with a snort.

Tara had her phone out and found the answer in seconds. "About fifty."

"That doesn't sound so bad." Alex sounded optimistic.

A derisive laugh from Juan shut that positivity down in a hurry.

"What?" Alex asked.

"Fifty miles in America may not take very long to drive. But that distance to Machu Picchu is a four-hour journey. One way."

"Oh."

"On top of that, once you arrive at Aguas Calientes, you have to take a bus up to the site. Or you could walk. I would recommend the bus."

"Four hours," Tara echoed, her voice distant as she stared at the pages. "No chance we're doing that tonight."

"No," Juan agreed.

"So, what then?" Alex wondered. "We go back to the hotel for the night?"

"That would seem to be the most prudent thing," Juan said. "You two have your crystals. I have mine. So, there's no chance that any of us are going to leave without the other."

"True. Not much point in that."

"Where are you staying?" Tara asked their new ally.

Juan raised his right eyebrow at the question. "I am sure you would like to know that. Perhaps you would come visit in the night and steal my crystal. I think it best we keep our accommodations for the evening a secret."

"Okay," Alex said. "Then what do you propose? Meet somewhere in the morning?"

"Yes. We should take the train, so I suggest we meet at Poroy Station. Is nine o'clock good for you two?"

"Works for us." Alex glanced at Tara. She nodded in agreement.

"Very well," Juan said, shifting in his seat. "I will see you at the train station in the morning. Unless you two have anything else you want to discuss."

The man sounded like he wanted to get out of there in a hurry, though they weren't sure why.

"No," Tara answered. "We're good."

Alex gave her a look that said he had more to talk about, but he bit his lower lip and kept quiet.

"Then I will see you tomorrow. Get some rest. You're going to need it." He started to stand, then paused as he leaned forward. "Oh, and you should probably get some medicine for altitude sickness. The mountains can make gringos like you two very sick."

His intention was to leave them on that sour, semi-insulting note, but Juan felt a hand on his right shoulder press down hard enough to keep him in his seat.

The two Americans had seen the man in the windbreaker stand behind Juan. They hadn't thought anything of it, not even when he took a step toward their new companion.

That changed the second he pushed the archaeologist into his seat.

"Fascinating discussion," the man said. He had the look of a bird of prey, with a strong, slim jaw and matching nose. His eyes were so dark they looked like black puddles in the dimly lit coffee house.

"What are you doing?" Juan demanded. "Who do you think—"

"Señor Orasco is not happy with you, Juan." He clicked his tongue and shook his head. "You should not betray a man like that. It is a bad idea."

"Betray?" Juan tried to shake free of the man's grip on his shoulder, but it was too strong. "I didn't betray—"

"Don't. Lie. To me," the man cautioned.

Alex shifted in his chair, as if to stand. "Get your hands off him," he ordered in a grim tone.

"Stay right there." The man pulled his windbreaker to the side and revealed the pistol concealed within. "I would prefer not to have any issues here. But if necessary, I will kill you all at this table in front of a room full of witnesses who don't know what they just saw, by a man they will not recognize."

"What do you want?" Tara growled.

"I want to take this conversation outside. From there, we will see where it leads. So, all three of you, stand up."

They hesitated. He cocked his head to the side as he squeezed Juan's shoulder harder, pressing his thumb into a pressure point to produce excruciating pain.

Juan winced and started to raise his hand to pry the man's grip away.

"Don't," the stranger warned. "If you so much as blink the wrong way, I will shoot you right here. Do you understand?"

Juan nodded rapidly. He'd gone from looking like a schoolyard bully to the wimpy kid in seconds.

The man reached into his front right pocket with his free hand, drew out a few bills, and placed them on the table.

"This should cover your bill."

"Thanks," Alex grumbled.

"Get up. All of you." The stranger reached into his jacket to grip the pistol in its holster.

"Why should we do what you say?" Tara countered. "I don't think we should make it that easy for you."

It was risky to call his bluff, but she wasn't wrong too. The man was overconfident. Killing three people in cold blood in the coffee shop would be witnessed by several people, not to mention all the others who would see his face on the way out.

Based on the weapon in his jacket, he might have had enough rounds to take out nearly everyone in the room, but there would be survivors. And they would talk.

"You should do as I say because there is a chance you might live to see another day. But if you refuse, I will kill you here, slip out the back, and disappear. I will never face charges. And it wouldn't be the first time I've had to kill in a public place."

She and Alex searched his eyes and his facial expression for any signs of a lie, but they found none. Only a cold, calculating, and probably sociopathic stare.

"We're not stupid," Alex said. "You take us outside where there are fewer witnesses, then kill us. I'll take my chances in here."

"Have it your way," the gunman said. "She dies first. And I'll scream that you did it. Won't be difficult to get people to believe it. You're an American. Everyone knows how much your kind likes guns."

He pulled the pistol out of its sheath. Before he could get it completely out of the jacket, Alex stopped him.

"No. Wait."

"Alex?" Tara protested.

"We'll go with you. Just, don't shoot her."

"So, you do have some intelligence after all," the gunman taunted. "Up. All three of you. Now."

He loosened his grip on Juan's shoulder, which produced a look of pained relief from the archaeologist. That expression disappeared when the man pulled him up by the arm.

"Move. You two in front."

The gunman kept his hand on the pistol hidden in his jacket as he ushered the three toward the exit.

No one paid any attention to the four. The young people at the tables and in the booths were busy talking, checking their phones, or poring over thick textbooks.

Alex got to the door first and pushed it open. He stepped outside, his mind swirling with wild ideas about how they could make their escape, but none of it would work. And he might get Tara killed in the process.

The door closed behind them, and they stopped on the sidewalk.

"Go right," the gunman sneered.

"Where are you taking us?" Tara asked. She knew she wouldn't get an honest answer, but she'd learned that in a situation such as this, it was usually a good idea to keep the guy with the gun talking.

"You'll see. Go."

They took several steps, getting clear of the last window of the coffee shop.

"Don't take another step," a familiar voice barked from somewhere to their left.

51

The stranger spun Juan around with a quick jerk, then grabbed Tara and wrapped his forearm around her neck.

He looked out to the street and saw the Americans' bodyguard stalking toward them with a pistol raised and aimed at him.

"Drop it," the villain warned. A second later, he had his own weapon raised and fired a shot Antonio's way.

He ducked with barely a fraction of a second to spare and took cover behind a gray Kia four-door.

The bullet sailed harmlessly across the street and struck one of the other cars parked along the curb.

Alex started to make a move to free Tara from the man's grip, but the enemy sensed the play and quickly adjusted his aim while he stepped back to put both Juan and Alex between him, Tara, and Antonio.

"There's no way out of this," Alex warned.

"We'll see about that."

Antonio peeked up over the back end of the car with his weapon aimed. The gunman fired another shot, this time through the vehicle windshield. The round exited through the back passenger window and ricocheted off the cobbled stones a few feet to Antonio's left.

The bodyguard was forced to hide again.

"You," the goon said to Alex. "Take his bag."

He motioned to Juan.

"What?" Alex asked.

"Take. His. Bag. Now. Or I kill her."

He squeezed Tara's neck harder.

She'd learned how to get out of holds similar to this, but the man's grip was strong, and he kept his feet positioned at an angle that made any sort of counterattack extremely difficult.

Juan started to argue, but the stranger turned the weapon to him and fired.

The archaeologist never knew what happened.

The bullet entered through his right eye and exited through the back of his skull. A pink mist plumed in the pale moonlight and the glow of the streetlights.

Juan's legs buckled. He fell to his knees and then prostrate on the sidewalk.

The pistol's suppressor offered only a click to accompany the victim's death. And it wouldn't have alerted anyone to the killing.

Tara gasped. Alex's eyes widened.

"Get his bag. Now," the gunman demanded. "Or she dies next."

Alex didn't hesitate this time. He stepped close to Juan's body, trying not to focus on the crater in the back of his head, and grabbed the man's messenger bag.

"Now move. This way."

The killer was already dragging Tara backward down the sidewalk.

"We'll never take you to the Temple of the Three Windows!" she shouted in protest, which quickly resulted in a tighter squeeze on her neck.

Antonio popped out from behind the car again. He tried to aim at the gunman, but with Tara as a human shield, there was no clear shot.

"If you hurt her," Alex warned, gripping the messenger bag.

"Shut up and keep moving," the gunman spat.

"You won't get away with this."

"Yes. Yes, I will." The killer turned his pistol toward the coffee house window at the nearest corner. The angle was sharp, but he was only aiming for the glass. He fired a single shot. The window spiderwebbed. Then he fired one more, and the entire sheet of glass collapsed.

The sound echoed across the street. Within seconds, it was joined by the screams of the people inside the coffee house.

The stranger led the two down to the next intersection where a cab driver waited next to a park bench.

He was on his phone when the gunman approached the vehicle and turned the pistol toward him.

"Out. Now."

Shock hit the man behind the wheel, and he immediately raised his hands in surrender before opening the door slowly and stepping out of the vehicle.

"You," the killer said to Alex, "drive." He opened the door and forced Tara inside, switching the aim back to her in case Alex was looking for a moment to make his move.

Alex reluctantly walked around to the other side of the car as the driver took off running the other direction. Once behind the wheel, Alex set his and Juan's bags down on the passenger seat and closed the door.

Once the gunman was in next to Tara, he closed the door and reminded Alex of his job. "Go. Now."

Alex shifted the car into drive and accelerated away from the curb.

"Where am I going?" he asked. Alex's voice filled with vitriol. He cursed himself for being so careless as to let this guy just saunter into the coffee shop and sit down next to them. Alex had even noticed the guy, recognizing him from when they'd left the church only a few minutes before. He should have been more suspicious, more aware of the threat.

He'd reasoned that the guy was probably just lost and trying to find the coffee shop for a date. That simplification had cost him. And to make things worse, Tara was in the middle of his mistake.

He knew she wouldn't blame him. She'd take just as much responsibility for the error, but that didn't make him feel any better.

"Just drive. I'll tell you where to turn."

"Where are you taking us?" Tara asked.

To her credit, she didn't sound afraid or pitiful like most hostages would in a situation like this. Instead, anger sharpened her tone. And if this guy made one lackadaisical mistake, she'd tear him apart.

"You'll see soon enough," the gunman answered. "Now both of you be quiet. And you," he spoke to Alex, "turn left at the next light."

52

Antonio growled in frustration as the two Americans and the gunman disappeared from view around the corner.

That was just the beginning of his problems.

The patrons inside the coffee house were in a full-blown freak-out, which he completely understood. If he'd been an ordinary civilian in a country with minimal gun crime, he would probably react the same way.

As it was, he stood on the street holding a firearm. And someone had just shot up one of the coffee shop windows. To those inside who hadn't seen what was going on, the logical conclusion was that he'd done the shooting.

The only thing he had going for him was the pandemonium spilling throughout the café.

People ducked under tables. Some screamed. Others tried to run out the back by way of the little hallway in the rear. The baristas were nowhere in sight, which he took to mean they'd either already made their escape or were hiding behind the counter.

Antonio considered stowing his weapon and going into the shop to calm everyone down, tell them he was with the good guys and a special agent with the Chilean government, but that wouldn't do much, especially here in a foreign country.

He might as well pin on a plastic badge from a Halloween costume.

He'd taken cover behind the car with the punctured windshield as soon as he realized what the shooter was doing.

Cops would be on their way soon, depending on the response time, and that would cause even more issues.

Antonio crept forward to the front of the car, poked his head around to make sure the shooter didn't take off the back of his head with an easy shot, and then sprinted to the next car in the row.

Again, he carefully moved forward, crouching low, and then checked the corner where he'd seen the three disappear.

This was pointless. Every second he wasted trying not to be noticed by the customers in the coffee shop was a second farther away his charges were taken.

He needed to catch up, and quickly.

Forsaking every concern for witnesses, Antonio dashed out from behind the car and ran down the sidewalk. He reached the next corner and skidded to a stop, held his pistol up high as he pressed his shoulder against the wall, and then spun around with the weapon extended.

He swore in his mind as he saw the gunman force a cab driver to exit the vehicle. Then the shooter shoved Tara into the back seat while Alex climbed in behind the wheel.

Antonio sprinted toward the taxi, but Alex sped away before he could close half the distance.

Jogging to a stop, Antonio knew he wouldn't be able to catch them on foot.

He heard sirens in the distance whining through Cusco's narrow streets. Their response time was faster than he figured.

He stuffed the gun into his holster, buttoned his jacket, and trotted down to the corner where the cab had been only moments before.

Antonio looked down the street in the direction they'd gone, but there was no sign of them. He did hear the squeal of tires, but he couldn't pinpoint where it had come from.

What was it Tara had said? Temple of something? Windows?

She'd yelled out the protest, as if she wanted to make sure Antonio heard it. But why?

He had to get off the streets. That much he knew. It wouldn't be long before one of the witnesses in the coffee shop told the cops they'd seen a man of his description with a gun out in front of the joint.

Unfortunately, he'd gone the opposite direction of the car, and to try to get back to it on foot would take up valuable time, and also keep him in view of any police that might come by this way.

His salvation appeared at the corner as headlight beams raked across the buildings and street signs. He looked back and watched the taxi pull up to the curb with a glowing sign attached to the windshield that declared the car open for hire.

He waved at the driver, almost unnecessarily since the man had already stopped, and hurried over to the door. Antonio opened it, slid inside, and shut it hard.

"Good evening," the driver said. He was a guy who looked like he was in his mid-fifties, with a thick push broom mustache, thick face, and a pudgy nose. He wore a New York Yankees cap over a thick mat of black hair.

Antonio wasn't in the mood, nor did he have the time for pleasantries. "Church of Santo Domingo," he said curtly.

The man looked back in the rearview mirror at the passenger, brow furrowed at the request. "Are you sure? That is just up the hill over there. Would take you less than five minutes to get there on foot."

"Do you want to make some money or not?" Antonio asked, shoving a generous cluster of bills into the deposit drawer. He closed it and pushed it forward so the man could see the money. "And take the long way."

The cab driver saw the cash, and his surprised reaction, both at the offer and at the unusual request to take the long way around, said it all. It was probably the first time in his career as a cabbie that anyone had asked for that.

Despite being in a hurry, Antonio couldn't risk going back past the coffee shop and the scene of the shootout. Cops were already on their way, and showing up there would make it way too easy for him to get caught.

Sure, he would be able to slither out of whatever trouble he got into with the local authorities, but he'd prefer not to put Carrera in that uncomfortable position.

"Whatever you want, sir," the cabbie said and stepped on the gas.

Antonio looked out the back window as the guy drove away from the corner. His thoughts hung on the words Tara had said.

"You realize the church will be closed for visits now," the driver said.

"Yes," Antonio lied. He didn't know that, but he figured telling the guy he did would shut him up. He could already tell that the driver was the talkative type. Not that Antonio blamed him. Most people couldn't tolerate long minutes of silence with another person within their personal space. It was human instinct to strike up a conversation about almost anything, or nothing.

He hoped the curtness of his answer would also stifle the man's apparent need for interaction.

It didn't.

"So, are you in town for—"

"Business," Antonio answered, cutting him off and driving a spike into the conversation.

The man took the hint and didn't say anything else. He drove to the next corner and then turned right.

Antonio checked the back window again, along with all the other windows in the car.

Windows, he thought, returning to what Tara had said.

She'd emphasized the statement for a reason.

He took out his phone and opened the chat bot app, then entered a query for the Temple of the Three Windows.

The AI answered the question almost instantly, filling the screen with the answer to his question.

The Temple of the Three Windows was a structure at Machu Picchu, and as the name implied, featured three windows in a block wall.

He read the rest of the details and then closed the app, opening another to do a search for images.

Antonio scanned through the resulting pictures. The place was nothing short of spectacular, allowing views of the mountains and valley beyond the high city.

What was so special about this place, other than it being an important stop on pretty much any tourist's visit to Peru? Machu Picchu was visited by over a million people every year.

"Unless." Antonio barely breathed the word to himself.

"What?" The driver asked the question with a note of relief in his voice, as if he could finally have the conversation he'd wanted to in the first place.

Again, his passenger shut it down. "Nothing."

"Oh." The guy was clearly disappointed. He slowed down at the next stop light, paused to look for traffic, and upon seeing none turned right again.

Antonio understood. He thought he did, at least.

Tara couldn't just tell him where they were going. The gunman might have killed them both for that offense. So, she'd done the only thing she could think of, using a false protest to relay the message.

Clever girl, he thought.

He reluctantly decided to throw the driver a bone. "How long does it take to get to Machu Picchu from here?" Antonio asked.

The man's forlorn expression brightened. "Around four hours. There are trains leaving from Poroy Station every morning that can take you to Aguas Calientes. From there you take a bus up to the site, or you can walk. Though, I'm not sure why anyone would want to make that hike. It's exhausting at such a high elevation."

"Thank you," Antonio said.

Poroy Station.

If Machu Picchu was where they were going, then so was he.

The cab driver made another right, and Antonio's car came into view.

"This is good," Antonio said. "You can drop me off here."

The man looked back in the mirror again. "Are you sure?"

"Yes. My car is here."

"Oh. Okay. No problem." The driver flipped on his turn signal and pulled up to the curb between a couple of compact cars.

"Thanks," Antonio offered. "Keep the change."

"Thank you."

Antonio was halfway out of the car as the man spoke, then unceremoniously shut the door and walked purposefully toward his rental car.

The cab driver passed him on the street, driving away to find his next fare. With the money Antonio had given him, the guy could take the rest of the night off if he wanted. But with the global economy in shambles, and Peru not being immune to those effects, the guy was probably going to keep working. Every little bit helped.

Antonio stopped at his car and looked around the street at the passing cars and at the homes surrounding him. A few people were out walking around, probably to hit the bars in the area.

The sirens screamed louder, and he saw the blue lights of the police cars splashing across the homes and businesses. Within seconds, the first car appeared at the corner, slowed down for a second, and then swerved onto the street toward the church and the coffee shop on the other side of the hill.

Antonio held his breath for a second, gawking at the emergency vehicle as it passed.

The car kept going, as if the driver hadn't noticed him at all.

Antonio exhaled, walked around to the driver's side, and climbed into the rental. He knew it was going to be a difficult night to get any kind of decent sleep. Not knowing where Tara and Alex had been taken, or what the gunman's plans were for them, left him in a terrible state of emotional limbo.

He hadn't gotten to know the two Americans that well, but they seemed like good people, and they loved each other. That much was clear.

They'd been brought here to do a job by the interior minister, and now their lives were in danger.

Antonio blamed himself.

It was his responsibility to watch over them, to keep them safe. And he'd failed.

Another negative thought coursing its way through his brain was the fact he'd let down Carrera on one of his final assignments.

This gig was supposed to be easy. Being a mall cop would be more difficult by comparison. And somehow things had gone awry in a spectacular fashion.

Antonio knew he had to update the minister. But that wasn't something he looked forward to.

Like ripping off a Band-Aid, he took out his phone and sent her a message.

"Found the Americans. They've been abducted. Suspect unknown. I know where they're going. Temple of the Three Windows at Machu Picchu. I will be there in the morning to handle the situation."

After typing out the text, he stared at the message for a minute in silence, then hit the Send button. He took several deep breaths, feeling an odd tightness in his gut. Anxiety hadn't been a problem for him in the line of duty. That wasn't to say the job was stress free. There were always things and people to watch out for. An unseen foe could appear at any moment. Antonio was good with all of that. He'd accepted the risks that came with the job.

This, however, had turned things on their head—within his own head. He felt guilty, angry, frustrated, impatient.

He turned on the engine, rested his hands on the wheel, and clenched his jaw. If Tara and Alex could survive the night, he would find them, and he would set things right.

53

Tara and Alex sat on the cold concrete floor in what had been an office at some point.

Alex had driven them to an abandoned knitting mill on the edge of the city. When they arrived, the gunman forced them into the derelict structure and then into the old office.

A metal desk still sat near one of the walls, but the chairs and all the other furniture were gone.

The only light they received came from the moon through a square window in the wall to their right. They would have considered using that as an escape, but there were bars over the glass. There was no way in, or out.

The gunman had barricaded them inside the room and remained outside. He'd told them to wait there, though he hadn't mentioned what, or who, they were waiting for.

The minutes turned into an hour. Then two. And their captor hadn't returned.

They both stood up numerous times to pace around and keep themselves awake, but as the night dragged on, fatigue started to grasp at them. Gravity pulled their eyelids together, and sitting on the floor against the wall in each other's arms, both of them dozed off for a few minutes at a time before inevitably waking again due to the untenable conditions.

Neither said much the first hour, except for Alex telling Tara everything was going to be okay. But after the first four failed attempts at sleeping, both knew that they weren't going to get any rest in this place.

"Who do you think we're waiting on?" Tara asked at the beginning of their second hour in the dumpy office.

Alex looked up at the cracked and falling ceiling tiles, then the dingy gray walls. Even after all this time, the smell of stale cigarettes still lingered from a period when smoking at work was common practice.

"I don't know," he said with a shake of his head. "If I had to guess, I'd say the guy's boss. Your guess is as good as mine for that one."

Tara sat on the floor with her knees pulled up to her chest and her hands interlocked around them. She stared at the far wall, her eyes distant and vapid.

"What was it like?" she asked.

The question was vague, and Alex didn't know what she meant.

Before he could inquire, she clarified. "Through your portal. What was it like? There were three trials. I assume yours was different from mine."

"Oh." He looked thoughtful for a second, sitting next to her staring down at the dusty floor. Bits of debris from the crumbling ceiling littered the surface. "I heard a voice while I was there. A woman. She spoke in a cryptic way. Didn't say much, actually. Only that faith and wits would pass the trial."

"Wits," Tara mused. "Good thing you went through that one, I guess."

"What about you?" Alex asked. "What was yours like?"

She didn't answer immediately.

"It's okay if you don't want to talk about it. I just figured—"

"No, it's fine, actually. It was weird. My trials were faith and courage."

"You've always been braver than me," he confessed.

"I don't know about that."

"It's true. You're always the one willing to take risks that I shy away from."

She shrugged. "The fear I had to face was a giant spider. It trapped me in a pit, and I had to kill it."

"Whoa. I know you hate those things."

Tara nodded. "Yeah. And when I say giant, I mean it was bigger than me. Like some kind of ultra-arachnid. I don't think those things exist in the real world. It was as if the cave I entered would conjure the biggest fear of whoever went in there."

"That's messed up."

"What did yours make you do?" she asked.

He inhaled deeply. "Well, mine was definitely weird. I had to keep my eyes closed the entire time in order to see. I figured that was the faith component. When I opened them, it was completely black in there. Like, beyond dark."

"Same with mine."

"Strange. And there was a bridge crossing this immense chasm. It looked like a bottomless pit. Did yours have that, too?"

"It did."

"I guess all three portals must have had that component. But I didn't have a spider. In my trial, the bridge moved in pieces, and I had to figure out how to get across without falling. It wasn't easy."

"And yet here you are. Clever as always."

"I don't know about that, but I'm glad I made it out. All I could think about the entire time was getting back to you."

They turned and met each other's gaze.

"I guess it looks like we're going to get to visit Machu Picchu," she said, cracking a smile.

"Yeah. I just wish that guy hadn't taken our phones. Would be cool to at least get some pictures."

Tara blurted an unexpected laugh.

The door creaked open and dim light poured in from the hallway outside. Two silhouettes stood in the entrance. One belonged to the man who'd brought them here. The other was wider and shorter.

Their captor stepped in first, and the other followed.

"So, these are the two who have been causing problems?" the shorter man asked.

He wore tan slacks and a navy-blue turtleneck that did nothing for his silhouette.

"Yes, sir," the hired goon confirmed.

Two other figures moved into the doorway behind them.

So, that's what we were waiting on, Alex realized. *Reinforcements.*

"What do you want with us?" Alex demanded.

The plump man took a step closer. The faint rays of moonlight piercing through the window barely touched his fleshy face.

"Do you have any idea who I am?" the man asked.

They shook their heads simultaneously.

"I am Manuel Orasco. I suppose since the two of you are from America, you wouldn't have heard of me. I am a businessman. That is all you need to know."

"You speak decent English," Alex said in Spanish.

"Ah. And you with Spanish, I see."

"What do you want with us?" Tara interrupted. "You have the crystals."

"Yes. And both journals. But I am, as I said, a man of business. Not history. You two, on the other hand, are experts in that field. Your expertise may prove useful when we arrive at Machu Picchu. So, I am keeping you both alive for now. Just in case."

They both noticed how he said the words *for now.*

"We leave in the morning. I expect both of you to cooperate. If you do, perhaps there will be a place for you in my new empire. If not, well, there are many long drops at Machu Picchu. And accidents do happen."

54

MACHU PICCHU

The Andes Mountains touched the heavens in nearly every direction. White clouds raced across the blue sky, some low enough to wash over the mountaintops and re-form on the other side.

The bus rumbled and squeaked as it bounced along the rough road leading up to Machu Picchu.

The springy seats reminded Alex and Tara of when they were kids traveling in a school bus.

This vehicle wasn't all that dissimilar to the ones from their memory. It had been painted a gaudy light red color that made the thing look like a deformed fire truck.

Orasco sat two rows ahead of Tara and Alex. Two of Orasco's men separated them from the tycoon, and the one who'd abducted them sat one row back, directly behind Alex.

Tara and Alex stared out the windows at the spectacular views through the jungle growing alongside the dirt and gravel road. They'd been forced to sit separately on either side of the aisle. Orasco was paranoid about letting them sit together.

They didn't know if he overestimated their capabilities or simply exercised an abundance of caution. But it irritated both of them they couldn't at least enjoy the ride up the mountain together before they were probably executed.

Even with that future likely hanging over them, they didn't appear to be worried.

Neither wanted to die, but they didn't fear it either. They'd seen enough, been through crucibles most couldn't imagine, that forged a respect for death—but not a fear of it.

Alex had started to say something to Tara as the bus lurched out of the pickup area, but Orasco had ordered them to keep their mouths shut.

So, they'd been left to their individual thoughts.

They weren't aware that private charters were available for buses up to the ancient city but also weren't surprised one had been arranged. Orasco, at least on the surface, appeared to be a powerful and wealthy piece of work.

He'd likely bribed one of the bus operators to hold one for him and his group, and paid a high price for it.

If that's how it went down, the man himself hadn't brokered the deal. He'd kept his eyes on them since they left Cusco earlier that morning.

The drive had been miserable. Four hours sitting in the back of a passenger van, dehydrated, and exhausted from the lack of sleep the night before.

Tara and Alex both hoped to sneak in a few hours of sleep on the long train ride to Aguas Calientes, but in the van catching some shut-eye had been nearly as difficult as sleeping on the floor in the knitting mill.

Up ahead, they saw the bus drop-off on the right at the base of Machu Picchu's iconic stone walls. On the opposite side of the turn-around, lines of queue rails stood empty. Later on in the day, the corrals would be full of visitors waiting to take the bus back down the mountain.

The only people here were some of the workers and guides. Other than that, Orasco's group was the first to arrive, which was no accident.

Orasco wasn't stupid. He'd planned the entire thing, including the group's departure at an unholy hour of the morning to get here just before sunrise. They wouldn't have much time before other buses started to show up. Then crowd control would become a huge problem and could turn into a full-blown international incident if Orasco weren't careful.

There would still be a few guides hanging around, but they could be contained with minimal effort if necessary.

The bus driver slowed to a stop then opened the door. "Welcome to Machu Picchu," he said with a tentative smile. He descended the steps and walked out onto the path leading up to the city.

"Up," Orasco ordered.

Tara and Alex stood, though they didn't want to obey the man.

They shuffled to the bus exit with the two guards Orasco brought leading the way. He and the other guy brought up the rear behind Tara and Alex.

The group exited the bus and passed the driver, who waved to them, still showing off a bright, toothy grin as they walked by. As soon as they were a few yards ahead of the bus, the man climbed back in, closed the door, and accelerated away.

The two Americans watched, despondent, as the bus drove around the circle and then back down the road.

"Keep moving," Orasco barked. "We don't have much time. Take us to the temple."

Alex and Tara were too tired for witty comebacks at this hour of the day, and with such little sleep the night before.

The guards in front of them had studied the layout of the site on the drive from Cusco and knew exactly where they needed to go.

Orasco and his men hadn't gotten much rest, either, but they didn't seem as tired—perhaps it was feeling the rush of power over other humans that invigorated the evil.

He remained behind the two hostages as the procession marched to a set of steps and then began the ascent.

The sun peeked over the mountaintops to the east, rays spraying across the stacked stone dwellings.

It was every bit as incredible as Alex had imagined, minus being held at gunpoint. Still, he caught himself staring at the mountains, the deep valleys, and the design of the ancient structures surrounding them. They walked for a few minutes, passing the houses people had called home centuries before along with gathering places that could have been used for ceremonies or celebrations.

The group wound their way through the maze of the old city until they reached a high point where a structure made of larger stones stood alone, separated from the other buildings.

It was built over a collection of terraces that staggered down the slope like giant steps with grass growing on the top of each. Most of the walking areas and open-air rooms had grass floors.

"Hard to believe this entire place was covered in jungle until 1911," Alex remarked. It was the first time either of the Americans had spoken in a while.

"Shut up," Orasco snapped. "I don't want to hear another word out of you unless I ask for it. Understood?"

Alex nodded silently.

The guards in front stopped just outside the entrance to the building. The stones were massive. They weren't all the same exact shape, but the masons who'd put them here long ago made each one fit perfectly to create the desired overall architecture of the temple.

"This is it," one of the guards said as he turned halfway around to face Orasco.

The boss stepped past the hostages and into the doorway, leaving only the assassin from the night before.

Tara and Alex had heard Orasco refer to him as Arturo a couple of times, though that name didn't sound familiar. The killer carried Juan's messenger bag, as well as another backpack that contained the two crystals the Americans had claimed.

Orasco stepped into the temple, looked right, then left. He almost appeared to be admiring the handiwork and precision crafted into the temple walls. A cubed stone pillar stood in the center, with several others of similar size laying on their sides next to it. Other smaller blocks were arranged around the front of the plinth toward the front of the building.

Orasco walked around the pillar and over to the wall opposite the door. He peered through the center of three near-perfect trapezoid windows.

After five seconds, he spun around and motioned for the rest of the group to enter. The guards shoved Tara, which sparked an instinctual and immediate response from Alex. He stepped toward the guy who'd done the shoving and started to raise a fist when his counterattack got cut short by an elbow to the kidneys.

He huffed and dropped to his knees, the throbbing pain coursing through him instantly. Tara looked back and reached for him, but the other guard cut her off and continued coaxing her into the temple.

"We don't have time for bravado, Mr. Watson," Orasco said. "Not to worry. It will all be over soon."

Arturo and the second henchman lifted Alex up by the armpits, forcing him to stand on wobbly legs. They dragged him over to where Orasco stood by the windows and let him go.

Alex doubled over, coughed a few times, and then stood up straight, as if to defy the men the pleasure of seeing him weakened.

"What do we do now?" Orasco asked, crossing his hands over his waist.

Tara and Alex looked at each other, then back to the man without saying a word.

Orasco sighed, already exasperated at the waste of time. He drew a hunting knife he'd kept sheathed inside his suit jacket and took a step toward Tara.

"Let me make this simple. Tell me what we are supposed to do here, or you get to watch me cut off pieces of your pretty little wife."

55

"If you hurt her—" Alex said.

"You'll be next," Orasco finished. The guard holding Tara by the arm wrapped his forearm around her neck and held her tight.

She squirmed, struggling to free herself, but the guy knew what he was doing. She couldn't wriggle enough to even head butt him in the face.

Orasco stepped close to her and dragged the blade tip down her right cheek from the corner of her eye.

"Okay," Alex surrendered. "Just don't hurt her."

"I had a feeling you'd see things my way," Orasco mused. "Tell me what we do with those crystals."

Alex had only started to recover his breath, and he still found it difficult to take air deep into his lungs, though the elevation wasn't making that any easier.

"You take the three crystals and put one in each of the windows. If you weren't so lazy, you'd have noticed that in the journals by now."

Orasco almost seemed amused by the barb. "I've built enormous businesses, am very wealthy, and can turn the tide of politics at my whims. That doesn't come easy, boy. And certainly not to someone who is lazy."

He looked to the other guard holding Alex at gunpoint. "Cover the entrance. I don't want any curious early birds poking around here."

The guard obeyed, returned to the doorway, and disappeared around the corner.

He turned to Arturo. "Place the stones according to how it is prescribed in Alsue's journal."

The assassin responded with a curt nod and set the two bags down that contained the crystal sculptures. He opened Juan's bag first and set the opaque crystal down on the hard-packed turf. Then he removed the other two crystals, each wrapped in rags to keep them from chipping during the journey. He unwrapped them and then took the journal out of the bag.

It only took thirty seconds for him to find the right page and match the symbols in the book with the carved statues at his feet.

Arturo stood, holding the first two, and walked over to the window on the left.

Tara and Alex held their breath as he carefully stood the carving upright in the window.

Sunlight glistened through it, but nothing happened other than a blue-hued beam radiating above them.

Arturo looked back at Orasco, who simply nodded—encouraging him to continue.

The killer stepped over to the center window and placed the statue Alex had recovered on the sill.

A red ray of light glowed from the statue, merging with the other. The two rays split off in different directions, now a dark purple.

Arturo returned to the last crystal and picked it up. He carried it over to the last window and paused. A cool, moist breeze blew over the mountain, tousling his thick hair. He released a breath and set the statue into the window.

He stepped back from it as the sun filtered through the pale crystal.

Beams of blue, red, and white angled in from each window and merged to become one lavender ray of light hovering eight feet above the ground.

Every pair of eyes in the group followed the new beam to the pillar in the center of the temple.

"Amazing," Orasco muttered.

He and the others watched as the ray of light seemed to hit something in the air above the plinth. Then, appearing from nothing, a shape emerged from the top down, as if melting into view from another reality.

At first, no one knew what shape was being created. At first there were only squiggly points, one in the center and two on either side. Then the top of a circle, more spikes, and then eyes.

By the time the new, golden crystal was halfway formed, Alex and Tara already knew what it was. The Key of Inti.

Everyone stared in awe at the stunning display until the image of the sun god was complete. Then, abruptly, the beams of light from the other keys disappeared, and the crystal sun remained alone, hovering over the pillar.

"Watch them," Orasco ordered, his eyes remaining fixed on the sculpture.

Arturo took a step toward Alex and drew his pistol. He kept it level around his hip, the sights pointed at Alex's torso.

Alex paid him no attention. He was mesmerized by the crystal sun, as was Tara.

"Only two may enter," a voice said, as if it came from the crystal itself. Unlike before, this voice was masculine, and sharp.

The guard whipped his head around, searching for the source of the voice. For a second, his grip on Tara loosened, but it wasn't long enough for her to free herself. He quickly recovered and squeezed harder than before, nearly cutting off her windpipe.

Arturo heard the voice, too, but he only checked to his sides briefly, knowing it was impossible that anyone had come into the temple without him noticing. The only obstruction was the pillar, slightly blocking the view to the door from his angle.

The voice only stalled Orasco for a second before he continued over to the base of the pillar and the massive block to the right of it.

He understood now why the stones had been laid in such a way. He stepped up onto the block and over to the pillar in the center.

Orasco gazed at the gleaming golden crystal as sunlight filled it, causing it to pulse and radiate points of yellow light down onto the temple floor.

He reached his hands up then held them aloft, pausing for a moment.

Alex and Tara could see the lack of conviction on the man's face, but that was quickly overridden by his pride.

Orasco brought his hands together and touched both sides of the crystal sun.

Nothing happened, which was both a relief, and a disappointment.

Had the man been transported into an alternate reality, the resulting confusion might have given the Americans a second of opportunity to get the drop on their captors. Instead, Orasco stepped down from the block, holding the sun in both hands.

He faced Tara and Alex, grinning devilishly from ear to ear.

"Now," he said, "nothing can stop me from opening the gates to the city."

"I wouldn't be so sure about that, Manuel," a familiar male voice said from just behind him.

Orasco turned toward the door, and his eyes widened with fear. A man stood just inside the doorway wearing faded blue jeans, hiking boots, and a drab green Columbia sports jacket.

He held a pistol in his right hand, with the barrel aimed at Orasco's head. Behind him, the guard's legs were within view, unmoving and sprawled out on the turf beyond the temple entrance.

Alex and Tara couldn't believe it, despite Tara's desperate attempt to convey their destination.

Antonio had figured it out.

56

Tara felt the man's arm around her neck go slack again, this time significantly more than the first time. Antonio's abrupt appearance had taken everyone by surprise, but she was ready when the opportunity presented itself.

She snapped her head back and felt the man's cheek smash into her skull. Before he could react, she stomped on the top of one of his feet with her heel, instantly breaking his arch. The arm loosened further as he leaned forward in pain—straight into her right elbow.

His nose crumpled against the hard bone. Blood gushed out, and he reached to his face out of sheer instinct.

Tara, on the other hand, reached for his pistol, grabbed it by the barrel, and twisted hard, wrenching the man's wrist into a nearly impossible angle. She heard a snap from his finger caught in the trigger guard.

He yelped and let go of the weapon, which she immediately turned around and aimed at the guy.

Alex's reaction was just as fast as Tara's.

He dropped one foot behind the other, closing the gap between himself and Arturo as the assassin switched his aim from Alex to the new interloper.

Alex moved like lightning.

As he stepped back, he twisted around and whipped his left fist into Arturo's jaw. The killer's head snapped to the side, and he tried to recover by turning the firearm Alex's way.

Alex anticipated the move and used his right hand to grab the gun and yank it down toward the ground.

The suppressor spit two rounds, then a third, but the bullets burrowed harmlessly into the ground.

Arturo shifted his weight and dropped down to one knee to get lower leverage against his opponent. The move threw Alex off balance, and he tumbled over in a roll. He didn't let go of the gunman's weapon, though, and his momentum caused Arturo's left foot to slip as he tried to pull against the weight.

The pistol's muzzle puffed two more times, sending more hot metal into the temple's floor.

They rolled over, grappling with each other for control of the firearm.

Tara shifted her stance so she could see what was happening, but she couldn't take the gun off the guard. The man was wounded but even so could be a threat if she were to lose focus for one second.

Alex rammed his right elbow into Arturo's rib cage. The man winced but replied with a knee to Alex's left thigh and then an elbow of his own to the gut.

Alex weakened for a split second, and the assassin tore the gun from his hands, albeit pointed in the wrong direction.

He tried to roll over to get a clear shot, but Alex wouldn't relent. He wriggled his left hand free and wrapped it around the man's head, then twisted to the right and looped his legs around Arturo's torso so that his ankles joined.

Arturo raised the gun to fire a shot, pointing the suppressor just by his left ear. Alex ducked to the other side as the man squeezed the trigger three times.

Tara ducked down and quickly moved to position the wounded guard between her and the fight on the ground. Orasco watched, while Antonio kept one eye on him and one on Alex.

Arturo tried to switch the gun to the other side of his head, but Alex pulled back on his chin while pulling his legs back and squeezing.

The maneuver sent a painfully awkward pressure through Arturo's spine. His finger tensed on the trigger, but before he could fire another shot, a pop came from his neck, and Arturo's body went completely limp.

Alex felt the neck break and the disturbing vibration from the popped bone resonate through to his fingertips.

He hadn't had a choice. It was him or the other guy.

Arturo had chosen his path.

Alex let him slump to the ground and then stood to step away from the body. He looked to Tara first. "You okay?"

She nodded. "Yeah. I'm good. You?"

"I'm fine."

They both turned to face Antonio.

"Nice timing," Tara quipped.

Antonio cracked a thin smile. "I wasn't going to mess up my last gig. That wouldn't sit well with me the rest of my life. I'm a perfectionist."

The two Americans grinned back at him.

"What should we do with these two?" Alex asked.

Orasco started laughing. It was a sinister, diabolical sound. "You know I'll never see a minute in jail. And what laws have I broken, anyway? None. Not to mention, you're out of your jurisdiction."

"I'm not a cop," Antonio said.

"Even better. You kill me, you're killing a man in cold blood. I don't think any of you three have the stomach for that."

Orasco faced the door with Antonio still blocking his path. "Now, get out of my way."

Antonio refused to move.

"I said—"

A click came from behind Antonio. Orasco's throat began leaking blood an instant after.

He dropped the crystal on the turf to his left, forsaking it to grasp at the hole in his neck. There would be no stopping the flow. The wound had severed the artery, leaving him scant seconds before he would lose consciousness, and then his life.

Orasco searched for his killer as the statue wobbled and then fell over a few feet away from Tara.

He saw a figure behind the Americans' bodyguard, but his vision blurred. He blinked rapidly as the shadows crept in around the corners of his eyes.

"So...fia?" He fell to his knees, teetered for a few seconds, and then fell face down.

Antonio spun around and saw his employer standing next to the guard he'd eliminated before.

"Minister Carrera?" Alex said, trying to make sure he was seeing correctly.

"Minister?" Antonio echoed. "You shouldn't be here."

"Yes, I know, Antonio. But I thought you could use a little backup. Can't have you getting killed on your last assignment."

He lowered his pistol, still staring at her in disbelief.

"Take this and cover him," Tara said quietly to Alex. He took the weapon from her and watched as she took two steps over to the crystal.

She bent down and picked up the object. The sun was roughly the size of her head, with the squiggly rays jutting out at seven inches each, the tips slightly blunted.

"Great work, Tara," the interior minister said. She stepped forward into the temple. "I must say, I had a difficult time believing any of this was real." She waved a hand around as if to indicate the mysterious occurrences of the last few days. "But now, we have the Key of Inti. And just in time for the solstice tomorrow."

Tara and Alex both thought it strange the woman wasn't lowering her weapon. The breeze blew across the mountain and tickled Carrera's ponytail. It shivered on the top of her red Marmot windbreaker.

She'd dressed for a hike and looked like a fish trying to run through the desert out of her normal business attire.

"You can put your gun down, Minister?" Alex said. "If you don't mind."

"I will," she replied. "When you give me the key."

57

"What?"

Alex and Tara's relaxed postures tensed simultaneously. They'd thought the battle was over, the mission accomplished, with the only piece left to travel to Devil's Point and unlock the gateway to a whole new world.

All of that evaporated as they realized what was going on.

"It was you all along," Tara said. "You were pulling the strings the entire time."

"A little," Carrera admitted. "I didn't hire the man Alex killed over there. That was Orasco's doing. But yes, I set all of this up. Always hedge your bets. I was the one who brought Orasco on board. He thought he had a mole in my office. His ambition and greed blinded him. I didn't fully trust him, though, which is why I brought you two down once I had a second journal. It was I who led Orasco and his archaeologist to Alsue's book. But with Buford's, I was able to pit you against Orasco. Either way, I win."

Antonio listened to her, his head going back and forth between the Americans and his employer.

"For what?" Alex asked. "You want access to the city? Why?"

"Because my entire life I have been the bridesmaid. So, I decided to take matters into my own hands. I couldn't rely on anyone to help me. And fate certainly wasn't going to give me what I deserve."

"You deserve to be in prison," Tara said.

Carrera snorted. She grinned derisively as she shook her head. "Don't you know? People at my level of power don't go to prison, Tara."

"You killed your husband." Antonio cut in. "Didn't you?"

For a second, the minister took her eye off the Americans and looked at him. "Oh, don't act like you didn't know. And don't pretend you're a saint, Antonio. I've seen your dossier. I know your past. I know the things you've done. Your ledger is far bloodier than mine."

Antonio couldn't believe it. And the look of utter betrayal on his face seemed to darken the bright morning sky.

Carrera returned her focus to the Americans, but in the moment she'd looked away, Tara lifted the crystal above her head and over a stone block at her feet.

"What are you doing?" Carrera asked. She almost sounded amused.

"You are not taking the key," Tara groused.

The minister's expression soured. "Is that what you think? I have waited my entire life to be the one on top. Under my leadership, the world will become an orderly, fair place to live. Everyone will be equal. No rich or poor. Don't you want that?"

"Of course, you'll be rich, though." Alex countered. "Right? And what you're describing isn't leadership. It's control. You want to rule humans like they're your pets."

"But think of how happy everyone will be." The look in her eyes said that she truly believed that.

"I've heard this kind of talk before. Fairness. Equality. They're just buzzwords to push the agendas of those who seek power. They tried that in the Soviet Union. Ask those people how much they loved all the fairness and equality for almost a century. And at the end of the day, the ones in charge had the biggest homes, the best cars, lavish lifestyles. Just like in any system. The only difference was, the people couldn't climb out of that one."

"You sound so American, Alex. Always believing that the American Dream is real and attainable. Only by being ruled can people be truly happy. When the responsibilities of life are taken away, they are free to pursue anything they want."

"Except meaning," Tara said.

"What?"

"The pursuit of meaning, what you give to the world and becomes your history. What you propose will take away all of that, and as well as the value people give to others, and themselves."

Carrera shook her head vehemently. "No. Enough of this. Give me the crystal."

"No."

"Fine." The minister turned her pistol, aiming it at Alex. "You already saw how good my aim is. Care to see it again?"

"Don't," Tara protested, fear rising from her gut.

"It's okay, Tara," Alex said. "Don't give it to her."

Carrera's nostrils flared with every angry breath. "If you break that crystal, humanity will be lost. Do you want that on your conscience, Tara? We are talking billions of lives here."

Tara knew what would happen if she surrendered the key. The moment Carrera and her bodyguard took it, they would kill the Americans and leave their bodies in the temple. The minister would tell everyone that a couple of gun-toting Americans had been involved in a gunfight with a Chilean businessman and his security detail, and that everyone had been killed.

People would believe the story. Few would ask why she'd been there in the first place. But any who did would be dubbed as conspiracy theorists, and immediately discredited. It was a tried-and-true trick, one she'd used more than a few times with the media, who always fell for it.

There was no way the woman was going to let them leave here alive. Tara figured the minister's next pitch was that they could join her if they just gave up the key. That she would let them live. But Tara wasn't stupid. She knew the truth. She and Alex were loose ends. And loose ends always had to be cut.

"People want to be free to choose their own path," Tara said. "Not ruled. No one should tell others what they can or can't say, or do for a career, or what they can eat, or what to drive, or where to live. That is what life is about. The freedom to go your own way."

"Fleetwood Mac reference," Alex whispered.

Tara cracked a smile. Even staring into the hollow eyes of the reaper, he still had that wit.

"I've had enough of this," Carrera snapped. "Give it to me. Or you watch him die."

Tara shook her head. "No."

Her hands moved forward and down.

Alex saw the movement to his right as if in slow motion.

Carrera did, too, and out of an instinctually perceived threat, twisted the gun to her left to retrain it on Tara.

The crystal slipped from Tara's fingertips and smashed into the stone block. It shattered into thousands of pieces. As the shards sprayed around on the turf, each one seemed to glisten with a spark as bright as the sun.

"You—" Carrera shouted.

The muted puff of a suppressor echoed almost gently around the temple.

Tara's eyelids opened wider. She stared at the minister, unbelieving.

Alex tore his eyes from Tara and looked to his left at the minister.

Blood trickled from a hole in her right temple. Her eyes remained fixed on Tara, though Carrera no longer saw her.

She fell over sideways and hit the stone floor with a thump.

Tara and Alex stared in disbelief at Antonio. His arm was extended to where Carrera had been standing. Smoke oozed out of the muzzle and dissipated in the breeze.

He lowered the gun, but his eyes remained on the minister.

"Antonio?" Alex said. He still wasn't sure whose side the bodyguard was on. "You okay?"

Antonio allowed an absent nod. "I spent years protecting that woman. I was loyal. I did everything to keep her safe." He pulled his eyes away from her and looked at the two Americans. "That was a brave thing you did. And you destroyed any chance at finding the lost city, and everything that comes with it."

"Maybe it's hidden because people shouldn't have access to something like that. Humans aren't ready for it. A place like that, they would just try to strip it of all its riches like we've done to everything else."

Antonio acknowledged with a thoughtful bob of his head.

Alex bent down and picked up a shard of the fractured key. It glimmered in the sunlight, spraying splintered rays onto his hand.

"Would have been cool to find it, though," he said, his tone reverberating the reflective moment.

"Yeah," Tara agreed. "It would."

She took a step toward the bags on the ground and pulled Buford's journal out of the backpack. She looked over it as if poring through a school yearbook.

Something caught her eye that she hadn't noticed before. She stared at the page, and the drawing of the rock formation at Devil's Point stared back at her, but in a light. Drawn to appear far away, a mountain at the other end of the valley rose to the middle right side of the page.

"Maybe we won't get to see the Wandering City. But we can at least visit the gate."

58

PATAGONIA

The sun climbed higher in the blue sky over the mountains of the Patagonia. In a few minutes it would reach its zenith and then begin the descent back toward the horizon in the west. From then on, the days would get shorter here in the Southern Hemisphere.

Tara and Alex gazed across the mountaintops. They stood under the shade cast by a curved, jagged rock outcropping. Snow swirled around their feet. The wind cut through their coats like the daggers of winter.

The snow motes gleamed and sparkled like powdery diamonds dancing in the air all around.

"How much longer?" Tara asked.

Alex pulled up his coat sleeve and checked the time. "One more minute."

They'd been there for almost an hour. There was only two chances a year at this, and if they'd been even a few minutes late, they would have missed this window.

"You ready?" She looked at him. If he could have seen her eyes through the sunglasses, he would have noticed the admiration in them.

"Yeah. I mean, it's probably not going to work. But it's worth a try."

"And if it doesn't, we got to spend the solstice in one heck of a cool spot."

He grinned behind the scarf covering his mouth and looked back down at his watch.

"Here goes nothing," he said.

The sun reached its peak with nearly imperceptible movement.

Suddenly, the swirling glitter of snow stopped. Millions of tiny flakes suspended as if time itself had halted.

"Whoa," Tara muttered.

"Only two may enter," a woman's voice breathed across their ears. "Present the Key of Inti, and enter the great city."

"We destroyed the key," Tara said, looking around for the unseen face.

"Then none will enter."

Alex took a step forward. His boots crunched in the hard snow. "A woman with evil ambitions sought the city for her own. It was better for the human race that the key be destroyed than to let her or anyone like her have it."

"We brought a piece of it," Tara said. She took off the glove on her right hand, unzipped her coat pocket, and pulled out a little wooden box. She held it out and opened the lid.

The shard inside was only two inches long and half as wide. But when the sun touched it, the crystal reflected the light in every direction, turning the icy diamonds around them the color of brilliant gold.

"You have made a great sacrifice," the voice said. "But without the key, none may enter."

The two expected that and nodded their disappointed acknowledgment.

"We figured," Alex said. He couldn't describe how absolutely strange it felt to be speaking to the ghostly, disembodied voice.

"However, because you chose the difficult path, I will give you a gift."

"Gift?" Tara wondered. "What kind of gift?"

"Anything the city may provide. The only exception is, I cannot return to you those who have gone to where dead things stand."

Alex and Tara looked at each other, uncertain what that meant. Though they both believed it meant the voice would not resurrect the dead if that was their request.

The statement did give them an idea.

"There was a man looking for the city, but he disappeared."

"Many have done so."

"Yes, but he vanished recently. If he is still alive, can you return him?"

The voice didn't reply immediately, as though it was considering the unusual ask.

"It is done."

The two immediately started looking around for the lost treasure hunter.

"Where is he?" Tara asked. "I don't see him."

"You will find him in the forest near Devil's Point. As for you two, you have not sought the city for glory or fortune. Perhaps the people of Earth have hope for the future if there are more like you."

Suddenly, the snow gleaming around them fell to the ground. The golden light radiating from the crystal shard disappeared.

The wind was gone, leaving the two standing in the warm rays of the noonday sun.

"I guess we should get to that forest," Alex suggested.

"Yeah."

THE SUN HAD DIPPED to just above the mountains in the west. Though there was still ample daylight, the forest canopy impeded much of it, casting a shadowy darkness throughout.

Alex and Tara had trekked back down the mountain and then made their way across the valley to the place Buford said he was going in his journal. The dense forest was just below the rock formation that pointed to the peak where they'd been hours before during the height of the summer solstice.

They'd started at the bottom of the forest near the road and worked their way up, going back and forth. When they reached the center of the woods, the two saw something sticking out from behind a boulder twenty yards away.

"Is that a leg?" Alex asked, uncertain he wanted the truthful answer.

"Sure looks like it."

"Do you think the rest of the body is attached?"

"We probably should have clarified that in our request."

"Right."

The two cautiously walked over to the boulder, ever watchful that something or someone might try to get the drop on them.

But nothing disturbed them, and the forest itself seemed to go silent as they rounded the edge of the boulder and discovered a man lying on the ground with his eyes closed.

Before either of them could ask if he was alive, his head rolled to the side and then back. He blinked several times and then rubbed his eyes. Even in the shade of the trees, the daylight was blinding.

"Michael Buford?" Alex asked.

The man squinted. He planted his right palm on the ground and pushed himself up into a sitting position. The act came with a groan.

"Who are you two?" Buford asked. "What in the Sam Hill happened?"

"I'm Tara, and this is Alex," she said. "Do you remember anything that happened?"

He blinked hard a few more times and rubbed his head, scrubbing the brown hair. "I... was up on the bald above the meadow. Then... I heard a voice. It was like it was calling to me. I followed it into the forest, then...." He faltered, as if he couldn't recall what happened next.

"It's okay," Alex said, squatting down next to him. "You're all right."

Buford looked into his eyes. Confusion was written in his gaze.

"There was a bridge. The voice... It said if I tried to cross it, I would be sent to the land where dead things stand, which was a strange expression I'd never heard before, so it stuck in my mind. So, I didn't move. I just... stayed there on the bridge. For how long I can't remember. After a while, time seemed to bleed into itself. Then I woke up here."

Alex looked up at his wife. She stared at the man in wonder.

"I must have slipped and hit my head on this rock," Buford went on. "I tell you what, that was one crazy dream."

"Yeah," Alex said. "More like a nightmare."

THANK YOU

Thanks for reading this story. Just like with all the books I've written, I hope you enjoyed the ride.

I did my best to include as many facts as possible regarding history and locations included in this work to blur the lines between truth and fiction.

If you did enjoy the story, and you get a moment, swing by Amazon or Goodreads and drop a review. They really help both authors and readers.

Have a great day, and thank you again for reading.

Until the next one,

Ernest

OTHER BOOKS BY ERNEST DEMPSEY

ACKNOWLEDGMENTS

As always, I would like to thank my terrific editors, Anne and Jason, for their hard work. What they do makes my stories so much better for readers all over the world. Anne Storer and Jason Whited are the best editorial team a writer could hope for and I appreciate everything they do.

I also want to thank Elena at Li Graphics for her tremendous work on my book covers and for always overdelivering. Elena rocks.

A big thank you has to go out to my friend James Slater for his proofing work. James has added another layer of quality control to these stories, and I can't thank him enough.

Last but not least, I need to thank all my wonderful fans and especially the advance reader team. Their feedback and reviews are always so helpful and I can't say enough good things about all of them.

www.ingramcontent.com/pod-product-compliance
Lightning Source LLC
Chambersburg PA
CBHW020932260626
47169CB00006B/1691